Frederick Exley's
LAST NOTES FROM HOME

LAST
NOTES
FROM
HOME

Frederick Exley

VINTAGE CONTEMPORARIES

VINTAGE BOOKS   A DIVISION OF RANDOM HOUSE, INC.   NEW YORK

Library of Congress Cataloging-in-Publication Data
Exley, Frederick.
      Last notes from home / Frederick Exley. — 1st Vintage contemporaries
ed.
        p.   cm. — (Vintage contemporaries)
      ISBN 0-679-72456-7
      I. Title.
[PS3555.X58L37   1990]   89-40088
813'.54—dc20   CIP

Manufactured in the United States of America
10   9   8   7   6   5   4   3   2   1

*This book
is for Aunt Frances
and for Frances and Connie.
In the order I met them it is also
for Letizia, Markson, Styron,
Loomis and Riedel.*

It is alleged by a member of my family that I used to suffer from insomnia at the age of four; and that when she asked me how I managed to occupy my time at night I answered, "I lie awake and think about the past."

—Ronald Knox

I have seen the hippopotamus, both asleep and awake; and I can assure you that, awake or asleep, he is the ugliest of the works of God. But you must hear of my triumphs. Thackeray swears that he was eye-witness and ear-witness of the proudest event of my life. Two damsels were just about to pass that doorway which we, on Monday, in vain attempted to enter, when I was pointed out to them. "Mr. Macaulay!" cried the lovely pair. "Is that Mr. Macaulay?" And having paid a shilling to see Behemoth, they left him in the very moment at which he was about to display himself—but spare my modesty. I can wish for nothing more on earth, now that Madame Tussaud, in whose Pantheon I hoped once for a place, is dead.

—Thomas Babington Macaulay
to Thomas Flower Ellis

A Note to the Reader

After parts of this book appeared in *Rolling Stone*, I received a letter from a prominent academic in the Southwest. Apologetic about reading *Rolling Stone*, explaining that his teenage sons subscribed to it, he wondered about the propriety of introducing a "real" brother, Col. William R. Exley (1926–1973), into a work of fiction. Had I then answered I'd have said I hoped my brother would have laughed. Were I answering today I'd say I'm sure my brother would have laughed. Jann Wenner, editor and publisher of *Rolling Stone*, in which four excerpts of this book appeared, was among the first to give me financial assistance. Yet another excerpt, in somewhat different form, appeared in *Inside Sports*.

Contents

Part One

PILGRIMAGE

1

At seven in the morning I go to Oahu. What was going to be a few jolly days of imbibing and, hopefully, copulating with heartbreakingly beautiful Eurasian girls (I was obsessed with loin fantasies of Tahitian nymphets) has turned into a deathwatch. My elder brother, Bill, with whom I was one day hoping to spend these larksome days, is dying of cancer, a malignancy that began in the caecum —a pouch or "blind gut" lying between the large and small intestines. Because cancer of the caecum, I am told by a top local thoracic surgeon, has such a high incidence of cure, I can only assume the Brigadier let it go until the pain was beyond enduring. The Brigadier, I should here append, was always, *always,* a hard head.

Although years ago I laid on him the cognomen of the Brigadier, Bill is only a full colonel. The Brigadier is a joke we had. Just graduated from Watertown High School, he entered the military at seventeen in February 1944. He served in three wars. He was much decorated, over the years being awarded the Silver Star, the Legion of Merit, the Bronze Star Medal, the Joint Services Commendation Medal, and two Purple Hearts. He rose steadily from the rank of private, and I used to chide him that he'd never know repose until he got his brigadier's star. Although in response Bill invariably grumbled *"Shee-it,"* he never denied it.

Convinced at length, however, that the footwork involved in promotion above the rank of full bird was more arduous and devious than he cared to cope with, that as a high school graduate competing with his West Point–VMI–Citadel brethren he would, for brigadier, be "passed over" for the first time (if one is twice passed over one's retirement is, at least tacitly, demanded), he decided to take his retirement in Honolulu where he is assigned to the 500th Military Intelligence Group, the army's top secret intelligence unit for the entire Pacific.

His plans were to remain permanently on Oahu with his army brat wife, the daughter of another colonel, and his fifteen-year-old son. The Brigadier owns a three-hundred-thousand-dollar home in Kailua, a Honolulu suburb on the northeast shore of Oahu much favored by the military. As nearly as I can determine, he was hiring out to a real estate firm to supplement his ample colonel's pension. He would sell property part time, sit at the edge of his kidney-shaped pool sunning himself, drink chilled Olympia (oh-lee) beer from the can, and call back the days of sacrifice and slaughter, of cannon and carnage, of madness, cowardice, and heroism. Although I ever so elegantly disapproved of it all—and the Brigadier damn well knew it (a lot he gave a shit!)—and there were times when I actually wondered how we could have issued from the same old lady's loins within three years of one another, I yet had hoped that on his retirement I might spend a year with him at the patio of that blue pool and that together we might relate the story of his life. The Brigadier served in World War II, Korea, and Vietnam, and I thought his tale might tell us something of the mid-twentieth-century American nightmare.

Alas, the Brigadier and I shall never—at least together—tell the story of his life.

The Brigadier was not sick. Rather, he was very sick and did not know it. The physical examination for the retiring military is scrupulous. Should a disease or injury incurred during one's term of service be detected, it may mean the difference between one's being retired at full or half pay. There is an ironic eye-expanding joke, doubtless apocryphal, among career soldiers that doctors always find something "wrong" with officers above the rank of brigadier and that they are thus always retired at full pay. In my brother's case, and though he wasn't really a brigadier, the joke did not apply. After the quacks kept calling him back for further X rays, they finally cut on him last November, took a peek, closed him back up, stitched him, and put him on the new cancer-controlling drugs. That was when the telephone wires between my hometown, Alexandria Bay, New York, a St. Lawrence River village just north of Watertown where I grew up, and Honolulu began crackling.

I can hear the word cancer (my father died of lung lesions at forty) spoken sibilantly the length of a football field. Still, I did not at first grasp the details or realize the full import of what was happening. At the time I was locked up in an upstairs study of my mother's house in Alexandria Bay, "the Bay," absorbed in writing *Pages from a Cold Island,* and as November became December, then January, the calls between the old lady and my sister-in-law became alarmingly frequent. Lifting my fingers from my typewriter keys, my ears cocked tensely, my breathing suspended, I could hear the old lady in her downstairs bedroom talking across the continent and halfway across the Pacific. In the early days she said oh and oh and oh as if she were being made to understand the situation. Then as the days passed she said *oh* and *oh* and *oh* as if in thrall to the desolation of the Brigadier's predicament. And always now I heard that demonic word cancer.

Unexpectedly we received a letter from the military surgeon attending the Brigadier at the Tripler Army Hospital in Honolulu. My twin sister is a laboratory technician at the E. J. Noble Hospital here in the Bay. The monies to build the latter were donated by the wag who started Life Savers, the candy with the hole in it, a guy much enamored of our Thousand Islands. My sister gave the letter to our friend, Dr. Bob Burtch, and asked his interpretation. Bob's interpretation was as succinct and hair-curling as masterful poetry. The Brigadier's case was terminal.

The old lady downstairs has had one stroke, has a bad ticker, high blood pressure, gall bladder trouble, and those various diseases attendant to aging. Thus Frances took her to Bob's office at the hospital, had him first check her blood pressure, then let Bob explain to her the hard unalterable facts.

From that day on the old lady began to weep a great deal, to wring her hands in anguish, and to make plans to visit Hawaii and for the last time see her eldest. Knowing the old lady's fear of flying, I did not think the plans would befall. Presently it was February and the entirely unexpected happened, something that was destined to take me from the ivory tower of my upstairs study and force my own confrontation with life's distressing eventualities, make me leave my cold and eyeless typewriter keys. The Brigadier, momentarily released from Tripler Army Hospital, called from Kailua. He talked at length with my mother, assuring her that everything was okey-dokey, and that the new "wonder" drugs were doing things just short of miraculous. Then he asked to speak to me.

The old lady called and asked me to pick up the upstairs extension. When the Brigadier heard her ring off, he demanded to know if she could hear my voice. I said no and that she did not hear well in any event. Now he spoke to me in the way he always had, with unflagging abruptness, as both Brigadier and older brother. Under no circumstances did he want the old lady, considering her health and her inordinate trepidation of flying, to come to Hawaii. He was being readmitted to the Tripler Army Hospital, he looked ghastly, man, ghastly, "like a piece of shit," and in no way did he want the old lady to see him in that condition.

"Do you know what I'm telling you, kiddo?"

I paused. I said yes. I wet my lips. Yet I paused again, my breathing labored. Taciturn, bewildered, painfully obstinate, I did not know what to say. At great length, and as though my voice were discrete and issuing from some soft-spoken man I did not know, I at last said I wanted to get away from my manuscript for a few days and might come to Oahu for an R & R. Knowing my pompously articulated distaste of the military, the Brigadier—as I hoped he would —got a kick out of my employing the jargon R & R. He laughed, around, I suspect, his ever-present Antonio y Cleopatra cigar. I said I could stay with my boyhood chum Wiley Hampson, with whom I'd started kindergarten and gone all through the Watertown public schools. Wiley had been on Oahu fifteen years, and from what I'd heard from mutual friends was doing well and owned a large pool hall and commercial fishing boats. As though it were a trifling afterthought, I said I'd then be able to get together with the Brigadier to chat and to tip ever so many drinks.

"That might be a good idea."

From the day of that circumspect conversation I, like the old lady, went on my own walkabout, sans hand wringing and tears, in my thermal hunter's underwear walking for miles on the Goose Bay Road with my boxer, the Killer. Atop the hill, where the February winds coming off the St. Lawrence whip furiously across the village's golf course, the gasping cold cut to the marrow and the Killer licked his chops uneasily, his cropped ears lay timidly on his fawn dome, and he looked bewilderedly and beseechingly at me. But still I did not weep. Walking with my tuqued head downward to the icy shoulders of the Goose Bay Road, my face burnt cerise by the cold, I was one day abruptly conscious of something hard, acrid, alien, and ugly in my mouth. I removed my glove, spat into my instantly frigid palm, and realized, astonishingly, that I had been gnashing my teeth so severely I'd loosened a great silver filling from an upper left molar. As if it could somehow be reused, I put the filling in my pocket. Turning swiftly on our heels, the Killer and I—*à corps perdu*—ran all the way home.

When we got to the house, both suffering tachycardia, I found a note from the old lady informing me she'd gone to Watertown shopping. Directly getting Honolulu information, I asked for Wiley Hampson's number and presently was through to him at his home in Hawaii Kai, a suburb on the southeast shore of Oahu, not far south of Kailua. I hadn't seen Wiley Hampson since 1949, during his mother, Ethel's, wake, when he'd joined me at the Crystal Restaurant on Watertown's Public Square and we'd tipped a few to help put Ethel's ghost on its way. So we exchanged pleasantries for a time, then I came to the point. My brother, Col. William R. Exley, whom Wiley had known as long as he'd known me, which is to say forever, was doubtless dying over there in the Tripler Army Hospital. I could not remember the doctor's name. Would Wiley get through to the attending quack and find out what was going on?

"Look, Wiley, old buddy. These fucking jokers are awfully jealous of their prerogatives and reluctant as hell to discuss cases with nonrelatives. I don't give a fuck how you do it. Explain you're a lifelong friend, say you're our half brother, whatever. But make the fucker tell you what's going on. And," I added, "the old lady's in Watertown shopping. So get back to me as soon as you can, will yuh?"

Wiley was back to me within an hour, when I was halfway through my third can of Budweiser. The Brigadier, according to the military surgeon, was not leaving the Tripler Army Hospital alive. If I were going to see him in this life, I'd better come immediately. Would I, Wiley wanted to know, stay with him or with my sister-in-law?

"Stay with me," he said.

"I probably will."

Now I called my sister-in-law in Kailua and explained to her what Wiley had just told me. She authenticated it. Had she made any plans to return the Brigadier's body to the mainland for burial? She had not. The Brigadier's request was that he be buried among his comrades in the famous Honolulu military cemetery in the extinct volcanic crater called Punchbowl. This did not surprise me. Although on the army's idiocy the Brigadier could be supercilious, caustic, sardonic, downright abrasive, he loved and took pride in the military. He had seen more friends than he could count fall in battle, and I found his desire to lie among them altogether in character. Telling his wife about the Brigadier's last call, in which he told me that under no circumstances did he want the old lady to come to Hawaii to see him, I said there was no way I could tell her I was going to Honolulu and get out of the house without her.

"For Christ's sake, she'll be sitting on her packed suitcase on the front stoop!"

If I couldn't dissuade her, my sister-in-law suggested I bring her with me, park her in the waiting room, and at an appropriate moment in the conversation explain to the Brigadier she was outside and wanted to see him. Knowing something of the Brigadier's temper and that ours is a family in which the elder's wishes are damn near commands (almost Italian in character in this sense), the prospect did not seem a happy one. But having no choice, I agreed.

I go forewarned. The Brigadier has wasted away. Besides his intestines, his liver and kidneys are now gone. There is a great amount of fluid on his stomach, and due to the "wonder" drugs he drifts between sleeping and waking, between rationality and irrationality. And as a weak man, and as rude as it may seem to my sister-in-law, I know I shall have no choice but to stay with Wiley. To get through this will take me a great deal of vodka, and the thought of doing a quart to a quart and a half a day in front of her, my nephew, and the old lady is—well—a dismally unnerving vision.

Ironically, and for whatever morbid or odd reason— perhaps simply because Bill was military—I have over the years, in one article or another, read about Punchbowl

Cemetery. Though dedicated as the National Memorial Cemetery of the Pacific in September 1949, the first interment or reinterment in Punchbowl actually occurred in January of that year and was the remains of an unknown serviceman killed during the December 7, 1941, Japanese attack on Pearl Harbor. Among those reinterred in Punchbowl that first year was Ernie Pyle, the World War II correspondent whom I've recently reread and was happy to discover read nearly as well as he had to a fifteen-year-old. Pyle was killed by Japanese machine gun fire at Ii-shima, a small island off the northern tip of Okinawa. It was of course the Americans' securing of Okinawa (within weeks of Pyle's death), a battle in which a hundred thousand Japanese were killed, that put our air force within easy reach of the metropolitan areas of Japan. At various times since the dedication, the remains of troops from World War II (reinterred), Korea (where the Brigadier received his wounds, the second time near fatally), and of course Vietnam have been buried there. Hence there emanates from this extinct volcanic crater a morose and ugly reminder of America's century-long preoccupation with the South Pacific. The Hawaiian word for the cemetery is *Puowaina*. During the Hawaiian monarchy years ago heavy cannon were mounted on the crater's rims to protect Honolulu Harbor. Depending on which Hawaiian is translating *Puowaina*, it means "reverence in the highest degree" or "hill of sacrifice." As much as I would later come to love Hawaii and the Hawaiians, I wonder if either of these translations is apposite to such a place.

2

Because the first leg of our American Airlines journey from Syracuse's Hancock International Airport to Chicago's O'Hare International—where after a forty-minute layover we were to connect with that line's nine-hour-plus direct flight to Honolulu—left at seven in the morning, my brother-in-law John drove us the hundred miles from Alexandria Bay to Syracuse in the late afternoon of the preceding day. At the airline counter we first checked our suitcases through on the morning flight to Hawaii, I holding out only my toilet kit, the old lady two small overnight bags. We then registered at the Airport Inn, asked that our room be rung at 5:30 A.M., and said thanks and good-bye to John, who promised he'd be in daily contact with us by phone. For an in-law John has had over the years a surprisingly close and harmonious relationship with the Brigadier, in many respects a closer relationship than mine.

After a solemn and speechless dinner in the dining

room of the inn, the old lady having deep-fried fantail shrimp (as with many people distress causes the old lady to eat more heartily than otherwise), and I nibbling at a dreadful charcoaled filet mignon which tasted of chemicals and an equally dreadful salad (all raw carrots and tasteless winter tomatoes), I picked up the old lady's two overnight bags, one a rouge zippered plastic satchel, the other an open black wool crocheted carpetbag patterned with red, orange, and yellow flowers, and led the way to our room. Detecting that the bags seemed inordinately heavy, I asked the old lady what the hell was in them. Rather sheepishly she explained she'd got a twelve-pound wheel of Heath cheddar cheese (probably the best in upstate New York) from the factory at Rodman, little more than a four corners southeast of Watertown, our county seat. It was a cheese the Brigadier much loved and was always asking to have mailed to him at the various ends of the earth where he was stationed.

Wiley had been in the islands fifteen years, and the old lady had cut the wheel in half and wrapped its separate pieces in aluminum foil as she felt it might remind Wiley of home. For the two of them she'd brought along some Croghan (another eye-blinking village in the area) bologna, which is shaped more like a sausage than the supermarket variety we upstate vulgarians call horsecock. Croghan bologna is terribly rich, terribly spicy, and terribly delicious. Both of these products are superb with saltines, horseradish, hot mustard, and a case of Molson's Canadian ale, lolling around with the guys watching Sunday football. Touched, and though I knew Wiley would appreciate the gifts immensely, I'd heard enough about the Brigadier's condition to know his cancer-ridden peritoneum wouldn't be holding down any cheddar, least of all that spicy and mouthwatering Croghan bologna.

At the dull, uniform, and nondescript room of the motel, which reminded me how far and how coarsely we have drifted from the American dream of distinction, I adjusted the color on the primordial ooze tube, then, on the pretext that the newsstand might not be open prior to our

6:30 A.M. boarding, and so that the old lady might make her toilette and get into the new nightgown I knew she'd purchased for her stay at the Brigadier's home, I told her I was going to stroll back to the terminal and get some magazines to read on the long flight. Buying the first half dozen publications I put my hand to, I walked to the bar, ordered a double vodka with a splash of tonic, no fruit, reached into my shirt pocket, removed two thirty-milligram Serax capsules, popped them into my mouth, and washed them down with the drink.

Abruptly, to my surprise and annoyance that I'd already ingested the downers which would very quickly be taking me into dreamy nether regions, I found myself talking with the Syracuse criminal lawyer John Ray, a fine, distinguished-looking, soft-spoken—no Kunstler courtroom tactics for John Ray!—and extremely considerate gentleman. Among upstate lawyers John Ray is considered the best in the area (I doubt he has ever lost a case—at least after appeals—up in our county of Jefferson). Many years ago, before the Appellate Division of the State of New York, he'd defended a friend of mine (alas, he'd lost this one!) in a disbarment proceeding brought by the grievance committee of the Jefferson County Bar Association, a case in which I was intricately and feloniously involved in a way that has no bearing on these pages. I had heard that John Ray had not originally wanted the case. The "rules of evidence," at which John Ray was of course extremely learned and adept, did not apply in such a proceeding. The prosecutors for our local bar association would be allowed, for example, to introduce as "evidence" my friend's drinking and sexual habits and so forth—his morality, which is of course utterly irrelevant in a criminal proceeding. Hence, an irony of ironies, attorneys don't accord their peers the same due process that is accorded a genteel "priest" like sweet Charlie Manson.

At first John Ray had recommended my friend to a Syracuse University law professor who had defended a number of lawyers against disbarment, sometimes successfully, sometimes not, and who was as good an authority on the proceeding as John Ray knew. But my friend was desperately adamant and told John Ray he was in trouble, man, trouble and that he'd put his faith in no one else but John Ray. While the latter was reluctantly pondering accepting the case, the entirely unexpected—or so the story goes—happened. It is said, apocryphally for all I know, that one or two Watertown establishment lawyers approached John Ray, said they'd heard he was considering taking the case, and told him they'd much appreciate it if he didn't.

Every time I heard the story I smiled sadly, and I desperately wanted to ask John Ray that night if it were true. Instead, against temptation, I squelched the urge to lure the great man into gossip. If true, such an intervention from one lawyer to another is not only unethical, it is grounds for severe rebuke from any bar association in America. More than that, though, and once again if true, it touchingly manifests the naïve provincialism of my home county and shows how little our local gentry understand of a man like John Ray. Like most great criminal lawyers, John Ray has always been a loner. I've heard his offices are as spartan as a monk's cell—no man for fancy carpeting, he! And though John Ray has been known to take more than several drinks (like most loners, I'd guess), he is totally abstemious when preparing and trying a case. An attorney friend of mine tells of the time he, John Ray, and a young lawyer were lunching across the street from a courthouse in which the young attorney was trying a case of his own. Detecting the young attorney was imbibing preprandial martinis, John Ray told him in his usual polite and gentlemanly way, but with no little severity nonetheless, that the young man was practicing the Law and had an absolute duty to his client not to do so with alcohol in him.

For whatever reason, John Ray at last agreed to accept my friend's case. At the airport bar we now bought each other drinks, with me going down, down, and down by the moment, talked about his summer home on Lake Ontario where he went to fish for bass, and then, and as was inevitable, came round to the Case. John Ray told me how much he'd liked my disbarred friend and his "lovely charming wife" and how sorry he'd been to lose that case above all. Five years later he'd petitioned the Appellate Court to have my friend reinstated, the petition being denied outright. And now—oh, my!—ten years had passed and the lovely charming wife was beseeching him to re-petition the court. He now asked me what I thought about it all. Flattered that the brilliant John Ray would seek my opinion, I said I knew my friend was doing well in the construction business but that for his three sons by his first wife, all now approaching college age and doubtless having received, as they were going through their formative years, no little abuse from their Watertown schoolmates for their father's disbarment, I suspected my friend wanted, if not vindication or exoneration, at least reinstatement as a sirely gift, humbly offered, to those sons.

"That's the point," John Ray said. "His wife wants me to re-petition on the promise that if he's readmitted he'll never practice again."

Gloomily I pondered that for many moments, sipping pensively on my vodka. Then I spoke.

"No, no, no. Under no circumstances would I ask those"—I almost said "fuckers" but knew John Ray wouldn't brook that kind of language—"judges down in Rochester to give him back his shingle on the condition it doesn't mean doodly-squat. I'd go in there with the idea that the guy's paid his dues, that he's supported and educated his children despite his disbarment, that he deserves reinstatement and that given his license back he can damn well do with it as he pleases. I know at his age he won't attempt to start another practice anyway. He's doing too well in the construction racket. But I certainly wouldn't approach those judges so abjectly as to have them imagine it was any of their business what he does if he gets his license back."

"I think you might be right."

Sorry that I couldn't get John Ray to reveal to me whether he planned to petition the court again (he was much too cautious for that), we shook hands and said good-bye. John Ray told me to give his affection to my friend and his lovely charming wife, and I dreamily, somnambulantly from the Serax and the booze, made my way across the parking lot to the Airport Inn. As I did so I was thinking how much the airport bar resembled every other airport bar in the world, with great picture windows opening onto macadam-and-concrete runways so we all could apparently go into orgies of ecstasy watching 747s land and depart. And I was thinking further that damnation might ultimately reside in having one's past catch up with him in the bars of distant terminals, say, Timbuktu, Perth, or Addis Ababa.

At the room the old lady, having taken her own pills, was asleep in her bed, her mouth open, her aging face wrinkled and drawn about the mouth and eyes. In vivid living color on the tube Matt Dillon and Festus in the persons of Jim Arness—also grown old with the times! Oh, no, not you, Matt!—and the shamelessly hammy Ken Curtis were in Matt's spartan weather-beaten wood-paneled marshal's office slurping black coffee from their tin cups. Festus had his spurs up on his desk and, prefacing his every high-pitched yap with "gol dangs" and "golly gees"—this in a frontier town where the American's love of the four-letter word was, if possible, even more pronounced than it is today!—was issuing his surprisingly acute and pertinent observations on the nature of life, while the ever-stoic and laconic Matt—all six feet seven of him from out of the Swede country of northern Minnesota—remained as word-less, stealthy, and scraggly as an old grizzly. To Festus's every remark Big Jim shook his head with a solemn, ponderous, and rueful petulance which seemed to suggest that if God did in fact lay a burden on each of us—to make one pay his dues, as it were—then assuredly Festus was the marshal's cross to bear.

That the old lady had fallen asleep spoke more eloquently of her grief than anything else could have done. *Gunsmoke* had been her and my stepfather Wally's—dead now six years himself—favorite TV show, one they had viewed religiously. To say the old lady "watched" is not precise. Although she has TV sets all over her house—it is she to whom the suave phrasemakers direct their nonsensical spiels and render the Ultimate Consumer—she presently (left to her own devices, her widowhood) has taken to falling asleep during a show, as well as we all should. The old lady had, however, taken great pleasure from Wally's pleasure.

Many years ago, before Henry Ford the elder rendered the horse obsolete with his assembly line and turned America into the most clockwork and wheel-spinning joke of a civilization that ever desecrated the green earth and forced Wally into the automobile spring business, Wally, like his father before him, had been a blacksmith. As an apprentice to his father he had traveled all over upstate New York shoeing horses. To this day the old-timers remember him as the blacksmith and not as the owner of the Watertown Spring Service. One of the antiquarians gave it to me as indisputable fact that once when trying to shoe a particularly churlish dobbin, Wally became so incensed that he doubled his fist, slugged the horse, and knocked it down. So it is that when I now watch the lead-in to ABC's *Monday Night Football,* and whether or not the old man's tale was fantasy, and see the cowboy-betogged ex-Detroit Lion tackle Alex Karras saunter up to a horse, punch it, and flatten it —assuredly a case of art imitating life—whereas I'm invariably watching this scene with fishing guide friends in the Bay and at this precise moment always feel crushed and walled in by peals of raucous laughter, I on the other hand am overwhelmed with nostalgic memories of Wally.

Although I'd had three or four double vodkas and was still going dreamily down from the Serax capsules, I couldn't resist—doubtless attempting to take my mind from the grave nature of the pilgrimage which lay ahead—watching the rest of the show. Removing my clothes except for my jockey shorts, and though it is ordinarily my wont to drop shirts and trousers in the middle of the floor where I stand, I now scrupulously folded them on hangers and hung them in the closet so that for the old lady I might look as spiffy as possible on the grueling flight ahead. Then I got into bed and snapped off the nightstand lamp, leaving the vivid multicolored TV image as the only light in the room. As was also my wont, I then started, sotto voce now because of the old lady's being asleep, yapping at the screen.

3

Well, Matt, old pardner, says I, like the rest of us you've grown old with the times. Your puss, old boy, is drawn with lines and wrinkles. There is melancholy in your blue eyes. Your jowls, Big Jim, are drooping down like cows' udders. That girth of yours appears to be held in by a corset, either that or that furry chest is sagging over your stomach. That Colt .45 sure don't clear its holster the way it used to. For sure, pardner. Excuse me for laughing, marshal. I was just thinking that if old Wally were still around I'm sure he'd express awesome admiration—doubtless incredulity!—for the miracle horse that could carry that lardass over scalding parched wastes and frigid rock-cragged hills. Well, that's okay, pardner. Shee-it, Matt, don't get me wrong. I forgive you and most assuredly don't mean to patronize. From the sidelines, and with the rest of us, you too have witnessed the jolly spectacles of Vietnam, the riots, the mindless and blasphemous assassinations, Haldeman, Ehrlichman, Colson, and that whole line of fascist pricks in their regimental neckties parading themselves before the very tube that you, Kitty, Chester—and don't forget the wise ol' Doc!—not only helped bring into every home in America but so institutionalized it became as sacred to the American as his odorless and spotless snowy vitreous china toilet bowl—yes, these tailored thugs parading themselves before your tube and straightfacedly confessing (manyof them educated to the law, Matt!) to one stunning felony after another.

Yeah, old pardner, the extent of your consternation and grief at the obscene spectacle America has become I can only guess at—Big Jim Arness from Swedish immigrant stock up yonder there in Minnesota, from Ms. Edna Farber's *So Big* country! Did you, too, have to read *So Big* in high school? Coming from your neck of the woods, you must have! My high school class loved the book. We laughed, we wept furtively, we were in thrall, we were fucking ennobled, old pardner, fucking ennobled! Of course Ms. Ferber's farmers weren't precisely Swedish or from Minnesota. Ms. Ferber's farmers were Dutch and did their truck gardening in Illinois. Do you remember Selina DeJong? By our teacher she was foisted off on us as one sensitive broad. She said things like "Cabbages are beautiful!" and into Ms. Ferber's prose there came a lot of "felicitous" phrases like "fresh green things peeping out of the earth."

Cabbages, Big Jim? Then there was Selina's son, Dirk DeJong—"So Big" himself! To his great misfortune the haughty Dirk didn't find cabbages in the least pulchritudinous. Dirk went on to make a lot of bread in Chicago, rode to the foxes with that snooty North Shore crowd, and, alas, ended up with a Jap (as Ms. Ferber called him) houseman and valet named Saki (I shit you not pardner!) and lying facedown on his bed among his proper Peel evening clothes. It is a pitiable, pathetic vision—Ms. Ferber's profound notion of the price one pays for scorning cabbages. And what can one say, save that these thirty years have rendered Ms. Edna Ferber and all her works as obsolete as the American Dream. Well, no, not entirely; one might take *So*

Big and a box of maple sugar leaves to a terminal case at Roswell Memorial.

We were lucky up yonder there in Watertown, though, marshal (as I pray you were too), for along with Ms. Ferber our teachers took Willie the Shake's *Caesar* and *Macbeth* and *Hamlet* and shoved them up our asses. And do you know the only thing I consciously retain from high school English—I mean, I was a fucking jock, Matt—after, lo, these nigh onto three decades? The prettiest girl in our class was also the brightest. She was tanned and blonde and rich and wore lemon cashmere sweaters. She owned the cold silent hauteur of her brilliance, could play the cello to break your heart—for fact, Big Jim—and when she strolled by between classes, great dark blue eyes so aloofly and coldly forward, her mountain of textbooks and notebooks clutched lovingly against and erasing the outline of her tender young breasts, she had the entire football team (me included, pardner!) stepping fiercely on each other's toes, self-consciously pummeling one another with our hands, ferociously butting heads, emitting great raucous belches, trying to score obscene "funnies" off one another, farting, spitting (yes, expelling flatus and expectorating right in the oily and hallowed halls of the old high school on Sterling Street!). We did anything that we might get her attention, anything that might crumple her stunning poise. Only once we wanted her to turn to us, if only in distaste, if only once we might get those great dark blue eyes to wince in nothing but dismay at our bestiality.

We never of course got any reaction whatever. And was it not astonishing, Mistuh Dillon? With all her distaff classmates mooning nightly by their phones for a call from one jock or another, she had at seventeen already put the thug and hooligan footballer behind her. Yes, great dark blue eyes forward and walking ever unwaveringly, that distressing pile of texts crushing her anatomy where even then a man's loving mouth should have been placing its wet caresses, she marched and marched and marched to some grander, nobler, more significant and dignified destiny.

It must have been our senior year, marshal, for we were into *Hamlet* and I was one day struck nearly speechless to see her raise a beckoning arm—nearly dumb, old pardner, because this sweety pants (as we cornily called them) did not just have smartness, the kind of smartness-smartaleckyness which like some monstrous sci-fi fungus thrives on letting itself be heard, which indeed cannot live without letting itself be heard. Au contraire, this golden maiden had brilliance and was awesomely and smugly comfortable with it and had no need whatever to assure herself or us, by the sound of her own voice, of that brilliance. Indeed, since junior high I doubt I'd heard her voice but twice.

As astonished as the rest of us, I think, the teacher deferentially acknowledged the questioning hand and whispering arm, sheathed in its lemon cashmere like a tulip peduncle in summer breeze, and my sweet cellist, to the incredulity of the entire class, and in very measured, articulate, and grave tones, expounded at no little length on the difficulty she'd had in absorbing Shakespeare since as sophomores we'd got into his heavier tragedies beginning with *Caesar*. Oh, as a freshman she'd liked *Romeo and Juliet* well enough, despite the unhappiness of its ending (that horny play was no play for freshmen, old pardner, but we were too dumb to know it, as was the New York State Board of Regents, never known for its wisdom), but since that first year it had been all madness, delusion, murder, vengeance, lies, assassinations, betrayal, mindless killing, fury, hatred, deceit, lust for power, incest—I didn't even know the meaning of the latter; I mean, I was a fucking jock, I've told you that flat out, marshal—ad infinitum. Yes, to the speechlessness of the entire class, this pristine golden cellist's litany was endless and almost stupefying in that she seemed to omit nothing that wasn't supposedly held most disgusting and abhorrent by man.

"It seems to me that Shakespeare," she concluded, and I remember her precise words, old pardner, "wants nothing less than to rub our faces in the muck of life."

22 ‡

But do you see what I'm driving at, Big Jim? Not only was that lovely brilliant young lady's uncharacteristic spiel the only thing I consciously took from high school English, but that catalogue of deplorable nauseous vices has turned out to be an apt description of our history of the three decades since that long-ago day. And I often wonder what my demure cellist does now. She's probably married to the chairman of the English Department at Northwestern, lives in twelve rooms in Winnetka, and at seven on Sunday evenings plays in a professional string quartet. Or, has she not made her adjustment to the hard facts of history, perhaps she huddles in a corner of a madhouse and weeps great scalding tears from out those dark blue eyes. Whatever, I wish I had a tape recording of her modulated, precise, and abrasive diatribe to send to Winnetka. No, no, Mistuh Dillon, no I don't. In retrospect that would be such a cheap malicious shot. For didn't we all, at seventeen, believe Willie the Shake rubbed our faces in the muck of life? It's now become so clear. Let's say good-bye, old pardner, to Ms. Edna Ferber and in apology tip our hats to Mr. Shakespeare. He may not have saved our reason, but were it not for him we wouldn't feel as comfortable with the stench we cast.

But peace, marshal. The Serax takes me down and down and at the moment I have neither the wit, cunning, nor arrogance of poise to sustain my ramblings. In any event, I forgive you your lardass, the crow's-feet about and the melancholy in your blue eyes. More than that, Big Jim, I'm sure I'd like you as a man. What little I've read about you indicates that, save for the millions which have obviously accrued to your fame, you carry your worldwide notoriety lightly and ironically. You have become somewhat hermetic and made yourself inaccessible to snooping moronic Hollywood reporters. You do not don the ludicrous red cummerbund and tuxedo of the popinjay and appear at "award-winning" ceremonies and kiss people you despise on the mouth. You refuse to let Johnny Carson get off his corny one-liners at your expense.

Ah, yes, good for you, marshal, beautiful! It is true I read someplace you were divorced. But who among us in the new America has not been divorced—I myself twice, Big Jim! Still, when we both look back, old pardner, and as Calvinistic and preposterous as it may seem coming from the likes of me, when all our one-night jejune honeymoons are over, I'm uneasily certain that wisdom will dictate that it would have taken infinitely more of what people used to call character to have hung in there with the same woman than to have walked away. I mean, look at the great Mr. Hemingway's first posthumously published book, *A Moveable Feast*. Above and beyond everything else, it was a valentine, a veritable valentine, to his first wife Hadley and suggested that all the women after Hadley were mere pilot fish. How that must have rankled Miss Mary! But why bother hanging in? Right? In our new affluent and mobile society it only takes about twenty minutes to pack one's bags and go out the door. I tell you this, Mistuh Dillon, because as I jabber away it occurs to me that had I wanted to I could have made it with either of my wives.

Too, and I hesitate to bring this up, Big Jim, but I read recently that your young daughter, like Papa Hemingway, died by her own hand. What can I say, old pardner, that hasn't been said throughout the ages? For her immortal soul I offer a prayer—I offer it at this very moment!—and for your grief and agony I extend my heartfelt sympathies. That said, I shall not grieve for her. What was it Kurt Vonnegut's son said? That in the world we live in "paranoia is an act of faith"? And that is the way I feel about suicide, marshal—that it too is an act of faith, negative faith though it be. For what thinking person among us has not looked about himself and seen the fascists, apes, and thugs who have inherited the earth and not at one time or another contemplated suicide? So that ultimately suicide becomes merely one's eloquent and dramatic way of announcing one will not live in a world controlled by goons.

Abruptly I found myself fiercely smothering my mouth with the palm of my hand to repress the uproarious laughter welling up within me, a laughter I feared would waken the old lady in the adjoining bed. Suddenly I recalled something I'd read about *Gunsmoke*. Some years back Big Jim's show had been suffering anemic audience ratings and was taken from the air for a couple of seasons. Then a Madison Avenue genius suggested what the obvious problem was. *Gunsmoke* had had a 10 P.M. time slot, and the suave merchandiser decided that, like Matt himself, his audience had all grown feeble with the times. We were all suffering from our maladies, "the thousand natural shocks that flesh is heir to," diabetes, piles, kidney stones, anxious bladders, cardiac trouble, prostate difficulty, discharging vaginas, ulcers, cancer, apoplexy, stroke, dementia, palsy, cabin fever, eczema, prickly heat, gout, general lassitude, heartbreak, manginess, morbidity, dyspepsia, squeamishness, paranoia, droopiness, chronic bronchitis, alcoholism, constipation, indolence, gastritis, circulatory problems, diarrhea, flatulence, laryngitis, biliousness, biliary calculus, varicose veins, graveyard cough, and the weariness of middle age, and that therefore, having taken our medications and Libriums, we were all comfy abed by 10 P.M. The thing to do, the Madison Avenue bright boy reasoned to the network moguls, was to reschedule the show to 8 P.M. and an hour we decrepit old farts could still keep our eyes open. It was funny, very funny indeed. Not only did the oldsters flock back to Dodge City and the Long Branch Saloon in droves, but a whole generation of youth discovered Matt, Kitty, Doc, and Festus!

Try as I would, though, to keep my mind from the Brigadier, I found I could not do so. The first time I ever saw *Gunsmoke* had been in the Brigadier's company. It was in his modest red brick home in Baltimore, not far from Fort Holabird, where as a captain he was teaching in that installation's top secret intelligence center and where he always maintained (facetiously one hopes) that West Pointers were his most intractable pupils. It must have been in 1957, for his son was still crawling around the living room carpeting in a baby-blue jumper suit with those built-in stockings to keep the feet warm. At the time I was doing my drunken "on the road" ramble, was on my way to Florida, and within months would be committed to an insane asylum and begin my three years in and out of those quaint places. The Brigadier sat in his easy chair, his shoes and necktie off, the silver bars of his captaincy pinned to the collar of his khaki shirt, an Antonio y Cleopatra in his mouth, his hair shorn close to his skull in the way of the lifer.

At ten o'clock he asked if I wanted to see *Gunsmoke*. When I said I knew nothing about the show and didn't care one way or another, the Brigadier expressed surprise until I explained that my moving about so much prevented my knowing hardly anything about TV. We watched together, the Brigadier, his wife and me. At the black-and-white climax, for the world was black and white in those days, Marshal Dillon had three young, mean, and scurvy hooligans with blotchy beards and crazy wild eyes—sort of youthful Jack Elam types—backed up against the side of a weather-beaten stable and petulantly debating whether or not to draw on him. At that moment, very evenly, in complete control, Big Jim issued his deadly menacing plea to the young thugs.

"Don't make me kill you, boys."

To this the Brigadier laughingly allowed, "They will. They'll make Big Matt kill them!" And sure enough, one of them went for his gun, and in less than a hotdamn Mistuh Dillon had cleared his holster and bam, bam, bam—wow! turning two of their number completely round and knocking the third back into the stable's facade with a force suggesting he'd been struck full in the face with Babe Ruth's outsized bat. When the smoke settled, the three miscreants lay piled up in a mound, limp and dead as mutton. Until that moment I had no idea of the violence being shown on TV and came unstrung, thinking the scene disarmingly powerful. Then I became aware of the Brigadier's wild mocking laughter.

"What's so funny?"

"So funny? See that goddamn Colt .45 cannon Big

Matt is using? In those days you'd have been lucky to hit Fatty Arbuckle the length of the bar in the Long Goddamn Branch Saloon. That cannon was about as accurate as a goddamn BB gun. And none of that shooting from the hip bullshit. You'd better hold that baby with both hands or you'd break your mother wrist. Worse than that, for Christ's sake, Big Jim would have to be using black powder cartridges—white powder didn't even come in until 18goddamn93!—and every time you fired those goddamn black powder babies you were all but overwhelmed with clouds of black soot. After the first shot you were lucky if you could see anything and even luckier if you didn't blow off your own goddamn kneecap!"

Having always known weapons, the Brigadier doubtless knew what he was talking about. It was then that the Serax took me all the way down. When the desk rang the room at 5:30 in the morning, the boob tube was still on but nothing emanated from it but a hum and a bright, bright ray of rectangular light. Laughing, I supposed this was the brightest thing that ever did emanate from the TV.

4

Until one has crossed the continent and half
the Pacific with an aging and ailing mother, a woman twice
widowed, a woman who nightly peruses her Bible and
accepts literally the three score and ten years meted man
by that book, a woman not uncognizant of having buried
two spouses and now en route to lay to rest her eldest
progeny, a woman doubtless mightily distressed at the unfairness of the Brigadier's being taken at forty-six and perhaps even chagrined and perplexed that her Bible had
seemed to betray her, until one has made such a forlorn
pilgrimage one can never truly comprehend the absurdity
of what the phrasemakers call the Jet Age.

The two-hour-and-twenty-minute flight from Syracuse
to O'Hare International was pleasant and uneventful enough.
Presently the captain, soothingly voiced, came onto the
loudspeaker. He told us the altitude at which we would fly,
twenty-six thousand feet. He announced our arrival time

in Chicago, 8:20 Central Standard Time. He informed us that Chicago's temperature was in the low twenties, which, having lived in Chicago and knowing that city's winds are no myth, I knew would chill to the marrow. As unflappable as a waiter at Le Pavillon, the captain said a fine snow was falling in Chicago and that the runways were "a bit slick."

"But," he hastened to add, "it's really nothing to worry about."

From me there issued a wheezing silent chuckle. If, I thought, there was nothing to fret about, why had the captain bothered to describe the condition of the runways? What pompous asses these commercial airline pilots had become over the years. Without doubt the captain was letting us peons in steerage know that we were in good hands, was assuring us, his palms and fingers cupped together lovingly upward, that we were "in good hands with American." For those of us whose childhoods had been spent in thrall to the comic books, the captain was *that* Smiling Jack who would get us through.

There was a distinction. Whereas my beloved Jack (I had a latent thing for Jack!) wore his captain's hat tilted rakishly to the side of his head, sported a white silk scarf which flew freely behind him in the propeller's furious draft, and wore, unzipped, one of those magnificent World War II leather army air force jackets (collector's items now) and always confronted the great inimical world with a large toothy Hemingway grin, my guy now up on the flight deck had grown dignified and somber (doubtless with the times) and wore his hat squarely on his dome. His white shirt was starched, impeccably knotted his black tie. His midnight-blue uniform, adorned with all those impressive hash marks signifying god-only-knows how many years and air hours, was custom cut. His shoes were immaculately shined to a sedate funereal black. One knew, too, that the captain never smiled. The task at hand was too awesome for that. For this reason, let us set his noble jaw more along the lines of Jack's brother-in-thralldom, Dick Tracy. By passengers, by first officers, by navigators, by engineers, by flight attendants he was supplicatingly deferred to. In the steerage section we exulted as the captain strolled chivalrously back from his flight deck, patted us comfortingly on the back, and in his correct masculine-timbered voice assured us that Everything Was Under Control.

In faraway motel rooms of Hong Kong, Istanbul, Rome, and Paris, even I'd guess in Mayor Daley's Chicago and the Waikiki Beach to which we now flew, the captain lay supine on beige bedspreads erupting into the hot moist mouths of lovely young attendants, those glorified and somehow touching hash slingers of the heavens. For who needed the captain more avidly than they? Hadn't stewardesses above all bought the entire dreary American mythology; and if, instead of being pawed by all those drunken humorless married electronic parts salesmen, if one day the young Aga Khan (one of their sisters had snared no less than Henry Fonda!) was to step into their cabin, take one look, and have his heart flip over, wasn't it compelling, nay, *imperative* that the captain get these hopeful young women back to the Big Apple, Chi, and Frisco that they might be primped and poised for the Khan on the next flight?

"Jack, sweetheart," says I, "you bring this crate nice and comfy down on those icy runways of O'Hare and I myself will suck your cock. For fact, baby."

On boarding in Syracuse, the cabin had been all but empty and to give each other legroom the old lady and I had taken seats on either side of the aisle. I did not talk with her. Her white head lay rigidly back against her seat. She had a tremendous dread of flying and was, perhaps, praying. In terribly strained repose her face looked more drawn and ancient than ever, a death mask. In one of the satchels beneath her seat—somewhere among the Croghan bolognas and Heath cheeses—she had bottles and bottles of her various medicines, including some Demerol the doctor had cautioned against taking until we had changed planes in Chicago. Now shaking the old lady's shoulder with gingerish tact, the attendant jumped back in alarm at the jack-in-the-box release with which the old lady sprang up.

"I'm sorry, *I'm sorry*."

"Oh, that's all right," the old lady said. She laughed by way of apology.

I had to laugh, too. It was as if the old lady expected to be told we were already making our descent into Honolulu. I had two cups of black coffee, the old lady had hers black, too, along with an emetic-looking great round orange pastry, which looked to me rather like one of those novelty store rubber puddles of puke practical jokers stick on the bar next to one's drink when one repairs to the *pissoir*. I didn't suggest as much to the old lady. Presently the captain was back on the intercom informing us that if we looked off to our right we could see Buffalo. Two or three people forward in the cabin, not seated at window seats, rose, slid between vacant chairs, and—I wish I were kidding—actually looked down on Buffalo.

Later, with a change of crew in Chicago for the direct flight to Honolulu, the new captain, sounding perfectly interchangeable with the one now up on the flight deck, would be yapping all the way across the western half of America, directing our attention to the headwaters of the Mississippi, the Continental Divide, certain peaks of the Rocky Mountains, whatever, never desisting until he pointed out an island some distance off the Pacific Coast which, thank the amenities, he said would be the last land we saw until we were making our descent into Honolulu, at which time the "big island," as it is called, of Hawaii, Molokai, beautiful Maui (where Charles Lindbergh chose to be buried), and the "pineapple island" of Lanai would come into view. Naturally San Francisco had been fogged and clouded in, and the captain had reached a kind of 1984 screwballness when he announced that though that hilly city by the bay couldn't be seen, if we looked down we could see the clouds blanketing that metropolis resting so placidly and smugly atop the San Andreas Fault, its inhabitants waiting in blissful obliviousness for that fog-enshrouded, gourmet-favored, cable-car fairyland to come tumbling down upon their Mickey Mouse skulls. All sorts of madmen would literally jump up and look down at the clouds below which, the captain had assured us, San Francisco sat.

In the utterly unlikely event I'd wanted to see clouds covering San Francisco, I'd have been unable to do so—as the reader shall soon see with our change of planes in Chicago, after which I'd be all but trapped in my seat. It was bad enough that in their attempt to take care of our most whimsical needs, attendants were overtrained to a near compulsion to slobber all over and drown one in vats of lachrymose smiles, now the captain had been rendered a Donald Duck tour guide director! But Buffalo at eight o'clock in the morning? I wouldn't be chauffeur-driven around that ghetto-ridden, factory-sated, pollution-enshrouded cesspool of a city at eight in the morning in a Mercedes 600, a curtain drawn discreetly between chauffeur-guide-coolie and me, a *Playboy* centerfold giving me head in the back seat.

In Chicago the old lady and I were spared the chill by one of those Brobdingnagian accordionlike hallways that snake out like tentacles of some undersea monster, are clamped to the cabin's exit, and allow the passenger to step out and walk into the terminal through a red-carpeted enclosure. The flight was ten minutes late, but we were already into the American spoke of O'Hare, did not have to clear security again, and after inquiring and being told from what gate the 9 A.M. flight to Honolulu departed, had to walk only a short distance.

At the boarding counter I presented both our tickets and was asked whether we wanted the smoking or non-smoking sections. When I, in turn, asked if the flight was crowded, I was told it was running "very light." In that case we'd take two in the smoking section on either side of the aisle from one another. Explaining the old lady had suffered a stroke and had a bad heart, I told him that with her medication she might, with legroom, be able to sleep the nine hours to Honolulu. The guy said he was sure she would.

On entering the steerage section there seemed to be no more than thirty or forty passengers, which makes a Boeing 707 appear as sparsely filled as the Wrigley Field bleachers on an overcast April afternoon. Placing the old lady's satchels beneath her seat, I clamped her seat belt, drew it tight, then took my seat across from her and clamped myself in. By now it was five minutes to nine or departure time, the engines were revving up vigorously. It'd been a damn near perfect connection. At precisely nine the engines moderated to an odd calm, then the captain came on the intercom and said he was sorry but there would be a forty-minute delay to pick up some passengers from Toronto. He said he'd probably then go up to thirty-five thousand feet, and that if anyone were waiting for us in Honolulu we'd make up the lost time and doubtless be only a few minutes late, if we were late at all. Abruptly someone up front drew the curtain between first class and steerage sections, perhaps suggesting that whoever was delaying the flight didn't want to be ogled by peons. Who the hell, I thought, had the power to delay a transpacific flight for forty minutes?

An extremely attractive attendant in her mid-twenties was coming down the aisle toward me. Her uniform was perfectly interchangeable with those of the girls on the Syracuse-to-Chicago leg of the trip, save that the predominant hue of the skirt and jacket was now an American-flag red, the blouse a checkered white and blue. Her red skirt was very tight, outlining precisely her fine full thighs. She was confidently aware of herself and walked with an oddly delicate muscular sureness. She had a great amount of black sepia—rather tobacco-colored—hair tucked neatly into her red, white, and blue cap. Her nose was chiseled fine, her mouth full and lightly painted. What startled more than her thighs were her eyes. They were huge and pale, pale gray flecked at the top with spots of vivid green. Save for the green flecks they were the biggest and most vacuous eyes I'd ever seen, something almost albino and haunted about them, something out of a horror movie. Like a traffic cop I threw the palm of my right hand rigidly upward to stop her. The identification tag on her red lapel identified her as *Robin*.

"Forty damn minutes to pick up a Toronto flight? This damn well better be Prime Minister Trudeau and his child bride."

Robin laughed and assured me it wasn't.

"Is Robin first or last name?"

"First."

"Last?"

"Glenn."

"Miss, Mrs., or Ms.?"

"Miz."

"Oh me, oh my."

Ms. Robin Glenn laughed again, with a shrill flightiness suggesting she might be as vacuous as her eyes, and in her muscularly delicate sure way proceeded to the rear of the cabin. I turned to study her bum moving away from me. I thought, "Oh, me, oh, my, *for fact*." Looking across at the old lady to see if she wanted to talk, I saw her eyes were closed in calmness, she was relaxed now, she had taken God only knows how many Demerol, she was thankfully going down.

5

I have always and forever feared, been ashamed of, and somewhat loathed the Irish within me. From where I write at the moment (and I shall write from many places, for many places shall be home), the upper story of my sister's A-frame on Washington Island off Clayton, New York, among the Thousand Islands, I can lift my head from this round card table, look out the vents of the jalousie windows, and, a short way downriver, see Big Round Island where, both before and after the turn of the century, my great-grandmother, Miss Fanny Maguire, worked as a cook and a domestic at the Frontenac Hotel, which no longer stands. In the 1850s the colleen Maguire had fled the potato famines of County Cork and settled in America—for that reason a "wild goose" to the Irish—and though, from what little I've learned of her, she herself was a woman of great character, industry, and forbearance, it is yet due to the Maguire strain that all my life I've heard about, and quake at, the tales of one great-uncle or uncle after another.

Each possessed his (it seems inevitable) drunkenness, garrulousness, wit, deviousness, scatology, humor, mysticism, blarney, amorality, poverty, xenophobia, blasphemy, reverence for language and tale-telling, his inclination to monologue, his bleeding leprechauns of Gort na Gloca Mora, ad infinitum, those things I despise, fear, and am most ashamed of in myself. This, then, is the distressing and somewhat frightening heritage with which I'm saddled.

Now, in Chicago, abruptly realizing, as laymen and nuns and priests began eagerly mobbing the economy section and settling into their seats, that the only reason an airline would delay a scheduled transpacific flight forty minutes was the almighty dollar a full complement of passengers would bring, I began to laugh aloud, which brought the old lady's alarmed eyes to me and had her wagging her head *no* as if she abhorred what she imagined my boorishness. Seeing how shabbily most were dressed, unable to comprehend a word they were saying so that I initially honestly believed they were blabbing away in some foreign gibberish—something Slavic, I guessed—I could see the old lady thought me laughing rudely at this rum randy group and I therefore clenched my teeth, compressed my lips, let my eyes roll histrionically up into my brows, and shook my head emphatically *no* to indicate she had misread my laughter.

So rapidly was the cabin filling up that I was on the verge of crossing the aisle and sitting in the center seat next to the old lady, so as not to be separated from her on the long flight, when two nuns, hands muffled in their billowing sleeves, bobbing their heads politely up and down the way nuns do by way of seeming to excuse themselves (for being alive? one always wonders), were sliding past the old lady's forcefully cramped-in legs and into the two empty seats. Before I could get her attention and hustle her over next to me, I was confronted immovably at eye level by the American-flag red of stewardess Ms. Robin Glenn's skirt, its tautness breathlessly suggesting the shape of her marvelous full thighs, and I hence looked questioningly up into her great gray vacuous and haunting eyes. Ms. Glenn informed me that every blessed seat on the flight would be taken but one, and as a member of the tour had broken his left leg asked if he could occupy the window seat and stretch out his cast in the space between us. Looking solicitously across the aisle at the old lady, I saw she was caught up in that farcical head-bobbing with the lady penguins and suddenly sensing how much comfort their proximity would provide her (this was, after all, a voyage to death), I said sure and asked Ms. Robin Glenn if this group was Russkis or Polacks or what?

"You are some kind of very funny man," Ms. Robin Glenn said. "By the looks of your kisser, you're probably one of them!"

Even then I had no idea what Ms. Robin Glenn meant. One skinny fiery runt of a hunch-shouldered, tottering, and rather maniacal-looking priest appeared to be the head honcho. His pallor was ghostlike, the glowingly pale folds of his skin fell so droopily and scarily away from his facial structure he seemed some grotesque from a horror movie. His snow-white hair, which might have lent him a somewhat distinguished look, was so tinged—out-and-out stained— an agingly discomfiting and sickening-looking yellowish orange, almost an ocher, that he looked some back-alley Fagin, some dirty old man given to popping out of blind alleys and for little girls displaying what would assuredly be a sorry shriveled specimen.

Quite as unsettling as his yellowish-orange hair were the index and middle fingers of his right hand. Between these—or pursed in his lips—he constantly held and puffed at a Canadian nonfilter cigarette whose brand I recognized and knew to be as head-swimmingly strong as those Picayunes the good old boys down in the country-and-western roadhouses of Yazoo County inhale to their toenails. Ms. Robin Glenn and another stewardess were scurrying up and down the aisle with the priest making sure the members of the tour, so rapidly filling the cabin, were settled snugly into their seats, their belts clamped firmly. Although I could not hear what the girls were saying to him, the NO SMOKING light was on, as it always is prior to takeoff, and I was almost certain that on two or three occasions they spoke to him about his smoking. His squinty little BB-blue eyes would widen in hurt apology, with a kind of terrible fury—not really anger, but his movements owned that terrible jerkiness indicating fury—he would jam the butt into the recessed ashtray of a seat's armrest and off he'd fly up the aisle, the breathless and intimidated stewardesses right at his erratic heels. The three would thereupon settle in the next members of the tour.

Almost immediately, and obviously totally unconsciously, the savage little squirt would reach into his pocket, without bringing out the pack, and remove another of those awful Canuck cigarettes, put it into his mouth, light it, and again be bounding up and down the aisle seeing to his flock. In a kind of terrifying way the little padre was rather endearing. There was something so excitable about him, a kind of Jesuitry gone bonkers, I couldn't help laughing, silently now to appease the old lady, and as much as for any other reason laughed at the poor man's utter helplessness to comply with the NO SMOKING sign. Far funnier than anything else, when he held his habitual cigarette pursed in his lips, like a delighted child sucking an ice cream soda through a straw and trying to drain the elixir in one extended draught, his cigarette would burn a third of the way down on one voracious drag. As it did so, and he fled airily, with something like hurricane stealth, up and down the aisle, the poor girls stumbling bewilderedly at his frantic heels, the cigarette's ashes would dribble snowily down his black silken rabat, forming a near-perfect four-inch column of silver gray running vertically from the base of his round collar to the bottom of his rabat and belt. It was rather as if he were from some privileged order of dandies given to designing their own priestly garments. There were three or four other priests, as well as eight or ten nuns and all kinds and shapes of ill-dressed lay people, both men and women, and as the priest ordered all of these about and seated them where he chose, I figured him for a monsignor at the very least, perhaps even a bishop.

When at length everyone was settled comfy in, a great hush fell over the plane, very amusing in its own way, the curtains separating the first-class and economy sections parted, my broken-legged seatmate came gimping through, and bedlam ensued. Great wild uncontrollable cheers rose up to greet him. Although he was dressed in layman's clothes, there was something so boundlessly shameless in the tumultuous accord with which he was being hailed by this staid religious group, I thought this preposterously sloppy man might be an archbishop or even a cardinal in mufti. In a grating crescendo these Russkies or Polacks or whatever they were, even the priests and nuns, though these acted somewhat more subdued, kept saluting him over and over again in some strange ritualistic chant which sounded like "Oh Too Me! Oh Too Me!" I could not imagine what this signified and for a time thought it might be some Slavic mystical chant translating as "Oh, come to me!"

Why I didn't then and there recognize the object, now proceeding down the aisle toward me, of this inordinate adulation as Irish I shall never know. For despite the farcical smile (so many even white teeth glowing—nay, gleaming brilliantly—with spittle that the smile all but obliterated his chin) with which he acknowledged these raucous hosannas, he was nonetheless drunkenness and defeat and death personified. He was fiftyish, with a full head of abundant and unkempt—Chicago windswept—graying wavy hair. His long forehead was one of the most pronounced I'd ever seen. It appeared hypertrophied, as if his entire brow had received a devastating blow from some aborigine's thighbone club and its swelling had obstinately refused to recede. His blue eyes were now so red and runny with drink he appeared to have pinkeye or terminal pneumonia. He wore a light tan suit of an obviously expensive winter gabardine, a chocolate-brown button-down shirt, and a snow-white worsted tie sloppily knotted and so far off center from his Adam's apple that most of the white knot was hidden by the right side of his chocolate-brown collar. There was something gangsterish in his choice of attire. Although his outfit had no doubt cost him dearly, he was so monstrously sanguine and brimmingly puffy with booze, his alarmingly flushed Irish cheeks pushing his red rheumy eyes right up into his copiously haired eyebrows which hung down, like black and gray bunting, from his massively precipitate forehead, his jowls dribbling like globs of dough over his chocolate-brown collar, his potbelly so saggingly and disgustingly pronounced it fell with a kind of damp obesity over his unseen belt, the enormous belly having undone or popped the bottom two buttons of his shirt revealing a pyramid of white undershirt framed in chocolate—so brimming with drink and gluttony and sloth that all his clothes appeared to be crawling up his person, his jacket and shirt up into his lardy neck, his cuffs snaking up his heavy hairy forearms, his breeches up into his balls and sphincter.

If his doctor had recommended crutches, the guy had scorned them and now made his way down the aisle on one of those knee-to-foot casts with built-in metal braces. Protruding from the cast's instep was a couple-inch aluminum pipe tipped with a rubber traction cup of the kind used on crutches. Never once abandoning the great spittle-toothed smile that rendered him chinless, he would take four or five wildly theatrical steps, putting his right leg scrupulously and precisely forward, now bending over and swinging his casted leg gingerly up beside his good leg, then pirouetting crazily on his rubber-tipped spoke, all the while his globular gabardine-covered ass swaying in monumental arcs from the seats on one side of the aisle to the seats on the other. Having painfully completed these few steps, he'd pause. In acknowledgment of the ritualistic cries of "Oh Too Me," he'd straighten up, stretch his arms so exuberantly and loonily Nixon-like above his head I thought his trousers would drop to his knees, a salute the tour members reacted to by going berserk with cheers and applause. Now the four- or five-step charade would begin all over again. "Oh Too Me!" As abruptly as if some laborer had flipped and hit me flush in the diaphragm with his sledgehammer, it occurred to me that this "revered" figure, hobbling gimpily down the aisle and almost upon me, the little padre and Ms. Robin Glenn solicitously bringing up his heels, was being hailed by his name, O'Twoomey. Lord have mercy on us all. This was a group of Irishmen!

As I now stood up, stepped first out into the aisle, then backward a couple paces so O'Twoomey could slide unimpeded to his window seat and thereby be able to extend his cast on the floor between us, O'Twoomey offered up his hand to be shaken.

"Hello, lurve," which I took to mean "love," "the name's James—call me Jimmy—Seamus Finbarr O'Twoomey." In a preposterously effusive way beyond my capacity to duplicate, Mr. James Jimmy Seamus Finbarr O'Twoomey told me what an altogether kind, generous, splendid, and lurverly chap I was, apparently for having done no more than stand up to allow him access to his seat. No sooner had he settled in and clamped his seat belt, I into my aisle seat and doing the same, Ms. Robin Glenn and the grubby priest hovering fawningly over us, when James Jimmy Seamus Finbarr O'Twoomey pointed at his cast, great histrionic hurt in his runny blue eyes, and demanded whiskey from Ms. Robin Glenn.

" 'Tis for the pain, me girl, 'tis for the pain!"

In the most good-natured and airline-trained way Ms. Glenn explained, with no little amused and exaggerated sympathy for O'Twoomey's plight, that the airline forbade "the serving of beverages" until the craft was airborne, which would be momentarily, and that she—with those large haunting eyes—would herself and personally, verily personally, see to it that O'Twoomey was served first. Ms. Glenn now pivoted and with her previously described walk of sprightly purposefulness proceeded toward the bulkhead. As I watched her walk away, having again fallen in thrall to her marvelous behind, the maniacal priest bent his screwy yellow head over between Jimmy O'Twoomey and me, his foul ashes now fluttering into my lap, and Jimmy O'Twoomey, not in the least inhibited by our American niceties and expressing my own thoughts to the letter, spoke to the padre.

"Wouldcha look at that wan, padre? Jesus, Mary, and Joseph! And all glory to the American colleen! An arse on her like two rabbits twitching in a sack!"

Sucking voraciously in on his foul-smelling and dizzying Canadian cigarette, the priest abruptly raised the nauseatingly stained index finger of his right hand and wagged it in a "naughty-boy" way at Jimmy O'Twoomey.

"Tut, tut, my lamb."

Now Jimmy O'Twoomey, in a typically circumspect and lyrical Irish way, said something about travel being "bruddening" and he thought—not thought but knew—that chatting "for some nice hours with 'an Irish Yank' " like me would be "lurverly, oh, the real cheese!" Here O'Twoomey reached over the empty seat between us and patted me affectionately, somewhat erotically, on the thigh.

Rendered near paralytic by O'Twoomey's so easily detecting my Irishness, I turned and spoke to him for the first time. With a very cultivated indignation in my voice —I was beautiful to behold!—I explained that my name was Frederick Earl Exley, the latter a quite prominent surname in England, and that in fact a certain Professor Exley, a cousin, I thought (I wasn't certain about the cousin aspect but the rest was true) was the headmaster of a very uppity English public school. Mr. Jimmy Seamus Finbarr O'Twoomey laughed heartily, gave his own thigh above the cast a resoundingly loving slap, and between gurgling laughs said he didn't much care if my name was Winston Churchill, there was "a nigger in the woodpile someplace, as you Yanks say," and that if I weren't Irish he would personally kiss my arse on the village green of Tara, the residing place of ancient Irish kings. Jimmy sighed. "And I wouldn't be found dead in bleeding Orangemen's country!"

Now hear me closely, gentle reader, believe me and try sincerely to imagine the extent of my ultimate humiliation. O'Twoomey, a great goofy and drunken smile on his face, said, "Well, Frederick Exley, my dear lurverly Limey, whatever you say. In any event, shake hands with my great and good friend, Father Maguire."

Mc-bleeding-Guire! My ancestral name on my mater's side! The awful cigarette pressed between his pursed lips, the padre extended his nicotine-stained hand, which I accepted as gingerly as I would that of a leper.

"Now there's a good boyo," Maguire said. He then turned and fled up the aisle toward the bulkhead. The plane began a slow taxiing toward the runway.

Thrown considerably off schedule by our forty-minute delay, the captain now announced there would be yet another few minutes' wait as there were a half dozen planes on the taxiway ahead of us awaiting the use of our designated runway. For that reason, he said, the stewardesses would use the time to acquaint us with the Boeing 707–323B, which American Airlines used on all its overseas flights. Although our plane had been moving steadily forward, and was now doing so somewhat jerkily as one after another unseen plane before us took the runway and became airborne, the truculent little Maguire—though, thankfully, he had been persuaded to discard his habitual cigarette—was the only passenger still standing. He was beside Ms. Glenn at the bulkhead. He seemed to be in some heated dialogue with her. Ms. Glenn had removed the microphone from its cradle attached to the bulkhead and apparently wanted to simper over the virtues of the 707–323B. As nearly as I could determine, she was refusing to do so until Maguire took his seat with everyone else. Presently, with no little angry frustration, she slammed the mike back into its cradle, pivoted and disappeared between the curtains leading into the first class section. Directly she was back with a uniformed man who, from his youth and the limited white hash marks on the sleeves of his blue jacket, was either the first officer or the engineer. That either officer would abandon his instruments so near to takeoff distressed me.

The officer, together with Ms. Glenn, now angrily engaged Maguire in what, had one been able to hear it, was as nasty and strident as outright name calling. At length, apparently exhausted by whatever Maguire's demands were and no doubt fearful of being away from his duties any longer, the officer conceded to Maguire, gave Ms. Glenn a rather hopeless little-boy shrug, rolled his eyes wildly around in their sockets, suggesting there was obviously no way of dealing with a loony like Maguire, pivoted, went through the curtains, and proceeded back toward the flight deck.

Throughout all this, I might add, Jimmy O'Twoomey sat there giggling drunkenly and sneeringly repeating, "Wouldcha look at that wan now, my dear Frederick, that bleeding arsinine culchie?" As O'Twooney had already made scatological references to Ms. Glenn's lovely, rather dream-of-sculptor's behind, I thought "culchie" was some indecorously Irish or downright obscene allusion to Ms. Glenn's vaginal area, say, as in "cunt," and that O'Twoomey was deriding her in the worst possible taste. My indignation was becoming sublime. Infuriated by the delay these Micks had already cost us, and further irked by the prospect of spending well over eight airborne hours with this drunken "boyo," I was also incensed that with the "courtesy" the airline had already extended his group by waiting forty minutes, O'Twoomey was so derisively and ungratefully able to deprecate the craft's personnel. Unable to resist it, and with a good deal of strained delicacy and circumspection, I pointed out to O'Twoomey that he and his brethren were "guests in our country" (I was beautiful to behold: I almost stood up and sang the national anthem!), that I knew regulations forbade the pilot's taking off until everyone, but everyone, "including your man of the cloth," is seated and strapped in. I saw no earthly reason, I added, for so nastily insulting Ms. Glenn for doing a job she had an absolute mandate to do. Jimmy hadn't the slightest idea what I was talking about.

"You called the stewardess a culchie," I said, whispering "culchie" and rolling the word with reverent naughtiness over my palate as though I were mouthing the ultimate Gaelic obscenity.

Jimmy O'Twoomey found my ignorance downright hilarious. He threw his head back, roared with laughter, rolled around in an abandoned giggle as though he were Silly Putty, then leaned wheezingly and intimately toward me, with his right hand again patted me with patronizing affection on the thigh, his mouth all drunken foamy spittle, and said, "No, no, me dear bucko, Frederick, not the lurverly colleen! What kind of a bleeding Irishman are ye! That wan, that wan, that dirty little pompous fol dol di do Jesuit!"

Unsettled that this Irishman, now embarked on what seemed a religious outing or pilgrimage, could be so derisive of a priest, I asked what a culchie was. Unable to accept that I knew nothing whatever of Ireland, with no little exasperation Jimmy O'Twoomey explained that a culchie was what we Yanks called a hick or hayseed or rube. When I said that from the rather magisterial way Father Maguire acted, I'd rather gathered he was the head of the tour, Jimmy found this unbearably funny and all but disintegrated with coughing, choking laughter. As he did so, his stubby fingers patting my thigh tightened fiercely, his thumb and index fingers coming together so excruciatingly at the inseam near my left ball I sensed the blood evacuating my face. And among maniacal demented shrieks, Jimmy told me that Padre Maguire was nothing more than "wan of Ryan's arse-kissing slaveys, brilliant though he may be, me boyo, just a bleeding Jesuit thug!" I had not the slightest idea who Ryan was and said so. My ignorance was severely trying Jimmy O'Twoomey. With an eye-popping and inflammatory impatience, coupled with that grating annoyance one employs with three-year-olds or retardates, and in pompously exaggerated and ever-so-patiently articulated words that rendered me rigid with a humiliation I didn't believe I had any obligation to feel, O'Twoomey informed me, with grand flourishes and pumpings of his arm, that "Dermot Ryan, for the sake of Jesus, Mary, and Joseph, is the bleeding archbishop of Dublin!"

"Oh, I'm sorry. So this group is from Dublin?"

"And where else, me boyo?" Jimmy sighed theatrically. "The bleeding prerogatives of an archbishop. When I set up this bleeding tour as a gift to some of our more deserving workers, I asked the great wan to give me anywan but Maguire to make the arrangements, handle the money, that sort of thing. Ryan saddles me with thees eejit anyway. Maguire's worthless at this kind of thing. He's nothing but a culchie who spent twenty years studying with the Jesuits, good for nothin' but scribblin' interpretations or apologies for Ryan's slightest pronouncements, written for those bleeding religious journals in that recondite gobbledygook which nobody but other culchie Jesuits can understand. I doubt he could find Hawaii on a map, lurve. And look at him now, me boyo, Frederick, just look at that wan! Thinks he's got a direct pipeline not only to Archbishop Ryan but to Jesus Christ Himself, sure he does—*the eejit*!"

Whatever Maguire's argument with Ms. Glenn, it was now resolved, for though she still stood watchfully beside him, she had surrendered the microphone to him and was explaining how a button on its side had to be pressed down with the index finger in order that the sound be heard. Apparently satisfied, Father Maguire looked beseechingly back to Jimmy, obviously seeking Jimmy's approval that he was doing a grand job. Still giggling drunkenly and repeatedly mumbling "the bleeding eejit, the bleeding eejit," Jimmy raised his right forearm limply up from his elbow in a weary Nazi salute and impishly waggled his fingers at Maguire by way of assuring him what a lurverly conscientious boyo he was. Father Maguire now pressed the button and asked our "indulgence." A stately silence engulfed the cabin.

"Jesus of Nazareth, King of the Jews, from a sudden and unprovided-for death deliver us, O Lord."

O Lord indeed! What a prayer to offer a jammed plane about to embark on a five-thousand-mile journey! Like the Pope on the balcony above St. Peter's Square on Easter Sunday rendering his hand benedictions to the mobs beneath, Father Maguire now blessed us in the same way, with his two yellow fingers repeatedly making the sign of the cross in the air space before his chest. All over the economy section passengers made the sign at forehead and chest and mumbled piously. Although O'Twoomey made the sign of the cross, all he mumbled, among dark, gleefully evil chuckles, was:

"The bleeding eejit, the bleeding eejit. It's all play-acting, me dear Frederick. I doubt the little culchie's administered the sacraments in his entire career and now wouldcha look at that wan? Just look at that wan! Play-acting the bleeding Pope for us. And sure he is!"

Memory is anarchic and I'm not sure I actually witnessed what happened next. I hope I did not. Ms. Glenn now had the microphone and welcomed us to American Airlines Flight 201, nonstop from Chicago to Honolulu. As though the group was indeed Russkis or Polacks in need of translation, the terrible little Maguire now usurped the mike and welcomed us to American Airlines Flight 201, nonstop from Chicago to Honolulu. Ms. Glenn said the Boeing 707–323B international model had twenty-two first class and 113 economy section seats. Maguire grabbed the mike from her hand and told us the same thing! Ms. Glenn informed us of the location of the lavatories and magazine racks. Maguire informed us also! On and on. Later, when we were airborne, which would be momentarily, the captain told us our cruising altitude, our arrival time at and the temperature in Honolulu, when he began pointing out the Continental Divide, a clouded-over San Francisco, and so forth, Maguire would leap furiously from his aisle seat hard by the bulkhead, snatch the mike from its cradle, and word for word repeat everything the captain had just told us. Did he really do that?

6

I don't know at what point I knew O'Twoomey was insane. In my days in the bin, I was on quite friendly, even palsy, terms with guys who had built structures in the skies—oh, fiefdoms and principalities and castles—every bit as elaborate (but nowhere near as brilliant) as Kinbote's lost Kingdom of Zembla. Had O'Twoomey's insanity been as jolly as that of the "happy" homosexual Kinbote, or that of some of my pals in the bin—one guy, nineteen years old, told me he had invented the process for iodizing salt and spent his days in the hospital's library preparing endlessly elaborate affidavits for suing Morton Salt and twenty-six other defendants—I would have been amused. Very early on, however, it became apparent that O'Twoomey's delusions weren't all that much "fun" and were charged with as much rage, malice, and prejudice as his person was brimming with booze.

As Ms. Glenn had promised, she took O'Twoomey's

order first. He wanted whiskey. What kind? With volatile impatience, O'Twoomey told her whiskey, girl, whiskey. Trying to help, I explained to Ms. Glenn that he undoubtedly wanted Bushmills or Jameson or Powers Gold Label. She said she was sure they had none of these brands. Jimmy laughed contemptuously, said he wasn't bleeding surprised that an airline as obviously barbaric as American—"It's hardly Aer Lingus, now is it, me girl?"—didn't know what whiskey was, then turned to me and asked what I drank. Looking across at the old lady to see if her Demerol was taking its effect (it was), and though I'd promised myself I wouldn't drink on the flight but now knew that without alcohol I could in no way endure this nearly endless journey with Jimmy, I said I drank the eighty-proof or red label Smirnoff vodka with a splash of Schweppes quinine water, no lime. Jimmy stiffened, sighed disgustedly, and told her to bring us two each of "what the bleeding Limeys would call 'a bird's drink.'" Returning with the drinks, Ms. Glenn lowered the trays from the seat backs in front of us and placed on them two clear plastic cups of ice, four miniatures of vodka, and a freshly opened bottle of Schweppes, still fizzing. O'Twoomey moaned and shriveled his rumberried nose in mock-horrified distaste. He asked me to mix our drinks the way I ordinarily did. As I did so, he spoke to Ms. Glenn.

"This is my friend, Frederick." He reached under the tray separating us and with the latent homosexuality so indigenous to the Irish again patted me lovingly on the thigh. "My dearest friend in all the world. If he should die before me, Lord forbid, may God have mercy on his immortal soul. Give him the check."

As I red-facedly stood up to reach into my pocket for the money (O'Twoomey had, after all, ordered the drinks), Jimmy popped off his first in one gluttonous gulp and Ms. Glenn was explaining to him that though he had chosen to sit in the economy section with his friends, Jimmy himself had first class accommodations and hence his drinks were included in the price of his ticket. Unfazed and watching me with amused smug skepticism, as though he doubted my financial ability to negotiate the five-dollar transaction, he promptly told Ms. Glenn to give me my money back as he was just testing "boyo Frederick here to see if he lurves me." He then told her to go forward and get the money from "whatziz-whozit, Padre Maguire or whoever in creation's damnation he is." Jimmy said that Maguire would pay for everyone on the tour, including his "new and lurverly friend, Frederick."

"That little culchie's got a whole gunnysack full of twenty-dollar bills and they're all mine!"

Jimmy threw his head back and roared. As Ms. Glenn began her turn to start toward the bulkhead and Father Maguire, Jimmy abruptly demanded to know what we were having for dinner. It was ten o'clock in the morning. Stopping joltingly in midturn, rather as if O'Twoomey had hurled an obscenity after her, Ms. Glenn turned back, widened those great gray vacuous eyes in amused irony, laughed, and said that dinner was a long way off. Soon we would have a sumptuous breakfast of choice of juices, scrambled eggs with ham or link sausage, toast or rolls with marmalade or jelly, a Danish if we chose, milk, and coffee. This was to be followed by "a super movie, Robert Redford in *Jeremiah Johnson*," then dinner, then Honolulu. Frederick and I, Jimmy assured her, wanted no bleeding mushy scrambled eggs, least of all did "we" want to view any "arsinine Hollywood flicker with a bleeding Limey named Robert 'Medford.' " We were going to have ever so many "bird's drinks," some lurverly talk, after which we would be famished. So what, he again demanded of Ms. Glenn, was for dinner?

Ms. Glenn's face reddened in stunned helpless sadness, excessively timid sadness, and I couldn't help remarking how much this ruefulness, on the face of a girl airline-trained to an effusive near-nauseating ebullience, lent her a truly alarming beauty. Oh, Jesus Christ, O'Twoomey, I wanted to bellow at him, I don't give a shit if you're the bleeding prime minister of the Republic! Would you for godawmighty sakes leave the poor girl alone so she can do her job? Ms.

Robin Glenn had by now explained the dinner choices in steerage were chicken luau or manicotti. Neither of these holding any meaning whatever for this porcine bleary-eyed potato-gobbling Irishman, he now demanded to know what was in them. Almost on the verge of tears, Ms. Glenn explained that chicken luau was a delicious dish of chicken fried in shortening, after which it was all mixed lovingly with spinach in a hot cream sauce made from coconut milk to create a casserole.

"Coconut cream?" O'Twoomey cried with shrill derision. "You mean it's a bleeding Hawaiian dish?"

"Yes."

Ms. Glenn was by now so intimidated that her affirmation made me recognize for the first time the validity of that cliché about people speaking mousily. Her voice was a demure peep. In the grand manner O'Twoomey threw his big hairy Irish head regally and haughtily back and proclaimed, "But I do not eat bleeding wog food! And manicotti?"

"Manicotti . . ."

Ms. Glenn hesitated, compressing her lips in touching bewilderment, and I could see she really didn't know what manicotti was. Her distress and frustration verged on the pitiable.

"Look, Ms. Glenn," I said, "you go take care of the rest of your passengers. I'll explain to Jimmy here what it is."

My effrontery in interrupting O'Twoomey was almost more than he could endure. Turning to me with a look of angry perplexity bordering on outrage, he instantly thrust his right arm and index finger violently outward, directed squarely at Ms. Glenn's striking cleavage.

"Stay, if you please, madame."

Now to his toothy mouth he lifted the second of his vodkas and quinine, which unbidden I'd already mixed (such was the extent of my own intimidation), and drank this down in one slurping draught, wiping his mouth with the back of his hand. With great ceremony he folded his arms across his chest, leaned back in his seat, looked straight ahead, and allowed his crossed arms to slide down to rest upon his chocolate-brown and white-undershirted belly where, I'd already detected, the bottom two buttons did indeed appear to have been popped. He lifted his chinless chin up in the regal way he affected, his lips formed a kind of Robert Morleyish fish mouth, and his words took on a tone implying that there lurked in his lineage baronets, dukedoms, and princedoms.

"Well, Frederick, me lurve, just suppose you tell me what manicotti is."

Jimmy sat there presidentially, rather petulantly Johnson-like, awaiting my arguments for pulling our troops from Vietnam. O'Twoomey was of course mad as a hatter. Insanity always instills in those of us who imagine we're still functioning a kind of eerie and queasy deference.

"Well," I hemmed, giving the petrified Ms. Glenn (for on O'Twoomey's harsh instructions to stay put she had literally frozen) a meek and helpless shrug. "One takes some long tubular—pipelike, you might say—noodles and stuffs them with a mixture of chopped chicken, veal, spinach, and onion fried up in butter and garlic. You then add some ricotta and Parmesan cheese to the mixture, stuff the ingredients into the cooked noodles, top the noodles with some thin slices of mozzarella cheese, and bake the whole business at a high heat, about 425 degrees, I think. This done, you smother the noodles in some hot Italian red sauce and serve. Quite delicious, really. But listen, Jimmy, I can't guarantee any food you'll get on an airline."

O'Twoomey of course picked up on one word only. "Italian?" he demanded, pronouncing it *Eye*talian and wrinkling his Santa Claus nose with monumental disdain. He looked on the verge of vomiting. "You mean it's a bleeding dago dish?"

"Yes," Ms. Glenn and I answered almost in unison. Our joint timidity amounted to no more than a sotto voce echo of one another, peep peep.

"But," O'Twoomey said, his arms still folded over his brown-shirted belly, his head thrown grandly back, his fish mouth forming his words with a suddenly introduced and painfully articulated Oxford accent, "I've already told you I do not eat bleeding wog food."

Ms. Glenn and I remained in trancelike and stunned silence. Presently Ms. Glenn reluctantly offered what she obviously prayed was hopeful solution.

"But, sir, you have first class accommodations. You can have just about anything you want to eat."

For the first time since Jimmy had withdrawn into himself, he turned to her. His great bleary blue eyes lighted up. He smiled with a childlike pleasurable warmth, exposing a mouthful of huge Irish teeth. With the palm of his left hand he joyously slammed his perversely pronounced forehead, causing his great mass of salt-and-pepper hair to fly abandonedly about.

"Is that so? Is that so? Ah, let me see—ah, yes, in that case Frederick and I shall have thump."

"Thump?" Ms. Glenn said.

"Thump!"

"Thump?" I said.

"Colcannon, Frederick. Jesus, Mary, and Joseph, lurve, I'm beginning to believe you really are a bleeding Limey!"

"But, Mr. O'Twoomey . . ."

Ms. Glenn started to explain, I imagine, that "just about anything you want" did not extend to having the airline prepare special dishes for O'Twoomey, when Jimmy interrupted by directing his index finger to a vivid green jade ring bordered in gold and worn on the third finger of Ms. Glenn's left hand.

"Is that a wedding band?"

"Well, it's not exactly—I mean, it's sort of one. It's a friendship ring the man I live with gave me until his divorce becomes final and we can marry."

Ms. Glenn broke out in a brilliantly hued embarrassment of having allowed this virtual stranger to intimidate her into revealing such intimacies.

"Ah," O'Twoomey cried, "you're a bleeding Prod, eh?"

"A what?"

"A Protestant, me girl, a bleeding Protestant! If you were living with a married man in Dublin, you'd be flogged, and sure you would, me lurverly colleen, and I do mean bleeding flogged!"

All teeth now, O'Twoomey was smiling with enormously sadistic pleasure, as though the very notion of stripping Ms. Glenn naked and beating her half to death with a truncheon appealed overwhelmingly to his Catholic morality.

"But enough of your harlotry for the nonce," Jimmy said. "Lend me your dastardly seenful ring and I'll show you and me lurve Frederick here how to make thump."

Dutifully, quakingly would be more in the spirit of the gesture, Ms. Glenn removed the ring from her finger, handed it to O'Twoomey, and said, her voice breaking with humiliation and hurt, "Please, sir, can't you just show Frederick? The plane is packed and I really have to—I mean, I must—help the other girls serve the passengers."

"Oh, be gone then and continue in your life of damnable seen!" Jimmy cried. "In Honolulu I'll have a Mass read for your immortal soul! Just make sure," he hastened to add, "that me lurve Frederick's and me glasses are bottomless. And wouldcha look at this, me girl, me bleeding cup already manifests a bottom."

I had taken but a couple sips of one of mine. Directly, and again unbidden, I mixed the second of mine and slid it across the tray toward O'Twoomey. In acknowledgment he gave me an enormously toothy smile and bobbed his head up and down with wooden jollity. "You are verily a lurverly chap, Frederick." His hand again came under the tray to rest sensually on my thigh.

"I will, sir," Ms. Glenn said. "I swear. I swear you'll get the best service on the plane." She then forced a smile of tentative, grievous artifice and flew away to the aid of her sisters. Again I scrutinized her behind receding up the aisle, as O'Twoomey of course did also. With his thumb and middle finger brought up to his pursed lips he blew a wog's kiss of delectation after her.

On the tray between us O'Twoomey now had the green jade ring, a white button he'd taken from the pocket of his tan gabardine jacket, obviously one of the buttons his enormous belly had forced from his chocolate-brown shirt, and a Kennedy half dollar he'd asked me for. I am in no way sure I can tell one what thump or colcannon is, nor can I be sure it is in any way as disgustingly nauseating as Jimmy made it sound. Thump began of course with peeled boiled potatoes put through a sieve, by which I gathered O'Twoomey meant mashed. Dripping spittle over his chin, he went on to tell me that any one of the "grand Irish potatoes" would do, even lovingly and salivatingly identifying, as only a bonkers Irishman would do, the pretentious and pseudo-blarney-poetic names of some of their fucking spuds, Aran Banner, Skerry Champion, Ulster Chieftain, the latter of course being "a bleeding Orangeman's potato." To these Aran Banners mashed in hot cream one then added half as much chopped boiled kale smothered in hot butter.

"Kale?" I said.

"Jesus, Mary, and Joseph, Frederick, I've given up— but given up—on your Irishness. It's a bleeding cabbage, a headless cabbage."

I could not even envision a "headless" cabbage but held my peace. Pretending now that one of his empty plastic cups was the kettle into which this slop apparently went, Jimmy now wrapped the button in a used damp cocktail napkin, threw that in the cup, followed by the jade ring and the Kennedy half dollar. With great hyperbolic vigor he twirled his chubby hand round and round, indicating he was violently stirring these three items into the mixture of buttered kale, potatoes, and hot cream. He then explained— still salivating of course—that one piled one's plate with a mountain of thump, with a spoon built a great volcanic indentation into the middle of this Aran Banner and kale Everest, and into this valley poured some lurverly hot melted butter.

"One eats from the outside, Frederick. You take a forkful, dip it into the melted butter in the middle, and simply let it ooze rather gloriously down your throat. Ah, and to be sure, me lurve, there's nothing like it on God's green earth."

Great and sudden wealth, according to Jimmy, would accrue to the one who got the coin in his mouth. The ring foretold an early and splendid marriage, and the button signaled to the recipient that he would walk in blessedness all his days, the button and ring being wrapped in paper so the "blessed soul" wouldn't swallow them. Reaching again under the tray for my thigh, Jimmy now brought his spittle-covered lips almost up to mine—I thought the zany bastard was going to plant one full on—and with an air of great secretiveness whispered to me.

"I was going to ask the colleen Glenn to join us, Frederick. But it's impossible, don't you see? I mean, supposing she got the button for single blessedness, living as she is in such seenful harlotry! Sacrilegious and all that, don't you know, lurve?"

Until we were a thousand-plus miles out over the Pacific, where Jimmy at last passed out completely and went into a deep heavy snore for the remainder of the flight to Honolulu, so that he would have neither chicken luau, manicotti, nor his glorious thump, his monologue was unceasing. As quickly as Ms. Glenn set up his vodkas, he'd down them, continue his lyrical and nonsensical spiel, throw his hairy head back into his seat, catnap and snore lightly for five, ten, fifteen, or twenty minutes, waken, furiously jab my elbow, and begin his rambling blarney all over again. No matter that I feigned reading magazines, that without turning up the sound I at one point put the earplugs in and feigned watching *Jeremiah Johnson*—the "Limey Robert Medford" had a lot of snow in his beard, throughout the flicker he kept looking higher and higher up some mountain or other, and at the climax—I think it was the climax—he single-handedly took on, *mano a mano,* a whole shitload of redskins—no matter what I did, the fierce jab at the elbow invariably came.

Whenever I tried to introduce more mundane subjects, hoping to bore him into silence so I could get back to memories of my brother, his replies to these timid overtures were, if possible, even nuttier than his nonstop monologue. When, for example, I asked him how he'd broken his leg, he told me that this tour he'd arranged for some of his "more deserving workers" (he'd tell me who they were soon enough) had begun in New York City. Upon their arrival, as was Jimmy's duty and custom whenever he was in New York City, he had one day strolled up to the archdiocese on Madison Avenue and had passed some lurverly hours swapping yarns with his great and good friend, Terence Cardinal Cooke.

"With whom?" I cried.

"Terence Cardinal Cooke. My bosom brother in Jesus, Cookie." O'Twoomey never batted an eye. "Jesus, Frederick, as a New York State Irishman you don't even know who your own bleeding cardinal is?"

Cookie indeed! I mean, really, what the hell could one say to this crazy bastard?

Whatever, it was after passing some lurverly hours with "Cookie," when Jimmy was leaving the cardinal's quarters and crossing the piazza separating the archdiocese's entrance from Madison Avenue's sidewalk that he slipped on a patch of ice and sustained a hairline fracture of the fibula in his left leg. Jimmy threw his great hairy head back and roared with laughter.

"Oh, Frederick, me lurve, didn't Cookie and me have a grand laugh over that leg! Here I am directly come from making sweet talk with a padre who practically sits on the right hand of God—yea, and to be sure, lurve, every bit as close to God as Dermot Ryan, Cookie is—just leaving this holy man's domicile and I break my bleeding leg practically on his stoop!"

O'Twoomey was quite beside himself with laughter. Again he reached under the tray, grabbed my thigh, pinched it at the inseam next to my left testicle, and again drained the blood from my face.

7

Mr. Jimmy Seamus Finbarr O'Twoomey was in public relations for Joe McGrath, Spencer Freeman, and the Hospital Trusts. For whatever reason, Jimmy appeared to find "public relations" a hilarious euphemism, for the term had no sooner issued from his furry tongue when he again, hysterically interrupting his own declamations, became somewhat sappily giddy with laughter, at the same time studying me diligently out of the corner of his rheumy eyes to determine if I had the foggiest notion what he was talking about. I did not. Detecting this, and with that somewhat terrifying impatience he'd already adopted regarding my calamitous ignorance of my Irishness, he now told me he no longer worked for Joe McGrath "as old Joe has joined the saints in heaven, God rest his soul," rather, he now worked at the Hospital Trusts for Joe's partner, Spencer Freeman, and Joe's son, Patrick McGrath. As I'm certain my expression registered nothing whatever, in very sharp and accusatory tones Jimmy accused me of not even knowing what the Hospital Trusts was. My muteness served as my confession.

Certainly I'd heard of the Irish Hospitals Sweepstakes? I'd heard of the sweepstakes but didn't know it had anything to do with hospitals. In fact, in all my forty-plus years, I said, I couldn't recall ever having seen a ticket, least of all ever having purchased one. With a kind of unspeakable and seething fury, Jimmy reached into the inside pocket of his gabardine jacket, violently ripped from it an expensive-looking and magnificently soft leather pocket secretary, sloppily wetted his fingers with his tongue and lips, snarlingly counted ten tickets onto our cup-stained vodka tray, loudly enunciating the number of each ticket as he counted, *one, two, three, four,* and so forth, ordered me to sign my name and address in the appropriate place, tear the ticket in half, give the parts with my name and address to him, and keep the other halves for myself. As I started to do so, I detected the tickets cost four dollars each, calculated immediately that the tickets would cost me forty dollars, and told Jimmy that one ticket would do me just fine.

"But, Frederick, me lurve, you don't understand—the bleeding tickets are on me! Look here what I'm doing, lurve. I'm transferring forty dollars from this slot in my wallet to this other slot with your stubs so I'll know exactly what it's all about if you win. Even I, you see, darling, in the very higher echelons of the Hospital Trusts' public relations—ha! ha!—have to account for every ticket which is dispersed. All the money, you see, goes to pay the hospital bills for Ireland's poor, impoverished souls. All of course but for some minute sums we hold out for mundane and worldly things like expenses, salaries, and that sort of unavoidable crassness. Who do you think all these gentle souls are? Nurses, doctors, hospital administrators, all with years and years of dedicated, utterly devotional service to curing the sick, the broke, the downtrodden, the devoid of spirit—the Gaelic crackpots, that is—aye, that's one of the reasons this bleeding tour was set up, a gift to the saintliest among us!"

"Oh, I see. I used to do public relations myself. Your job is kind of employee relations, setting up tours like this, planning annual company picnics, that kind of thing?"

"Oh, no, Frederick, me lurve. Don't slight me. As I've said, this tour is only one of the reasons that this outing was set up. My personal public relations is a rather more discreet and delicate operation than this little group would suggest."

Although O'Twoomey would say no more, I never for a moment doubted that sooner or later he would. Shortly before Jimmy passed out completely, when at last I could get back to the memory of my brother, when we were about midway between San Francisco and Honolulu, Ms. Robin Glenn, inevitably joined by Padre Maguire, who would take the mike from her hand and repeat her every word, gave us American Airline's canned spiel on the Hawaiian niceties. Across the aisle, the old lady, her head back, her mouth open, the Demerol doing its work, still slept. A must word in the islands was *mahalo*, which meant "thank you." Ms. Robin Glenn pronounced it for us, as Father Maguire did directly after her. "Maw-*how*-low!" In unison we were all asked to pronounce it. Save for O'Twoomey, we did so. "Mah-*how*-low!" (In the first bar I would enter in Hawaii, that of the Honolulu International Airport, a classily dressed mainlander, after having a mere two highballs, would leave the bartender a five-dollar tip and start for the door. "Mahalo!" the bartender would cry after him. The guy would turn back, smile, wave and say, "Yeah, bah-fungoo or whatever!") We had of course all heard the word *aloha*. This meant both hello and good-bye and many other things as well, as, for example, in the expression "aloha spirit" which would be interpreted as "the true spirit of hospitality." Parroting both Ms. Glenn and Father Maguire, we all, save Jimmy, twice chirped "Ah-low-*haw!*"

With abruptly seething, near-obscene, and terrifying bitterness, Jimmy grumbled, "Aloha, me bleeding arse!"

Alarmed, nearly unmanned at the vastness of Jimmy's

loathing, I, agape and wide-eyed, turned to him. Jimmy gave me a rueful but sneering smile of apology, the smile seeming to suggest that of a rabid fox.

"Oh, I forget, lurve, this is your first trip to Hawaii. I suspect you imagine it Elysium. It is true, Frederick, as your Mr. Samuel Clemens has claimed, that they are the lurvliest group of islands on God's green earth. It's what's on them that sours the bleeding stomach and has one eating Tums like popcorn. Nothing but a bunch of bleeding wogs and dagos, bleeding savages come right down to it. They can't even speak English, Frederick. You'll have the bleeding devil's time trying to comprehend a word the bleeding eejits are saying to you."

Here, adopting his most hyperbolic Oxford accent to date, Jimmy gave me a lesson in the pidgin he claimed all Hawaiians used. When they want to know where you have "been" (Jimmy said "bean"), "Instead of saying, 'Where have you bean?' these wogs say, 'Where you went?' " For "What do you want?" it was, "What you like?" Rather than answer, "I do not want anything," one heard, "I no like nawting." By this time Jimmy was working himself into such a state—he'd already told me "I'm peloothered, lurve, bleeding peloothered"—that I felt he'd be unable to proceed, so excruciatingly difficult had it become for him to form his fish mouth and articulate. But proceed he did, his exasperation far outweighing his inebriation.

"Suppose, Frederick, I wished to exhort you to make your best effort. Do you know what these bleeding wogs will say to you? These bleeding dagos will say, 'Geev-um!' Now tell me, lurve, if I hadn't told you that, would you have known what anyone was saying to you when you got to Hawaii? Of course you wouldn't!"

"Nevertheless, having read a lot of Irish writers I know that 'peloothered' would be the equivalent of one of us quaint Yanks saying he was 'drunk out of his skull.' But how many Hawaiians would know what you were saying if you threw peloothered at them?"

"Peloothered can be found in any serious dictionary in the English-speaking world!"

"I take serious exception to that. If it were found at all, I'm sure it would be either slang or a colloquialism."

"To hell and back with your bleeding exception!" Jimmy cried.

If I found myself eating with any of these bleeding wogs, I shouldn't be allowed to say, "It tastes delicious." I'd have to say, "It break da mouth." But even this was inaccurate as these bleeding savages were incapable of handling an h. "It break da mout." For some reason I found this vastly amusing and was thinking what a field day Ireland's James Joyce would have had in Hawaii. I almost said as much to O'Twoomey. Not only did I suspect, however, that Jimmy would deny James Joyce's existence but O'Twoomey's monologue was not about to be interrupted. Something as simple as "How are you today?" became "Howzit?" When and if I finally became accepted, I'd know because "these creatures or whatever they are" would start calling me "brother." Of course these "dagos" couldn't be expected to handle anything as simple as "brother." This came out "bruh-duh" or, even worse—and here Jimmy shook himself feverishly, as though the malaria was on him—simply "bruh." "The day you are completely at one with them, Frederick, you'll be walking down the street and on meeting you every one of these apes will cry, 'Howzit, bruh?' " Jimmy turned to me, his hand slid under the tray and came over to pat me affectionately on the left thigh. He sighed. "I told you I was going to tell you something, lurve. Then I told you what I said I was going to tell you. Now I'm telling you that I've just told you. You get my point, Frederick?"

Oh, dear reader, Jimmy sat there as complacent as Gibraltar. The pleasure he took in himself had its boundaries somewhere in infinity. It was at this point I thought I might slip in my observation on what Ireland's Joyce would have done with pidgin. There would be no such luck. Jimmy had removed his hand from my thigh, had gone back to looking straight ahead, and as he again began talking his head bobbed up and down and his mass of graying hair flopped all round his enormous forehead.

"To the heart of the matter, Frederick. Who in Christ's damnation wants to be accepted by these savages? Like your bleeding niggers, lurve, these people have no written history, no literature, no nothing but rice and shrimp. For that matter, and come right down to it, the Irish have produced the only writers of enduring value. Shaw, Yeats, Synge, O'Casey. Ah!" Jimmy sighed with immeasurable nostalgia. It was the sigh of the gods, coming, as it seemed to do, from that far-off and clouded-in Olympus.

I absolutely refused to let that slip through. "Well, Jimmy, there was Shakespeare, you know?"

"Overrated," Jimmy sneered.

What the hell could one say to this Irishman?

It was now Jimmy's moment to set me straight on any fallacious notions I might hold of Hawaii's being a paradisiacal mixture of racial and ethnic groups. Listening to Mr. James O'Twoomey—the most biased man I'd ever encountered in Christendom, a not uncommon phenomenon among the Irish—lecture me on the bleeding evils and seenfulness of racial and religious prejudice stupefied and undid me to the point where I sat in a kind of mind-blowing euphoria, imagining that I was caught up in some unending improbable dream. It was rather as if I'd reached that eminence whereon I'd been granted a private audience with the Pope and the Pope had spent my allocated five minutes proselytizing the health-inducing—high color to the cheeks, peace of mind, calmness of spirit—advantages of frequent participation in wildly abandoned sexual orgies.

The most despised man on the islands, according to Jimmy, and as I would find out soon enough, was the white man, who was invariably referred to as a *haole* (*how*-lee), which was the equivalent of a mainland "nigger" calling a white man "a fucking honky." As it was the first time in our conversation—that is to say, Jimmy's monologue—that Jimmy had used the all-purpose adjective "fucking," he abruptly and violently cupped his mouth with the palm of his chubby hand, rather as if he expected his Jesuit school-masters to be waiting in the wings ready to cane him half to death, his eyes opened wide with the horror of his indelicacy, he removed his hand from his mouth, apologized profusely, and promised he wouldn't let that awful word slip out again.

"Swear!" he cried, raising his right hand to the heavens. Racial and ethnic slurs were rampant, epidemic, flips for Filipinos; nips or Buddha-heads for Japanese, chinks or pakes for Chinese, yobos for Koreans, borinques for Puerto Ricans, popolos for "niggers," and even the pure Hawaiians suffered the derogation kanakas. As to the poor Portuguese or Portugees, as they were called, they had been reduced to being absolutely interchangeable with the Polacks of our mainland jokes. The only group who had avoided any ethnic slur was the bleeding Samoans.

"Why is that, Jimmy?"

"Oh, Frederick, me lurve, your ignorance of the islands borders on the unforgivable. Nobody dares cast an ethnic slur on Samoans. All Samoans"—Jimmy raised his right hand to the heavens once more—"stand six feet seven, weigh 275 pounds, and have a thirty-two-inch waist. If they can make an X on a piece of paper, they are transported to your mainland universities to play that absurd mutation of the Irish game you choose to call football. If they are unable to make their little X, they muck about Honolulu and work for loan sharks and collection agencies, breaking the arms and legs of the poor souls who can't pay. I must say, though, in all fairness to them, lurve, and unless their employers are really angry and want the kneecaps broken, these lads can give you some marvelously clean breaks." Jimmy now instructed me as a fellow *haole* how I ought to approach a Samoan should such an unthinkable confrontation arise. Shoving his chubby hands up into the sleeves of his gabardine jacket, suggesting the way the Japanese put their hands into the billowing sleeves of their kimonos, he began bobbing his head up and down in the Orientals' gesture of politesse and, as though he were I addressing that imagined monstrous

Samoan, kept repeating over and over, "You my brud-duh, you my brud-duh, you my *bruh!*" Unhappily, the Samoans did some rather nastier things than breaking legs and for that they should have to pay dearly. I had no idea what Jimmy meant by that but also didn't doubt that he would tell me.

8

Jimmy now had his elbows propped on the tray, was cradling his jaw in his clenched fists, staring directly at me, and as I returned his stare, he rolled his eyes wildly and secretively to the left, indicating I should come closer. Even with my face almost up to his, he rolled his eyes yet again, suggesting I come even closer, and my face ended up almost lip to lip with his. "Of course, Frederick," Jimmy whispered, "when our little group leaves these paradisiacal islands, there's going to be about six less Samoans!"

"There's going to be what?" I cried.

Jimmy raised his index finger to his lips and shushed me so violently that his spittle sprayed all over my face. "I mean," he said, "we are going to get some shotguns, blow their goddamn thick skulls off, stuff them into the trunks of Toyotas, and leave the cars in the long-term parking lot of Honolulu's International Airport. It's not only a reprisal, it's an out-and-out warning to their employers, the bleeding eejit pakes and yobos."

"But why in the world would you want to do that, Jimmy?"

"Because the bleeding eejit pakes and yobos want a dollar a ticket, that is, a fourth of our total Hawaiian take, for insurance purposes only, that is, insurance that our distributors and sellers will be able to move freely in Honolulu. They themselves won't do a blasted thing, distribute, sell, anything else. They just demand a fourth of the take to ensure our people will be able to move about the islands unmolested. I mean, godawmighty, Frederick, your own Mafia, knowing the monies go to the poor, the sick, the downtrodden of our beloved but impoverished Ireland, don't interfere with our operations."

"Who fixes that for you? Cookie?"

"Now, Frederick," Jimmy said, smiling despite himself and patting me lovingly on the thigh, "don't be a naughty boy, lurve. In fact, your Mafia volunteered to come over here and intercede in our behalf, but we refused and told them we were quite capable of handling our own affairs, thank you, ma'am. Besides, one does not accept favors from the Mafia. Their bill always comes due, if you know what I mean? You see what happened, we told these bleeding eejits in Hawaii to ram it up their bleeding arses and they, in turn, put some double-aught buck into a sawed-off shotgun, blew away the head of our distributor—the cutest little Buddha-head you ever saw—threw the poor bugger's body into the trunk of his Toyota, and left him in the airport's parking lot. The poor chap's decomposing body lay there so long that by the time they discovered him he had stunk up the whole airport."

"But listen, Jimmy, I don't understand this at all. I thought you said this was a pleasure outing for the more deserving workers of your Hospital Trusts."

"Well, it is and it isn't. There can hardly be any harm in mixing a little business with pleasure. Aboard this flight are three superb gunmen, one from Dublin and two we picked up in New York City, members of the Irish Republican Brotherhood."

"Is the Irish Republican Brotherhood the same as the Irish Republican Army or IRA?"

"Oh, no, the IRB is strictly an American organization. As it happens, these two chaps we picked up in New York City were formerly with the IRA but things became extremely uncomfortable for them in Belfast and Derry and they were forced to emigrate to the United States."

Against the possibility of any reason, judgment, or sanity, I found myself so caught up in O'Twoomey's lunacy that I started craning my neck up and down the cabin's aisle trying to isolate these "superb gunmen." Jimmy laughed heartily and told me not to bother as I wouldn't spot them in a million years. "Let me say only that their leader is old enough to have stolen the Peking Man!"

"To have stolen *what*?"

"The Peking Man!"

My ignorance of archaeology verged on the sublime but I did know what the Peking Man was. In a limestone cave near Peking, during approximately the decade between the late twenties and the late thirties, anthropologists had uncovered human skulls, limb bones, jaws, and teeth, which were said to predate Neanderthal Man by at least five hundred thousand, perhaps six hundred thousand, years. However, with World War II looming, a decision was made to move the bones to the United States for safekeeping during the war. The relics were thereupon packed into two redwood chests and moved by train from Peking to the port of Chinwangtao, where the chests were loaded aboard the S.S. *President Harrison* for shipment to the States. From December 7, 1941, the very day the Japanese attacked Pearl Harbor, the redwood chests were never again seen. Moreover, I knew that after these nigh onto four decades, there was still outstanding a substantial reward—perhaps as much as fifty thousand dollars—for their return, no questions asked; but Jimmy scoffed at this and said the reward was a hundred fifty thousand but with some hard bargaining one could easily reap at least two hundred fifty thousand dollars.

"But, Jimmy, why in the world would you want to steal the Peking Man?"

"Frederick, lurve, sometimes your ignorance appalls me. Pius XII couldn't very well sit still for that kind of blasphemy, a bunch of crackpot scientists uncovering a bunch of bleeding monkey bones predating Christ by perhaps more than one or two million years and having the audacity to claim they were men."

"If you don't mind my asking, where are these relics now? Underneath the Vatican in the room adjoining the Pope's pornography collection?"

"Oh, Frederick, you really are choosing to be a naughty boy, aren't you? As a matter of fact, the remains are right in my Dublin flat. They are magnificently polished and cleaned and I use the skulls to serve my Guinness in. You come visit me one day in Dublin and I'll serve you some splendid dark in one of the skulls. Word of honor!"

All the time Jimmy had been talking I once again had been looking loonily up and down the aisle and now told Jimmy that the only man who appeared old enough to have pulled off the Peking Man caper seemed to be Father Maguire. Jimmy threw his head back and roared with laughter, told me I might just be right, lowered his seat, told me he must, absolutely *must,* sleep, and asked me to awaken him in Honolulu. "You really are a truly lurverly chap, Frederick," he said. He then went into the deepest most nerve-wracking snore I'd ever heard. James Seamus Finbarr O'Twoomey snored all the way to paradise.

9

Now on American Airlines Flight 201, I was trying to remember the Brigadier, My Lai 4, the entire senseless war, recriminations, past hurts inflicted or imagined, all those things that members of a family seem somehow less able to forgive in each other than strangers are able to. I found that for the moment at least I was in no way up to recalling these things. Our tall, sturdy-legged, sprightly, and vacuously gray-eyed stewardess, Ms. Robin Glenn, happily injected herself into my consciousness for the nonce and prevented my recalling an unfortunate confrontation I'd had with the Brigadier about Vietnam.

Ms. Glenn's haunting eyes were a constant recrimination telling me she thought something was wrong with me, something not at all right. It wasn't as simple as having refused her breakfast of scrambled eggs and sausage, of having forsaken the movie *Jeremiah Johnson* with Robert Redford, or even at that moment of having refused the economy section's dinner choices of chicken luau or manicotti. It was something a good deal more distressing to Ms. Glenn and perhaps something not notably indigenous to her generation. I was not jolly. I am unable to pinpoint the precise moment Ms. Glenn abstracted the lack of felicity within me but I do know that from the time she did so she set herself the improbable task of instilling in me what her employer doubtless would have called "the aloha spirit."

Our bargain had been simple enough, though my part of it was utterly tacit. In exchange for refilling my vodka tonic on the rocks whenever it was discovered empty, my obsequiously laconic smile had seemed to suggest I would refrain from breaking wind, wouldn't pick my nose and wipe the viscous waste on those damp cocktail napkins Ms. Glenn had to retrieve, and wouldn't vomit in the laps of any passengers in the completely jammed steerage section. Mentally or physically, Ms. Glenn's part of the bargain required no great effort. I was nursing no more than one drink every forty minutes or so, perhaps as few as one an hour. To my agitation, however, Ms. Glenn seemed to materialize every quarter hour, would myopically scrutinize my plastic cup, satisfy herself that it still contained vodka, and then would wordlessly retreat into the darkness of the forward bulkhead area. Alas, when my cup was found to be empty, Ms. Glenn at some unhappy point decided, or apparently decided, that what I needed was a little prodding into the grand adventure called Hawaii. In two hours the captain would be announcing our impending descent into Honolulu and such was the enormous altitude at which we flew that descent would take yet another hour after his announcement.

Like that good old boy from Plains, Georgia, who had the whole country by the balls before the country even realized he had its fly unzipped, Ms. Glenn began her campaign to lure me into gladness gingerly and tactfully enough, even in what I suppose she imagined was a kind of quaint, charming subtlety. Whereas she'd previously been taking my empty cup unbidden, filling it, and returning it to my tray with nary a word, she now began to hover over me until I was forced to look up into a doll-like smile of great artifice and in gratingly lyrical tones she'd ask the obviously rhetorical did I "care for another" or how would "a nice lovely fresh one" do me? Invariably my answer was a vigorous but mute nod of affirmation. Despite the fact that Ms. Glenn spoke quietly and that I didn't speak at all, I began to suspect, as only an alcoholic in thrall to his own and inevitable paranoia can suspect, that these exchanges had become matters of sympathy or alarm to those passengers in our immediate vicinity and it was all I could do to refrain from saying, "Goddamnit, yes, I'll have another drink. And to allay your obvious qualms, you ought to know there have been times in my life I needed a pint of this stuff to rinse my mouth mornings. You know, the way you use Cepacol?" In my fantasy I even appended, "Incidentally, as a practical matter and for a survey I'm conducting for Erica Jong, do you use Cepacol before or after giving head?"

In the course of putting down a drink Ms. Glenn wanted to know if it was my first trip to Hawaii. I said that it was. She said I must be thrilled. I said I wasn't in the least thrilled. When I looked up into her large, gray, haunting, and vacuous eyes, I detected in them a perplexity of which I hadn't credited her capable and hence was compelled to offer a smile by way of apology. Ms. Glenn wanted to know if I was staying on Waikiki. If I was I must absolutely stay away from the hotel bars and the floor shows featuring "the Steve and Eydie–Tony Bennett–Don Ho bunch." That was all part of Waikiki's "flagrant, unarmed robbery." Again I smiled in deference to Ms. Glenn's perception. She had no trouble detecting I hadn't any shekels. Ms. Glenn recommended a lot of sun for me. When I needed my vodka tonics she told me to walk to the corner of Kalakaua, Waikiki's main drag and "a depraved pigsty after sunset," and Lewers Street and at the Holiday Hotel—not to be confused with the Holiday Inn, "another trap"—I'd find a most comfortable little bar with a naval decor where I could get a drink at mainland prices. The place was called Shipwreck Kelly's. Evenings the place also featured an authentic

Hawaiian group. Again I thanked her but told her her information was gratuitous as I was staying with friends in a Honolulu suburb pronounced, I believe, Hawaii Kai.

"Hawaii Kai!" cried the lovely Ms. Glenn. "That's where I live! Where in Hawaii Kai?"

It was some street with a kanaka name I could neither pronounce nor spell.

"Hey," Ms. Glenn said, "I thought you'd never been to Hawaii. Where do you get that kanaka stuff?"

I pointed at my seatmate, Mr. James Seamus Finbarr O'Twoomey, the totally insane and drunken Dublin Irishman who had long since passed out.

"That figures," Ms. Glenn said. "I'll tell you this, though, as a stranger and a white man—a *haole*, did the informed Mr. O'Twoomey give you that expression?—you'd better be careful how you throw that word kanaka around on Oahu."

I promised I'd be a good and obedient boy.

"My fiancé and I share a houseboat at the marina in Hawaii Kai. The Coco Marina. It's right behind the main shopping plaza there. Your friends will know where it is."

Was this an invitation to a ménage à trois? Perhaps Ms. Glenn's fiancé was one of those pure Hawaiian flower children. She had certainly been indignant enough at my use of kanaka. Abruptly I grew giddy and ethereal with mirth, thinking I might laugh in the bewildered Ms. Glenn's face. I had conjured up this vision of Ms. Glenn, her kanaka fiancé, and myself, all naked except for leis and exuberantly smearing one another with coconut oil, about ready to abandon ourselves to the houseboat's water bed and thereupon defile the smug suburban ambiance of good old Hawaii Kai. I was mortified and turned my back on Ms. Glenn and took comfort in Jimmy O'Twoomey's drunken snoring, thinking that at least I'd heard the end of him until we reached Honolulu.

By then *Jeremiah Johnson* was long since over, the houselights, as it were, had gone up, and my fellow passengers, having placed their orders for either chicken luau or manicotti, were awaiting their dinners and reclining in a stunned loginess induced by the incessant drone of the engines and the near-interminable length of the flight. It was when I adamantly refused both dinner choices that my dialogue with Ms. Glenn turned somewhat heated, then disintegrated completely and I again sensed the blood rushing to my face, certain that the passengers in our proximity were picking up every nuance of my supercilious replies. By then I had determined to get Ms. Glenn away from me at any expense.

Surely I would have a tossed salad and some rolls? Most surely I would not. Did I want to spend my Hawaiian "vacation" in a sickbed? For most of my forty-plus years I'd been "an ambulatory, invalided outpatient" but had somehow managed to survive without this being readily detected. Assuredly there must be something she could do for me. Ms. Glenn not only had left herself wide open for my reply, she had all but invited it. Snapping my head angrily round to her, my eyes falling precisely at the level her tight American-flag-red skirt clung tautly to her fine full thighs and revealed a suggestion of her Venus mound, I hung on my face a demented, eye-crossed, and near-drooling lust, then snapped, "There is most absolutely something you can do for me!"

To my extreme discomfort this did not appear to have the desired effect. Ms. Glenn's firmly planted legs neither moved nor even twitched; and after what seemed an eternity, with my head all the while ballooning with burning vertigo, I looked up, my neck seeming literally to creak as it did so, and into Ms. Glenn's huge gray eyes to see they'd misted over to a stunning violet, deep, deep lavender, the way I'd seen them do at the beginning of the flight when the drunken, sleeping Irishman next to me had been badgering her unmercifully. Before I could say that I was sorry, genuinely sorry, that though my trip was not in the least a pleasure outing I had no right whatever to lay the sadness of it on her, Ms. Glenn whispered violently at me, "You rotten SOB," the SOB sizzling out like *esss ohhhh beeee*. When Ms.

Glenn stormed away, I'd seen the last of her insofar as her attempting banter. She was to serve me two more drinks before the plane at last settled onto the runway of the Honolulu International Airport, but at these times she was grimly efficient and avoided my eyes as she set the plastic cups on my tray.

This seems an inauspicious beginning for what was to follow. Ms. Glenn would not only make up a significant part of the canvas of the ensuing week's deathwatch and burial but was to become a large part of my life during the next four years, at least those months of my life I spent in Hawaii. It ended—well, no, not really; it hasn't ended yet— one sunny Easter Sunday when we were occupying a room in the Towers of the Royal Hawaiian Hotel, Waikiki's legendary Pink Palace, and in some ultimate pique of passion Ms. Glenn hurled a double-pronged steak-grilling fork at me and it lodged in my chest (as I type I discover my fingers have unconsciously left the keys to rub tentatively at my sweatshirted chest where the two round BB-size purple scars still exist), yes, lodged in my chest to, I might add, a drunken and raucous laughter emitting from me. I expect it couldn't have "ended" any other way. Unlike the narrator I call Exley, who can "lie" about anything unless it might significantly hurt or damage someone, Ms. Robin Glenn lied about everything and it wasn't so much that she didn't care what these tales might do to another as that she was totally oblivious to the irreparable damage her meretricious slanders were initiating. Her fantasies were boundless and in the matter of sex she was and always had been the femme fatale victim. Beside Robin's sexual hysteria, that of Susan Brownmiller's *Against Our Will* seems a quiet and brilliantly reasoned academic treatise.

10

At the fashionable prep school Robin had attended in New England, for example, an elderly, decrepit janitor had entered her room one witching hour when her bunkmate was confined to the infirmary with the flu and on muffling her strangled, painful cries had there had his way with her, taking her virginity in the process. At the time Robin was fourteen and out of fear of the humiliating repercussions hadn't informed the authorities. Had it happened again? "Only twice." This came from a demure and maidenly Robin, her large, haunting eyes avoiding mine as they always did in her confessional moods. I don't think the evasion of eyes was so much that of a liar—though she was certainly that—but that with each telling her stories so ballooned, took on such different and ghastly implications, that she must have sensed those hauntingly unsparing eyes, had she riveted me in their relentless regard, would have so discountenanced me as to render me hideous, doing this at the same time that, even conceding the pitiable and thrillingly lovely Robin may have been doing nothing more than groping, in her loony way, for some glimpse of the truth, I yet arrived at that absurdly existential moment I couldn't believe a word she said during these "confessions" and came not only to smile during these sob-ridden, body-contorting soliloquies but had to muster the Spartan regimentation of a marathon runner to prevent my laughing right in Ms. Robin Glenn's tear-disfigured face.

The elderly decrepit janitor turned out to be twenty-year-old Dick Brophy, the junior quarterback at either Williams or Amherst or Colby or the University of Vermont or whatever college was located in the same town as Robin's prep school (though Robin finally settled on the participants, the town, the prep school, and the college changed with each telling). As part of Dick Brophy's athletic scholarship, he'd been guaranteed a job and, between the evening hours of nine and eleven, he'd swept and mopped the halls and lavatories of Robin's particular prep school dormitory, this among his other, rather more strenuous and seemingly inexhaustible exertions. Nor apparently had there been any need for Robin's roommate, Ms. Priscilla Saunders, to be confined to the infirmary during these assignations, which did not happen "only twice" but were nightly sport. Dick Brophy serviced both Ms. Robin Glenn and Ms. Priscilla Saunders. Although Robin reluctantly allowed that Dick Brophy had been "real cute," even "superneat," he was an awful coward for "a hoity-toity swaggering jock" and in some ways so disgusting as to be "ugh." Even though he paid for them, Dick Brophy's pusillanimity took the form of making the girls buy the condoms as in a small prep school–college town he didn't feel it would be good for his "icky all-American, golden-boy image" to be walking into drugstores and ordering Trojans.

"Either you buy them," Dick Brophy had menacingly told the girls, "or get your asses knocked up. And if that happens, I won't know from nothin'. *Nothin', yuh heah me?*"

It goes without saying that Ms. Robin Glenn had been

much too timid for such a sleazy mission. But, brother, should I have known that Ms. Priscilla Saunders! "Balls! Balls you wouldn't believe!" Ms. Priscilla Saunders would don panty hose, pumps, a dress, a little makeup, strut into a drugstore as bold as a sumo wrestler into a fag bar and walk out with "Golden Trojans by the orange crate." In the matter of Dick Brophy's "ugh," whenever one of the girls was menstruating, Dick Brophy forced her to——. Silence descended and Robin's swimming and now stunningly violet eyes came to rest pleadingly on mine, forcing my own to erase their wry twinkle and my lips to desist from their randy smile. Now Robin pointed with histrionic poignance to her mouth.

"Suck his cock?" I volunteered.

"Jesus!" Robin cried. "Do you have to be so nauseatingly disgusting and cruel when I'm trying with all my heart—*all my being!*—to get you to understand me? *Me! I'm somebody, too, you know, Frederick?*"

"Robin, let me remind you that not an hour ago I was lying topside getting some sun and reading the new Travis McGee when you came up and announced, 'Come below. I want to suck your cock.' That's what you said. 'I want to suck your cock.' And that's what you goddamn well did."

"That's now! That's now. This was when I was a goddamn fourteen-year-old kid. A goddamn baby!"

"Let me remind you further, dear, dear Robin, that this tale has gone from an 'elderly decrepit' janitor's twice raping you to a guy about fifty to forty to thirty to the twenty-year-old 'real cute, superneat' Dick Brophy, the Bowdoin quarterback or whoever the fuck he was. Still further, not only was there no rape involved but apparently you and Ms. Priscilla Saunders were such willing participants in these nightly ardors that the ballsy Ms. Saunders even purchased the cocksafes!"

Ms. Robin Glenn was deathly silent for many moments, pondering. Her eyes again narrowed and became evasive. She spoke in a holy whisper.

"None of this would have happened if Priscilla's and

my fathers hadn't started us on sex the year before, when we were only thirteen. I mean, honest, Frederick, once you get started on balling, it's worse than all the drugs combined, you know that."

"*Jesus Christ, Robin!* Are you telling me that Mr. Anthony Glenn, the Exxon vice-president headquartered in Paris, started having sex with his daughter when she was thirteen and that at approximately the same time, someplace else in America, perhaps Dearborn, Michigan, let's say, a Mr. Anthony Saunders, no doubt a General Motors vice-president, introduced his virginal daughter to lust and that's why you girls had to have your nocturnal fucks from janitor-quarterback Dick Brophy? Is that what you're telling me, *for Jesus H. Kheeeriiist's sake*?"

"You're goddamn right that's what I'm telling you! Both our mumses found out about it and herded us off to that Gestapo prep school, as though it was our fault! Jesus! Daddy's the one who should have been put into solitary confinement! Should have been castrated!" Robin sighed. "That's why I only spent a year at the Sorbonne."

"I thought you went to Vassar."

"Smith. Smith! But I did my freshman year at the Sorbonne. That's where I really wanted to graduate. Both Mums and I thought when I came back to Paris as a young lady Daddy would leave me alone. But of course he didn't, the scum. That's when Mums shipped me back to Northampton."

"Well, of course. Why not? Anything you say. I understand everything now."

Robin's father, Anthony "Tony" Glenn, lived in Queens, where he had been born. Her "mums," Evelyn Glenn (née Flaherty), had been born and raised in the Prospect Park section of Brooklyn. They had been married thirty years. Robin was their only child. Tony was a plumber retired from George Meany's old local; also retired, Evelyn had been an executive secretary for Con Edison. Robin's secondary education had all taken place in the public schools of Queens. She had been an A student. She had then completed two years at the State University of New York at New Paltz where, before getting an "itch to see the world," she had enrolled with a view to becoming a secondary school English teacher, Lord forbid. Moreover, when on one of my later trips to Hawaii I found myself, incredibly, seated next to Tony and Evelyn Glenn in the coach section of a United Airlines 747, I wasn't half an hour into the conversation (I never mentioned knowing Robin and such was their pride in her they expressed no surprise at my curiosity about Robin or themselves) without being unequivocally certain that Tony Glenn had never touched his daughter save in the utmost paternalistically loving fashion, such parental adoration there was in their voices when they spoke of Robin and her "wealthy fiancé" who was, according to Tony, paying for "me and Evy's thirtieth wedding anniversary trip" and putting them up at the Holiday Inn "right on the beach, big swimming pool, the whole shebang!" I waited years to confront Robin with the "truth" of her heritage. I simply became so bored with her stories that I grew angry with weariness. That was the Easter Sunday I got the steak-grilling fork hurled into my chest.

I am trying to understand. At the time of our initial madly desperate coupling, I was forty-three, Robin twenty-three. As I write I am forty-eight and Robin is twenty-four, by her own incomprehensible geometric progression having added only one year in that period I have added five. Robin's persistently repetitive insistence on her age has me moronically counting those years over and over again on the tips of my fingers. Whenever I laugh at her age claim, Robin angrily swears she possesses a State of Hawaii driver's license to prove it. On the occasion I laughed too heartily, Robin tore the houseboat apart, oh, frantic she was, dumping the contents of her purse and wallet onto the galley floor, emptying the dresser drawers onto the beige carpeting of what she calls "the fucking master suite," even hurling the contents of the galley drawers and cupboards, knives, forks, spoons, spatulas, corkscrews, cans of Comet, Lemon Pledge, the whole caboodle all over the place. On finishing, Robin had the place looking like typhoonland. She then dropped in a histrionic faintlike dreamlike motion to the floor, laid herself out spread eagle among the waxy rags, carving knives, boxes of Supreme Steel Wool, plastic jars of Lestoil and Johnson's Future Floor Wax, closed her eyes, with her arms formed a folded rood across her chest as though she were doing her mortuary bit, sobbed of course, and hissed at me.

"I know that goddamn fucking driver's license is around here someplace!"

"Don't worry about it. I can never find mine either."

This is patently untrue. Having just removed my wallet from the back pocket of my Levi's, I discover four items therein: a valid New York State driver's license, expiration date 3/31/82, free of traffic violations and markless save for an X preceding CORRECTIVE LENSES; a colored snapshot of my beautiful ten-year-old daughter by my last— oh, most emphatically and hopefully my last—wife; the phone number of some broad I must have found a good deal more than amusing in bed. In a drunken scrawl I have written, "Don't forget the nasty Irishperson! Wow, pal, she showed you stuff never dreamed of in"—I think it says— "Oriental erotica." This is followed by a seven-digit phone number from which, alas, I can decipher only four digits, the first, fourth, fifth, and seventh. As we have a fishing guide in the village, the Duke, who is a mathematical genius, I asked him the odds against putting the illegible numbers together in proper sequence and after a quick mental calculation he told me 1,752,647 to 1. Hence I spend a whole helluva lot of my waking hours summoning up names. Fallon? No. O'Brien? No. Duffy? No. O'Halloran? Last there is a recently dated prescription for a hundred thirty-milligram capsules of Serax, one of which has the potency equivalent of a blue bomber. My doctor, a very lovely, very bright, very attractive analyst, long ago threw her arms up in outraged dismay and despair at our sessions together, telling me I was too hopelessly imaginative to treat, too much of a tease and a con, and adamantly and menacingly advised that I not drift far from people who know I am bonkers.

The prescription even contains Alissa's—her handle, and what else could she be but an analyst with a moniker like that?—BNDD number so that I will have no trouble filling it if I get caught someplace among strangers. Alissa doesn't believe me housebroken enough to move among civilized people without being heavily sedated. These paltry items, then, are the accumulated remnants of a mismanaged life. When good buddy—as the CBers sign off—Alissa finally gets around to reading these pages—she's heavily into fiber diets and a group thing called Beta—I know she'll write me a five-page, single-spaced, typewritten letter telling me what the skimpy contents of my wallet signify.

Please don't, Alissa. I beseech you.

Yes, I am trying to understand. But it is unequivocally not Robin's lying I am trying to understand. I do in fact find this aspect of Robin's character rather endearing. In it there is—as there is in her lovemaking—something wild and intelligent and abandoned and imaginative and rather terrible as opposed to the awful sincerity of so many women. How drearily cumbersome I find both a sincere woman and her lovemaking. How creepy-crawly tentative and tippy-toey calf-eyed and poignantly pouty-lipped she comes to one who, unbeknownst to her and the virginal aura in which she has swaddled herself, is dying of boredom and yearning to snap, "Hey, listen here, what is this? Are we gonna fuck? Or do you want the cameras dollied in so we can consecrate this scene for the big screen? Say, like Jane Fonda?" At least Robin could walk through a screw without getting dust on her handsome shoulders. No, I am trying to understand her morbid, nearly self-flagellating need to confess. Perhaps it is because I am—I find my nose shriveling in very real self-mockery and distaste at the thought of even saying it—"a writer." Only three people in my life, other than Robin, have ever called me Frederick—my friends dubbing me Ex, Dopey Dildocks, Nutsy Fagin, Goofy Gumdrops, or whatever moves them—and these three have all filed and, don't ask me how, have had approved the most preposterously irrelevant, ponderous, and hilariously verbose master's theses, anchored by pages and pages of bibliography listing an awesome wasteland of portentously academic and psychological tomes with which they actually believed they were explaining "their Frederick."

Calling me Frederick, then, suggested that Ms. Robin Glenn saw me as a writer first, perhaps as just another screw second, and possibly even as a fellow human being third. Thus I suspect Robin believed she would show up "enshrined" among the pages of this book. Any number of times I tried to dissuade her from that absurd hope.

"Robin, if you're telling me all this stuff thinking I'm taking mental notes for putting you into words, get that right out of your head. I mean, get it out of your head but now! There's no way I'd ever admit to having fallen for a loony like you, least of all attempting to guide you into typeface so you'll be right out there where God and Mums—as you call her—could see it!"

"What an incredible prick of an egomaniac you are! Who'd want to be in one of your books? They're so dull and morbid and—and, yes, goddamnit, pornographic. Filthy! Fallen for me? That's the best line you've ever come up with. You don't even come to Hawaii to see me. You travel five thousand miles to put all those expensive flowers and leis on your brother's grave at Punchbowl, then come back to the houseboat, stay sloppy drunk on vodka for three days, and keep mooning and mourning about continuing to say goodbye to another generation. Fallen for me? Bullshit! You've never once—*not once!*—even told me you love me."

I said it then. I said, "I love you, Robin. I love you much more than I can ever tell you."

I wished I had left it at that and hadn't felt the need to qualify it.

"If those flowers and leis were expensive, you're the one who picked them out and damn near had me evacuating my bowels when one of those cute little Buddha worshipers laid the price on me. Not only that, you've recorded my every pilgrimage to Punchbowl with the six-zillion-dollar Nikon your fiancé or whatever he is gave you. Once, for Christ's sake, you even tried to get me to bow my head at the grave site. Ho, ho, ho! Exley in a posture of supplication. Recorded for posterity, no doubt!"

"You prick! I thought that's what you old farts did. You smug nothing antiquarians! Worship not only your gods but your family, your ancestors, your lofty notions of duty, honor, loyalty, crap, crap, crap, and more crap. All that shit that made your brother and his ilk send thousands of young boys to their deaths in Vietnam. How I loathe all of you. How much you make me want to puke. Yes, puke!"

11

In the three days of the Brigadier's dying, Robin did not make a single trip to Tripler Army Hospital to see him. She did not know him, of course, but her main reason was that being a child of immediacy, youth, and health she could not "abide sick people." For all that, she had an absolutely morbid fascination to be filled in on every blessed detail of my visits, how he looked, what was said, how much time I thought he had, and so forth, all of which she listened to with an intenseness I have never seen in her since. I went with my hosts, Wiley and his Hawaiian-born wife, Malia; my mother went with the Brigadier's wife, with whom she was staying. Occasionally our visits overlapped, occasionally they did not. On the last night of the Brigadier's life, Wiley and Malia and I remained longer than usual as the Brigadier seemed inordinately heavily sedated and drifting from irrationality to abrupt catnaps to infrequent periods of sense. During one of the latter periods he suddenly asked if someone would go to the soft drink machine at the end of the corridor and get him "a couple of cold cans of somethin'," preferably the noncarbonated orange drink.

Wiley and Malia and I had already been severely admonished by the nurse, one of those smugly efficient dyke types the army seems to attract, not to comply with such a request should it arise. As we were lay slobs outside the esoterica of her calling, she didn't deign to explain why but one didn't have to be a Mayo Clinic internist to fathom the reason. The Brigadier's cancer had become so pervasive that both his liver and kidneys had failed; indeed, they had placed a sheeted cage discreetly over his stomach to protect our virginal eyes from the severe distension of his abdomen, and it was apparent that any additional fluids would force the doctor the inconvenience of employing a catheter to draw off the excess urine. When we protested his request, the Brigadier's smile was utterly devoid of bitterness, rue, regret, sorrow. Then the Brigadier threw his arms out from his sides in the most good-natured gesture of futility, as though to say, "C'mon, guys, is it going to make any fucking difference?" and Malia, still laughing, went and fetched the orange drinks, which the Brigadier drank in long, embarrassingly grateful gulps, followed by lengthily unavoidable, near-painful belches, after which, poor Malia, in guilt I suppose, and certainly in trepidation of that formidable nurse, ran the empty cans back up the corridor and put them in the disposal container next to the machine. Late the next afternoon, the Brigadier's wife called Wiley's house, asked for me, said, "It's all over," and hung up.

For whatever reason, it was this story of the deathwatch that fascinated Robin above all the others and she had me repeating the story over and over again until she had every nuance of it down pat and kept saying, "Good for Malia! Good for Malia! And fuck the doctors! Fuck the doctors!" However, as the years passed, and she took to telling this story to her Hawaiian friends, she had somehow placed herself in the hospital room with us and as she told her version, her arm resting on the spine of the couch, her legs crossed in an arrogantly purposeful way, her left hand holding a lighted, mentholated More cigarillo with which she jabbed the air emphasizing her points, she began saying, "Yes, I'm glad we did it! Glad, glad, glad! And fuck the doctors!" Ultimately, of course, as even more time passed, and, I might add, she never blinked an eye telling the story in my presence, it hadn't been Malia at all who had fetched the orange drinks, it had been Robin.

"The Brigadier asked me for the soft drinks. And I goddamn well got them! What would you have done? Put yourself in my place. You'd better believe I fucking well got them! And I'm glad! Glad, glad, glad! And fuck the doctors!"

What a strange, haunting, loony, and touching homage to the Brigadier she'd never met and the man who had "sent thousands of young boys to their deaths in Vietnam."

But now we are pinpointing Ms. Robin Glenn's need to confess, albeit that her confessions were more often than not unadulterated lies. Whereas I was a child of the thirties, forties, and fifties, Robin was born in 1949, four years after we had dropped the bombs on Hiroshima and Nagasaki and, for all practical purposes, and dates notwithstanding, with those bombings began what we have come to call the twentieth century, born to a time when, if nuclear arsenals had eliminated one's need to ponder a possibly nonexistent future, they had also eliminated the need to encumber oneself with literature, history, art, music, all those things we lump together under the sweeping banner of culture. With the elimination of both past and future, Robin, together with her coevals, was a child of now and what she did not understand about us antediluvians and the absurd rituals, decorums, and loyalties with which we had been saddled was how much we—or at least I—envied the compulsions of Robin to sate thoroughly and irretrievably every passing whim, from seeing the latest "in" movie to an abrupt urge for "a cheeseburger with the works" within an hour after we'd finished a more than ample steak dinner, once even dragging me from the middle of a John Barth reading at the

University of Hawaii's Kuykendall Auditorium simply because she wanted to copulate.

Robin's confessions, as unlikely as it may seem, were born out of her love, however shabby that may have been—and probably still is—for me, her need to free herself from the narcissism and hedonism of her existence, and her desperate attempt to try to come together with me at that bourgeois—as opposed to the merely sexual—level where we both had histories replete with tipsy, wealthy, and slightly dotty aunts, mumses, lecherously incestuous fathers (in Robin's case, in any event), prep schools, proper universities, and so forth. "I'm somebody, too, you know, Frederick?" Robin had cried at me; and each time those huge, gray, haunting eyes avoided mine and she began a new penitential soliloquy charged with sighs, lavender tears, outrage, indignation, absurdity, she was adding to a history that in some subconscious way she actually believed was bringing our ages, if not chronologically, at least timelessly closer together in experience, no matter that the dimensions she was adding to her character were almost invariably pure fabrication. Dotty as it may seem, I'm positive Robin told me these stories because she loved me and prayed that the character she was creating in her image would provide those slings and arrows, the bruises, batterings, and hurts of time that would bring her ever nearer to me. Dottier still, on the day I told Robin I loved her I did.

12

Since puberty Robin had never been to a gynecologist who hadn't attempted rape. When I tried to get the name of one of these cunt consultants in order to write nastily eloquent epistles to the American Medical Association, I was told that "no, no, no, you'd do something crazy. Go down and beat the shit out of him or something," a most improbable Exley to the rescue on a white charger. Indeed, Ms. Glenn could not attend an afternoon movie without returning from that sparsely filled theater and in shaking horror telling me that though there were only a dozen people attending the matinee one ugly dwarf had settled himself smack down beside her and had there masturbated to his heart and cock's content. As the seventies progressed, bringing with it what psychologist R. D. Rosen calls psychobabble, i.e., designating a moody person a "manic depressive," saying "I'd like to get into your head" for "I wish I understood you," calling one "uptight" when in fact he might be in a state of severe clinical depression, when Robin went through her encounter group–primal scream–please touch–sensitivity training phase, found no relief there, and began hopping and skipping from one analyst to another, she did so because not a single one of these professionally trained analysts, male or female, had been able to keep his hands from her!

Robin's classic was delivered shortly after she returned from a two-week vacation to Italy, one of those free trips she was entitled to as an airline employee. At a cocktail party in Rome she had met the legendary fashion designer Emilio Pucci, who had insisted on the spot that Robin become one of his stable of models. Robin had been exorbitantly thrilled. There'd be no more slinging hash—or trying to sling hash—at drunken slobs like me, no more waiting to be fed bones from the likes of her fiancé. To seal their verbal contract Emilio had taken her to dinner at a snazzy trattoria on the Via Veneto, where they had occupied a private alcove off the main dining room. As the superb food, the dago red, and the exuberant chatter had flowed in profuse deference to the born-again, soon-to-be-famous Ms. Robin Glenn, Emilio had abruptly reached over, cupped the nape of Ms. Robin Glenn's regal neck in the palm of his strong hand, and furiously slammed her face into his lap, where to her eye-watering, nauseous disgust she'd discovered his fly unzipped. To Ms. Robin Glenn's present indignation and chagrin, and though I was totally unable to prevent it, I laughed hysterically at this tale. In the highly unlikely event that a junketing airline stewardess would find herself in old Italia in the same room with Emilio Pucci, I knew his girls were invariably size six and Robin hadn't seen that size since she was that age. With her Hawaiian tan and her marvelously full figure, Robin might have done just fine parading swim-suits around Malibu Beach for Mr. Jantzen and company but the closest she'd ever get to *Vogue* was subscribing to it. Ironically, Robin wasn't so much ired at my explosively derisive laughter as at my neglecting to ask her what happened.

92 ‡

"I don't know what you mean. There's more to the story? All right. What did happen? You take a little Guinea sausage into your mouth or what?"

Robin had kept gagging until she finally threw up her linguine and red clam sauce all over the great Mr. Emilio Pucci's seven-hundred-dollar suit.

"That's what fucking well happened!"

That vomiting had ended Ms. Robin Glenn's high fashion career right in its glorious incipience.

Robin's friend was not a kanaka but a *haole* and save in Robin's mind he was certainly not a fiancé. He was a very wealthy, very handsome blond man my age whose seafaring Nantucket ancestor had sailed to the islands shortly after Captain James Cook's arrival in 1778. That ancestor had jumped ship and had flourished, as all of his progeny had done since him. Robin's friend was a partner in a corporation consisting of five stockholders, two from old-family *haoles* and three Japanese-Americans. They owned a dozen first class resort hotels spread out among the various islands. With an individually owned construction company he built condominiums and shopping plazas. He lived with his beautiful wife, whose family went back in the islands almost as far as his, and two adolescent sons in a $1,750,000 oceanfront complex on the southwest shore of Maui. I know his wife was beautiful because one lunchtime in Lahaina Wiley and Malia pointed the two of them out to me at the bar of a restaurant owned by the ex-Dodger pitcher, Don Drysdale.

Although she wore no makeup and her long, naturally blond hair fell rather casually, even sloppily, over her shoulders, there was no mistaking the beauty of her facial structure or disguising the strikingly tanned figure beneath her elegantly custom-cut gray slacks and off-white blouse. Like so many people of old wealth she was devoid of ostentation and wore no jewelry save for a simple engagement ring and wedding band, both of white gold. She was drinking a John Collins. On the other hand, he wore loafers without socks, dusty khaki pants, and an equally dusty faded denim shirt completely unbuttoned. Sweat ran down his tanned, muscular chest and taut stomach past his beltline and into his trousers. Obviously he was building something around Lahaina and had just come from the construction site. In the manner of his laborers, he hurriedly drank three beers from the bottle. The sweat dried, he refused to have lunch with his lovely bride as—I think I heard him say—"we're pouring piling" and, kissing her with genuine affection, he left her to order another John Collins and a roast beef sandwich. On his way out he called back to the bartender and told him to put everything on his tab, the company's, not his personal one. He also told the guy to write himself in a five-buck tip. We did not look anything alike but, save for his build being muscular while mine ran to sedentary flab, we were both five-ten and weighed about 180 and I suddenly understood where all Robin's gifts to me had come from, aloha shirts, V-necked yachting and tennis sweaters, khaki, denim and Bermuda slacks, socks, sandals, deck shoes. She had bought them for him and after banging her he'd departed without even re-membering to take them with him. I don't know that I'd have bothered either. After his departure I spent a lot of time staring at his wife. For all of me she could have been the biggest bitch in Christendom but she gave off class the way boxers give us the lilt in their walks.

Over the years Robin has tried repeatedly to convince me, but mainly herself, that by fornicating on his houseboat we were not only in dire physical danger—"With his con-nections in these islands he'd probably have us both killed!" —but that she was jeopardizing her entire future right at that moment he was on the verge of divorcing his wife and marrying Robin. When he unexpectedly showed up on the houseboat, according to Robin, he demanded that she be there and if he ever caught her with another man—Robin leveled her joined index and middle fingers at me, made what she imagined were the reports of an army-issue .45-caliber sidearm but which sounded more like a sneezing fit, *cahcheeew, cahcheeew, cahcheeew,* then raised her two joined fingers up and feigned a gory slashing of her lovely throat. All this was manifestly ridiculous. If Robin were lucky, he came to the houseboat twice a month, more often than not only once, and on these occasions he telephoned her two or three days in advance to give her his anticipated arrival time. He knew his mistress all too well. Besides the houseboat and a Master Charge for groceries and whatever else she needed (that card, too, was in his company's name), he had bought her a sun-yellow Porsche and had presented her with credit cards to Liberty House and two expensive boutiques along Kalakaua. On the consummation of our first violent copulation, which took place within twenty-four hours after she'd hissed at me her "rotten esss oooh beee" high above the imperially azure Pacific, violent in only the way the specter of the Brigadier's imminent death could make it violent, Robin leaped instantly from the bed, pranced to the dresser, picked up a brush, and with furious jerkiness began brushing her hair, as she did so studying herself with incredible intentness in the dresser's mirror. When I started to light a cigarette, she demanded I abandon it, rise, walk to her, stand behind her, put my arms around her waist, and by thrusting my chin over her right shoulder place my cheek against hers and study her image in the mirror with the very intentness she was studying herself.

"See what you did to me?" she demanded. "See what you did!" I did not see. "The color, the flush in my cheeks. You did that! Who needs makeup after a screw like that?"

Assuming that was meant as a compliment, I summoned up an appropriate modesty and said, "Well, you helped, too, you know?"

"No, you did it! You!"

As it turned out, Ms. Robin Glenn never did anything to herself. People did things to her. Like a dozen other women I have known, Robin had this laughably preposterous need to convince her lovers that if they weren't getting a virgin—as they most certainly weren't—they were staking out unique claims to all sorts of firsts "inflicted" upon her body. No matter that Robin could wet her pants by just dancing solo around the living area of the houseboat listening to Andy Williams sing "Didn't We?" on the stereo,

I was the first man who ever made Robin "come" (Jesus, gang, it's time to go pop a can of Genesee Light on that one). Although Robin had never been into oral intercourse since those unbearable, nightmarish days with Dick Brophy up at the University of New Hampshire, naturally my semen was the first she'd ever taken into her self and fed upon. On the first occasion I had anal intercourse with Robin, her comment on its consummation was that it was not only another "first" but that "I knew that you absolutely had to do that to me and get it out of your system," no matter that Robin had brought me to erection orally, then with all the aplomb of a diagnostician looking for rectal trouble and preparing to shove that ghastly looking proctoscope into one, had reached into the drawer of her bedstand, had brought out a tube of K-Y Jelly, as though she had no doubt that that universal balm of the gay world had reached such ubiquity that it was to be found in the nightstands of every bedroom in the republic, had lathered me up, and had directed me in.

When I came from the shower the next morning, I found a bikini panty-clad Robin cooking her idea of breakfast, two hamburgers on toasted English muffins loaded with pickle relish, to be washed down with Cokes. Expecting affection or a show of warmth for our nightly labors, I found instead a Robin on the attack, eyes flashing.

"Jesus, Frederick, if you ever have to do that disgusting thing to me again, you'll have to use prophylactics." I liked the delicacy of "prophylactics." "When I walked naked into the galley this morning, all your rotten icky muck plopped out of me right onto the goddamn floor. I almost puked cleaning it up. Why do you have to do such crummy things to me? Why, why, *why?*"

Within two days, frantically searching for a pencil to do the Sunday crossword puzzle, I had occasion to look into Robin's nightstand and discovered next to her tube of K-Y Jelly, if not an orange crate, enough condoms to have anal intercourse three times a day for the next six months. Apparently Robin had come a long way from the timid little girl who had let the ballsy Ms. Priscilla Saunders perform such sleazy pilgrimages to the drugstore. Men did things to Ms. Robin Glenn. On the Sunday she buried the steak-grilling fork in my chest, within an hour after she'd done so she'd convinced herself beyond all doubt that I'd also done that to myself simply to hurt and spite her. But that is enough of Robin for the moment. She is to occupy a much larger place in these notes than it makes me easy to contemplate. After my return to Alexandria Bay I would hear from her very often but never by mail. I made the mistake of telling her that tomorrow was spelled with one "m" and not "tom-morrow" as she had spelled it in a letter. The last words she ever put on paper were on a postcard reading, "Go f. your-self! You snobbish so-called intellectual P————k!" What they made of that card in our quaint and proper little village post office I don't even like to imagine.

For a time Robin's messages were conveyed to me by phone and received about six in the morning. It was mid-night her time and invariably she was slightly in her cups. Three months after I met her standing statuesquely and hauntingly above me as I was seated in a 707 on a Chicago runway waiting to pick up some passengers from Toronto so we could proceed to Honolulu and the Brigadier's death-watch, American Airlines discontinued its Hawaii flights, and as I understand it all personnel, save for some senior captains who would have to deadhead back to the mainland to connect with their flights, were forced either to return to the mainland city in which their flights originated or to re-sign. Robin resigned. From tidbits she's dropped over the months, both when I've been there and during these drunken erratic calls, I gather her "fiancé" has given her the title to the lovely houseboat, ironically named *Cirrhosis of the River,* ironical in the sense that I doubt that there's a river on Oahu wide enough for it to navigate upon or that he drinks enough to come up with a name like that. Robin, however, claims he can go through a quart of Tanqueray gin between six in the evening and midnight, which did not at all coincide with that three-beer virile construction boss I'd seen at Drysdale's bar in Lahaina.

13

Robin still had the sun-yellow Porsche, a new one at that, the credit cards, and so forth and she would tell me she was working but the job varied with each telling. At one time she'd be managing one of those expensive boutiques where she used to charge hand-wrought leather belts, at another time she was the hostess at the Monarch Room of the Royal Hawaiian Hotel, at still another she was lifeguard at the pool of the Kahala Hilton where she has become chums with Debbie Reynolds, Johnny Carson, Lucille Ball, Jack E. Leonard, and Joan Didion who, Robin gloatingly didn't hesitate to tell me, "thinks you're a lousy writer!" Whenever I was in Hawaii, and though I spent some of my time with Wiley and Malia who had moved to the island of Lanai, twenty-five air minutes from Honolulu, Robin always seemed to be on vacation from her job. From what I'd guessed and pieced together her fiancé spent less and less time aboard the *Cirrhosis of the River* but his business acquaintances passed all kinds of time there for much more negotiable pieces of paper than credit cards. Robin has never admitted to me that she was hooking but at the gut level I knew that she was. There is a very nice restaurant and lounge fronting the marina and once when Robin and I were leaving there I distinctly heard this exchange between the bartender and a waitress: "I'd give a month's salary for just about ten minutes with that." The waitress replied, "It'd cost you more than a month's salary for ten minutes with that." When I got back aboard, I poured myself a triple vodka and grapefruit juice, drank it in one gulp, walked immediately to the head, and threw up.

Taking Robin's calls at six in the morning was a distressing, humorous, frightening, crazy, somewhat terrifying experience. She was not only invariably tipsy, she was sobbing so heartrendingly that for the first three or four minutes I was unable to make out anything she said but what a no-good nothing slob of a tramp she was. I'd spend those minutes listening to this awesome self-flagellation, interrupting when I could to assure and reassure her what a lovely, loving, generous, sensitive, intelligent, and altogether stunning young woman she was. If this was so, why didn't I come to Hawaii? Because I hadn't any money. Robin had enough money for two. Within three days there would be a first class plane ticket in the mail. I didn't like the idea of having to move out of the houseboat on the frequent nights her "fiancé" came over. Why didn't I get a job like everyone else and then I'd be able to have my own place? I was never going to finish my book anyway. "Even if you do, it'll be a bunch of shit like the other two." This hurt. I held my peace. Did I love her? Would I say it? Yes.

Now then, this is the way it always ended. What am I doing now? I'm waiting for her to hang up so I can urinate, make a cup of tea, and do some scribbling on the shitty book I'm never going to finish. Do I ever think of her? Yes. In what way? In all kinds of ways. Am I alone? Yes. Will I do "that" to myself and think of her while I'm thus engaged? Robin will do the same thing and it'll be as though we are together. Once she asked me to call her when I'd finished to see if it had "happened" at the same time. That was too expensive. All right, Robin would call me. "You cheap bastard!" I'd had just enough time to micturate and get the teakettle humming nicely when the phone rang. I laughed. "Jesus, that was quick."

"You prick! You once accused me of being the horniest broad in the Western Hemisphere. But see how basically shy and retiring I am? How quickly I can bring it off when I'm by myself? You really are a prick, you know that, don't you Frederick?"

Did I ever participate in this absurd ritualistic autoerotic surrogate copulation with a partner five thousand miles away? Does it make any difference? In all the sad and illusory, the laughable and perspicacious, the unbearable and joyous days of my life, I was yet addressing myself to love.

Part Two

INTERMENT AND NEW BEGINNINGS

1

Listen, Marshal Dillon, I suspect I've bent your ear quite enough, but please believe me when I say that I am in no way up to this ceremony and have neither the character, strength, nor will to get through this interment without your aid. I realize that my saying I was certain I'd like you as a man hardly gives me the right to demand you reciprocate my affection, so if you feel you'd like to prop your size-thirteen boots up on your desk, lean back in your chair, push that ten-gallon baby over your grizzled face and catch a little shut-eye, please feel free to do so. Ironically, the Brigadier's fifteen-year-old son, Scott, is into his Rock period, as Picasso was into his Blue. His sun-bleached hair, worn in a ponytail, is down to the small of his back, and realizing how out of place he'd be in this oppressive milieu, he absolutely refused to attend. This of course infuriated me, as I'm sure it would have you, Matt, for I could only visualize him thirty years hence, stuck between flights at a bar in the San Antonio Airport, pensively sipping his drink and excoriating himself for not having gone to his father's funeral. In other words, Jim, I didn't want to see him set himself up for the kind of remorse none of us needs in middle age.

But now, staring across the Brigadier's bier at the seven-man honor guard, their rifles at port rest, I understand Scott's decision completely, as I'm sure his father would have, and know he did the right thing by staying away. Whether the guard is from the Twenty-fifth Infantry Division (James Jones's outfit) or Fort Shafter, I don't know, marshal, but from their vacant-eyed mute rigidity, I would suspect they had all spent one too many days in the line in Nam. As we are the only family represented, the old lady is standing between my sister-in-law, Judy, and me in the front row; in the row directly behind us I've spotted a couple of one-stars, the rest of the row being made up of guys holding the Brigadier's rank of bird colonel and in the rows behind them, in the very stylized and hierarchical way of the military, light colonels, majors, captains, lieutenants, warrant officers, sergeants, and so forth, respectively, entirely too much brass for the honor guard and for me.

Sweating under their field helmets, their necks encased in white silk scarfs worn like ascots, the honor guards stare so unseeingly I suspect that though laymen might view this as cushy duty, one or two of these guys—especially the one who, doubtless having sensed my own abundant discomfort, stares so eerily at me—would prefer being back in the line in Nam, killing Cong.

Robin is not here, the selfish bitch, having explained that she cannot "abide dead people." In the week I've been here I've become terribly smitten with her, as smitten, Big Jim, as I guess I've ever been. And though in fairness to her she told me repeatedly she wouldn't come, and in fact I never asked her to come and can in no way articulate any obligation on her part to do so, I yet had hoped she might. James Seamus Finbarr O'Twoomey, accompanied by this monstrous Samoan dude, Hannibal I believe O'Twoomey called him, a guy O'Twoomey claims to use as a bodyguard when he's in the islands, is here. Astonishingly, my best friend from Alexandria Bay, Toby Farquarson III, is also here. When I decamped from the funeral limousine and was making my way across the beautifully cropped grass of Punchbowl toward the bier, I had a chance to speak briefly with both of them. O'Twoomey told me he'd read the Brigadier's obituary in *The Honolulu Advertiser*, and as Exley wasn't that common a name he'd made the association with me immediately and had decided to do me the courtesy—"don't you know, lurve?"—of attending. Four days after I'd left the Bay with the old lady, Toby decided that as he'd never seen Hawaii, the Brigadier's death, though he hadn't known Bill, was as provoking an occasion as any for coming over. And of course my childhood friend, Wiley Hampson, and his wife, Malia, with whom I spent the past week's deathwatch, are here, all standing awkwardly back there behind me in one place or another, like characters waiting to be introduced into a novel. Wiley, Big Jim, is so very much family that he and his wife could as well be standing up here in the front row with us, to help leaven the oppressiveness as it were. The Brigadier would, I know, have very much liked Wiley to be in the family place.

2

On arriving in Honolulu, the old lady and I were met by the Brigadier's wife, with whom my mother would stay, and by Wiley and his petitely stunning wife, Malia, whom I was taken aback to discover was part kanaka, part Chinese, part Filipino, part French, one of those veritable chef's salads of racial and ethnic genes so indigenous to the islands. Directly the old lady and I had scented leis about our necks, had received our mandatory pecks to the cheeks from Judy and Malia and the aromatically funereal odor rising from the flowers seemed somehow appropriate and not nearly as frivolous a ritual as I'd so often envisioned it. Wiley exchanged phone numbers with Judy, told her he'd be in touch as soon as he had me settled in, kissed my mother again, and said he was looking forward to talking with her that evening at Tripler Hospital. On the expressway driving out to Hawaii Kai, Wiley pointed out "all the shit" that had, since his arrival fifteen years earlier, sprung up in the form of hotels, high rises, condominiums, and housing projects, not to mention "the fucking smog." Wiley used kanaka names for most of the developments, which meant nothing to me, told me he'd fled Los Angeles fifteen years earlier for the very same things that were once again "crushing in my fucking skull," interrupting himself again and again to address himself bitterly to the Brigadier's plight.

"Forty-six years old! A bird colonel. Three fucking wars! Silver Stars, Bronze Stars, Purple Hearts coming out his tuppy. Then the Big C starts eating away at his interior. How do you figure it, Ex? It isn't fair, you know?"

When Wiley would turn to me, seated next to him in the MG, his upper lids and lashes would flutter furiously and for the first time I oddly understood his childhood cognomen of Twitch. When he took his wild eyes from the freeway and turned back to Malia, who was seated in the jump seat of the brilliant red sports car, he'd be poised and primed for new horizons.

"You know what I'm going to do, Malia? I'm goddamn well selling everything, the house, the pool hall, the fishing boats, the cars, every goddamn thing and moving to Kauai or Lanai. Yeah, Lanai. No Cadillacs, no smog, no concrete, no hotels, no nothin'! I don't give a shit if I have to go into the field with the flips and pick pineapple! Mark my word, Malia. It all goes so quickly, you know? Unfair. *Yeah, unfair.*"

When I'd turn back to Malia, she'd wink at me, I at her, our way of agreeing that the Brigadier's imminent death had sent Wiley round the bend and into some deranged region. At forty-three, Wiley and I had been born in the same year, the same month—though different astrological signs—and Malia and I were agreeing that Wiley had made his life and that there were now no islands left for him. In either of our lives, I doubt Malia and I would ever be more smugly in error.

At Wiley's typically suburban three-bedroom two-bathroom house, Wiley went agape with pleasure at the old lady's gifts of Heath cheese and Croghan bologna, and before I'd taken a sip of the Budweiser he'd given me he was preparing grilled cheese sandwiches with half-inch-thick slabs of Heath, cutting Malia great chunks of bologna, and off on a nonstop reminiscence of home. In droll exasperation, Malia at length interrupted by saying, "Lanai? Why don't you go back to your precious St. Lawrence River?"

"Naw," Wiley said. "I really don't miss anything about that goddamn freeze-your-goodies-off place. Oh, maybe Ex here and a couple of other guys. Yeah, and one other thing —*Guinea food*. These chop-chop slant-eyes don't even know what wop food is, Ex." When I looked at Malia to study her reaction to "chop-chop slant-eyes," she was laughing affectionately and I understood that Wiley's chatter was the kind of rhetoric allowable between lovers. It was Wiley's salivating memories of Italian food that sent us to the supermarket at the Coco Marina Plaza in search of ingredients for lasagne.

We'd go to the hospital that night, we decided, and before returning there the following afternoon I'd make Malia and Wiley the biggest pan of lasagne ever seen in Christendom or, I added, in Buddhadom, nodding in amused deference to Malia, so much that they'd have to cut it into portions, freeze it, and be eating it for the next eleven and a half years. At the supermarket, as I hadn't any idea how long the Brigadier's dying would take, and as Wiley had told me he'd neither fish nor bother going into his pool hall however long it took, I first bought six quarts of Jim Beam for Wiley, six quarts of Smirnoff red label vodka for me, and, though Malia protested she didn't drink, I bought a gallon of good dry white Chablis for her.

"You guys," Malia said in mock and humorous disgust.

In the months ahead Malia would say *"you guys"* very often.

"It's the Irish way, Malia. At a wake one drinks himself into a stupor, sings songs about his mom, and no one ever dies."

Trying to find the lasagne ingredients from the long detailed list I'd made up, I'd been in the supermarket twenty-five minutes when I bumped, in the literal sense, smack into Ms. Robin Glenn. Like comics in a high hedge-rowed maze, I came from the paper towel–toilet tissue–baby diaper–Kleenex alley, Ms. Robin Glenn from the canned tomatoes–tomato puree–pasta–condiments alley, we turned directly into each other, and our carts met head-on. At first I did not recognize her. Her tobacco-sepia hair was down and brushed so lovingly and lengthily below her shoulders I was amazed to think she'd ever got all that tucked up beneath her petite American-flag-red-white-and-blue attendant's cap. She had scrubbed every trace of makeup from her face and she had on a pair of great round black shell-rimmed prescription glasses, a man's chocolate-brown full-sleeved velour shirt too big for her, and a pair of torn faded Levi's. She was barefooted. Behind those huge spectacles those equally huge gray haunting and vacuous eyes came to mine, told me nothing and to my "Excuse me" she spoke nary a word or even nodded, apparently still angry from my treatment of her on the flight. Abruptly she withdrew her cart three steps, started around us, stopped joltingly, turned to me, and said, "These must be your Hawaiian friends?"

"Malia and Wiley Hampson, Ms. Robin Glenn, the flight attendant I was lucky enough to draw on my way over."

So it ends and so it begins. Bird colonels don't die from the shrapnel in their legs and back but are eaten up by a carcinoma of the soul. Old friends don't miss much of home but Guinea food, and the last Watertown Exley male bumps his silly wired grocery cart into that of perhaps one of two women he'd ever love.

By the next day at noon, Wiley had gone from the simple ravings of the disaffected to the kind of hysterical monologue that under its own momentum achieves after a time its own inner logic, and though, behind Wiley's back, Malia and I continued to twirl our index fingers at our temples, our smiles grew increasingly forced and implied we'd begun to understand that, at forty-three, Wiley intended doing everything he damn well said he'd do. Wiley's life, as I knew better than anyone, had been the pursuit of some last island and I could see and hear in his endless ranting some need to exalt his life from merely pretty achievement to a plateau in the realms of art.

A month after the old lady and I returned to the Bay, she asked again if I'd sent Malia a thank-you note. I said no but I'd do so that day. I did so and ten days later the letter was returned stamped GONE, LEFT NO FORWARDING ADDRESS. Two days after that, Wiley called, exuberant. He and Malia were on Lanai, living in a rented plantation house, he was working in the pineapple fields with the flips, he'd sold his pool hall, his commercial fishing boats were on the market, and Ms. Robin Glenn was house-sitting his three-bedroom home in Hawaii Kai, trying to find him an appropriate renter, the monies from which would take care of the house's mortgage. "When are you coming over, Ex? It's paradise, fucking paradise."

If Wiley had been hyper driving from the airport to Hawaii Kai, he was, as I say, demented the next morning after having seen my brother the night before at Tripler. Wiley hadn't, I suspect, seen the Brigadier since Bill had entered the service in 1944, a very tall, very handsome, very slender young man of seventeen; and what Wiley'd seen the night before was a young man old at forty-six, his close-cropped hair having gone gray, his limbs wasted—he weighed only 120 pounds over a six-two frame—and that sheeted cage over his distended stomach. Malia had invited Robin over for brunch, and Malia and I were enchanted with both Robin's beauty and the history (we did not then know how much of it was pathological bullshit) she revealed at Malia's and my eager solicitations. Wiley was not impressed. Eyeing us over his bloody Marys and his uneaten scrambled eggs and bacon, he brooded on the Brigadier and his own dream of some final island, once actually sneering at me when he thought I'd laughed too effusively at one of Robin's tales, as though he were telling me that he found my gushing attempt to strip Ms. Robin Glenn of her panties nothing short of despicable at such a time.

In many respects the bonds between the Brigadier and Wiley were far stronger than any brothers' blood ties, characterized as they were by impossible codes, a lofty-toned morality, Watertownians' esoteric handshakes reinforcing our unswervable belief that where others didn't we knew precisely what was right and wrong with the world, that there was, as there was for everything, a time to die, and that at such a time a gentleman went into a limbo of mourning and would never think of laughing rather too affectedly at Robin's trite tales or giving her affectionate pats on her full Levied thighs. Wiley sneered. For thirty years I'd owed Wiley an apology, for reasons I'll go into, and the reason I'd never been able to make it was that the very self-righteousness he was revealing on this morning in his Hawaii Kai kitchen, while we drank and made our lasagne, was the kind of smugness that would not have allowed him to accept my apology gracefully.

Wiley and I'd met when, freshly scrubbed of an early September morning in 1935, we were taken by our separate mothers to the Academy Street School in Watertown and enrolled in Miss Whitney's kindergarten class. Neither Wiley nor I has any memory of that meeting and are united only in the memory of Miss Whitney and Old Charlie Reilly. Miss Whitney had snow-white, frazzled curly hair, the result I expect of too many permanents, a red face, and deceptively hawklike features, deceptive in that she was a tolerant charming woman who had an easy way with children. In the morning we were given chocolate milk in half-pint bottles, straws through which to drink it, and cookies. In the afternoons we took enforced naps on tumbling mats we used for exercise. We did projects and projects and projects, the only one I recall a watercolor of anything we chose to paint. At the time the Brigadier, my sister, and I were heavily into cowboys and spent a good deal of our home hours drawing, over and over again, the same cowboy, my sister and I copying or practically tracing the Brigadier's.

As he was older, at a higher grade level, and had therefore been subjected to more lessons attempting to reproduce the human anatomy in some semblance of dimensional perspective (as yet Grandma Moses hadn't reached her sixtieth birthday, begun her art career, and with her paintings tacitly proclaimed to the world, "Fuck perspective"), I took my lead from the Brigadier, drew a cowboy cum Stetson, neckerchief, chaps, boots, lariat, cacti, mountain horizon, the works, and mine was deemed so superior by Miss Whitney that she paraded me from classroom to classroom and had me display my creation before my more learned upper-grade school mates. When we entered the Brigadier's room, he put his head down on his folded arms on his desk, hid behind the kid in front of him, and sneered. To this day I don't know what he sneered but whenever I summon up the incident I project the adult Brigadier into that third-grader, put an Antonio y Cleopatra into his mouth, and around it have him saying, "Look at that frigging hot dog!" Despite the Brigadier's grandiose condescension, that plagiarized son of the prairie was the apex of my otherwise utterly undistinguished academic career in the Watertown public school system.

Old Charlie Reilly was principal. His office was on the same side as but at the opposite end of the corridor from our kindergarten room. As mysterious and omniscient as the Dalai Lama, he sat behind his closed office door. He had the blackest hair I'd ever seen, was the constant bearer of a formidable and apparently ineradicable five o'clock shadow, and also wore the thickest glasses I'd ever seen. In the seven years I was in his charge I can honestly say that though to my recollection his eyes were brown I was never able to get them into focus long enough to know their precise pigmentation, such was the eerie effect of his prescription. During his childhood in Albany, Old Charlie Reilly had been inadvertently hit so severely in the eye with a baseball bat that the eye had been dislodged from its socket and the specialist had pleaded for its removal, which Old Charlie Reilly and his parents adamantly declined, ending forever Old Charlie Reilly's dream of green, green outfields and leaving him with one eye so maverick in its cavity it seemed literally to hop and to skip behind those spooky lenses.

Far worse than anything else for Old Charlie Reilly, somewhere along the line he had cultivated a love for literature and, against his doctors' strenuous objections and doubtless any number of new prescriptions for ever and ever thicker lenses, he read eight, nine, ten books a week, holding the volumes four to five inches from his eyes, a good deal of this reading taking place behind the closed door to his office, where I doubt his administrative duties were all that burdensome.

Notwithstanding that Old Charlie Reilly was a lover of, a man obsessed with, words, we were impressed from the day of our enrollment in Miss Whitney's kindergarten class that the last place in the world we wanted to be sent was to Old Charlie Reilly for disciplining. From the moment one reached the second or third grade, however, this prospect held out little trepidation to the students and by the time we graduated into junior high school it held out no fear whatever. By then Hitler had invaded Poland, the evacuation of Dunkirk had come and gone, the Japanese had attacked Pearl Harbor; and Hollywood, fantasies at the ready, had joined the fray to make the world safe for democracy, General Motors, U.S. Steel, and Hollywood. A recurring vignette had the archetypal ugly Gestapo inquisitor confronting the befuddled bespectacled academic, always played by Hume Cronyn, and invariably the moment arrived where Cronyn dropped his glasses to the dungeon's sleazy floor, and the rodentlike, swastika-emblazoned Gestapo officer, who held his cigarette cradled up between his middle finger and thumb and sucked on it in the most voraciously erotic and suggestive way, perpetrated the ultimate cruelty, smiled and ground the glasses back into sand beneath the heel of his shimmering black boot. I always imagined Old Charlie Reilly the hapless helpless academic.

On the wall of his office Old Charlie Reilly actually had a razor strop mounted in a locked glass case but to my knowledge the case was never unlocked. It is true that he kept a wooden hazing paddle in his desk, and that he did not hesitate to administer corporal punishment to the bent-over student's backside (fully condoned if not outright applauded by one's parents, who were caught up in a Depression which allowed them to fret about little other than getting some macaroni and cheese or Spanish rice on the supper table), but he had no real facility for meting punishment and more often than not didn't seem to know or care for what he was paddling a student. Once I took Old Charlie Reilly a note from our teacher seeking our class's permission to go on an outing (oh, joy!) to the Roswell Memorial Library. Without reading it, Old Charlie Reilly told me to bend over, grip the edge of the desk, and assume the position. When I suggested he read the note before he began his lackadaisical business, he did so and told me *yeah, Exley,* it was okay and I could tell the teacher so, after which he excused me with a waft of his paw. Talk about trafficking with one's luck. I might have interrupted Old Charlie Reilly when he was getting into Dante! Old Charlie Reilly died of uremia in 1951, age forty-nine. When Wiley and I had become his wards in 1935, Old Charlie had been thirty-two.

It is little wonder then that, spending such crucially formative years under the abstracted, unseen and unseeing eyes of Old Charlie Reilly, Wiley and I were neither model nor well-behaved students. Wiley was the richest kid in Academy Street School, or at least I thought he was. He wasn't—there wasn't any real money in the Academy Street School district—but he wore the same elastic navy blue socks and Buster Brown grained Bass shoes worn by doctors' and lawyers' sons west of Washington Street who went to Sherman Street School. Perhaps that was what delayed an early friendship between Wiley and me.

During the Depression any outward display of affluence aroused envy, bitterness, and even overt gestures of anger in one's peers and by the time we reached South Junior High, where we had to bring our lunch ("brown-bag it") in lieu of walking home for it, we thought anyone who brought chopped egg or tunafish sandwiches was hotdogging it. If the poor bastard brought roast beef or ham and cheese he wasn't even allowed to sit at our table and bask in the stimulation of our newly acquired four-letter-ridden conversations. That's if he were lucky. If he wasn't lucky, he got mucked about a bit, a few cuffs to the ears, some solid sucker shots to the humerus muscles of his arms, had his roast beef sandwiches taken from him, and had them replaced with our peanut-butter-jellies to get him through the afternoon.

Sy Hampson, Wiley's father, had attended Cornell, a family tradition. He was an extremely nice and easygoing man, always classily dressed in a three-piece suit, a starched white shirt, and a striped tie. He owned an auto parts store off Public Square on State Street, but though he was very bright and quick-witted he didn't really have any head or affection for business, he drank too much, and I'm sure he always wished he were doing something else. I don't know what Sy wished he were doing. At the back of the auto parts store Sy had a makeshift office with a half beaverboard partition behind which, between customers, he could hide with his whiskey glass. When one walked by and looked through the display windows from the street, one could see only a partially visible desktop atop which the propped-up heels and soles of his shoes could be seen, ankles crossed.

"The old man at work," Wiley would say, after which, and not in the least a disparaging way, he'd spit on State Street, an adult spit.

"Yeah, the old man at work," I'd say and I'd spit too.

Sy liked all Wiley's friends and called me Ex, after my father, with whom he was on amiable terms, no doubt a drinking camaraderie. Unlike Wiley's mother, Ethel, whatever Wiley and I were going to do was okay with Sy. If we were going to the fairgrounds to sneak into the high school football game, Sy said, "I wish I could go with you." If we were going to the evening movie, probably to sneak into that too, Sy said, "I envy you." Had we said we were going to knock ourselves off, I suspect Sy would have said, "I wish I had time to join you."

By the time we were thirteen Wiley and I were hanging around the Victory and Eleanor diners on State Street until two or three o'clock in the morning, in blissful ignorance talking girls and smoking Camels and also those Wings and Sunshines which moved onto the counters when Lucky Strike green went to war. Wiley taught me how to inhale. Sy and Ethel didn't really have any control over Wiley and by that time my father had begun his long losing ordeal with lung cancer and my mother was so preoccupied with that hard fact she had no idea where I was.

In the early years, before alcohol had done its thing, when he was still the dapper and handsome, the three-piece suit and striped tie Sy, he one day after school, highball and cigarette in hand, read Wiley and me James Thurber's "The Secret Life of Walter Mitty" from his current issue of *The New Yorker* (I find myself wondering what that issue in mint condition would be worth today). Although Wiley and I were suitably impressed and at the appropriate moments laughed with glee, clapped our hands, and did a good deal of histrionic rolling around the Hampsons' Chianti-colored carpeting, I now so equate Walter Mitty's drab life made bearable only by his hilariously touching fantasies with what may or may not have been Sy's life that for years I have found myself unable to reread the Thurber classic.

Barbara Jane Hampson, Wiley's sister, was four years older than we and moved in an entirely different circle, one that Wiley and I in our naïveté had sneeringly and derisively dubbed "the goddamn four hundreds," naïve in the sense that though Barbara Jane's group was what we would now call upwardly mobile we had no executive class in Watertown, no money at all in the sense of Back Bay or Southampton money, so that to be a four hundred one had only to be a doctor's or lawyer's child or be bright, well dressed, and attractive enough to be admitted into this rather touchingly amusing group west of Washington Street whose idea of a full life was getting into the right college (Cornell in Barbara Jane's case), being admitted into the right sorority or fraternity, marrying well, and returning to Watertown to live in a large spacious-roomed red brick house on Paddock or Clinton street.

Barbara Jane Hampson was bright, lovely, and incredibly well built and I expect that half her male contemporaries must have been in thrall to the possibility of being loved by her. To Barbara Jane Hampson, Wiley and I were just two bugs to be walked by, often walking by us half-dressed as though we had no existence whatever for her, and this at a time we were just discovering our cocks and were pulling our pollywoggers forty-two times a day. (I have just made a note to ask good buddy Alissa if Barbara Jane was not uncognizant of our sweaty-palmed, hollow-stomached, thrillingly lusty, and achingly forbidden desires.) Wiley and I showed each other the hair on our palms. We looked cross-eyed all the time, scientifically demonstrating the Boy Scout maxim that masturbation was rendering us crazies. Our favorite expression was *Smile if you jerked off last night*. Wiley and I smiled all the time.

In all those years I remember Miss Barbara Jane Hampson directing her attention to me only once. Trying to act casual, she one day asked if Bill Exley were my older brother. I told her that the Brigadier was indeed my brother. As she turned her eyes away and it became apparent she was going to leave it at that, I started in search of Wiley only to hear her say, "Boy, if I were a year younger, could I go for him!" How proud I was, speechless, for if she could go for the Brigadier, could she not one day, when I "grew up," go for me?

I put this down as having happened in the spring of 1943, for Barbara Jane would graduate that June, the Brigadier a semester later in January 1944. As that was the only conversation Barbara Jane ever initiated with me, and

I could unearth no ulterior reason for her having done so, I did what I thought was expected of me and told the Brigadier. The Brigadier laughed, laughed at Miss Barbara Jane Hampson's thinking he was the goods! He said, "She's some fine-looking specimen, baby brother, but that chick's not ready for me." Nor was the Brigadier in the least kidding. Whereas I was so sexually naïve I thought the penis went into a girl's belly button until I was twelve, the Brigadier had been staying out all night since he was fifteen. I had no doubt he knew exactly where it went, and I'm also sure that Barbara Jane wasn't in the least ready for him.

It was about this time, too, that I entered into the world of the jockstrap, a journey on which Wiley had neither the inclination nor the talent to travel. And though Wiley's genuine grief, near hysteria, at the Brigadier's predicament indicated he had long since forgiven me, I had never really forgiven myself for the hard abruptness with which I'd cut him from my life.

3

Although I know that subtlety and irony don't
rest easy on the biscuit-beefsteak-eating cast iron stomachs
of the folks out yonder there in Dodge City, Matt, I nevertheless ought to tell you, old pardner, that Secretary of State
John Foster Dulles and his brother, Allen, who for a time
and as a front for his brother, Foster, headed our Central
Intelligence Agency, were from Watertown, the sons of our
Presbyterian minister. I shit you not, Matt—from Watertown! The red brick First Presbyterian Church of their
father, Alan Mace Dulles, still stands at the corner of Washington and Academy streets, a mere two blocks from our
Public Square. Implanted in the facade of the church is
a plaque commemorating the elder Dulles's pastorship.

Watertown and Jefferson County also gave the world
Robert Lansing, President Woodrow Wilson's secretary of
state. Charles M. Yost, an undersecretary of state and ambassador to the United Nations, was from there. And

Charles (Chip) Bohlen, the Soviet expert and ambassador to Russia, spent a good part of his youth at Cape Vincent, twenty-five miles upriver from where I now live. On holiday, Bohlen would continue to return to the Cape all his life, as the Dulles brothers continued to return to Duck Island. Indeed, so much did Watertown's view of the world permeate America's that once, many years ago in Washington, I was told by a guy conversant in the way of the capital that there was a clique in the State Department known as the Watertown mafia; and though I later tried unsuccessfully to verify that any such epithet ever did exist, I still laugh heartily in the knowledge of understanding completely what the guy meant. It has something to do with the impertinence of imposing a WASP–Old Boy Club mentality on a world that could care less.

But bear with me, Matt, for out of necessity I am forced into circumspection. If, for example, we all come from Yazoo County, as Willie Morris came to understand, then we all also come from Watertown and Jefferson County. And what has been both very right and very wrong with America for the better part of this century is what was both very right and very wrong with a Presbyterian minister's son and by extension both very right and very wrong with Watertown and Yazoo City and Duluth and Ogden.

John Foster Dulles, Big Jim, was an enigmatic, perfervid, devious, and infuriating man. Until 1939 he was nothing more than the successful lawyer son of a tank-town Presbyterian minister; and in that capacity had risen to a partnership in Cromwell & Sullivan, America's leading corporate law firm, where one of his clients was a group of New York City bankers with heavy holdings in German bonds. The Nazi regime seemed not to arouse the moral furor of our minister's son. The first we hear of him on the national scene he is excoriating the Franklin Roosevelt administration for supporting England and France against Germany. A month after Hitler's invasion of Poland, he is still insisting that the only way the United States can "fulfill its destiny" is to stay out of the war.

In 1943 our minister's son accepts his first prominent political position as foreign policy advisor to New York State Republican Governor Thomas E. Dewey, who is preparing to run for the presidency against Roosevelt in 1944. In that campaign Dewey (almost as if our minister's son were holding him on his knee, à la Charlie McCarthy) puts forward the idea of a postwar world with a "lasting peace" that would of course exclude our ally Russia, an idea that could only further stimulate the paranoia of Stalin and drive him further and further into his demented self. Such an idea also infuriated the Roosevelt administration, whose wartime policy was that any lasting peace must include not merely Mr. Dulles's Anglo-American Big Two but all the allies, including Russia, which had after all, marshal, endured the siege of Stalingrad and was just as committed—if not more so—to the defeat of the Axis as we.

By 1946 our minister's son has moved from the shameful isolationism of his 1939 hope that we wouldn't intervene against Hitler to become a flagrant, verbal, nearly hysterical internationalist and in his public utterances is given over to phrases like "the menace of Sovietism," to calling Russia "atheistic and materialistic" (this, Matt, coming from a citizen of the most materialistic nation in the history of mankind and a nation whose very constitution guarantees one's right to atheism), to saying the Soviet regime "rejects the concept of moral law," and it has become apparent that our minister's son who, as late as 1943, was advocating a "Christian" postwar peace with Il Duce and Hitler's thugs is now advocating a "Christian" war with Russia. It becomes apparent, too, that his isolationism of 1939 had not so much to do with his legally representing New York banks holding German bonds as with his "Christian" loathing of the possibility of any accommodation whatever with "the godless Bolsheviks." By 1947 he has become the most feared and despised man in Russia, the object of searingly vitriolic attacks by Vishinsky. Our minister's son has almost single-handedly become the architect of the Cold War. From 1947 on, in his capacity as delegate to the World Council of Churches, to the United Nations, as Republican party advisor to Truman's secretaries of state, and finally as Ike's secretary of state, our minister's son is everywhere—but everywhere, Big Jim—spreading the Cold War gospel of the Soviet menace. It was a dormant Cold War destined to volcanically erupt in both Korea and Vietnam.

Do you know, for example, old pardner, where our minister's son was on June 19, 1950, a week before the North Koreans crossed—on June 25—the thirty-eighth parallel into South Korea and the Korean War began? As "nonpartisan" Republican Party advisor to Democratic Secretary of State Dean Acheson, Foster Dulles was in Seoul, South Korea, huddled with that runt Syngman Rhee, whose Republic of Korea was hardly a republic. President Rhee's little paradise was rife with rumors that it was a police state that would have warmed Himmler's heart. Rhee's republic was further beset by the known fact that the majority of its citizens favored reunification with the Communist north, a possibility which, had it become actuality, would have left Mr. Rhee sucking hind tit and Mr. Dulles's godless heathen occupying more earthly space.

How this must have galled our minister's son, not to mention our old-soldiers-never-die guy sitting like an emperor in his Dai Ichi headquarters in Tokyo. Emanating from South Korea at least since May there had been intelligence reports, even published newspaper reports, of massive buildups of North Korean troops along the thirty-eighth parallel; and though on June 25 General Douglas MacArthur would express shock at their crossing the parallel into South Korea, later, before a congressional committee, the head of MacArthur's own G-2, Maj. Gen. Charles Willoughby, a Kraut with a pronounced Teutonic accent born to an American mother and a German aristocrat named Tscheppe-Weidenbach, would in a circumspect way seem to contradict his commander's prerogative to shock.

From my reading of history, marshal, whatever machinations were conceived between our minister's son and

President Rhee in that week before the war will never be known, but it is certain that Mr. Dulles flew directly from those conferences to Toyko, huddled with MacArthur at Dai Ichi, and then, amusingly, instead of flying home he went holidaying in Kyoto, where for three days he lolled about as if waiting for something, as indeed he unquestionably was. On the North Koreans' moving across the parallel (some intelligence reports indicated that rather than assuming a defensive posture Rhee's Republic of Korea troops had crossed into North Korea first, provoking the attack), our minister's son flew immediately back to Tokyo, again conferred with General MacArthur, and what might be justifiably called the Dulles–MacArthur–Rhee War was under way.

Within hours after the June 25 outbreak of hostilities MacArthur received permission from Commander in Chief President Truman to use American air power, within days permission to use American land forces. Be that as it may, with his war against the godless red menace heatedly and furiously under way, our minister's son flew happily (at least one imagines him happy) back home, stopping off in Honolulu long enough to tell assembled reporters that though he knew the situation in Korea had been critical, that attack had come "sooner than expected." Brother!

You tell me, Big Jim, that out yonder there in Dodge City the folks ain't all that unsubtle and yet you cannot grasp wherein my irony lies and that you further challenge everything I've said about Dulles. Okay. Peace. We had another man from Watertown, who even now lies before us in his bier, and boys from all their various Watertowns (didn't even you, old pardner, have your own Watertown up there in that cold Swede country of Minnesota?) who for the past twenty-five years have been the well-disciplined instruments of our minister's son's zealous missionary dedication to ridding the world of the heathen. There is, however, a world of difference between sitting in the very highest seats of power formulating policy and becoming a pawn-like tool in the execution of that policy.

Whereas I'm certain, Big Matt, that our minister's son died smugly (let me not be that unkind and instead say "self-righteously") in Maryland's Walter Reed Hospital—not comfortably as he, too, had the cancer and for any pain he suffered I'm genuinely and truly sorry—in the knowledge he'd done what he must to bring the wrath of God down upon the godless, the Brigadier, on the other hand, and as a finely honed utensil of our minister's son, somewhere along the line became not only somewhat brutalized by our minister's son's Christian wars but became a rather more dedicated advocate of clearing the world of our enemies than even Watertown's patron saint, Mr. Dulles, was. I think, Big Jim, I can even isolate the moment this change began occurring.

On November 21, 1950, the Brigadier's (he was a first lieutenant then) regiment, the Seventh Division's Seventeenth Regimental Combat Team, commanded by Col. Herbie Powell, was standing at Hyasenjin on the Yalu River, looking over the mostly frozen gorge of the river into the frigid barren mountains of Manchuria and spitting contemptuously into the narrow and unfrozen stream which trickled and twisted serpentinelike through the Yalu's icy banks. Despite what you may have heard from bullshitters in bars, Big Matt, the Brigadier's regiment was the first to reach that river and stare haughtily into the nearly mythological and mysterious depths of Manchuria.

Speaking of guys, marshal, from all our various Watertowns fighting in the wars of our minister's son, do you know who the first three guys to reach the Yalu were? I have their pictures at home and the men's names and ranks are stamped as indelibly into my mind as the frozen mountains of Manchuria in the background. They were Sgt. Peter Rupelnas of South Boston, Massachusetts; Cpl. Mayford Gardner of Royal Oak, Michigan; and Pfc. Tommie Robinson of Las Cruces, New Mexico. I kid you not, Big Jim! As much as the names and hometowns sound like the creation of some hack screenwriter who wrote those fairy-tale B war movies in which you, and most of the other stars, doubtless began your careers, these were the first three guys to reach the Yalu. Sergeant Rupelnas is kneeling in the crusty snow taking a picture of Mayford Gardner and Tommie Robinson, parkaed and field helmeted, M-1s at the ready, the partially frozen Yalu behind them, and over the way beyond the river the craggy snow-covered mountains of Manchuria. Yes, marshal, Mayford Gardner and Tommie Robinson standing at the very top of the Korean Peninsula—there is great gravity in their faces—announcing to the world that the Seventeenth Regimental Combat Team has secured and battened down North Korea for our minister's son.

4

By then, MacArthur, the smell of blood in his nostrils and heady with victory, is crustily urging his commanders to take the Seventeenth Regimental Combat Team as example and push on to the Yalu. Once there, he assures his commanders, he will relieve them with South Korean troops. In one of those bursts of trashy sentimentality of which the general was capable, he tells his commanders he has promised "wives and mothers the boys will be home for Christmas." In a visit to his field commanders on November 24, three days after the Brigadier's regiment arrived at the Yalu, he told Maj. Gen. John Church, commander of the Twenty-fifth Division, "Don't make a liar out of me"—presumably with the wives and mothers—"Get to the Yalu and I will relieve you." The general then boarded his private plane, the SCAP (Supreme Commander for Allied Powers) for his three-hour flight back to Tokyo and his headquarters. On his way he decided to fly over Hyasenjin and salute the Seventeenth Regimental Combat Team for its audacious run to the Yalu. As he passed low over Hyasenjin, he ordered his pilot to tip the plane's wings in recognition of that regiment's courage. For this the Air Force awarded Gen. Douglas MacArthur the honorary wings of the combat pilot and the Distinguished Flying Cross. Would I kid you, marshal?

Had the general been able to land SCAP at Hyasenjin, he might, according to what the Brigadier later told me, have awarded every member of the Seventeenth his own honorary wings and Distinguished Flying Cross, though how a rifleman would explain such paradoxical awards to the boys in the neighborhood bars back home—assuming he got back home, and many wouldn't, Big Jim, *many would not*—is another question. A week before the Brigadier's regiment walked warily—M-1s and Thompsons at the ready—into this tin-hutted mud-floored village, planes from carriers in the Sea of Japan had bombed and burned 85 percent of it and Hyasenjin lay, for all practical purposes, devastated as though on Judgment Day.

Although the day before—on Thanksgiving, November 23—the general had so suavely (Old Mac had style, marshal, you got to give him that) tipped his wings in homage to the Seventeenth, the troops had been air-dropped shrimp cocktail, roast young tom turkey, cranberry sauce, candied sweet potatoes, stuffed olives, fruit salad, fruit cake, hot coffee, and minced pie—I know I sound like some wise-ass, Mistuh Dillon, but it's true, *true*—even this reminder of wives and moms back home in South Boston, Royal Oak, and Las Cruces—no, even this heat-generating orgy of calories could not compensate for what the general would have discovered had he been able to land SCAP at Hyasenjin.

On the night the Seventeenth walked into Hyasenjin the temperature dropped to thirty-two degrees below zero. As we would begin discovering in our hometown newspapers some weeks later, the Seventeenth Regimental Combat Team, like so many troops in Korea, was in no way equipped for this near-arctic fighting. Many troops were without gloves. Although they all had combat boots, they were not the insulated kind suitable for winter fighting. Most had parkas, but many were unlined and not the arctic kind the army used for winter fighting. A week before, in the valiant and furious drive to reach the Yalu, troops of the Seventeenth's Third Battalion entered the Unzi River and began to ford it in what they believed was ankle-deep water, only to find themselves waist deep in heartstoppingly icy waters. Eighteen of them suffered such severe frostbite that their uniforms had to be cut from them. Water-soluble medicines froze. Blood plasma had to be heated an hour and a half before it could be administered to the wounded.

Nor were the cold and the poor planning for winter combat the least of it, old pardner. On the same day General MacArthur was tipping his wings in salute to the Seventeenth and adding ribbons to his chest, the CIA was telling President Truman that the Chinese would indeed cross the Yalu, subject our forces to a "prolonged attrition," and maintain North Korea as a political entity, and told the president further that the Chinese possessed sufficient troops to do so, an incredible six hundred thousand troops amassed around the bridges leading into North Korea. Nor could this possibility have ever been far from the general's mind, suggesting that at age seventy he may have been walking about in fairyland talking only to the noble multiwinged seraphs.

But the rest is history, old pardner. On November 26, two days after the general had flown over the victorious Seventeenth at Hyasenjin, the Chinese came storming across the Yalu by the thousands, by the tens of thousands, by the hundreds of thousands, and this same Seventeenth which only days earlier had stood so arrogantly and proudly, spitting so disdainfully into the freezing waters of the Yalu and staring so contemptuously across the way at the snow-blanketed mountains of Manchuria, after being bivouacked for a few days of cold uncomfortable rest right at the very Chinese border, now found themselves fighting desperately back—with the First Marines covering their retreat at the Chosin Reservoir—to the ports of Hamhung-Hungnam, where in that now historic evacuation they would be taken by ship to the southern tip of Korea, and, after regrouping, have to begin the long arduous fight back to the thirty-eighth parallel.

Even then the Seventeenth Regimental Combat Team was luckier than most. As is well known by now, Big Jim, Chou En-Lai's main thrust was directed against Johnnie Walker's Eighth Army in the west and entire battalions under Walker's command not only ceased to exist as fighting units but simply ceased to exist. By January 22, a mere two months from the day the Brigadier's regiment had stood so haughtily on the banks of the Yalu, the Chinese had driven the United Nations forces seventy miles below the thirty-eighth parallel.

It was about this time, old pardner, that I began to detect a change of tone in the Brigadier's letters. At the time I was a sophomore at the University of Southern California, books containing the wisdom of the ages in hand, strolling about wide close-cropped green lawns shaded by swaying palm trees and surrounded by gaggles of some of the loveliest, most golden coeds imaginable, hardly the place to react to the bitterness and brutality seeping into the Brigadier's letters. Much has been written about the near-hysterical abandon with which the Chinese fought in Korea.

"The Chinese," said Gen. Matthew Ridgway, who replaced Johnnie Walker after his jeep-accident death, "was a tough and vicious fighter who often attacked without regard for casualties."

Most of the American troops believed, in fact, Big Jim, that such recklessness as the Chinese displayed was spurred by marijuana smoking at the very least, more probably by opium smoking, and into the Brigadier's letters there now came this new and biting hatred. By then his regiment, along with the rest of the United Nations forces, was slowly and agonizingly fighting its way back to the thirty-eighth parallel, and I one day received a letter—and

I remember the Brigadier's precise words—in which de-humanization entered into the Brigadier's service in behalf of our minister's son. Writing in not nearly the restrained tone of General Ridgway's saying the Chinese "attacked without regard for casualties," the Brigadier said that "the fucking gooks came at you in such a way it was like picking off fucking ducks in a shooting gallery." Although the Brigadier admitted it was shameful of him, he wrote that he "laughed like a fucking hyena when he saw the fucking gooks piled up like cordwood, like mountains, baby brother, like fucking mountains!"

Don't get me wrong, marshal. The Brigadier was my brother, and even in the very groves of academe and walled in by all those stunning and proper golden girls from Beverly Hills and Bel Air, I laughed like a fucking hyena too and prayed, yes, *prayed,* Big Jim, that the Brigadier would kill a few thousand fucking gooks for me. So in the service of our minister's son the process of brutalization is passed from brother to brother, from brother to friend, from friend to friend, and goes on forever, world without end.

Alas, marshal, the Brigadier would never make it back to the thirty-eighth parallel, where the war ended at the very place it had begun. The second time the Brigadier was wounded, his hip and his pelvis were crushed. He was flown from a M.A.S.H. field hospital in the line to the Tokyo Army Hospital, thence to Tripler Army Hospital (where some twenty-odd years later he would die), thence to a military hospital in Waltham, Massachusetts. After many months the surgeons succeeded in putting him back together again. Whether the good doctors ever succeeded in putting the Brigadier back together mentally is another question.

What is my point, old pardner? It is simply the age-old and proverbial one of power awesomely corrupting its beholders, as it most certainly did with Dulles and MacArthur. Let me be more specific, Big Jim, and say I believe the much-revered MacArthur was a fraud and a fucking liar into the bargain, that despite his protestations of shock at the Chinese entering the war en masse the general never for a moment doubted they would do so and that he stood prepared to sacrifice, like pawns in a chess game, his most forward elements, including the Brigadier's Seventeenth Regimental Combat Team, to the Chinese in order to get Congress's permission to wage nothing less than an atomic war of attrition against the godless Chinese, a war our minister's son doubtless would have endorsed. It is a very harsh accusation, I agree, old pardner. For all that, and though the Brigadier would give the army another twenty-two years of his life after finally leaving the hospital in Waltham, I have reason to know he was forever haunted by the possibility that MacArthur had been rendered so blasé in the execution of what one calls *Command* that he had become a moral monster. You wince with distaste, Mistuh Dillon?

5

If I say that I'd long owed Wiley an apology
for the hard abruptness with which I'd cut him from my
life, I mean that at fourteen I entered the haughty world of
the jock and in those days in Watertown jocks had no time
for anyone else but other jocks. Of course I did not know
that day at the bier that I had become so smitten with
Robin that over the next year I'd make an incredible five
round trips to Hawaii to see her, staying on the *Cirrhosis of
the River* at the Coco Marina in Hawaii Kai—she'd rented
Wiley's house—for as long as up to two months, when her
Maui boyfriend would call her and announce he'd be over
in a couple days. I'd then move on to Wiley's in Lanai.

Nor did I know that directly after the funeral we'd
repair to O'Twoomey's second-floor suite in the original
part of the Royal Hawaiian, where my best friend, Toby
Farquarson III, from Alexandria Bay, or wherever he was
from (no one was ever quite certain), would immediately

hit it off with O'Twoomey—at their first meeting at the suite they were huddled whispering in a corner—or that O'Twoomey would not return to Dublin with his Hospital Trusts pilgrims and would instead stay on Oahu. For whatever knavery on which he was embarked, he hired Toby to work for him that very day. For that reason, whenever I returned to see Robin, I would stay for a day or two at the Royal Hawaiian to see how the other half lives, as it were (O'Twoomey always picked up the bill), then go out and stay with Robin on the *Cirrhosis of the River*. During my stays with her, we would always take the time to make the thirty-minute flight to Lanai and spend three or four days with Malia and Wiley. One night on the *Cirrhosis* Robin introduced a subject that led me indirectly to telling her why I had been forced to cut Wiley from my life.

At supper Robin brought up a matter that was causing her considerably more anguish than it was causing me: my drinking. Each time she brought up alcohol and lolled it around on her palate as lovingly as if it were a delicious piece of gossip about a movie actor's recondite sexual habits, she'd ghoulishly apologize and solemnly swear never to mention booze again, only to bring it up two nights later. It was as if she saw vodka as *the* obstacle in what might otherwise be a blissfully beau-ideal relationship. On this night, obviously piqued at having flogged her subject to death, at having explored all its avenues, byways, nooks, and crannies, oh, its obscurist tributaries, at having exhausted her subject with such devotion I was on the verge of booting her in the behind and she damn well knew it, Robin leaped in one breathtakingly absurd moment from the conclusion that I was a hopeless drunk to the idea that I wasn't in any way an alcoholic.

"Christ, Ex, I've seen you drink a quart of vodka a day for days at a time, then one morning just get bored or whatever, get up and walk ten or twelve miles on the beach and go off the booze cold turkey. I mean, drunks start talking to the dicky birds, have to be lugged to the heebie-jeebie ward on a stretcher, and get massive intravenous doses of

B_{12} and God-only-knows-what-all medications. You don't have to do that. You'll concede me that?"

"It's something I learned from a guy a long time ago."

"You mean like a guru or holy man or priest or Hare Krishna or someone like that?"

I laughed. "Yeah, Robin, someone like that."

My guru was our high school coach. Although we had a parochial school in Watertown, if one wanted to play football and basketball against the Syracuse and Buffalo schools, against those in Utica, Albany, Schenectady, Binghamton, Rochester, Elmira, Rome, White Plains, Erie, Pennsylvania (once even Clearwater, Florida), one had no choice but to enroll in Watertown High School and pay the exacting price demanded by the coach, a big, brawny, handsome, tawny-skinned, cigar-chomping, awe-inspiring Woody Hayes type who struck rigidity not only into his players but also into the other students and even his fellow faculty members. With the exception of a half dozen more principled teachers, in whose classes we were cautioned against enrolling, he was perfectly capable of having marks upgraded to keep his needed jocks—he didn't worry about Nixon-like third-stringers—in uniform. The distaff teachers were so much putty in the coach's hands. He was not only bright, intimidating, and handsome, he could be extremely gracious, and he did not hesitate to use that charm to his advantage.

He was also a gifted enough coach to be on palsy terms with Notre Dame's Frank Leahy. At a football seminar held in the Adirondacks at the coach's summer boarding camp for affluent kids, Leahy gave him the T formation, which he promptly introduced in the prehistoric year of 1943. Thus for six, seven, eight years, well into the 1950s for that matter, Watertown played against single- and double-wing formation teams that hadn't the foggiest notion what we were doing on offense. He had not only varsities and junior varsities, he had junior junior varsities. He did not call them that; he called them the North and South Junior High School teams. He gave these coaches his T formation playbook and conned the Frontier League, made up of smaller high schools in the surrounding area (including Alexandria Bay, where I now live), into accepting Watertown's junior high schools into their midst. Thus we thirteen-, fourteen-, and fifteen-year-olds, just the far side of puberty and not really physically ready, were learning the coach's plays and competing against—and, more often than otherwise, beating—seventeen- and eighteen-year-old juniors and seniors. By the time we moved into the tenth grade and the old high school on Sterling Street and on to either the junior varsity or varsity—the latter if we were very, very good or very, very lucky—that is, by the time we moved into the coach's imposing presence, we not only knew his playbook, we had had our physical baptisms against much larger, much stronger boys. Even that did not prepare us for the price the coach would exact.

He did not hesitate to put his hands on his players. Laughingly—I say laughingly *now*—I recall his once stopping a scrimmage when our starting right tackle missed a blocking assignment, taking the left end instead of crossing over and taking the right linebacker. The coach whistled the scrimmage dead, nonchalantly walked over to the right tackle, unsnapped and removed the right tackle's helmet. In embarrassment, we all stared at the cleated grass. A stunning, hallowed silence whistled around the Knickerbocker practice field. The coach raised his doubled fist high and with seemingly savage fury brought the heel of his fist smack down atop our right tackle's dome. Today I'm sure the coach didn't hit our right tackle hard; in fact, with his absurdly histrionic sense he pulled that punch. It was as if he were trying to get a comic strip light bulb to glitter poppingly above our right tackle's head that the tackle might get the idea of the coach's maxim: Every play is a touchdown if properly executed. Nonchalantly, the coach replaced our right tackle's helmet and snapped it firmly on his chin. Nonchalantly, he told us to run the play again.

We did. He told us to run it again. We did. He told

us to run it again and again and again. This was in September before Daylight Saving Time had changed to Eastern Standard Time, and the coach made us run that accursed play into dusk and then turned on the klieg lights and made us run it more. By then the coach and his covey of assistants were standing beyond the range of our blinded visions, beyond the lighted practice area, laughing and joking, the kind of laughter that suggested they were swapping raunchy jokes. We were almost sure they weren't even watching us, but how could we be absolutely certain? So the hitting and the hurting and the thirst and the exhaustion went on.

When at last the coach blew his whistle and bellowed "enough," it wasn't enough. He ordered us to run four laps around the quarter-mile track encircling the field, then run the half mile up Thompson Boulevard to the field house, take our showers, and get some sleep. Directly the coach departed with his laughing assistants. We did our four laps, ritualistically removed our cleats, tied their strings together, threw them over our shoulder pads so we wouldn't leave cleat marks on the lawns of the upper-middle-class homes along Thompson Boulevard, and, too weary to run another ten steps, strolled slowly in our stocking feet, heads downward in embarrassment and tiredness, moving in and out of the light and shadows of streetlamps. Vividly I recall our right tackle's saying, "Sorry guys, sorry guys, sorry guys," and our replying, "Screw it," and "So you blew one," and "What's the diff?" and "It could happen to anyone." But who would ever miss another assignment? Well, I would. But that is only incidental to this tale.

Abruptly we heard a car's brakes screech to a halt behind us. Turning in panic at the sound of the careening rocking vehicle, we saw the coach emerging from his station wagon. *Did we call this running?* The coach removed the belt from his pants, left his wagon idling smack in the middle of the boulevard, and doing his Mr. Hyde laugh, chased us along the macadam, with his wide leather belt lashing out at the slower-moving buttocks all the way into the locker room. That was one of the half-dozen nights during my football and basketball days under the coach when I put my head down on my folded arms and fell into the stolid sleep of utter fatigue while my mother was re-warming a supper eaten hours earlier by the rest of the family. So bad was it on this night she could not even rouse me until 3 A.M., when she again tried to feed me. But I waved the food scornfully away and barely struggled up the stairs and into bed, while the old lady in her house-coat stood at the bottom of the staircase and moved me on with a whispered hand-wringing litany of "Dear, dear, dear, dear."

Was it worth it all? To this day I don't honestly know. I do know that we won and we won and we won. I also know that to win and to win and to win leaves little time for anything or anyone else, including Wiley. I did not learn to play a musical instrument or join the glee club. After that Stetsoned son of the prairie I'd produced in kindergarten, I never did another watercolor. I never tried out for the school play. Even today my ignorance of music appalls me. Writing a speech for President Reagan would be beyond me. I could list the gaps in my education until the reader slumbered. One might well ask, then, if being a jock cost me so dearly in other disciplines, why my feelings are in the least ambivalent. When after World War II we arrived in the presence of the coach, his whole bearing tacitly articulated to his players what he doubtless could not have put into words: *Listen to me. Do what I ask. Give me your regard. And I in turn shall show you the way to the world's regard.*

"How could you learn anything from a tyrant like that?" Robin said. "And I don't see the bloody relationship between going cold turkey and that bully." Of course Robin knew everything about the Depression, to which we players had been born, from her father and couldn't comprehend the "abhorrent ambivalence" that forced us old farts into speaking of a period of "economic deprivation"—academic claptrap—with such loving and mawkish sentimentality.

In my senior year, I told Robin, as starting offensive

‡ 137

center and, depending upon who was hurt, either nose guard or linebacker on defense, I cost Watertown an undefeated season. In our fourth game at Auburn High School in gale-like winds and rain, I was called for holding on their one-yard line on fourth down. We scored, had the play nullified, were penalized fifteen yards, and on the replay from sixteen yards out, we failed to put the ball in. In eight games that year, I continued, though I suspected I myself was talking to the dicky birds by then, Watertown scored 157 points and gave up twelve. "Imagine!" Six out of eight teams we goose-egged. We took our opener 21–6, our second game 41–0. Each week awards were presented to both the out-standing defensive and offensive players, the prize being a free steak and spaghetti dinner at the New Parrot Restaurant. After the 41–0 game, when I won the defensive award, the coach suspended the prizes, saying our defense was so good the award should have gone to the entire defensive unit, which would have cost the owner of the New Parrot, our line coach, Jake DeVito, a small fortune in T-bones and pasta.

"Still, Robin, I got mine. And you know what? That was the best meal I ever ate!"

"Jesus, Ex!"

Because our third game was at Rome Free Academy under the lights on a Friday night, the coaches from the five teams remaining on our schedule were in the stands scouting us. We won 21–0, and the next morning we picked up the newspaper to learn that Dave Powers of Oswego—he was this venerable white-haired dude who'd been coaching up-state forever—was quoted as saying we were the best high school football team he'd seen in ten, maybe twenty damn years. I sighed. "Boy, was Auburn waiting for us."

Rising to my feet, slightly inebriated, I assumed the offensive center's stance and tried to tell Robin what had happened at Auburn. The winds precluded our even trying our passing game, which was great. The water was ankle deep, so running the ends would have been blatant wanton-ness; even off-tackle plays turned out to be reckless shilly-shallying. In the end, losing 6–0, we drove downfield "right off the cheeks of my ass." Slapping my right haunch, I explained to Robin that that was the "one hole," my left haunch the "two hole" and that we marched down the field never varying from those two holes. "You know, Robin, the shortest distance betwen two points." In the huddle at their one, our quarterback, Bill Reynolds—"he's still a good friend and a hotshot trial lawyer in Buffalo"—called a forty-one on hut, and I said to myself, "No, no, no! Jesus, no, Bill. They're going to throw their linebackers and entire secondary into those two holes." And I was right. Snapping the ball, I just veered to my right, the "one hole," taking as many guys as I could any way I could. Out of the corner of my eye I saw Joe Guardino break two tackles, slip past my right hip and into the end zone. Then I went to the ground and when I looked up I saw the referee throwing a white flag at my knees, grabbing his right wrist with his left hand and beginning to pump his right arm fiercely up and down.

"That's it, Robin. We blanked the rest of the teams on our schedule, Oswego, Massena—they came down undefeated with an all-state halfback, Gilbert "Gibby" Granger —Onondaga Valley of Syracuse, and Lackawanna of Buffalo."

"So every time you go straight, you're making penance for a mistake you made in a dumb football game thirty years ago. Jesus, Ex!"

"Not at all."

"If that's not true, when you go on the wagon and start walking, you invoke some mental image of this coach that sustains you?"

"Yes."

"What?"

"That's easy. When I'm walking, I remember the coach chasing us up the street-lighted boulevard and snapping our asses with his belt. You see, Robin, he was a teacher in the true sense of the word in that he taught us all we could be someone we never thought we could be."

"Jesus, Exley, I swear you make me want to puke."

6

If one is as amoral as I, it is little wonder that my best friend in the Bay was—I'll call him Toby Farquarson III, for he looks like nothing so much as a Toby Farquarson III. Toby seemed so to symbolize, nay, epitomize that younger revolutionary generation relentlessly committed (armed conflict if necessary) to a confrontation with the Establishment, that from the moment I learned who and what he was, Toby never ceased riveting my attention, though even I was astonished that he'd shown up at the Brigadier's funeral. Toby's revolution rose up from some dark excessively hurt and grieving place within himself, and his sometimes violent "cause" was executed in behalf of no one, *absolutely no one*, but Toby Farquarson III. Shortly after we met, when the front pages of every newspaper in America and Walter Cronkite and brethren were rendering us comatose (who needs Serax?) with that stultifying fairy tale "about" Ms. Patty Hearst, "about" that pompous barrister Mr. F. Lee Bailey (I could have given that emaciated poor little rich girl a better defense than he!), "about" Bill and Emily Harris and their salvaging of the Symbionese Liberation Army, I somewhat guardedly asked Toby what he thought of the entire business. Here I couldn't resist a wry smile.

"From a professional's point of view?"

We were in the Adirondacks on a snow-splotched dirt road the other side of Harrisville, one that ran by Totem Camp where the upstate affluent had used to unload their bothersome kids during the ten-week summer recess, a camp once owned by my twenty-three-years-dead high school football and basketball coach (how all these upstate locales conspire to haunt and close me in). In his deep blue leather bucket seat Toby was at the rich-looking polished wooden wheel of his sixteen-thousand-dollar 1972 Aston Martin DBS. Toby had dual points on the distributor; had added a high-output coil, modified the manifold to get exhaust in and out as quickly as possible, changed the gear ratio and cam shaft to give the vehicle a better "lift," and bolted lead weights to the frame. With these modifications Toby claimed the car would cruise at 150 miles per hour and that no trooper in New York State could even have the Ass, as he called it, in the range of the trooper's vision after a chase of a paltry five miles. When I responded I didn't much care for cruising at 150 miles per hour and asked how he evaded roadblocks, Toby said he never did anything "naughty" at a location where his route of flight wasn't protected by at least a half dozen side roads, adding that he knew the precise destination of every one of these roads and the precise speed at which he could travel them.

"Still, Toby, the Ass has absolutely to be the most watched and scrutinized vehicle in upstate New York. Don't you think it a rather ostentatious car for a rising young man in your line of work?"

"Jesus, Exley, sometimes I think you're as dumb as

the troopers! Only a state policeman would be thick-skulled enough to be looking for the Ass."

As he said this we were traveling Route 12 upriver to Clayton and passing a weather-beaten barn-red farmhouse. In the yard stood an old wooden spinning wheel and an antique wooden butter churn. In front of these a black half-inch pipe had been driven into the yard, and to the top of the pipe was attached a prepainted red-on-white FOR SALE sign of the kind bought in a five-and-dime. From the odd location of the sign one couldn't understand if the antiques or the farm and the whole kit and caboodle were being offered up for one's consideration. A 1970 green Ford half-ton pickup truck, all of its fenders battered and rusty, sat in the cindered drive. Toby now pointed at it.

"I might even use that. Afterward I might—I say, *I might*—drive up to the Schine Inn in Massena, put it in the parking lot in the rear, go through the back door, stroll as pretty as you fucking please through the lobby, step out the front door and into an Impala or Lincoln or Caddie next to a perfectly proper businessman—I have a few who owe me, baby" (probably men for whom he'd torched businesses, poor bastards!) "and get my ass royally chauffeured to Platts-burg or Rouse's Point or Ogdensburg where maybe, that is, *fucking maybe,* I might move in with a lovely half-breed nurse of my acquaintance, or with a fifty-two-year-old widow who likes to mama me, or maybe even with the mayor's wife. After a week or ten days of lolling about getting my cock sucked, I'd have my Iroquois maiden, my fifty-two-year-old mama, or His Excellency's wife drive me home."

"And where the hell is *that*?"

"Hey, man, we got a bargain. Remember?"

This was true. Our deal was that if Toby were ever in trouble, no matter how desperately so, he'd never seek refuge in the old lady's house. He'd never tell me of any of his capers on which the statute of limitations hadn't expired. Above all, Toby would never tell me of anything he had on the drawing board. My part of the bargain was simple. I would never probe him about that mysterious Shangri-la he called, for whatever reason, "home."

On the day we were on the dirt road cruising at seventy further up into the mountains, the early April snow melting and rendering the road soupy in spots, the lovely tall pines so encroaching our passage we seemed to be moving cramped between high stunning green cliffs, on the day I sought Toby's opinion of *l'affaire Hearst*, we were on one of Toby's drives. Every ten days to two weeks he'd walk through the front door, charmingly salute the old lady (she thought him "a nice guy"), ascend the stairs to my attic studio, inquire if I weren't sick of working on *Pages from a Dum-dum Island*, and ask if I wouldn't like to take a drive. Invariably I said I was indeed sick of Dum-dum Island and would indeed like to go for a drive.

These drives always carried with them a delicious forbidden tension. During them Toby never talked save when, as in the case of Patty Hearst, I initiated the conversation. Toby never talked but his eyes were everywhere. On these drives I got to know my home state almost as well as Toby. We'd go as far north as Malone (where my father was born), to Geneseo, south of Rochester in the west, southeast in the Mohawk Valley to Gloversville, to Waverly on the southern tier. Toby always drove on back roads through New York State towns which in my mid-forties I'd never known existed. It was as if we were somehow moving through a dream or nightmare of endless Thornton Wilder *Our Towns*. Whether Toby needed gas or not, he stopped at isolated gas stations, bought a Coke, some peanut butter–cheese crackers, and a Hershey bar with almonds, and struck up a conversation with the grease monkey.

"Who's the genius who decided to stick fuel pumps in this godforsaken place?"

If a cocky and indignant attendant snapped back, "Don't worry yourself, fella, about what goes into that register," I always moaned and thought, *"That poor bastard."* On arriving back in the Bay, Toby would always empty the glove compartment and give me piles of peanut butter–cheese sandwiches and Hershey bars with almonds. He told me I could give them to the old lady or throw them into the garbage as I saw fit.

In Waverly or Gloversville Toby'd abruptly brake the Ass in front of the local bank, histrionically slam the heel of the palm of his hand against his forehead, and with grotesque and laughable sincerity explain he'd offered to buy dinner that night but had only two one-hundred-dollar bills on him. He had to get them changed as the owners of these "shitkicker eateries" were always rendered epileptic at the sight of a C-note. When I baited him, as I invariably did, by saying I had plenty of smaller bills, Toby always replied with feigned outrage that he'd invited me and would goddamn well observe the proprieties by playing host. In his observation of life's amenities, Toby was truly wondrous to behold.

I had Toby's modus operandi down pat. He'd never go near a bank on a busy day, Monday or Friday. He was strictly a Tuesday-to-Thursday man and he'd never change these hundreds save at slow hours in the morning and between 1:30 and 2:30 in the afternoon. To break two hundred-dollar bills into ten twenties never took him less than fifteen minutes, sometimes a half hour, occasionally even longer. When on his return I asked, as I also habitually did, if the cashier were a slow counter, one of those unfortunate souls who reads with his lips, Toby always roaringly gave his ritualistic reply—one cockamamie tale or another.

"My god, no. There wasn't anyone in there but this uglie-buglie skinny four-eyed nineteen-year-old. Not bad boobs, a rather curiosity-arousing ass. I felt sorry for her, started making with the palaver, and turned on the charm. Within five minutes the pathetic creature wanted my cock in her mouth"—right hand off the wheel and raised Boy Scout fashion: Toby the Good making vows to a jury—"so badly her salivary glands were pumping like the pistons on the Ass. She's been married six months to little Jimmy Thaxton who works down the street in the hardware store.

They're saving up for a down payment on a split-level. She showed me this wretched little costume jewelry wedding band. It made me want to weep, Exley. I almost came out, slid under the Ass, grabbed the magnetic box I've got built into a lead weight, and gave her one of those thousand-dollar diamond-inlaid white gold bands. I might have, too, had not her salivary secretions become so pronounced the spit was leaking all over her funny little chin. Imagine, Exley! Six months married to little Jimmy Thaxton down there in Scrooge's pots-and-pans emporium and she wants to blow me! What the hell are these kids up to today? And can't any of these young bucks take care of their child brides? I mean, it's sad, *really sad*, but kind of nauseating! You know what I mean?"

7

Toby Farquarson III was indignant. As I say, when Toby Farquarson III became indignant at the absence of morals in the modern world, he was astounding to behold. And for all I knew the cashier had been a haggard doddering spinsterish seventy. What I did know was that when it was to his advantage, Toby had the charm and boldness to initiate and perpetuate conversations with all manner of people, and that with cashiers he would assuredly be convivially chatting away and listening with half a cerebrum, the other half being utterly devoted to a relentless scrutiny of every nook and cranny of the bank. Toby was never more outraged than at my having the dense audacity to introduce Patty Hearst into the chatter of one of those stealthy searches he called "drives." It was rather as if I'd condemned the entire medical profession for the proverbial solitary quack who leaves a scalpel where the appendix had been. That sick clamp-toothed smile which always somewhat unnerved me froze upon Toby's countenance. Then, as if he abruptly realized I was the only one in the world to whom he confided (with others he claimed it was "making palaver"), he unclinched his teeth, opened his mouth cavernously, and began to roar.

"*You goddamn fool! You goddamn fool!* Were there any justice Hearst shoulda got burned to a cinder with the rest of that Moo-moo Liberation Group in that dump in LA. What do those meatballs know about freedom? You know who's free?—*you horse's ass! I'm free!* That's because I work alone—the same as you do, baby. I mean, we're both fucking paranoid psychopaths. All writers are! The only difference between me and you guys, you ain't got the balls to shove a sawed-off shotgun in a bank manager's face. Can you imagine taking that drippy-nosed teeny-bopper Hearst on a fucking bank job? Sheer lunacy! That'd be as irresponsible as putting your boxer Killer behind the wheel of the Ass. And the fucking FBI? Who can ever take those clowns seriously again? You know—and I'm not shitting you, Exley—a few months back I actually thought seriously of going to whatsiz-whozit—you know, Hoover's replacement—*Kelley!*—and telling him that for a hundred big ones I'd find Hearst and the Harrises within six weeks and bring them in or take my twelve-gauge, pop in some lovely double-aught buck, and off their fucking skulls. Yeah, I'd'a found 'em in six weeks and I don't even know the fucking West Coast. And I'd'a offed them too! Offed them for the magnitude of their imbecility. You know, the way the parents of that Betty Lou Schlock wanted to pull the plug on that lump of protoplasm down in Jersey?"

"Karen Ann Quinlan," I said.

"Incidentally, writer man, the way Ms. Karen Ann got to be mush was mixing alcohol with too many of those funny pills you keep mooching from me! And you know what's so wildly ironical—*farcical*? From what we now know about that prick J. Edgar, he'd of probably given me a contract for a fucking hundred grand!"

Toby Farquarson III was legendary in upstate New

York, a victim of upstate, of the times, and of himself. About "himself" I didn't for a long time learn much more than everyone else knew. I'd heard about Toby for months, had even become friendly with him without realizing it was he because he was not at all what I'd envisioned and because, whereas he'd introduced himself to me as Toby, everyone else spoke of him, even when he spoke in whispers —and one always spoke of Toby in whispers, looking over his shoulder as he did so—as *Farr*. It was *Farr* this and *Farr* that and *Farr* the other thing, a recurringly whispered paranoid-hued din.

"Don't you know Farr, Exley? Sure you do. I've seen you with the fucking guy!"

"I don't know him."

Farr's story varied with the teller, it being agreed only that he hailed from the Adirondacks. It was said that Farr came from Old Forge or Tupper Lake or Lake Placid and was the most gifted athlete to come out of upstate in years. On scholarship he'd gone to Ohio State or Michigan or Notre Dame or Oklahoma and there he'd severely torn cartilage in a knee or suffered a concussion that had kept him unconscious for a week or had one of the worst shoulder separations in clinical history, this as a sophomore when he was already starting. Whatever the injury, Farr had promptly dropped out of college and entered his chosen "profession," one not as unlikely as it seems.

In upstate, boys grow up with guns in their hands, learn early on a weapon's awesome capacities; and I know, for example, there are more guns in the Bay than there are people, that is, more guns than the number of people who make up our permanent winter population. According to one story, Farr's injury hadn't dissuaded the New York Giants. In their leanest years a few years back, it is told that representatives of Jim Lee Howell, the Giants' director of player personnel, made repeated trips to the mountains (how they ever unearthed Toby escapes me!) and pleaded with Farr to let their surgeons repair him. To shore up their amusing "defense" they were going to make him a corner-back. Reportedly Farr told them to buzz off, his athletic days were done, man, *done,* and he was "doing well in business." If this were true, I could visualize Toby telling them between his clinch-toothed smile. When I got to know Toby as well as one can know him, I asked him about his athletic prowess, what college? what injury? what about the Giants? Toby answered with his typical live-for-the-moment evasiveness.

"Who the fuck cares? That shit is all in the past. I never even think about it anymore."

People said Farr seduced any woman he wanted to seduce, though whenever his name came up in mixed company, girls gagged exaggeratedly and mimicked a furious throwing up, hyperbolic theatrics which always seemed to me so strung out as to suggest that whoever Farr was, he undoubtedly was oblivious to the particular girl doing her fierce feigned puking. People said if you crossed Farr he'd kill you fucking dead, if not with one of his sawed-off shotguns, with his hands.

"Lord awmighty, one night at the Edgewood I saw him go outside with the biggest sonofabitch you ever see—a fucking lumberjack, a baby fucking whale! Farr hit the poor slob a dozen times without the gorilla ever getting his hands up. We had to take the guy's remains down to the candy-with-the-hole-in-it hospital. The patient didn't leave his sickbed for ten fucking days!"

People said Farr made fools of the New York State Police. They said the troopers were weary unto death of it, up to here with it, the hand knifed and slicing enthusiastically at the Adam's apple. Supposedly a top honcho investigator in the state's BCI office in New York City had told local troopers if they knew for certain it was Farr fleeing a crime, there wouldn't be any need extending him the courtesy (a few stout fellow winks here, one imagines) of inviting his surrender. The troopers were to "blow Farr's pretty fucking head off!"

People said they wouldn't mind Farr all that much if he didn't push dope.

"What's the diff? He doesn't sell to kids. In fact, he doesn't sell to anybody he doesn't know. He's too cute for that. The fuzz want him for so many other things, they'd love to bust him for pushing. He'd get the maximum, for fact. And who you shittin'? You get your grass and uppers from him, don't yuh?"

"Gawd, what a *weirdo*. Nobody even knows where he lives. He's supposed to have one place right in this rinky-dink town, and nobody even knows where that is. I mean, *really*! How can anyone disappear in the goddamn Bay?"

None of these Farrs was the Toby I'd known without realizing it was indeed Farr I knew.

Whenever during the tourist season (Memorial through Labor days) I left my attic studio and the manuscript of *Pages from a Cold Island,* ten or fifteen bucks in my pocket, and strolled the crowded streets from bar to bar, drinking a couple beers here, a couple there, I was usually alone. Except for a year at one time, a year at another, spent teaching at local rural high schools—and I viewed these as only interim stints to stake my return to Florida—I really hadn't lived at home for a quarter of a century, since I'd entered college in 1948. Hence I knew hardly anyone but older bar owners and fishing guides. Two or three times I observed Toby in Cavallario's Steak House. I never saw him come in. I'd look up and he'd be standing at the far end of the bar from the end I favored. He was about thirty. I took him for a dentist or surgeon or rising young bank executive, the latter of which he was in a way. He always wore immaculately pressed basic-colored golf shirts with little alligators sewn on the pocket, extravagantly colored, neatly pressed, expensive-looking plaid golf slacks. He shod himself in equally expensive-looking Scotch-grained custom-made shoes.

Except for his very blond wavy hair parted in the middle and brushed lovingly back to the middle of his ears in the Prince Valiant pageboy style of the time, he looked astonishingly like a young Michael Caine, though, unlike

Caine's thicker black rims, Toby favored the brown-speckled-with-yellow thin rims Ivy Leaguers wore in the fifties. There was in his countenance, for example, Caine's sadness and irony, his cynical vulnerability, his innocent decadence, his sinister childlikeness, even his effeminacy. And yet one somehow knew, as with Caine, that he wasn't that way and that the smug aloof bastard was doubtless devastating with women. Materializing at the far end of Cavallario's bar, he would have a bottle of Heineken set before him without his asking, he would lift the bottle directly to his mouth, take a long cool draught as if he'd just come from doing twenty-seven holes, return the green bottle to the bar, sip slowly after that, and never drink more than two. Although from where I stood I never heard how people addressed him, everyone seemed to say hello. If he deigned to acknowledge these greetings at all, he did so with the most cursory of nods. It was as though he were returning salutations from bugs. Looking suddenly up, I'd discover he'd exited with the same silent stealth he'd entered.

To my surprise and uneasiness I one night saw him bent over in eager sibilant conversation with the bartender, Jimmy Tousant, and from that night on, to my embarrassment, he sipped at his Heineken and stared at me. Entering Cavallario's on the July Fourth weekend, I found it so crowded I had to reach over a three-deep mass to get my Budweiser, after which I retreated and rested the small of my back against the frame of the picture window fronting on the street. Abruptly, and without again having seen him enter, not to mention fathoming how he'd got his Heineken so quickly, I sensed he was leaning against the wall right next to me. He did not turn to me.

"Somebody said you're Exley."

I said I was Exley.

Still looking straight ahead and with his left hand holding the bottle he even now sipped at, he proffered his right hand palm upward for me to shake.

"I'm Toby."

Although in his handshake there was a definite warmth and firmness, Toby did it in such a way as to suggest he was offering it up, Pope-like, to be kissed.

"You been away from home a long time."

"Yeah, *a long time*."

"I've read *A Fan's Notes*."

Unless one is a writer, it is difficult to comprehend with what passionate depths one comes to loathe one's own creation. (I don't mean to romanticize the writing racket. Most of us are simpering bohunk egomaniacal pricks just as in thrall to our advances, reviews, and royalty statements as the chairman of U.S. Steel is in thrall to the net earnings figure in his annual report.) For years I had not kept a single copy of that book within a country mile of me. Neither had I kept a single review nor letter in praise of it. Had I elected to keep a scrapbook at all, it would have been comprised of articles and letters damning the book out of hand. In the bathroom, framed and mounted on the wall next to the medicine cabinet, I did have artist James Spanfeller's excellent dust jacket for the original Harper & Row edition. Regally seated on the throne mornings, I could stare at the purple and red psychedelic dust jacket and re-mind myself of how abysmally short of its conception the book had in fact fallen, pull up my Levi's, flush my ugly wastes down the vortex, and return to my Smith Corona determined that this time out I'd consummate my vision.

My Random House editor Bob Loomis was kind enough to say only good writers sneer at and derogate themselves. Loomis said when his hacks come to town he takes them to lunch at swank restaurants, hoping that the sumptuous food and wine will distract them but that, in-variably, he has to sit stupefied for three hours listening to the *various levels of meaning* (oh, my!) on which the hack's book *works*. Before he retires, Loomis swears he's going to sit dopily (he claims these sessions cause constipation) through one of these endlessly dreary monologues, then solemnly remove the habitual cigar or pipe from his mouth and say, "Your book doesn't work on any level whatever, which is not to say that Newhouse and Random House don't hope it sells a hundred million copies." My case wasn't so much hate as love-hate. Years before, when I'd owned a copy, I'd found that on those nights I came home drunk I invariably picked up the book, opened it to any place it happened to open, and moaned or went *ahhhh*. It was a kind of did-I-ever-write-that-badly?-did-I-ever-write-that-well? thing. On the night it became a continuous moan I descended the stairs, went out the back door, opened the garbage can, stood over the banana peels and discarded potato salad, tore out the book's 385 pages, and let them flutter into the pork gravy, salvaging only Spanfeller's dust jacket.

"You must be one of the six guys who did read it," I said.

Toby laughed, then remained silent for a long time. Finally he said, "You wanna get laid?"

"You and me?"

"No, not you and me, you asshole!"

Toby again laughed and for the first time looked at me. "Okay, then."

For the first time I found myself seated in the deep blue leather bucket seat of the Ass. At eighty miles an hour Toby drove the two-lane Route 12 upriver to Clayton and parked the car behind O'Brien's Hotel, a watering hole for the younger crowd. When I opened the door and started to climb out, Toby said there was no need for my doing that. Inquiring if I shouldn't go in, meet the girl he had in mind for me, and observe the amenities by at least buying her a single drink, Toby said there was booze at the camp where we were going and not to sweat about getting laid.

"These cunts do what I tell 'em to do."

8

On returning with the girls, Toby introduced them as Corrine and Vivian.

"Vivian's yours."

Toby told them to sit in back on the cramped blue leather jump seat. Both were quite pretty but neither particularly striking. What they had was youth, neither appearing to be much more than twenty, and youth always has its magnetizing effect on middle age. Toby drove to what he claimed was a "borrowed," beautifully furnished camp at Millen's Bay. As the night chill had come in off the St. Lawrence, Toby lighted the pilot light of a gas furnace in the living room, got both Vivian and me a bottle of Heineken from the kitchen refrigerator, and took Corrine immediately to a bedroom off the living room, closing the door behind him. Vivian and I drank two bottles of beer and talked. The ambiance was so throbbing with awkwardness —already pleasurable mating noises emanated from the bedroom—I remember very little of what I said. Vivian was attractive in a buxom, dark-eyed, and pouty-lipped way. She said she'd been a nurse at Watertown's House of the Good Samaritan ("Good Sam") for three years, which happily put her a few years past twenty. What she said next was not destined to make me happy. Vivian said her father had been a high school classmate of mine! She said he hadn't liked *A Fan's Notes*—"your book"—because he hadn't liked the "bad language" and really hadn't understood it but that he remembered me fondly as a jock.

"He said you played center on one of the great Watertown High School football teams. He said you were even better in basketball."

I do recall what I then said.

"Pure nostalgia." (Banal and sham modesty in my manly utterance.) "I'm unequivocally certain that the kids of your generation are bigger, faster, and more aggressive than we ever dreamed of being." I was pensive for many moments, trying unsuccessfully to rebuke myself for my predicament. "I wish you hadn't told me about your father. Not about his not liking the book. I don't like it either. About being a classmate. It makes it rather—?"

"Crummy?"

"And sleazy and discomforting and sort of incestuous. Yeah, deed it do. *Deed it do sound crummy.*"

"Don't worry about it. If it makes any difference, I won't tell you my last name. Not that you'd remember my jerk father anyway. Besides, he gave up—*ha, ha*—on me ages ago! As if there was anything special to give up on! In the age of the pill and the IUD! As if I was into anything all that monstrous, anything everyone else isn't into." Vivian did an *ugh*. "That drunken self-righteous slob!"

On finishing her second Heineken, Vivian entered a bedroom on the opposite side of the living room from the one Toby and Corrine had entered. She left the door ajar. On finishing two more Heinekens, I entered the room and closed the door, feeling sad, as heavy as an ogre, and about as unclean. I undressed and slipped stealthily into the bed next to a naked Vivian. Pale light from a near-full moon came in a window and during interim respites, while Vivian poutily slept, I scrupulously studied her face, trying to call back that of a high school classmate's. I had no luck. Fucking Vivian I would ask her if I were her daddy and Vivian would say that yes and yes and yes I was her daddy!

In the next weeks Toby fixed me up a dozen times in the same way, though on each occasion we went to different bars to pick up different girls (perfectly interchangeable, however) and different domiciles to copulate, to farmhouses in Rutland or Copenhagen or Burrville, to cottages in Adams Cove or Cape Vincent or Hammond, to apartments in Gouverneur or Mannsville or Pulaski. What invariably startled and distressed me was that, though the owners were never in residence, the places always appeared to have been vacated only moments before. Dirty dishes were piled in sinks. In bathroom baskets were recently used Kleenex. Medicine cabinets were full. Fresh puddles lay on the floor of tiled shower stalls, the nozzles still dripping, hairs like question marks beneath the water. Damp limp bath towels hung yet on racks. Once, logs were still smoldering in a stranger's fireplace. When I later learned that Toby and Farr were one, I told him with great and aggravated earnestness that I hoped he wasn't intimidating anyone into clearing out of his own goddamn house just so we could get laid.

"My word, no! These people are my friends!"

As far as I knew, Toby had no friends but me. On discovering Toby and Farr were one, I had a stock reply whenever the girls on the jump seat asked our destination.

"To one of Toby's *safe houses*."

Toby always laughed and exclaimed, "You goddamn fool!"

At seven one night Toby climbed to my attic studio and told me he wanted to take me to a new place down around North Syracuse. After the name of the play it was called The Devil Made Me Do It. Toby'd heard that "the cunts are swinging from the rafters" and wanted to have a "look-see" for himself. Toby had no girls lined up, but who knew? I declined, explaining close friends had been vacationing in the Bay for a week and that, though Budweiser had carried me well enough for two days, I'd spent the rest of the week swilling vodka.

"As I get older I find it increasingly difficult to get off the sauce. I've had the gruesome wild willies all day, just quieted down after supper a few minutes ago. Now you expect me to start all over again. C'mon, Toby, be a friend!"

Toby told me not to fret. He'd give me some pills. I should take one before I went to sleep and he guaranteed I'd wake without any nervousness whatever. He told me to get an empty aspirin or prescription bottle or "even a fucking envelope will do." In the upstairs bathroom I found one of the old lady's empty brown plastic prescription containers. It had one of those new tops that are supposed to prevent three-year-olds from ODing. (Without a great deal of sweat and cursing, the only ones who can fathom the opening's intricacies are three-year-olds!) Instead of traveling west to Interstate 81, Toby first drove east on Walton Street, turned northeast on the Goose Bay Road, and went up past the golf course. In a small dell the other side of the course, just before one again turns left on the road running to Dingman Point, there is an abandoned dirt road which runs unimpeded for thirty feet and then is lost in high reedy swamp grass and bramble bush. Toby drove right into the grass and when he braked and put the Ass in park, the reedy grass was swishing harshly at the windows on either side of the car. Getting out, Toby lay on his back in the stiff pulpous grass and pulled himself beneath the car, reappearing almost instantly. As though we were kids exchanging jelly beans, he let the red and white capsules sift sievelike through the bottom of his fist into my cupped palm.

"Take one tonight. You'll sleep the sleep of the innocent. If you can't sleep for the next couple nights, take a couple more. But do not—I repeat, *do not*—continue taking them and drinking. These babies are heavy, love. Thirty milligrams. About twenty will take you all the way, right up to see Big Daddy in the sky."

Dr. Toby was dispensing clinical wisdom.

"What are they?"

"Something new. Serax. In fact, they're using them mainly on drunks like yourself. Only known side effects are possible skin rashes, perhaps a little nervousness in your bladder. Might cause a little fluttering in the kidneys and you'll be ah-drip-dripping into your jockeys. I myself am not much into the evil pills. Occasionally if I don't feel like grass, I pop one of these and put a couple Joni Mitchell albums on the stereo. Great dreamy soothing fucking or masturbating time listening to Mitchell on these."

Oddly, I did not even then equate Toby and Farr.

The Devil Made Me Do It was packed. Toby elbowed me a place at the far end of the bar next to the section piped off for waitresses serving tables on the floor, laid a fifty on the bar, ordered a Heineken, and told the bartender to "give my gramps here some vodka on the rocks with a touch of tonic, no fruit." Two big construction guys stood next to us at the bar. They still wore their dusty orange hard hats. Their khaki shirts, trousers, and hands were covered with the grime of their day's labor. Live country-and-western music emanated from a dance hall hard by the bar and lounge. Nobody looked over thirty save the hard hats and me. Doubtless they'd started drinking at the five o'clock whistle, had got drunk, and now found themselves caught up among the younger nocturnal crowd. The one closest to me really enjoyed Toby's calling me gramps. With him it apparently passed for wit incarnate. He slammed the bar with the palm of his big dirty right hand, giggled coarsely, pointed a stubby index finger at me, and spoke to Toby.

"Izzee really your gramps? *Izzee really your gramps?*"

Paying him no more attention than he paid any other stranger, Toby started circulating among the tables in the lounge. The hard hat was very put off. Into Toby's appearance he misread the effeminacy I have remarked. He let his dusty knobby hand go limp at the wrist, and for his partner affected a lisp.

"Oh me, oh my. Ithent he some kinda pretheus Ivy League queen?"

Toby wandered from table to table, pulling up at those occupied by unescorted girls. Toby was doing what he did best when the spirit moved him—exuding charm. From those tables came squeals of high shrill girlish laughter. One had to hand it to Toby. He was good, as good as I'd ever seen. When at length he smilingly started walking back toward me, I thought he'd settled on two and was going to fetch me to join them. Instead he told me he had to drive into the heart of Syracuse to the Presidential Plaza Apartments (high rent) and "see someone on personal business." He'd be gone only an hour and did I mind waiting?

When four hours had elapsed and Toby still hadn't appeared, I was inebriated and extremely agitated. The hard hats had become obnoxiously drunk and were baiting me constantly.

"Hey, gramps, where'd your pretty-boy grandson go?"

"Hey, bartender, give ol' gramps here another drink!"

"Hey, gramps, aren't yuh gonna buy one back?"

In a depressingly ostentatious attempt to display their affluence and outdo each other, they had already bought one another so many they had a half dozen full bottles of Ginny backed up before them on the bar, growing warm and flat.

"Look, I'm trying to mind my own business. I didn't ask you to buy me a drink. I don't want you buying me drinks!"

"Well, gramps, if you wanna be a *cheapo*, we'll buy the fuckin' drinks anyway."

Finally, in exasperation, and because the bar was still so crowded, I asked the bartender if he'd watch my drink and save my place at the bar. He said he would but recommended I take my change with me, the dwindling change from Toby's fifty. To my astonishment the Ass was still parked in the back lot in the precise spot we'd left it! Bringing my hands up to my temples like horse blinders,

I brought my nose up to the glass, looked into the front seat, then into the back seat. Toby wasn't there. Now I did the same thing with every blessed vehicle in the parking lot. The only people I found were a couple kids copulating in a Volkswagen camper. The camper had curtains, but apparently the kids' anxiety hadn't allowed time to close them. The guy wasn't Toby. Bewildered and despondently alarmed, I walked slowly back into the bar.

At five minutes before closing time Toby appeared all smiles, profusely apologetic and sanguine with some cockamamie tale of having to drive his "personal business" friend over to Fulton and back, a matter of great urgency.

"Life and death, baby. I wanted to call you but couldn't find anything listed for this dump."

The hard hat nearest to us rose up from his stupor, put his heavy dirty arm around the shoulder of the inky-blue V-necked cashmere sweater Toby wore over his golf shirt.

Toby spoke with deadly even menace.

"Take your fucking grubby paws off me."

"Oh, my, pretty boy's a tough guy. And, yeah, so does an elephant piss lemonade."

The hard hat closed his arm around Toby's neck in a mock-furious wrestler's hold. It happened with such shocking celerity I could not take it in completely, rather as if it were the projected images of a movie camera gone mad. Toby hit him only—I think—twice. He hit him first flush on the nose, out of which there gushed immediately a profusion of thick rich-red blood. With his right fist Toby next connected viciously to the guy's left jaw, I heard something snap, hoping it wasn't Toby's hand (it wasn't), and the hard hat settled ever so slowly down on his hands and knees, then to all fours. He remained that way shaking his head as if his skull were underwater. The shaking didn't so much reflect his awesome disbelief and chagrin at what had happened as it seemed to express a reflexive twitch, as though his temple had been grazed by the lead of a .50-caliber shell and he were waiting horrified for death.

By now the bar had completely emptied except for the

four of us and the bartender. The latter had pulled the zinc trash cans full of empty bottles from beneath the folding service bar, had lidded them, and they now rested at the nape of my knees behind me. He was obviously going to take them out back at our exiting the bar. He stood as stunned as I did. The other hard hat, though terribly drunk, too, was much bigger than the first, his gnarled dirty hands from wrist to clinched fist looking somewhat like moldy overgrown zucchinis. As he lunged furiously toward Toby, Toby grabbed a lid from one of the garbage cans, turned it so he gripped it by its edge, then swung it high over his head and brought it so ferociously down on the man's head (he'd made the mistake of setting his hard hat on the bar) that Toby seemed to leave the floor and the metallic sound of lid against head seemed as someone hitting a great Oriental gong with a sledgehammer. Now the hard hat settled slowly to his knees, at which time Toby kicked him violently in his heavy belly, and immediately the guy also went to a doglike all fours, perfectly juxtaposed with his friend, and was throwing up puddles of sickish bile-looking Ginny. Now Toby did an unforgivable thing. With his heavy Scotch-grained custom-made right shoe he kicked the first to go down in the ribs, and I definitely heard something snap. With amazing swiftness he moved behind the other and with equal fury kicked him high on the bottom, right at the coccyx, causing him to topple over and settle face down in his own nauseating emissivity. The room had started going round and round on me—I was becoming sick myself. I was so petrified I was unable to move, and Toby had to take me firmly by the arm and drag me to the Ass. Behind us an equally amazed bartender issued an ironically meek "Hey, Jesus." Toby said, "Don't follow us to the parking lot or you'll get worse. Like maybe your fucking head blown off."

Of course I knew who Toby was then. But I didn't say anything until we were halfway home on Interstate 81. My face was red with embarrassment and chagrin that it had taken me so long to put Toby and Farr together. When we had gone on our erotic outings ("people said Farr seduced any girl he wanted to seduce"), I'd noticed, the following mornings, when Toby and I and the girls were lolling about the cottages in our underwear, how surprisingly muscular and well built Toby was (the Giants were to make a corner-back of him), a physique which had been disguised by the formal cut of his Ivy League duds. As Rizzuto is reported to have said of Mantle, "He grows bigger as he undresses." I didn't say anything for a long time because it also took a long time for Toby's anger to abate. His right hand was hurting him badly and he kept removing it from the wheel and shaking it as if to prevent swelling. When at length he slid a Stevie Wonder tape into the slot beneath the dash and was driving with his "wounded" hand, was humming and keeping time to the music by tapping the palm of his left hand against the wooden wheel, I spoke.

"I got to tell yuh, Toby. You're the meanest son of a bitch I ever saw. The quickest too. And the fucking most violent. It wasn't in the least necessary to administer those final *coups de grâce* by kicking those slobs."

Toby laughed loudly. *"The devil made me do it."* Now he fell silent and grew solemn. "You're a sucker. Don't you understand about pigs like that? They were determined to get it—begging for it. If I hadn't done it for them, they'd have ended by pounding the piss out of each other. Disgusting fucking pigs, the long and the short of it." Toby paused and smiled. "As to my being violent, my dad told me he only ever met one guy tougher."

"Who's that?"

"Your dad."

"Your father knew my father?"

"Yeah, years ago when your father was a lineman with the Niagara Mohawk."

"Your father was from Watertown?"

"No, no, *no*. We used to get bad ice storms up around Wanakena and extra gangs from Watertown used to come up and help repair the wires. My father said it once took six troopers twenty minutes to subdue your father in the bar of the hotel up there. And the fucking troopers were using their billies! The old man said your dad was a better athlete than me, too."

"Is that where you're from—Wanakena?"

"Forget about where I'm from."

"Where's your dad now?"

Toby seemed equally reluctant to answer even that. Finally he said, "He's dead."

"I'm sorry."

"No need to be."

I don't know why I started anything as manifestly academic as I now started.

"How do you spell your last name, Toby?"

"F-A-R-Q-U-A-R-S-O-N."

"Are you the one they call Farr?"

"Yeah, who the fuck'd yuh think I was?"

My irritation mounted moment by moment but I didn't say what was really bothering me until we had left Interstate 81 at the Bay exit and were ten minutes from the old lady's house.

"Don't you ever, *ever* do that to me again, Toby!"

"Do *what*, for Christ's sake?"

"The Ass was in the parking lot all goddamn night, right where we goddamn well left it! Wherever in hell's half acre you went, you went with somebody else, hot-wired a car, or walked. You went on a fucking caper, one that took you a helluva lot longer than you figured!"

"So what if I did?"

"So what if I did? *So this if you did*: if you think you're ever going to set me up for a perjury rap by telling troopers you were drinking with me all night in some crowded bar— oh, very conveniently crowded!—you are bonkers, Toby, *bonkers!*"

Parked in front of the old lady's house, we struck our "bargain" that night, shaking hands on it, the bargain in which I had only not to probe Toby where "home" was.

Toby never set me up again. Unlike the old lady's pre-
scribed Demerol, I got whatever Serax I couldn't get from
Alissa from Dr. Toby Farquarson III, unprescribed and
gratis. Toby Farquarson III was also part of home. And
is it any wonder that he and the nefarious James Seamus
Finbar O'Twoomey hit it off so quickly?

9

Well, marshal, if you've hung in there with me this long, I imagine you have the stamina to hang in with me a moment more. About all that remains is the honor guard's mock-firing their M-1s in salute to the Brigadier, the escort's weapons being brought to order arms, the playing of Taps, the folding of the American flag into the shape of a cocked hat, and the presentation of it to the Brigadier's widow, Judy, accompanied by the standard words, "From a grateful nation." They do, I understand, have a prefolded flag and will present it to the old lady, with of course the same words. As I know Taps to be among the saddest, most mournful sounds in the world, I have stiffened my back and upper lip against it and my prayer is that the bugler hasn't the artistry of James Jones's Pvt. Robert E. Lee Prewitt. If he does, I'm not sure I have the strength to keep my grief at bay.

The only thing, Big Matt, that will surprise—*astonish* is perhaps the better word—is that at that moment just after

Taps a very strange dude with a black eye patch and a black leather left hand, dressed in a double-breasted brown suit, shall step from a command car, scurry across the lawn to the end of the bier, accept and present the flags to Judy and the old lady, then vanish as quickly as he appeared.

Speaking of James Jones, one night after we'd visited the Brigadier at Tripler, Malia and Wiley took me for a drink to the top of the Sheraton Waikiki to the Hano Hano Room, where we were to meet Robin. As the back bar is floor-to-ceiling plate glass, they wanted me to see the glittering night lights along Waikiki. As I had been thinking a lot about Jones's Twenty-fifth Infantry Division having its permanent home at Schofield Barracks in Honolulu, I abruptly found myself thinking of the scene in *From Here to Eternity* where Privates Prewitt and Maggio, drunk, are sitting on the curb in front of the Royal Hawaiian, nipping at a bottle, and debating whether to go in and make out with the movie actresses.

Years later, in a wonderfully poignant eulogy written on Jones's death, Joan Didion would also call back that scene and when I asked Malia where the Royal Hawaiian was, to my astonishment she said it was right next door, to take the elevator to the lobby, walk out to Kalakaua and turn right. I did so, accompanied by Robin, and though I did not attempt to find the curb space Prewitt and Maggio had occupied, I did raise my plastic cup of vodka and take a sip, my salute to Jones, to which Robin of course laughed cruelly. In one of those grand ironies that Jones would have loved, the Japanese now own the Royal Hawaiian, as they do eleven of the fourteen first class hotels along Waikiki, and whereas on that, my first view of the Pink Palace, one could see across a wide expanse of beautifully cropped lawn, gardened and lighted up by Oriental lanterns, the Japanese have now built an architectural monstrosity they call a mall, a building so relentlessly ugly the locals call it the Fortress, and the Oshkosh stroller on Kalakaua can no longer get even a glimpse of Waikiki's most legendary hotel.

If the milieu of Dodge City, Big Jim, is divided into

white and black Stetsons, I ought to say that for a good part of the ceremony I found myself thinking of the writings of Edmund Wilson, and especially of a brief passage in his attack on the Internal Revenue Service, *The Cold War and the Income Tax*. There had been a period in my life when I'd gone systematically through every book Wilson had written (he not only taught me how to read but did more for me than any psychiatrist had been able to do), and I was thinking of this particular passage because it illustrated that all members of the State Department's Watertown mafia were not ipso facto black hats.

When I said earlier, for example, that for all practical purposes the twentieth century began with the atomic bombing of Hiroshima in August 1945, it is because of one of the Watertown mafia, Charles "Chip" Bohlen, our man from twenty-five miles upriver at Cape Vincent, that we now know the twentieth century—at least the abomination we have been forced to live with—need never have begun at all. According to Wilson, it had been known for some time before the attack on Hiroshima that the Japanese had told Stalin of their desire to negotiate a peace. For a long time we made Stalin the fall guy by claiming he withheld this information in order to prolong the conflict so he could declare war on Japan and, in victory, claim his share of the booty. According to our Cape Vincent man, Chip Bohlen, however, Stalin fully informed President Truman at Potsdam and Truman refused to listen to this peace initiative. Oh, how very different, Marshal Dillon, the twentieth century might indeed have been.

10

Ln early spring 1969, I was informed by the National Institute of Arts and Letters that *A Fan's Notes* had won the Rosenthal Award "for that work which, though not a commercial success, is a considerable literary achievement" and that for the May ceremony at the American Academy of Arts and Letters, in Manhattan, a number of tickets for relatives and friends would be made available to me. Not only did I expect the Brigadier to refuse my invitation, I expected his refusal to come in the form of no response whatever. It was, therefore, much to my surprise when he accepted and hence I phoned him at his home in Springfield, Virginia, and gave him the name of the Manhattan hotel where my publisher had reserved a room for two.

The Brigadier (at forty-three, he had made his bird) had only a few months before returned from Saigon, where he had been assigned to General Westmoreland's staff (he did not of course report directly to Westmoreland) at the

Saigon airport or what was familiarly known as Pentagon East and living a short distance away at BOQ One. He had been there during the Tet offensive, the worst of times, the Cong or Charlie or the Gook was in the streets of Saigon, the Brigadier and his friends were working eighteen- and twenty-hour days and so unsure of getting back to BOQ One for four hours' sleep, they were carrying army-issue .45 sidearms and automatic weapons to ward off ambush. It was during this time that the now famous film of the police chief of Saigon blowing away the head of an alleged Cong in the middle of a street came out.

Arriving at the desk of the midtown hotel, I asked if a Col. William Exley had checked in, was told no but that a Bill Exley had. I smiled. Although the distinguished reporter, Seymour M. Hersh, hadn't as yet broken the complete story of My Lai 4, morale in the military was at an all-time low. They had been stripped of any remnants of pride. Gone were the pomp and ceremony. Not only did they never caparison themselves and primp about in their uniforms, they seldom if ever volunteered their rank. In response to what he did for a living, I'd once heard the Brigadier say he was "in government." Learning that there was a refrigerator in the room, I walked across the street and at a grocer's bought two six-packs of Budweiser, for which, in 1969, they charged me seven dollars apiece. Welcome to Manhattan. Then I returned to the lobby and stepped into the elevator. I was ready for the Brigadier and was going to do it to him good.

When I unlocked the door and stepped into the room, I intended to say, my voice brimming with histrionically amused irony, "Hey, Brigadier! Hey, old pukka sahib, how's your good buddy—ha, ha, ha!—Willie Westmoreland?" One had only to look at the Brigadier to think better of any such opening sally and to my abruptly culled alternative, "Hi! How are you? I brought you some beer," he neither responded nor even looked up from his chair or the movie he was watching on TV. Indeed, so much had the Brigadier always intimidated me that I, who was going to be in complete control, abruptly found myself in a damn near hysterical monologue.

"That's either channel five or channel thirteen," I capaciously and gingerly volunteered, rather as if the Brigadier was a spaced-out muscle-bound dude with a switchblade at my Adam's apple and I was coweringly offering up my wallet. "They show great old movies down here in the afternoon. Late at night too. Anyone with chronic insomnia ought to move into the Manhattan area *al instante*. No shit. A fact. Besides, the Establishment—you know, the multinationals, the guys on the floor of the exchange, Kojak, the various intelligence services"—that didn't even get a rise!—"et cetera, et cetera—can keep Negroes and Puerto Ricans off the streets during the witching hours. They're all home watching Jimmy Cagney plan his bank heists. You and me? During the commercials we go to our Sears Coldspots, make a ham-and-cheese sandwich. These guys? They lift up boards in their floors and pore with loving myopia over their caches of bomb components, Pento-Mex and ammonium nitrate, their M-16s and sawed-off shotguns. They're all going to skyjack a 747, fly down, suck Fidel's cock, and luxuriate beneath palm trees drinking coconut milk and copulating with chiquitas. Nobody's told them Fidel throws their sorry asses into a pokey that makes the Tombs look like the Yale Club. Even if they read it in *The New York Times*, they wouldn't believe it. To them the *Times* is written for Jews and liberal Episcopalians, the *Daily News* for the fascist hard hats and mackerel snappers. Since Muhammad Ali, all these guys have become Muslims. What else can they do but gloat over their alarm clocks and dynamite sticks? They don't have ham or cheese or Sears Coldspots."

The Brigadier did not look up from Bogart–Edward G. On the dresser's plate glass cover he had quartered three or four limes with his pocket knife and the opened knife, the lime pieces, and the lime juice spread out in an eerie Rorschach design atop the glass. The solid maple stand next to his chair held a quart of Gordon's gin, a quart of Canada Dry quinine water, an ebony glass ashtray for the ashes of his Antonio y Cleopatra Grenadier (stuck as always in the side of his mouth, Bat-Guana fashion), and a half-empty gin, tonic, and squeezed lime in an escutcheoned gold leaf hotel glass. A small brass bucket placed between his feet held ice cubes. Although the Brigadier could easily do a case of beer a day, even when he was working, he seldom if ever drank hard stuff and I was surprised to see him doing so. I didn't then know he'd been into gin since his return from Nam.

More than anything else, it was the Brigadier's farcically touching attempt to travel in mufti that disarmed and amused me. At that moment I of course did not dare laugh. As always, his hair was shorn skin-close, still dark and vigorous at the dome, the bristles at his temples touched with gray. He wore his glasses with thick black shell rims; as his Antonio y Cleopatra was a constant in his mouth, he might have been said to be wearing that too. For the rest, he wore a button-down shirt of candy-striped white and pastel blue. Beneath the knot of his fortyish thin black knit necktie, as though for security reasons he were "double-checking his coordinates" as he hadn't faith in his "shirt-buttoned right flank," he had also attached a gold collar pin. His Weber & Heilbroner suit was of an expensive summer sharkskin, finely patterned with nubbly microdabs of red and gold and over all a more dark than medium blue. His feet were shod in those thick dark burgundy cordovans indigenous to the marine corps and other young males of the forties and fifties, perhaps the last shoe made in America, like the Model A Ford, which didn't contain built within itself its own obsolescence. Staring at those shoes, I had to summon all my discipline to stay the laughter. In the late sixties there was no place in America, least of all would there be the next day at the American Academy of Arts and Letters, where the Brigadier wouldn't instantly be recognized as fuzz, military, FBI, or CIA. To distract myself from the silliness welling up within me, I tore the cardboard from the six-packs, then put the cans of Budweiser into the refrigerator.

"Guess you don't wannany beer, huh?"

The Brigadier did not deign to respond. For the first time he looked at me. With his index finger he slid his black shell-rimmed glasses up to the bridge of his handsome nose, his way of conveying to me he had me in riveting, inescapable focus. Under any circumstance I did not appreciate the Brigadier's looking at me. He had a mocking, impertinent way of staring at one's lips as though he were sardonically prepared for any idiocy that might fall from them. He had a face bereft of flesh, candid eyes, a nose too sane and knowing, and a slender neck topping his slender frame. His whole bearing suggested the cynicism and skepticism of the Greek, and like the Greek he seemed forever poised to counter one's notions with a dazzling piece of sophistry. Long ago I had determined that he always unraveled my premises with what surfacely seemed the most rational and stunning counter-arguments, but on a day or two's hindview I would be able to see—too late, alas, for our immediate dialogue—that not only hadn't he addressed himself to my arguments, he hadn't really said anything at all. I wondered if this knack wasn't something he'd picked up in one of the spook's training schools. It probably was. He was also Greek in his unflagging belief in the moral rectitude of military might. Looking at him, though, I could see he no longer possessed the Anglo-Saxon stamina for field command, that he had cultivated a Gallic respect for the quick flourish, the abrupt insight, the devious thrust, that he was in effect perfect for what he was doing.

Abruptly the Brigadier began to laugh derisively. When the Brigadier was solemn, I didn't trust his laughter anymore than I trusted his reined-in but palpable stillness, and what followed made me understand that for whatever reasons he had been sitting there reviewing his life. "Did I ever tell you about seeing the movie version of *From Here to Eternity*?" Having risen from the ranks, I expect the Brigadier's sympathies had always been with the grunts, as I expect that this conversation was the reason my thoughts so often went to Jones four years later at the Brigadier's Hawaiian death-watch. "It was in Berlin in '54 or '55 when I was a pinchbeck lieutenant or captain. In those days the army got first runs before the Berliners did and to see it I hence had to go to a post theater. At the time the officers sat sequestered on the right side of the theater, the noncoms in the middle and far left sides of the orchestra. Halfway through the flick, at that point that feeble-minded Polack sergeant—a helluvan actor, one of those guys whose stage names you never remember—finally provokes Private Robert E. Lee Prewitt into a fist fight in Schofield's quadrangle and Captain Dynamite Holmes stands idly by and allows the fight to proceed—remember that?—at that point, anyway, some tight-assed brigadier down front comes up ramrod straight in his aisle seat, pivots, and marches thunderously out of the theater and every chickenshit officer on our side of the orchestra leaps up and storms out after him—all this, I might add, to the deafening applause, whistling, Bronx cheers, and foot stomping from the darkness-protected noncoms.

"Every officer but me, that is. Man, I was still limping from Korea. I figured, screw these silver- and gold-laden tin soldiers, I'd paid my quarter or thirty-five cents or whatever it was in those lovely days when we were so sure we knew who the enemy was, I was enjoying the movie and hadn't any place else to go but the officer's club to get drunk, which I was going to do afterward anyway. Amusingly, if my brethren had waited two more minutes the camera would have zoomed to the upper balcony of Schofield Barracks and they'd have seen two staff-level officers talking, the senior officer ordering the lesser to get Holmes's name and bring him to the former for an ass gouging. Admittedly, it was a scene Jones never wrote. Not that I remember. I expect it was a compromise Hollywood made with the Defense Department to get its cameras into Schofield. I wonder what Jones thought about it all. He probably needed money. Writers always need money. Writers ought never to need money."

"Let me have five grand."

The Brigadier chose not to hear.

"Still, I can't believe that in my lifetime in the army

that ludicrous scene occurred and those officers charged out of that theater in Berlin. *Kheeerist!* We don't even have dishonorables anymore. If some fag rhetorician fresh from the editorial pages of his college rag decides he wants to go home and have his mums continue his breast feeding, we even ease his passage to those sagging withered udders. We shake his hand and wish him lah lah *lah-dee-dah* luck! It's a wonder Congress doesn't pass legislation instructing us to blow these fruitcakes before they leave. That'll be next."

I couldn't help laughing—the Brigadier was so frenzied, so uncharacteristically verbose, so straining to seek out the utmost horizons of man's more preposterous antics—even though I sensed in his zany nonstop monologue a volcanically simmering rage which, by some enormous regimentation of his will, he kept obstinately repressed beneath his loftily grand and comical demeanor, even though I chuckled throughout his entire erratic spiel, I knew even as I did so that he was close to a hysteria verging on dementia. Brother or no brother, the Brigadier was cracking up. And I didn't much know what to say but I knew I had to get him off his mutually purgative and self-destructive binge.

And wherein did the Brigadier's madness lay? It was, I thought, all the schooling to kill the "enemy," all the strategies, the logistics, the weaponry, the intrigues, all the battles, all the dead friends, all the dead period, all the years —twenty-five in the Brigadier's case, twenty-five, *his life!*— all fallen before a long-haired, geetar-strumming, pot-smoking, toot-sniffing, pill-popping, terrorist-inclined, rock-oriented, please-touch, denim revolution he neither understood nor could have appreciated had he understood.

But with what little regard I convey the Brigadier's intelligence. What I was too dense to understand that day, even though the Brigadier tipped me off in a hundred small ways, was that he had long since ceased to trouble himself with triflingly imperceptive middle-class questions as to whether we were going to have a revolution in America and if so when it would come and how violent it would be. To the Brigadier—and he was right!—the revolution had come and gone! And what was needed was a willing adoption of a whole new set of vantage points from which to view both America and the world, an adoption the Brigadier was incapable of making. And what galled him more than anything was those politicians who professed a sympathy with and comprehension of that revolution, not in the least understanding that Vietnam was lost, the revolution was complete, and the implacable, laughable, and laughing Russkis had altered their goal of world domination not a whit, a domination that would bring with it its strident and real—as opposed to the Brigadier's rhetorical—anti-Semitism, repression of the artist, et cetera, all those things we "freaking intellectuals" so professed to abhor. As the Japanese physicists were said to have wired congratulatory messages to our counterparts on our development of the atomic bomb, the Brigadier told me he was seriously considering wiring congratulatory messages to some Soviet spooks he knew.

11

"You want a vision of insanity?" the Brigadier said at one point. "Don't look to General Westmoreland. Conjure up McNamara with his eighteen-ninetyish greased-down hairdo, his prissy rimless glasses and schoolmarmish pointing stick, his incredibly detailed and brilliantly hued charts and diagrams explaining in that remote gobbledygook —as euphemistic as a freaking Nazi justifying the final solution to the Jewish problem!—what we were supposed to need in Nam to see the light at the end of the tunnel. He thought he was still selling his Harvard Business School background or whatever to the stockholders of the Ford Motor Company. He was really incapable of making any distinction between prosecuting a war and Henry the Elder's assembly line. You know, the invincible American know-how would bring us through, 'when Johnny comes marching home, tra la, tra la.' Yeah, just conjure up the picture of the early and mid-sixties McNamara and you recreate some ultimate vision of lunacy.

"It makes *1984* look as shallow as a futuristically inclined comic strip. Is it any wonder the 'body count' mentality seeped into the military and turned ninety percent of our ambitious field commanders into goddamn liars? They began to feel they were Pinto dealers whose franchises would be yanked if they didn't somehow account for more dead bodies or Fords or whatever it was we were supposed to be selling in Southeast Asia. Or take Teddy Bear Kennedy— and you can have him! He comes over to Nam for a whirl-wind tour to get a 'firsthand look' at the situation and goes back to Capitol Hill and tells his colleagues, those decrepit drunken old whores, and the American people that he was appalled at the corruption he found from top to bottom in Vietnam, from the province chiefs to the village mayors right into the South Vietnamese Army. Shit me a vanilla cup-cake, will yuh, baby brother? Those gooks don't have any translation for our concepts of corruption, bribery, extortion, and so forth. To them it's all some time-honored and admired Oriental tradition and one that very early on the military had to learn to live with and adjust itself to."

For the Brigadier my heart leaped suddenly out in sympathy, perhaps love. He was to be pitied. He was to be pitied in the way the archaeologist who carries with him some stamp of mourning for the passing of the dinosaur is to be pitied.

"You ought to get out of the army."

"Get out of the army? What the hell would you imagine I'm going to do? Hang around in that limp-wristed undisciplined Cub Scout pack? I'm seeing Nam through to the end" —the Brigadier would not of course make it to the end— "and then the army and I shall quit each other, kaput, slam the door in each other's faces. And may God have mercy on us both. Especially the army."

"I guess you'll never make your brigadier's star."

"*My brigadier's star! My star!* It was never *mine*. It was always yours, for Christ's sake. It was some power fantasy you were living out through me. What kind of a chance did you imagine I had, a high school graduate and a two-bit reserve officer into the bargain? You got any idea what it means to make bird colonel as a reserve officer? You know how many light colonels there were, say, last year at the height of the Tet offensive—we called it the counter-offensive, for Christ's sake? Seven thousand! And you know how many would be passed over for bird? Plenty, freaking plenty, and I'm not only talking about guys like myself or even freaking college ROTCs, I'm talking about regular skinheads from the Point, VMI, and the Citadel. I never even got to the war college at Carlisle, a must to make general. Even had I been in the right place at the right time —and you can be sure, baby brother, that I usually made damn sure I was *in the place at the time*—I still never would have made my star as a reserve officer."

The Brigadier was laughing. It was a silly, derisive laugh, causing his tall angular body to seem to creak about at the joints.

"In the last twenty years you know how many reserve officers have been offered their stars? Guess? Don't bother. I'll tell you. *One!* One goddamn reserve officer! And you know what he did? He told the Pentagon to shove its star up its ass! *True.* True story. I shit you not. The guy is still a legend in the army. I can't think of the admirable gentle-man's name. Let's say it was Hobbs. Whomsoever, as a member of the joint chiefs might say when testifying before a congressional committee, whenever old Hobbsie's name comes up, one of the guys at the club invariably sighs and says, 'Yeah, old Hobbsie, ain't he the guy who told the army to empty its bladder on its star?' And everyone cries '*Yeah, yeah*,' takes a morose, pensive sip on his drink, and shakes his head in wondrously awed salute to old Hobbsie. You know the kind of thing. Everyone wishing he had the balls and the opportunity to tell the army the same thing. Hobbsie, the last pariah. *The Last Pariah*, a title for you. Gratis."

So the Brigadier, who would never be a brigadier but forever a colonel, and the army would after Nam call it quits, kaput, slam the door in each other's faces, and may God have mercy on them both, especially the army. For a flashing instant I facetiously wondered if, on retirement, the Brigadier would have his name listed in the telephone directory as Col. W. R. Exley but the thought no sooner entered my mind than it exited because I knew that when the Brigadier quit something he owned the obstinacy to quit it forever.

Like the members of any profession, I said, guys in the army had an annoying habit of working on the tacit and smug assumption that laymen knew precisely what they were talking about. Not only didn't I understand the regular-reserve distinction, I said ("What the fuck's the difference if either designation of officer has been in twenty-five years?"), but I also thought he'd been to every command school the army had to offer and didn't understand this war college at Carlisle abruptly becoming an obstacle to his making general.

It was very simple. At any point in his career the Brigadier could have applied for a regular commission, but he had no doubt that without a college degree the commission would have been denied him, despite the honors bestowed on him. He probably should have applied and made the overture anyway. "The goofy bastards always want to know if you love them, you see. They want to know whether you are serious, interested in doing thirty years and assuming responsibility at staff level or whether you are a hot-dog dilettante just pulling your pollywogger and biding your time until you get your twenty in, any time after which you might pull out, buy a motel and beer bar in New Smyrna Beach, Florida, sit in the sun, and let the regulars suck ass, jockey deviously, and cut throats to achieve rank. However, some time in the fifties they introduced some fine print into the regular's contract, some fine print that made a lot of us very nervous. If, for example, I'd become a regular and on retirement had moved over to Langley or into the Department of Defense, my regular's pension would be cut and adjusted to the salary I was receiving from the CIA, whereas if I made the move as a reserve officer I'd draw both full pension and full salary—double dipping, as we say, on the exalted level. It was the army's way of assuring themselves that regulars had no incentive for leaving the army until they had thirty years in. Hence, from the day I refused to make an attempt to meet requirements for a regular commission, say, picking up a degree at night school, whatever meager—and it was very meager indeed!—chance I had of going to Carlisle—believe me, kiddo, the Harvard or Cambridge of the army!—or achieving general staff level was nonexistent. Non, non, non, *nonexistent*. The choice was easy for me, though. I was never that fond of the army in any event."

"I don't believe that at all. And such restrictions seem silly as hell to me. I mean, with your obviously not undistinguished military career."

"Silly? Say what you mean. It's freaking absurd, like everything else in the freaking army."

Later, I told the Brigadier I was going to have a good scrubdown in the shower, after which I was taking him to a small bistro in the Village and letting him buy me dinner.

"Scrub up all you damn please but I've already made plans to have dinner with a friend. At a place in the Village called the Coach House. Do you know it?"

"Yeah, I know it. It's not far from where I'm going. I'll walk you there when we get off the subway. I just hope your pal has a lot of loot. The cheapest thing on the menu is chopped steak and that goes for eight hundred dollars. And the menu is à la carte!"

"My friend is treating."

"What the hell does he do?"

"As it happens, he's a captain in the New York City police. Intelligence."

"A *captain?* How old is he? And if he's a captain, he won't have to go for dime one, even at the Coach House."

"Probably not. We served together in Berlin in the fifties. Let me tell you, baby brother, this guy was the best I ever saw. He and another guy, a Top, once walked right through Checkpoint Charlie to get a look at the Russkies' new T-54 tank."

"And just how the hell did they do that?"

"Swedish passports. Listen, allow me to spare details, will yuh? You might learn something. When they got to the tank, they discovered the Top had forgotten the film for the freaking camera—I shit you not! So this ballsy bastard, my pal, and this Top, knowing precisely what time the Russian sentries would come by, kept crawling in and out of the tank to avoid them, and they stayed in an hour longer than they were supposed to (I know because I was waiting for them!), adding, as you can well imagine, more brown stains to their skivvies than they ever did in combat, as well as adding no few to mine. With a tape measure my main man measured everything on the tank, length, width, thickness of armament, estimated the caliber of the weaponry, and so forth. Even then our boss—that chickenshit prick—was so furious about their forgetting the film that my guy said, fuck it, he'd walk back in and get the pictures. The Top said, 'Not with me you fucking won't walk back in!' " The Brigadier laughed heartily. "And a week later my guy did walk back in and came out with the pictures. I mean, this guy I'm meeting is the best."

When we'd left the subway and I'd walked him to the Coach House, the Brigadier tried to persuade me to join them for dinner, explaining that their conversation would be the same old nonsense, how much the cop wished he'd stayed in the army and how much the Brigadier wished he'd have joined Manhattan police intelligence and could bug marvelous characters like Joey the Meathead Gallo. When he saw that I was adamant, feeling, as I did, that I would severely hamper their conversation, he started up the Coach House steps, stopped, turned, and with a bitingly ironic laugh issued the Irish platitude, "Up the revolution." I winced. That was more meaningful than one of the last things the Brigadier would say to me from his deathbed:

"I wonder if anyone ever told Dustin Hoffman he overacts."

Part Three

IN THE DAYS
BEFORE I SHOT
MY SISTER

I don't know if the following epistolary indulgence—my paranoia run amok?—will ever reach you. When I walked to the post office for the morning mail with Hannibal Cooke and he caught me trying to post a letter to the Maui County authorities, reached out, grabbed my left wrist, snapped it as though it were a parched twig, then relieved me of the letter and handed it over to O'Twoomey for his clangorous scrutiny and sinister caveats about any such future actions on my part, even then no one believed me and the explanation was given out that while drunk I'd fallen from bed. I doubt there is a resident of Lanai who didn't accept that as readily as he knows he'd be jobless if pineapple were abruptly found to be a carcinogenic agent.

At the hospital, when Dr. Jim was X-raying the wrist, taping it, and capping the tape with a tautly drawn leather wrist band, I kept trying to signal him with what I imagined were foreboding winks. Then Hannibal, with that uncanny animal instinct of his, sensed nervous duplicity on my part and placed his six-feet-seven-inch, 275-pound, lean, and bemuscled frame directly behind Jim so I was unable to make a gesture Hannibal couldn't see. Not that Jim picked up on anything. In distress he has a nervous habit of twitching his mustache and blinking his eyes. Perhaps he thought I was mocking him, perhaps he feels I suffer the same distracting tic and that we are brothers in affliction. Whatever, his ministrations completed, he gave me a hail-fellow jovial poke between my shoulder blades and assured me I'd be back on the golf course within two weeks.

God of Israel, Alissa, if I am forced to play another eighteen holes with O'Twoomey, Hannibal, and Toby, I shall go round the bend completely. My so-called oldest pal in the world, Wiley Hampson, about whom you've heard so much from me, says I'm that anyway—"the most mental," he said, "I've ever seen you." One night when he was drunk the infuriating bastard had the audacity, in oh-so-high-and-mighty and censoriously slurring tones, to tell O'Twoomey that if he were really my patron, as O'Twoomey claims to be, he'd have me institutionalized in some decorous asylum Wiley knows of on Oahu.

"Tut, tut," said O'Twoomey. "My dear Frederick shall prevail. Yes, Frederick shall prevail."

Wiley is so obsessively absorbed in building his new prefab house that he apparently doesn't notice I can't go to the can without Hannibal deciding his bladder needs relieving at the same time. On those infrequent occasions I've got Wiley alone for a few seconds and told him with menacing earnestness that I am literally O'Twoomey's prisoner, he gives me a simperingly absurd smile, erratically twirls his index finger round and round at his temple, and repeats the same tired lines.

"You got it made, Ex. You got it made. The Counselor was right. Boy, was the Counselor ever right."

The Counselor was a mutual friend, with whom we had gone to high school, and his cynically endearing description of me was: "Exley could go into a strange town and be fixing parking tickets for the natives within two weeks." In other words, Alissa, my pal Wiley is not only insensitive to what's happening and believes I've so exercised my alleged guile on O'Twoomey (who—you must believe me, Alissa— is the ultimate paranoid in this scenario) that I live in regal splendor on O'Twoomey's largess and that I'm little more than a slob and an ingrate and ought in thanksgiving to be kissing O'Twoomey's reeking scaling feet.

Two nights after Hannibal broke my wrist, Malia and Wiley had us over for mahi-mahi baked in some lovely way Malia does it with lemon, onion, garlic, and mayonnaise, accompanied by cauliflower, green corn, and those petite red-skinned boiled potatoes, a concession to the harp O'Twoomey of course. Save for an infrequent glass of Chablis, Malia doesn't drink, Hannibal and Toby both use *pakalolo* (Hawaiian for "crazy smoke"), but before dinner O'Twoomey, Wiley, and I were putting away the Jameson's in majestic style. Suddenly Wiley repaired to the john to take a leak. I leaped to my feet, followed him into the can, and moved him to one side of the bowl as though my urgency was such that, as we had as kids, we'd have to pee at the same time.

"Hannibal broke my wrist when he caught me trying to mail a letter to the Maui County police chief."

"Jesus, Ex. You get off that nonsense before the men in the white jackets *really* do come after you. I mean, c'mon, pal, *get off it*."

Hannibal burst through the door, stood hovering intimidatingly behind and above us. "Quick. Hannibal go too." Which is the way Hannibal talks.

Wiley said, "Piss between Exley's legs."

Alissa, O'Twoomey is going to kill me and the irony is that I haven't the foggiest idea why. Do you know the only thing that saved my ass when he read that aborted letter? Although to the authorities I stated in unequivocal terms that I was being held captive on Lanai, I did not mention who my abductors are and went on to say that it is all some grisly and ghastly joke. Before God, Alissa, I honestly do not know

‡ 187

—or most of all care—what nefarious nonsense these guys are up to, which doesn't negate that whatever it is involves staggering amounts of money—forget that innocuous crap I told you about sweepstakes tickets—and that at one awful moment they unjustly assumed I had overheard a conversation or come across some document relating to their enterprises.

It has been two years now. If after our last meeting you can believe it, I miss you, Alissa. My menopause has run its course. My breasts sag doughily. The collops about my waist balloon. My genitalia shrivel. My semen diminishes. My cigarette consumption is consummate, my imprisonment complete. And the only fragile hope I have is O'Twoomey's daily assurance that once his "business" is done I shall be free to go as I please, "with a nice lurverly bonus from me, dear Frederick, for the inconvenience, my dear."

Fat chance. If O'Twoomey and Toby are into something odious enough to quarantine me for something they think I know, I'm a goner, Al. Another time when I got Wiley alone long enough to plead my case, he laughed and said, "Well, Ex, at least you're a prisoner in paradise." So in the unlikely event this missive ever reaches you, and as I've spent so many hours boring you extolling the breathtaking loveliness of Lanai, do me the kindness—for you really are a plumed cocksucker, Alissa—of not issuing that throaty lyrical chuckle and saying, "Well, if nothing else, my pal, star, and least tractable patient met his Maker in paradise."

And about our last meeting, I'm sorry, dreadfully so. We sat at the bar of the Dockside, the fishing guides' hangout, where you try with such syrupy urgency to be one of the guys but believe me, Alissa, as an island person you'll never be accepted there, and all I said was that I was again returning to Hawaii, did not know for how long and wanted enough thirty-milligram Serax capsules to last me indefinitely.

"Exley, I shall give you enough Serax to last you a lifetime. But only on one condition. That you never seek out another session with me. You are a psychopathic personality, incapable of telling the truth, and though with my training I ought to be sympathetic, I can't be. I considered you my friend, at one time my dear old grizzly head. But how unbearable the pain is to lie in the night with a man who has never told you a solitary thing about himself, to continually take a stranger's semen into yourself, to lie with all your orifices dripping the wetness of a man you, as a trained analyst, can find no way to recognize. Believe me, Ex, it is a far more degrading experience than that of those wan and pathetic souls who find 'love' in a singles' bar. Yet each time I questioned one of your tales, and I questioned all your tales, for I always felt you were bouncing fiction off my head, to see how it would play, as it were, or tried to get you to submit to an amobarbital, you fluffed me off as though I were a semieducated bumpkin. There came the point I could no longer sleep with a stranger and believed that all our sessions together, including those endless nights lying together smoking Colombian and talking to the ceiling, were nothing more than con jobs to get more Serax. So awful did it become for me, and God forgive me for it, I actually came to wish you'd wash a whole bottle of Serax down with that quart of vodka you swill a day, never wake up, and put both you and me out of our misery. Incidentally, and now that I'm clearing the air, you owe me something over three thousand dollars, you've never offered me thirty dollars of it, huh, thirty cents of it, and yet you seem to come up with all the money you need to fly to Hawaii to see your precious Robin Glenn, who by your own admission is little more than a whore and who, for all I know, is just another figment of your diseased imagination."

Hence I struck back in rage, rage that brought you to those heartrending tears I gloried in, tears that exalted me, for every word you told me about myself save for Ms. Robin Glenn, my love for whom I have come to loathe in myself, and the fact that you'd throw a bill in my face when you begged to treat me as some kind of challenge to yourself. You have never once presented me with a statement, you have even purchased my unending supply of Serax, you have more money from your mother's estate than you could spend in five lifetimes—spend? give away—yes, every word you told me about myself was the truth, and all our sessions together except for the aforementioned Robin and my name, rank, and serial number were unadulterated bullshit. *But you must know why.* Because I never liked you as a person. Oh, you were generous enough in bed, as you certainly were with your pocketbook, but what was past enduring was that urbane hubris that comes with wealth and being fourth-generation Harvard. What acrimony that aroused in the son of a man who climbed telephone poles. I couldn't bare my soul to a woman who offers a stranger a forthright firm grip in handshake and says, "Hello there. I'm Doctor Alissa Tunstall-Phinn from Belgravia Island. I was out of Harvard Law at twenty-one, decided the law wasn't for me, returned to Cambridge, and had my residency in psychiatry at twenty-five."

La. Di. Da. Of course I was cruel, for I was doing nothing other than seeking your tears. Admittedly, you have too much class to append all that crap about your educational background, in fact, don't even preface your name with Doctor, but you yet seem to have no idea how much "Hello, I'm Alissa Tunstall-Phinn from Belgravia Island" grates on us locals, we who have spent our lives mowing your lawns, cooking your food, building the docks and boathouses for your cruisers, serving your drinks, and in general running errands for and kissing the asses of your wealthy friends who flood in there from May to October and imagine those lovely islands are theirs. It is pathetic. By your own reckoning, Alissa, your impoverished forefathers arrived here from England in 1729, they made the American experience their own, prospered beyond measure, and no doubt now muck about wailing eerily in their tombs witnessing the obscene spectacle of you and your equally fraudulent father affecting the offhand gentility of the English aristocracy, witnessing the desecration of your denial of them by trying to reclaim an escutcheoned heritage that was never in fact yours. Tunstall-Phinn indeed! Your name is Phinn and most Americans spell it Finn, as in Huckleberry.

And so on autumn Sundays, as only one example, you came to the Dockside to watch the last quarter of the Giants games with us, came in your ninety-dollar designer jeans mouthing your bubbly inanities: "Oh, my, are the Giants really, *really* ahead?" and "Which guys are we—the white or the blue?" and that most democratically memorable of all your banalities, "Hey guys! Hey guys! I bet that big black dude—what's his name? Bad Joe Greene?—would give a girl a fuck that would have her throwing stones at clowns like you." How that jammed barroom rocked with laughter, did so until I had you fiercely by the wrist and was blindly dragging you toward the door, the nape of my neck burning with humiliation because I knew that, mouths agape at my uncharacteristic violence, the guys' trite reading of my response was as one of schoolboy jealousy. But you knew better, didn't you, Alissa Tunstall-Phinn?

Out into the fall downpour we went and back into the narrow alley between the Dockside and the Aragon, where the steep pitch of the roofs caused the autumn waters to cascade over us as if we were taking a shower massage together. Slamming your back into the barn-red clapboard, I fervently slapped your face once, then twice, then yet again. You spoke nary a word, those calflike gray-green eyes of yours more chameleon than I'd ever seen them, the waters matting your long lovely russet hair to your beautifully formed Brahmin head, turning the hair the most vivid auburn I'd ever seen it. Abruptly you reached up and put your arms about my neck, pulling my face down to your already swelling cheek where I could feel the hot tears mingling with the cool rains. Such a noble and forgiving gesture on your part, Alissa, as though you were saying, "You see, Ex, how badly you need my help?" knowing even as you continued this charade that only you and Exley knew, whether you read Jung and Fromm and Adler and the guys in Cambridge and he read them as a bum on a Florida beach, that in slapping you as terribly as he had he was crying out for you to stop committing these abominations against your person.

I'm sorry I was too debilitated with anger to do what I intended, drag you by your clenched hair back into the bar and cry, "Listen, guys, listen to me. In mitigation of what you have just seen, Alissa here knows more about football than any guy in this room. Two years ago I invited her to a Giants game, she said she knew nothing about football, spent three hours in the public library, and by the time we reached the Meadowlands the following Sunday she was explaining to me the circumstances under which a defensive secondary would be most apt to move in and out of zone and man-to-man coverages!" A slap is a slap is a slap, but the total humiliation of a fellow human being is something else again. Bad Joe Greene? And just as I'm sure you also knew would happen, the next day a couple guys said, "Jeeze, Ex, that was a mite unnecessary, wasn't it? I mean, the Doc was only joshing. Everybody thought it was funny but *you*." So I said, "I'm sorry," allowing you to transfer your putrid guilt to myself. But it would all become clear in the library of London's British Museum, wouldn't it, Alissa Tunstall-Phinn? The transference completed itself and the lineman's son became analyst, the Harvard magna cum laude damn near incurable patient.

2

But on that other, that day of terrible confrontation, it was of course when I got on to that hot-dog
expatriate father of yours, one Anthony "Tony" Tunstall-
Phinn, now a citizen of Her Majesty's government residing
in tastefully languorous splendor in his town house in Wilton
Mews, Belgravia, that dear Alissa's tears became profuse.
Tony claims to have been Alger Hiss's best chum at Harvard, to have entered the State Department with him, and
that on Hiss's conviction for perjury Tony left America and
has never again set foot on our soil. In the first place, I have
read every volume I could find pertaining to the Hiss-
Chambers case and have never once come across Tony's
name. In the second place, I have three times written both
the State Department and Alger Hiss asking them about the
relationship and have never had the courtesy of an answer
from either. Unless the question is totally meaningless to
Hiss, why doesn't he step forward to identify a man who

cared enough about him to deny his country for what he considered a malignant miscarriage of justice? Hence I have never for one second believed that Tony is living in grandiose exile entirely on monies from the family's patrimony.

At Christmas 1972, just prior to the Brigadier's unhappy death in February 1973, I hadn't the money to go south, you said why don't you come to London and spend the holidays with Tony and me? I said if I couldn't make it to Florida I could hardly be winging to Great Britain to share drumsticks and cranberry drippings with Tony.

"Who said anything about money? This is my treat."

(Is this also part of the three grand you suddenly decided I owe you?)

So I finally went. And on the very first day Tony took us for lunch to the Hard Rock Cafe on Old Park Lane for cheeseburgers and steak fries (a disenchanted exile's fare, for Christ's sake?), thence to the Tower of London where to my utter astonishment he not only explained in meticulous detail the elaborate security system of Wakefield Tower, the fisc for the Crown Jewels, but even how to get around that system and get those gems out. On returning to the Wilton Mews town house that night, I scrupulously took down every word I could remember Tony's telling me, I still have those notes among my papers, and if finally I can see no way from my imprisonment I fully intend to turn those notes over to O'Twoomey and Toby and buy my way out. What a mouthwatering field day those two lunatics will have pondering that delicious job. Knowing he can't fence them, O'Twoomey would of course steal those baubles if for no other reason than to drop his pants before the Coronation Chair in Westminster Abbey and defecate on them, so irrationally certain he'd be that they were paid for with the blood of Irishmen. As indeed they probably were.

It wasn't so much Tony's Wakefield Tower esoterica that gave him away as something other than an expatriate claiming to have spent the past thirty years on what he says will be the most alarmingly recondite translation of the *Iliad* and the *Odyssey* ever rendered. On the day he took us, at my request, to Grosvenor Square, at least three young people said "Hi, Tony" to him, said it with that bouncy Iowa enthusiasm, more people than ever said hello to him in his own Belgravia neighborhood. Now even I, Alissa, who know nothing of London, know Grosvenor Square is overrun with employees from our embassy and to Londoners is known patronizingly as Little America. How those jubilant youth from America's heartland—corn silk sprouted from their noses—would have a first-name familiarity with a man who turned his back on his homeland thirty years ago—is he a cult hero to them?—is not only laughably mystifying but unanswerable save by some other explanation. Whether Tony is CIA, Department of Defense, Army or Navy Intelligence is beside the point; unless I miss my guess Tony doesn't know Zeus from Menelaus, Andromachē from Leda, Achilles from Hector. On Christmas Day, moreover, after Mrs. Dobbins had served us that wonderful steak-and-kidney pie Tony had had the chef at Marcel make up the day before, he said something while drunk that so disarmed me I couldn't finish eating and this, together with his boorishness on Boxing Day the following morning, left my holiday in ruins.

My main reason for initially declining your London invitation until the last possible moment was, as you know full well, Alissa, that that autumn had been my season of love for you, when I did not know from one anxious second to the next when I'd be utterly helpless to overcome my desire to ram, jam, stab, impale you with a prick and I confessed—sins monumental!—that it would drive me mad being under the watchful eyes of your father and denied the social license to stroll into the bathroom right at your heels, sit down on the lid, reach up, strip you from your panties, and maneuver your healthy thighs above my lap.

With the Giants leading by a point and five minutes remaining, I had that fall taken you at dusk's end from the Dockside to the front seat of your Mercedes and fucked you in the pale glare of a streetlamp, only to return to the bar to find the Giants had not only lost—what else?—but that in those clocked five minutes (twenty in real time) the Eagles had scored two touchdowns and a field goal, fate's revenge for my walking out on my team. And there was that incredibly embarrassing day when I went to Syracuse for pizza supplies for Mike, almost made it out of the city without seeing you, but suddenly found Mike's station wagon parked in the driveway of your home-office. Surprised to find a patient with you—do you really practice? —as well as another in the anteroom, I somewhat hysterically demanded to see you immediately (those patients took me for "very disturbed," didn't they?), you asked your patient to wait in the anteroom, and, slamming the door behind me, I fucked you on that rich tan leather couch on which, you tell me, no patient has ever lain. When you came to the Bay that evening and we were driving around the back roads you said with great disparagement, "Don't ever, *ever* do anything like that to me again," pensively adding, "All you want to do is fuck me." "Shut up," I said. "Is that *all* I want to do, fuck you? If that is so, at least you're getting my total and undivided attention and I'm not wasting waking hours daydreaming of fucking someone else. *All I want to do?* Shut your mouth." Whether in trepidation or in comforting gratitude, your right hand left the wooden wheel and came to rest on my thigh. And the Mercedes came to a stop at the side of the road.

When I shied away from your London invitation because of my infantile inability to keep my hands from you and the terrifying trepidation of humiliating us both in the eyes of Tony, you said, "Tony? Are you talking about Tony, for Christ's sake? I'm thirty-two, he knows you've been laying me on and off since I was seventeen, and though he certainly doesn't know what you've been going through this fall—as I'm not sure I do either—we'll be able to make it about anytime you choose. If you can handle it, though, I'd prefer you didn't shove me against the preserves counter at Fortnum and Mason and remove my knickers on the spot. For propriety's sake and in deference to Tony's generation, I'll have my own room and have to be back there by morning so he can do his ritualistic waking of me. Since I was a kid, he's always wakened me by ripping the covers to the floor and giving me a crack on my bare bum. Of course only a degenerate like you, Exley, would read anything sexual into it. I don't know what it is really. I think it reminds him of when I was a baby, when he was happy with Mum before he got caught up in that awful Hiss business and Mum died." Mum committed suicide, Alissa, but I saw no need to say so or point out that many people other than degenerates would see in Tony's method of waking you something very sexual indeed.

3

Βut you were wrong, as you often are, Alissa, about Tony's sophistication. On Christmas Eve he made the applejack eggnogs too potent, he tactlessly wept when reminiscing about Mum. Because of the drinks we slept through the alarm and when he found your bed unused and without so much as a hem or a haw charged into my bedroom, pulled the covers from both of us, and, *swaaat*, did his thing on your bum, I heaved a great sigh of relief. However, when I arrived downstairs and found him voraciously wolfing the bloody Marys at ten A.M.—so very unlike Tony, don't you know?—I knew he hadn't taken our naked spent entwined limbs as sportingly as you'd led me to expect he would. All day long, and what an interminable Christmas it was despite Mrs. Dobbins's never permitting our cut glass tumblers to be empty, Tony continued to ask those asininely rude questions a prospective father-in-law asks only in unreadable English and Boston novels. And to my own incredulity I found myself telling him about my grand-parents, my aunts and uncles, my parents, my two sisters and the means by which their husbands supported them, my niece and eight nephews and their parents' hopes for them, even about my two ex-wives and my two daughters, one by each, and my earnest estimate—pure bullshit on my part, of course—of why my marriages had failed. They failed, Alissa, because I'm a drunk.

By then it was 4 P.M., we were all to the point of in-ebriation past having even a pleasant time, digging into the steak-and-kidney pie and sundry other goodies and I was waging my not-so-subtle war with the insufferably Chesterfieldian Mrs. Dobbins, a war of which Tony had become eye-archedly and ironically aware. Three times in the first two days of my visit, Mrs. Dobbins had had to lean down close to my ear, as though at table we had forty guests to be excluded from her tart remonstrances, and remind me that when she'd served me I should return the sterling forks and ladles to her dishes convex side up so the utensils wouldn't slither into the food mucking up the handles for the next chap. Chalk it to my shanty Irishness, Alissa, but with that third reminder Dobbins had drawn the line in the dirt before me, intrepidly defying me to step across, and I not only returned the servers convex side down, giving them a slurpy little push as I did so, but began looking forward to the nice runny gooey tomatoeylike dishes, the only one on Christmas Day being that marvelously liquescent creamed corn, peas, and mushrooms concoction. "Please, Mrs. Dobbins," Tony said, "if you don't mind," and an utterly enraged Old Dobbie snapped out the linen she had folded over her apron string and without taking her harried un-forgiving little eyes from me wiped the handle as clean as if she had silver-polished it.

"So you have a brother who's a bird colonel in the 500th MIG," Tony said in response to a meager recitation I'd given on the Brigadier, the last member of my family I'd chosen to discuss. "An interesting outfit, the 500th MIG. That would be headed by Colonel X." My abrupt loss of appetite wasn't so much the result, Alissa, of Tony's using what was to me the unfamiliar army shorthand MIG, when I had used Military Intelligence Group, as that, thirty years a Homerian scholar in exile, Tony apparently still had some inexplicable need to know who was running our various intelligence agencies. And he did know, *Tony did know*, for on our returning to the Bay my first order of business was to write the Brigadier and ask him if Colonel X was the commandant of the 500th MIG—he was indeed the commandant—and when I suggested to you that this was wondrously idiosyncratic information for Tony to possess you said only, "Tony knows the goddamndest things."

As dinner was breaking up Tony asked me, somewhat mystifyingly, if I'd mind meeting him in his study at ten the following, Boxing Day, morning. As drunk as I was that night I slept only sporadically with my door locked against you (no more scenes, thank you, Alissa), thinking the dotty bastard had summoned me there to ask how I intended supporting you, to explain how wealthy you were—as though I didn't know!—and the responsibilities of money, to express the hope that I'd continue writing rather than devote my life exclusively to the enchantments of vodka. Imagine my surprise then, Alissa, when I arrived at the study to find this niddering popinjay Mr. Fowler, Tony's tailor from Anderson and Shepard, 30 Savile Row, who, our hands having just separated from their limp introduction, began flitting around appraising me as though he were the casting director for an X-rated movie. Then suddenly he spread his tape measure across the unimposing breadth of my shoulders, dropped to a knee and with laughable British reserve measured my inseams not by flicking a ball aside and running down the inside but by coming down to the instep from a dimple in my haunch just below my ass.

"I didn't believe you'd come to London, Fred, until I picked Alissa up at Heathrow and actually saw you there. Yesterday I was embarrassed having no gift for you and as I was being fitted for some spring clothes today, I hoped that by way of apology you'd accept a suit to take back with you."

Tony did not of course ask me if I'd like a suit, least of all enquire what in the world I'd do with one in Alexandria Bay. Nor was it lost on me that Tony had had well over a week to get me some small gift and that seemingly he'd purposely chosen to present mine on Boxing Day, the day the gentry throw alms to their retainers who, for reasons quite unfathomable to an American, are rendered simperingly and absurdly appreciative. En route to the study I'd stopped by the kitchen for coffee and Mrs. Dobbins, profuse tears of gratitude in her eyes, had shown me her new blue leather gloves, her red knit scarf, and her GE electric Teflon fry pan you'd neglected, Alissa, winking at me as you did so, to declare at customs. After she'd poured my second cup of coffee, and knowing full well that, despite my promise to myself that morning to declare a truce, the war in all its majesty would begin anew, I said, "For all my kidding around, Mrs. Dobbins, your food is entirely too wonderful to cook in a piece of shit like that." On the flight back to Montreal, you told me that Mrs. Dobbins had told Tony, spelling it out, s-h-i-t. I said, "Good."

As for the gift of the suit, my humiliation, Alissa, had never been more complete, my face throbbing with embarrassment, my body stony with shame, and for reasons that will become apparent I found myself thinking of a legend my grandfather in his dotage had used to repeat over and over again, that of the Irish schoolmaster Wright, a teacher of languages sentenced to five hundred lashes for a seditious note written in French and found on his person. Although the evidence suggested, if not proved, that the note had been composed by one of Wright's pupils, the infamous magistrate, Thomas Judkin Fitzgerald, himself dragged Wright to the whipping triangle where, after fifty lashes, Wright's entrails stood exposed, only to have Fitzgerald demand yet another hundred strokes. Wright was then cast into the mud to die.

Despite my rhetorical and bombastic folderol directed

against my Irishness, the Maguire in me had never been more salient than it was at that moment, and each time Mr. Fowler pinched, poked, prodded me with his tape measure, my body screamed and reeled with an agony nearly as excruciating as that of Wright's feeling the cat. Yes, for the first time, Alissa, I truly understood empathy and the whole bloody and shameless history of England's genocide of the Irish ran before me as in a nightmare. Had I not suddenly recalled that Wright had lived—yes, Alissa, Wright endured—I doubt I ever would have found the courage to break my clench-toothed silence. With a nonchalant shrug, which implied that my words had been inspired by the bookishness of Tony's study, I said, "Tony, do you know Washington's comment on the Irish Brigade who volunteered their services in the cause of *our*—should I say *the American?*—revolution? No? General Washington said that if defeated on all other fronts it was among these Irish troops that he'd take his final stand for freedom."

Tony arched that eyebrow, smiled, and said, "Oh" as though my words were completely lost on him. And then you backed him 100 percent that afternoon when we were, at my instigation, on our way to the library of the British Museum to see where Marx had done his research for and a good deal of the writing of *Das Kapital,* the polemics of which could hardly have found a more amenable milieu in which to be honed than among the most insufferably class-conscious boobs in the world.

"Oh, oh, oh!" you screamed at me in the tube, and in case you hadn't noticed it, Alissa, since the day you arrived in London the subway had become the tube, the TV the telly, the toilet the loo, panties had become knickers, a sausage a banger, a can of soup a tin of soup, and my all-time favorite, for which you damn near got a kick in the ass, a party became a rave-up. "That's what I'd have said, too! Oh, oh, oh! You're being measured for a suit that might be a gesture of generosity on Tony's part because he likes you—likes? I think he's afraid of you. What a joke!—and your sickening paranoia turns it into some attempt to humiliate you on Boxing Day. Hence you come up with a totally asinine piece of pedantry about George Washington and actually expect my poor father to make a connection between something as manifestly simple as Mr. Fowler's fitting you for a suit and that cabalistic piece of Americana. Oh, oh, oh! You're goddamn right that's how I'd have responded. Under the circumstances what sane person would express anything other than the bewilderment Tony did? Oh, oh, oh!"

"Shut up, Alissa. Did you just get As at Harvard or did you maybe once or twice draw analogies among what all them mugs were saying in all them fat books at Widener?"

We neither of us spoke or touched for perhaps an hour. Like an obedient and tentative little girl at my heels, sensing my enthralldom shrouded in fury, you followed me about the maze of the library. Then to rest we sat at that librarylike table in that alcove and you placed your leather-gloved hand on my inner thigh. "No." "Please, Ex, don't turn away from me now and stomp off in your churlish and childish anger. Which has, be honest, been the story of your life." So in the most explosively erotic scene to which I've ever been a party, your russet hair came down spreading like a silken web over my lap, I gently stroked the back of your head, and then, at last and finally, I came. And though we would make love a few more times before I went to Hawaii to bury the Brigadier and there met Robin, it was never quite the same because you had to turn the heart-wrenching spontaneity of that moment away from love and make it yet another noble gesture whereby, in an almost clinical way, you were simply abating my psychotic hostility.

Yes, it had been at that moment, more than at any other in our unending relationship as adversaries, when I saw not obscenity, as that laughably startled Limey who strolled by had, but love coupled with groveling penance, supplication, and heartfelt apologies for Tony's unforgivable behavior to me, that moment when, as I have said, you became patient—and what so-called civilized person would not have viewed your sucking my cock in the British Mu-

seum library as an act of the most appalling dementia?—
and I the vessel of your most repressed desires. Indeed, so
much are you able to take things as they were and recon-
strue them to your liking that I learned at our last unhappy
meeting two years ago that in lieu of my taking up with
Robin you had stopped spreading your legs for me because I
was a psychopath. But this is nitpicking. When I said above
that I didn't like you as a person, and therefore was unable
to tell you about myself, I also neglected to say that I've
loved you since you were a child. Let me then attempt to
put aside my contempt, Alissa, and try to make a new
beginning by telling you about the time I shot my sister.

4

In the days before I shot my sister I spent endless time cultivating my left hand and cleaning the Brigadier's guns, either activity able to fire in me sappy dreams of illustriousness. It was Llewellyn Rexford Bean, known interchangeably as Lew or Rex or Marilou Ellen, who as he jogged by the hour above me on the concave corrugated track—slap, slap, slap, slap, slap, slap, watching me with wary intentness from the downward corner of his eye—grew piqued with my continuing to come from the right side, swoosh and swoosh and swoosh and swoosh, and suggested that if I weren't going back to school I might put the days to better use by trying the same thing from the left side. Resting his elbows on the top pipe rail of the track, his hands folded, his right sneakered foot up on the middle rail, his thick blond curly hair—beneath his crazy green-and-white stocking sweatcap—so thick with perspiration it looked in the afternoon sun streaming through the windows a brownish red, Rex leaned his green-and-white head far out into the void above the gym and hollered down at me.

"Hey, Ex, my sweet pal, you got the right side down pat. There's no place from the right side you can't hit. Besides, you're boring me to tears." As though Rex weren't boring me, slap, slap, slap, slap. "Tomorrow, why don't you start from the left side? You know, try the left-handed layup, then when you get that down just keep moving out and out and out, the same way you do from the right side."

"Hey, good idea, Rex!"

Rex beamed, proudly thrust out his chest, flicked his nutty stocking cap back over his right shoulder, pulled away from the rail, and once again began his distracting slap, slap. So it was the following morning at nine, about two hours before Rex, invariably hung over, showed up, I began the schooling of my left hand. It was the war year of 1944, I was fourteen and a couple years from my top height of five-ten. Because that would be as tall as I'd get, it is impossible not to credit Rex's suggestion with my one day making the league all-star team, one of the dreams that turned out not to be as sappy as I'd supposed.

Other than Rex's being rich, having his undergraduate degree from Princeton and his law degree from Yale, I can't imagine anyone's calling him Marilou Ellen or believing him a sissy or effeminate. Because my friends and I were poor and uneducated, I expect that Rex's being all the things we weren't not only aroused our envy but necessarily mitigated against him. Rex was thirty, tall and blond and stunningly handsome, always a sartorial vision in the clothes he ordered by mail from Brooks Brothers, and though his two older brothers, Jonathan and Hardy Bean, were fledgling surgeons—everyone said it was a toss-up who would become the best in the area—Rex neither practiced law nor did much of anything but greet and entertain our returning furloughed servicemen, attend all the high school games, work out, eat, drink, and woo an entire generation of the most marvelous-looking girls to blossom in upstate

New York. This is not to say that Rex didn't claim to work. But he wasn't in the least earnest about his claim.

On Clinton Street Jonathan and Hardy, whom Rex referred to as Rick and Dick or Dick and Rick or sometimes as *Rickahdickahdoo,* had built the first professional or medical arts building in town, a tasteful one-story limestone and white-shuttered affair with only enough space for themselves and Rex. Fronting the street was a large spacious beautifully appointed common or waiting room, dominated by one of the most impressive limestone fireplaces I'd ever seen, in which on fall and winter afternoons there was always a splendid crackling log fire. Behind the waiting room Jonathan and Hardy had posh offices and diagnostic cubicles for themselves and another lavishly carpeted book-lined suite for Rex, commanded by a huge antique mahogany desk and oil paintings of Lincoln and Justice Holmes. On one of the two occasions I ever saw Rex partially serious, he told me the only time he'd ever used that magnificent desk he'd drawn up wills for himself and Jonathan and Hardy.

"One of them suckers, either Rick or Dick or Dick or Rick, is gonna go with a coronary before he's forty—so devoted, don't you know, Ex?—and old Rex has got to get his share of the swag to keep him in his old age."

Even when Rex pontificated, as he often did in the days I was acquiring the left-handed touch and he was none too subtly trying to get me to do what I must do—horrible, abominable thought!—to be readmitted to school, he was totally incapable of carrying it off.

"Well, Ex, my luscious pal, as my old pappy used to say, 'I gotta work, you gotta work, we all gotta work,'" after which he'd throw his head back and roar with idiotic, inner-directed laughter. Rex's father had foreseen the market crash of 1929, had done what money people did acting on that happy piece of sagacity, had gotten out forty-eight hours before that dismal October day, and as ostentatiously given to homilies as that father may have been—apparently he'd succeeded with Jonathan and Hardy—he had, leaving his sons those millions to do with as they damn pleased, failed out of hand with Rex. For example, Rex was at his loony best when, at four, after a day's workout, he'd say, "Well, Ex, my sweet pal, I reckon old Rex ought to meander back to the sweatshop and answer the afternoon mail." Then he'd literally double over, fiercely clutch his stomach, and go right off his tree with orgiastic laughter, enlisting me in his uncontrollable zaniness. When his laughter subsided, Rex would lean back against his locker, spread his legs so his balls rested on the bench, light a Camel, and smile his perverse smile. Certainly without insolence, Rex's smile was nevertheless that of a man privy to insights not given to other men and those insights appeared to have confirmed his preconceived notions that none of the clichés of the workaday world—"I gotta work . . ." "I reckon old Rex ought to meander back to the sweatshop . . ."—were essential to sanity.

By then Rex would have showered, he'd be waiting for the steam to lift so he could see in the mirror to shave and outfit himself in a beautifully cut tweed jacket, neatly pressed gray flannel slacks, and custom-made shoes, and from the pile of filthy sweat clothes at his feet he'd pick up a sneaker, a jock, his crazy stocking cap, take a long loving whiff of it, grimace in odoriferous but ecstatic agony, and say, "Jesus, Ex, my sweet pal, decadent, I mean, *depraved*. Remind me to bring some fresh workout clothes tomorrow." When I was supposed to remind him I hadn't the foggiest, or did I have any doubt that Rex didn't want reminding. Early on I'd discovered it wasn't the Brooks Brothers suits that were Rex, that his essential being of boyish randiness (goldfish in the mouth, toads in the pocket, garter snakes in mason jars) was more readily epitomized by those foul putrefying garments than by those ironically worn double-breasted navy blue polo coats with great mother-of-pearl buttons. It was a randiness I'm certain proved a challenge to be remedied by that unending parade of nubile beauties on his cashmere-covered arm. In those days at the Y it was as if I were playing hide-and-seek with a child.

Although it was permissible to peek through my fingers to see where the kid had hid, it would have been grievously unsporting to find him out too quickly. And though I doubt any of those girls understood the true extent of Rex's adoration of the indecorous, when I at last read that smile, as though caught hiding behind the ancient stand-up Hoover in a distant closet, and learned that he'd elevated the raunchily trivial to a godhead, that he was congenitally promiscuous, lovably rotten, and hopelessly ribald, I knew he was beyond the redemption of any of those girls he was said to take at bar's closing to the Clinton Street office where, after banking a fire in the great limestone fireplace, he'd lay them—we hoped he did—on the carpeted forefront of the hearth, throwing kisses, one somehow imagines, at Rickahdickahdoo as he did so.

Finally dressed and ready to face his day, Rex'd shake my hand formally and say, "See you tomorrow, my luscious pal. Boy, that left hand is coming swell. You're gonna be a hummer, pal, and I do mean *a hummer!*" Going out the door, he'd holler back, "And don't forget, my dear pal, who it was that taught you!"

Rex did not know how to dribble a basketball. When Rex left the Y at 4:30, everyone in Watertown knew he trotted across lower Washington Street, crazily zigging in and out of the rush-hour traffic, actually feigning stiff-arming the hoods of honking overanxious cars. On gaining the other side of the street, Rex'd turn left at Smith and Percy, take a hard right at Stone Street, thence another hard right into Duffy's Tavern, which was the meeting place for our servicemen on leave. He'd order his first martini of the day and search the bar for faces he recognized, despite the strange uniforms beneath the faces. If Rex saw any, he'd buy a round, there'd be embraces, laughter, tall tales, and they'd be mapping the evening's strategy, all of which Rex would take care of, the drinks, the food, the girls. Although

I never asked Rex, there were delicious rumors in town that Jonathan and Hardy's secretaries and nurses had used to arrive at eight to find Rex, his on-leave pals, and various young ladies drunk and passed out all over the posh waiting room, so that on rotating weeks the girls now took turns getting to the office by seven to assure the party was sent on its way and the office stood in comely sedateness for its first patients.

If Jonathan or Hardy ever reprimanded Rex, I'm sure he did so with long-suffering head-wagging good humor. As everyone knew, Rex was the most pampered, coddled, and deferred-to kid brother ever reared in upstate New York, impossibly spoiled not only by his brothers but by everyone in the community. When Rex was eight, either Jonathan or Hardy had become enraged during the course of a children's game and had coshed Rex over the head with a pinch bar, laying his skull open to the gray matter and sending him into a coma where for days he lingered near death. By the time he came round, the X rays had already indicated brain surgery, he was flown to New York City, a metal plate was inserted into his skull (the cause of the army's rejecting him), and forever after his aberrant behavior was explained by our tapping our forefingers gravely at our temples and darkly whispering, "Brain damage." As Rex had been Phi Beta Kappa, the damage hadn't, apparently, impaired his learning or memory.

Although at fourteen I accepted this diagnosis as readily as everyone else did, in retrospect I'm not at all certain Rex's peculiarness would have been markedly different had he not suffered the trauma. Cynicism had only recently, with the onset of puberty (aching, burning nipples, pubic hair, an ashamed need to strangle my cock every twenty seconds), become a part of my being, I wouldn't understand for years that cynicism is nothing more than a mask that represses all enthusiasms for fear that that to which one lends an ungloved willingness of the heart might prove unworthy of one's regard and that Rex's behavior may have been as simply explained by saying he was without cynicism. Assuming that Rex's problem was brain damage, it must have occurred to that area of the brain where the superego resides, for in the loveliest of ways Rex was utterly without the restraints that make for civilized behavior, marvelously oblivious to any sense of suffocating politesse.

Whether in the Y locker room lovingly scratching his balls, whiffing his sneakers, or in his insane cheering and various other shenanigans at the high school games, Rex embarrassed us only to the extent of our inability to unshackle ourselves from our own inhibitions. When Rex stormed rabidly onto the football field or basketball court to confront the officials, his camel hair coat and regimental necktie flowing crazily out behind him, his blond hair in great disarray from his theatrical pulling on it, his vivid blue eyes turned inward with indignant hurt at the obscene unfairness of the officiating, we laughed uproariously at his antics. Our faces red for him, we nonetheless applauded his sticking his nose smack into the face of the referee, à la Billy Martin, by wildly cheering his "cause," knowing even as we did so that the official, like a plate umpire calling a third strike for which he'll brook no quarrel, was even then dropping his right shoulder and contracting his right arm to throw it furiously out toward the nearest exit, signaling Rex was out of the game, which invariably rallied the crowd to one standing, sustained shriek of *Boooooooooooooo*. Rex was the only fan in Watertown to be ejected from games more frequently than our coach.

In sports it was all very simple to Rex. There were our guys and there were their guys, never the twain should meet, our guys never committed a penalty or foul, never missed a long gain or twenty-foot jump shot which wasn't the result of the other team's knavery (undetected to everyone save Rex) and woe to the official who didn't view the game through the same magically wondrous lenses as Rex. In the basketball season of 1942–43, our small parochial school, Immaculate Heart Academy, had been loaded with talent and our coach, with the greatest reluctance (everything to lose, nothing to gain), had scheduled them twice. Each time IHA tied the score or went into the lead, Rex, who sat with the town elders at the opposite side of the gym from the student bleachers, would cross his blue eyes, stick his thumbs into his ears, crazily wiggle his fingers at the officials, and let his tongue droop dopily out and blow on it, creating the harshest, wettest, eeriest, most tasteless raspberries imaginable, all of which sent the students into paroxysms of ecstatic hostility.

During the first game the referee, unable to stand it any longer, violently blew his whistle, pointed directly at Rex, and bellowed *"Technical!"* Onto the court came our coach and though it was too noisy for the crowd to hear, I was the ball boy seated on the bench and heard it all.

"How the hell yuh gonna call a technical on my crowd for something that crazy bastard Bean does?"

"Okay, Bill," the referee said. "I shouldn't have pointed at Bean. But Bean's got this crowd out of control, you're responsible for it, no matter the instigator, and IHA gets a free one."

During the second game poor Rex didn't make it to the buzzer signaling the end of the first quarter before that same referee, detecting Rex's tongue gingerly beginning to dangle with idiotic slack wetness over his chin, blew his whistle, pointed at Rex and screamed, "Okay, Bean, out, out, out, out, OUT!"

The two on-duty cops were detailed, one on each arm, to escort a dignified Rex, shaking his head from side to side in incomprehensible hurt at the majestic injustice of it all, from the premises, while the high school fans screamed bloodcurdling epithets to the effect that the cops were unredeemable "fascists," a word that had of course come into great vogue in those years. People said that Rex could not have gone into an alien community and lasted five minutes without getting himself locked up, the keys thrown away, our way of congratulating ourselves on our tolerance. Like Highwater Louie, who had been shell-shocked in World War

I, and Woody, the peanut man at the games who drew pennies and nickels from the ears of pop-eyed little kids, Rex was one of our town's acknowledged and protected eccentrics, Rex was, as it were, *ours*, as familiar as the Roswell P. Fowler Memorial Library at the bottom of Washington Street.

5

Ordinarily on Friday nights Rex was the first fan at the gym, accompanied by his latest girl, who was, "Can you believe it?" we'd say, wagging our weak noodles in wonder, even nicer than her predecessor, arriving and taking his seat even before the jayvees had taken the court for their warmups. Hence I expect we should have known something was amiss when he not only showed up unescorted one night, for Rex without a girl was as a mutant camel without its hump, but during the jayvee game seemed abstracted, nervous, and so pensive he only challenged the referee's calls nine times. Then, five minutes into a varsity game which already promised to be a corker, an unearthly stillness permeated the crowd and looking round for the reason I stared, with everyone, across the way and beheld Miss Sally Jane Hannigan dressed in a black Chesterfield coat with black velvet collar, black high-heeled pumps, and dark suggestive silk hose, her incredibly beautiful anthracite-black shimmering hair parted in the middle and flowing luxuriantly down to the small of her back. The hair framed that placid deep olive mask and those great bottle-green eyes covered with even greater great round black horn-rimmed glasses. Yes, Miss Sally Jane Hannigan stood there as cold and as calm as a corpse in deep freeze, her black leather-gloved hand cradled in the crook of the sleeve of Rex's coat, which was, we could hardly credit it, a black Chesterfield precisely like that of Sally Jane!

All the guys called Sally Jane Hannigan, without irony, "the Princess." She was eighteen, extremely intelligent, beautiful beyond adolescent fantasies, so retiring the older guys in the locker room made book that butter wouldn't melt in her armpit ("I'll bet hair doesn't even grow there!") and that, assuming she mounted the throne mornings as other people did, which the older guys in the locker room, shuddering distastefully, said she obviously didn't do, oh, no, not the *Princess*, she defecated lilac stalks in the full fruit of their fragrant cluster of white and lavender flowers.

Everyone liked her save our parents, who did not know her but did know that her mother, Jenny Hannigan, who looked, *really*, a more stunning, sexier kid sister to the Princess, was the undisputed luminary of Hilary's brothel on Court Street and was said to have been, hands down, the particular favorite of the Oklahoma Indians of the Forty-fifth Infantry Division. Having trained at nearby Pine Camp, the Forty-fifth Infantry Division, under Patton (who else could have commanded them?), had invaded Sicily that July, going in at Scoglitti. By January 1944, as support troops to General John P. Lucas's Sixth Corps, they would enter Italy at Anzio. When called upon to check the Germans' Twenty-sixth Panzer Division at the Carroceto Creek on the Albano-Anzio road (how even today these names resound and permeate my being), they fought with the desperation, savagery, and nobility of their ancestors, thinking of Jenny, one somehow imagines, as they did so and happy that the historical stars had been in such conjunction that they could have left her a wealthy woman in Watertown.

Astonishment does not do justice to what the crowd was undergoing. It would be more accurate to say that for no few moments everyone's heart stopped beating. In the first place, no one had ever seen the Princess with a boy other than her cousin, Juice Dooley. On December 7, 1941, Juice's father had been a pilot in naval reserve, he'd been called back, and because Juice's mother had wanted to go with him (she was now in Honolulu, where he was training carrier pilots), Juice had moved in with his Aunt Jenny and the Princess. Like the Princess, Juice was very bright, except for grotesque ears he was very handsome, and, as anyone who'd ever mentioned his aunt's occupation to him knew full well, he was "one tough Mick." He and the Princess had graduated near the top of their class in June 1943, Juice had gone into the navy as a seaman, and the Princess had enrolled at St. Lawrence University at Canton, New York, where she'd dropped out after a few weeks, claiming it was too easy and that she'd come home to await the following fall, when she'd deign to enroll in a university better equipped to challenge her intelligence. Although I was only thirteen the winter Rex took up with her, I never believed the older guys in the locker room when they said the reason they didn't take the Princess out was social pressure from their parents. Nobody asked the Princess out for fear of her demurral.

In the second place, our incredulity rose dizzyingly because on what was obviously their first date the Princess was in such complete control that unlike her predecessors she wasn't about to sit through a dopey jayvee game. Like those New York City sophisticates who pay thirty bucks for a theater ticket and arrive near the close of the first act, she'd had the serene audacity not even to show until five minutes after the varsity tipoff. Moreover, with mysterious guile she'd persuaded Rex, an authentic maverick, and *our* maverick at that, to wear a costume matching hers, and all during that first evening they sat, the two of them, and gave us a preview of what we might expect throughout that endless winter. Yes, all that winter they sat, the two of them, the pain in the asses, their hands folded primly on their laps, attired in matching clannish tam-o'-shanters, yellow slickers, navy pea jackets, beige camel hairs, the perfect couple—*ugh*. That night Rex never once leapt from his chair or allowed himself any gesture but that of polite applause, at which the Princess would allow that calm olive mask to open, exposing the most perfectly beautiful great white teeth imaginable, a smile of approval at Bucky Donahue's displaying his breathtakingly nonchalant left-handed hook shot.

It was the weirdest scene I'd ever witnessed, and it would, as I say, continue that way to a lesser degree throughout the season. It wasn't so much that the Princess diminished Rex but that by diminishing him she diminished us. Since we were toddlers we'd looked to Rex to take the lead at games and now that his eyes had glazed over; now that he bore a permanently absurd, rather crapulous smile; now that he was living concussed, conversant with cherubims, suffering brain trauma more severe than anything he'd known as a child, oblivious to everything but the warm pulsing presence (and, oh, dear heart, what a presence!) of the Princess; now that he was unmistakably in love and we knew in the discomfiting place where truth resides that the Princess was one girl—despite our parents' suffocatingly moral hackneyisms to the effect that, like her mother, the Princess was damned and doomed—who wouldn't be lying down on the rich carpeting before the great limestone hearth; now that we knew if the Princess ever did lie down, it would be at her time on her direction (poor Rex had been rendered such wispy flesh he couldn't have directed a girl to the ladies' room); now that, as abruptly as the guillotine does its bloody work, Rex was no longer among the living, what a sad and sorry, dejected and listless, rudderless and skipperless crowd we became, adrift on silent measureless seas.

No, I'd never seen anything quite like it. Watertown lost that first night 58–57, with the score changing hands at almost every turnover of the ball, and what ordinarily would have been a full-fanged ravenously lunatic crowd sat as forlorn as basset hounds, our hands buried beneath our stolid thighs, looking with sick unbelieving longing across the way at Rex. Over all, I'm sure, there was this sense of irreparable injured betrayal at the same time we thought, wrongly of course, that at any moment he would throw off his cancerous aberration, rise up from the yoke of his palpable and diseased apathy, and rally us by at least allowing his tongue to slither out or stuff his thumbs into his ears. In our ingenuousness that was how little we knew of the murderously numbing effect of love on the human heart. In their snug-fitting short purple satin skirts the cheerleaders' bums looked as appetizing as ever. Rena Ruth Gillis still had her lovely old wazoos. Even in defeat in the locker room, Bucky Donahue could yet say of Inez Sue Dobbins that his vision of the beatific death was to go with his head between her thighs. Save for Rex—now gone somewhere far, far away—the participants were the same, but as hard as the poor girls tried they were quite unable to ignite the crowd and they finally gave it up and sat in stunned disbelief with the rest of us.

6

Had not the Princess died that spring, on June 6, 1944, the day the Allies invaded Normandy, I could not have got as friendly with Rex as I did the ensuing fall at the Y. Although Rex had been out of law school for six years, he had yet to pass his New York State bar examinations, indeed had not even bothered to take them. That spring, however, and I have no doubt he yearned to appear as solemnly industrious in the Princess's eyes as he'd begun to appear at the basketball games, he spent a lot of time in Albany—we missed him at the baseball games—taking cram courses for those exams. Had she lived, Rex not only would have been practicing law by fall but would have forsaken both his role as Watertown's one-man stage door canteen and that of upstate New York's most eligible bachelor.

To this day I'm not precisely certain what happened to the Princess, though I like to think of her being as much a casualty of war as some of Jenny's Injun pals had been at the Carroceto Creek in Latium. In February 1944, her cousin, Seaman First Class Juice Dooley, had been forced to abandon his destroyer escort in a battle, near Kwajalein, for the Marshall Islands. Before he was picked up from the ocean he'd received oil burns on his upper torso, as well as first- and second-degree sunburn on his face and neck. By late May he was home on thirty-day leave, an authentic walking wounded and Pacific hero, looking handsomer than ever despite his strange ears. That night the Princess was said to have had her usual date with Rex, he'd dropped her home at midnight, and by 2:30 she was dead on arrival at the House of the Good Samaritan. As nearly as I could determine, after going into the house she and Juice had decided to go for a nocturnal spin in Jenny's 1940 Cadillac convertible, had ended in the lovers' lane we knew as the Gotham Street stone quarry, a "loose" rock had fallen from high up the quarry's cliff, had hit the Princess on the head, and by the time Juice Dooley carried the bloody and—oh, my—naked Princess into the emergency room she was already dead.

Two nights later I was at Wiley Hampson's for supper. Wiley's father Sy had gone into the kitchen to help Mrs. Hampson with the dishes, and suddenly Wiley was violently shushing me that we might hear their conversation, a conversation that was, in unending variations, being bantered about in every kitchen and bedroom in Watertown. Mrs. Hampson demanded to know why the Dooley boy hadn't had the decency to dress the Princess before rushing her to the emergency room, then added that as cousins engaging in sex they were nothing more than lace-curtain trash and God—"the Devil, I should say"—would have done well to take them both under an avalanche of stone.

Usually a mild-mannered man, Sy Hampson would nevertheless have none of this and I'd never heard his voice so angry. He pointed out that the Princess's and Juice's mothers were stepsisters, that no blood was binding Juice and the Princess, and that there was no way their acts could be construed as incestuous. Sy Hampson said further that it was certainly not unreasonable, indeed it was doubtless inevitable, as the Dooley boy had certainly taken enough lumps defending the honor of both the Princess and her mother Jenny, that the Princess would be in love with him. Who else had the girl had to turn to in all her years of isolation from the community? In all the years Mama Hampson and the rest of the town biddies had ostracized her for her mother's vocation? In the brief year since the Dooley boy had left home he'd undergone his boot training at the Sampson Naval Station (he'd been taught how to react, that is), he'd fought the battle for the Marshall Islands, he'd been left in Pacific waters for three days before being rescued, he'd become a man, Sy Hampson's voice seemed to suggest, and to expect him to waste time bothering to reclothe a beautiful, intelligent young woman with blood gushing from her scalp, that he might spare the sensibilities of Mrs. Hampson and her sisters in charity— "Talk about lace-curtain trash!"—was so laughable as to be demented.

"Go tell it to your precious Reverend Donaldson. You know what he'll tell you, don't you, Ethel? He'll tell you to mind your Ps and Qs."

About the whole business Wiley and I kidded ourselves that we didn't harbor a terrible secret. We never spoke of it. The Gotham Street quarry was in our, the Thompson Park, section of town and since we were kids we'd sneaked from the house on Friday and Saturday nights, had made our way up a trail on the back side of the quarry, and had rained pebbles down on lovers' cars. During puberty, sensing that at thirteen we were only three or four years from parking there ourselves, Wiley and I had abandoned such foolishness, which is not to say we hadn't initiated younger kids in the neighborhood into the "sport." And though everyone in Watertown seemed perfectly willing to accept the Princess's (she was after all the daughter of the infamous Jenny, an Indian love goddess) demise as an act of God, in that a rock as big as a melon loosened itself and fell from high up the precipice smack atop her astonishingly lovely head, in fact everyone had known for years about the "park rats," as we were called, and our causing *coitus interruptus* in uncountable upstate lovers. Balming my conscience all these years has been no easy matter. Without ever having checked—I daren't do so—the morgue of the local newspaper, I've chosen to believe the weather was cloudy that night, the sky moonless, and that one of our nitwit park-rat protégés, standing so high up there in the darkness, had only been able to make out the vaguest outline of Jenny's convertible and had no idea whatever that the canvas was down.

So Rex, at least surfacely ungrieved, went back to the Y and Duffy's Tavern and his furloughed pals and his girls and his late-night revels at Rickahdickahdoo's on Stone Street.

As I address myself to forty years ago, I don't remember for what offense (could Don Juan remember his conquests?) the high school principal, Bill Hewitt, opened the door for my prolonged sabbatical in the autumn of 1944, four or five months after the Princess came to her untimely end. What I do know is that it must have been a lugubrious offense indeed. Hewitt was ordinarily satisfied that the student take a note home to Mums and from her return with a note to the effect that one's behavior would assuredly improve; if it were a somewhat more unhappy dereliction one might have to return with Mums in tow; and when Hewitt ordered one to return with one's father it was so serious as to be, as they say nowadays, the pits.

"No note, no Mama," I recall his saying. "I want your father in here with you, and I frankly don't care if I ever see your face again until I see you with Earl. For some reason I abruptly find myself too inarticulate to explain the rules to you, Exley, and perhaps Earl will have better luck detailing them for you than I've had. In fact, I'm quite confident Earl will."

Of course Hewitt knew damn well that in Earl's case, as a lineman for the Niagara Mohawk, having to come to school with me would cost him a day's pay, no small thing for a man with a wife and four children (three now that the Brigadier was fighting in the Pacific) to feed, and this at the tail end of the Depression economy. What Hewitt hadn't bargained for was the morbid romanticism which so obsessed me in those years, dreaming of Scoglitti and Anzio and the Carroceto Creek and Campoleone and Kwajalein and Tarawa and, since the Princess's death, Saipan and Leyte and Omaha Red Beach and Bastogne, that I owned such a majestic contempt for the pedestrian world of plane geometry and translating the campaigns of Caesar that, quite honestly, I simply refused to tell my father that Hewitt wanted to see him. Moreover, as I write it occurs to me that had I not had a twin sister who would eventually, more from fear of my failing all my courses than any malice on her part, for my sister was without wickedness, tell my father I'd been going to the Y instead of school, I might have continued running and jumping and bombing until the summer recess and ended not only a high school all-star but playing in the NBA, such was the fury of my dedication at the Y. It was the inappropriately mad enthusiasm an adolescent employs to obliterate the guilt of one day's missed school becoming two, then three, then a week, then yet another, and now abruptly a month of unlearned geometric relationships and Latin syntax. And all the while above me, rather fittingly like the Oriental water torture, the ceaseless slap, slap, slap of the strange cuckolded Llewellyn Rexford Bean.

And of course, as was my sister, the Brigadier was always with me, and I can't tell which bedeviled me more, the unjustified suspicion that from kindergarten on my sister, being in the same grade, had always ratted on me at home or the palpably envious possibility that as I missed day after day of school and went swoosh and swoosh and swoosh, while above me the wretched Rex tried with all the desperation at his disposal to jog the Princess from his soul (how could he have when across all these years I can see her as vividly as if she stood before me now?), the Brigadier, over yonder there in the wide Pacific, might even at that moment have one of those slimy slant-eyed little Nips in his gunsights. Neither bedevilment, as it happened, was warranted.

In the first case, my sister was one of those grotesquely irritating people born utterly free of envy, malice, or the capacity to ridicule. In all the years we were growing up I can't once recall saying that someone was a jerk or a prick or a fag without her responding "He's okay when you get to know him," or "I think he's nice," or, that most grating of all responses, *"He's a human being, too, you know,"* replies that with their implied remonstrances all but sent me round the bend in agitation. If one cannot enlist one's twin sister in his more cynical, hateful, and ultimately unmanly visions of the cosmos, who the hell can one enlist? I suspected wrongly that the paranoia which in my late twenties would lead to mental hospitalization could be blamed in no small part on a much too intimate sibling proximity. Of course, I turned that proximity into a rivalry that never existed save in my sick fantasies. Now I know that except for an inadvertant slip of the tongue at supper my sister never told or even suggested to my parents just how nasty a guy I was—and I was *bad*—until that fateful day when, out of what must have been for her this terrible trepidation that I'd fail everything, she at last told my father I'd been out of school for a month and going to the Y. It was for this that I'd blow her away, pathetic luckless girl.

For what I must have put her through that month—when I wasn't cleaning the Brigadier's guns and cultivating both my left hand and my friendship with Rex—it's a miracle she didn't end up in the loony bin (for she did survive, though only God knows how) in lieu of me. Whenever, at supper, the subject came round to how we were doing at school, I'd catch my sister's eyes, let my own droop crazily cross-eyed to the bridge of my nose, let my upper teeth come over and bite furiously Dracula-like into my lower lip, all the while with my flattened right hand making razorlike slashing motions at my Adam's apple, indicating with a horrifying finality that should she breathe a word I'd steal into her bedroom that very night, bury my cuspids in her lily white neck, and drain every blessed drop of blood from her body, do this even while she dreamed of high school fullbacks and senior proms and white picket fences and whatever in the hell it was that fourteen-year-old maidens dreamed of.

Enter my schizophrenia, a schizophrenia damn near as hopeless as that which English writers have claimed to be the very essence of the British malaise. Whereas on the one hand I insisted—absolutely demanded—the right to do my own thing, to be utterly free to choose what was good for me (certainly not biology and world history), to cherish and coddle, à la the English, my own eccentricity, on the other hand I brought the militant discipline required to maintain the disastrous notion of Empire to my daily practices at the Y and my nightly cleaning of the Brigadier's guns. The Brigadier had worked (A&P bag boy), horse-traded, and damn near worn himself out acquiring that collection. On his induction into the service it was the only thing I'd sworn—as solemn as the Eagle scout I'd been—to look after.

And what a collection it was, guns that would be worth a fortune on today's market. In handguns alone, the Brigadier had a Model 1911 Colt .45 automatic, a toggle-action 9mm Luger, a Walther P38; that little sidearm jewel carried by Italian officers, a 7.65mm Beretta, and, among rifles too numerous to mention (twelve-gauge Browning shotgun, .22-caliber Winchester pump long rifle, that kind of nothing stuff), an original .30-06 Browning automatic; the M-1, a lightweight beauty which had cut nearly four pounds from the BAR; and my lovely lovely favorite, a Model 98 .30-06 Mauser, topped with a Mossberg 8A scope. In expert hands, the Mauser will of course take down an elephant, and if one has never heard the report of this gun—it'll set tremors shimmering in the windows across the street—one does not know the true sound of guns.

Regarding my unjustified bedevilment in the second case, the Brigadier never fired a shot in anger during World War II and would not get into the earnest business of killing until Korea when, as I've elsewhere said, he'd write me that he'd reached the point he could laugh when he saw Chinese troops stacked up like cordwood. Other than his immediate superior, the guy giving him orders (the most memorable enemy to most servicemen), the Brigadier never got a glimpse of the antagonist in what Archie calls the Big One. And hence my daily ritual, buoyant with envy of and chagrin at him for slaughtering the heathen while I kept moving farther and farther and farther out from the left side, was all so much nonsense. Each night, with my Hoppes cleaner, my Birchwood blueing, my rod and pack, my spotless rags, I had that collection not only ready to join Jenny's Indian chums at the Carroceto Creek but so gleaming that the meanest mother sumbitch Texas top sergeant would, on inspecting it, have promoted me two grades on the spot.

Nor were my dreams confined to killing alien grunts. Even as my texts lay by my bed unopened and unread, those books I so dutifully carried to the Y each morning, the Saturday matinees grew more imaginative and with them so did I. Eventually I became Wild Bill Donovan's top OSS guy, the one they parachuted into the Black Forest of Deutschland, the Italian Alps, the very heart of Tokyo, my feet heavy with hiking boots, my disassembled Mauser and Mossberg scope in my rucksack with the ham-and-cheese sandwiches and thermos of black coffee. Yes, believe unequivocally in my grim-visaged sincerity when I say that at one time or another I had them all—I mean all, Hitler, Heydrich, Himmler, Mussolini, Admiral Yamamoto, General Hideki Tojo—in the spiderwebbing cross hairs of that Mossberg 8A scope.

One night my father said, "How's school going with you, Fred?"

"Good, great."

Silence.

"How can it be going great when you haven't been there for a month?"

An excruciating pause.

In a voice that signaled ultimate anger. "Get away from this table. Upstairs. I don't want to look at you."

From my mother a genuinely mind-boggling piece of foolishness. "Don't you want him to finish his supper?"

"I want him out of my sight."

Of course I had no choice but to blow my sister away. Assuredly she had been dutifully and fairly though ominously admonished. And the worst of it was I'd have to do it that night while my father was out on what we in the Thompson Park area ever so solemnly called Night Patrol. At the outset of the war, the old man—he was thirty-six in 1941—and the other men in the neighborhood, as men did from all the wards in Watertown, went nightly to the Elks Club on Stone Street where, abetted by an instructor, a projector, and slides, they learned to identify the various aircraft of the Luftwaffe and the Japanese Imperial Air Force. In this way they could take their rotating four-hour shifts and on their assigned nightly watches intently scan the dark forboding skies of Watertown for the Nip and the Kraut. As I had no way of knowing that Mr. Ball, our neighbor, had for business reasons changed shifts with my father and that therefore my father would be in the house, I went blissfully on, with excruciatingly demented fastidiousness cleaning the Mauser and the scope. Prepared at length, I studiously put a .30-06 cartridge into the chamber and yet another into the magazine.

The latter cartridge was reserved for me. The execution of one's sister would require nothing less than that afterward I do the decent, obligatory thing and commit the American rural version of the time-honored Japanese harakiri, lie down on my bed, put the barrel into my mouth, and activate the trigger with my big toe, which I'd already practiced, sans cartridges, any number of times. After what seemed an eternity I heard her drawing her bath (it was fitting that she die cleansed and, hopefully, at peace with her Maker), thinking that if I could only make it another half hour until she got to her bedroom and before her vanity had begun that endlessly infernal brushing of her hair, I had it made. Now suddenly, hearing the bathroom door open and close, then the one to her bedroom do the same, I knew it was time. Placing myself, legs apart and set, at the far end of the Brigadier's and my bedroom, the Mauser's brilliantly polished stock braced snugly to my shoulder, the cross hairs of the 8A scope zeroed in at the estimated point her monstrously freckled face would enter the room, I called her name.

"What?"

"Come 'ere."

"Fat chance."

"I ain't mad. *Seriously*. Look, I just want to talk about the assignments I've missed."

"Fat chance."

"*Seriously*."

"I had to tell Dad. Mr. Hewitt told me you'd been out of school so long that if I didn't you had no chance of passing, plus which he himself was coming up here tomorrow night and tell Dad. *Brother*, I can see that. All I did was spare you a real hiding."

"Look, I'm not even thinkin' about that. That's all in the past. Gone with the wind. Just my schoolwork. *Honest*."

So she came, impetuous ingenuous girl, the door hesitantly opened, into the room in her flannel nightgown she stepped, her hairbrush still held innocently in her lax right hand. Then the tip of her laughably freckled though patrician nose came smack into the spiderwebbing and *BRRRRAAAAAaaaaaammmmmm*. The jolly freckles on her face dissolved and vaporized into nothingness, her hands went clutchingly to her throat, the hairbrush clacked to the floor, and she slid ever so slowly and histrionically down the door casing to the floor, going *ugh, ugh, ugh.*

"Bye-bye, you squealing rat."

"What in Christ's name was that?"

Having taken two steps toward my bed to complete

my untidy Oriental ritual, and having realized—oh, malevolent fate!—that it was the voice of my father, I literally dropped the Mauser to the floor and by the time he'd turned into the bedroom, having taken the staircase in three preposterous leaps, the old lady right at his heels, I was already, in horrifyingly frightened self-vindication, bellowing, *"She's fakin' it, for Christ's sake! It's only a blank cartridge, for Christ's sake! A fucking blank cartridge!"*

One can only judge the genuine extent of my fear by understanding that in my house in those prehistoric days using the word *fuck* was a more serious offense than shooting my sister.

"She's in shock," I heard my father say to my mother. "Draw some cold water in the bathtub. Then come back here."

When my mother returned and had her cradled in her arms and she had at last stopped choking and gone to hysterical tears, the old man, with a finicky deliberation that did not bode well for Master Frederick Earl Exley, walked slowly to the middle of the room, picked up the Mauser, and threw it right through the glass of both the inner and the storm windows. Then, with equal gravity, all the Brigadier's beautiful guns went, one after another, through the broken windows and out and down onto the hard fall frosted yard between our and Mr. Ball's houses.

That collection got sold the next day, the money banked against the Brigadier's return, and it goes without saying that on his next leave I paid all over again. But the Brigadier hadn't the heart for his business. He got halfway through slapping the shit out of me, bouncing me off the bedroom walls, when he abruptly stopped and doubled over with laughter.

"You goddamn fool. You fucking jerk. Had you ever stuck that Mauser in your mouth the velocity would have given you a concussion bad enough to kill you. And the powder is so old in those blank cartridges half of it wouldn't have burned until it reached the inside of your mouth. You know what a hot fudge sundae would taste like after that?

Like uncooked dandelion greens, that's what. I mean, what a fucking jerk. To think I ever gave you a key to the gun case in the first place! That's what kills me—how fucking stupid I was!"

Prior to this incident my mother's *you just wait till your father gets home* had been a standard joke in our house. No matter how elaborately or with what urgent intricate melodrama my mother related our misdeeds, my father, looking up from his breaded pork chops, would only say, "I hope you booted him in the ass" or, "What do you want from me?" or more humiliating than anything for my mother, he'd find the story droll and begin to chuckle. Now of course he had no choice.

As he had me by the shoulder dragging me down the stairs, my pain-in-the-ass sister, to the end as incapable of vengeance as any other of the base impulses—the "even Fred's okay when you get to know him" syndrome—kept calling through her tears, "Don't hurt him, Dad. *Please don't hurt him.* He was only kidding." Hence what business my father had with me was done openhandedly, in the cold hard yard next to the forlorn pile of shimmering guns, my noble ghoul of a sister spared me a couple well-deserved broken ribs, and I hadn't even the satisfaction of having my torso taped so that, on my return to school, I couldn't for the guys in the shower make up some grand adventure of what had happened to me in the Black Forest during my month's sabbatical.

7

On Christmas Eve, when the rest of the family was out caroling with the neighbors (I'd been grounded for the remainder of the school year), Rex telephoned to find out where I'd been and also to tell me he'd taken a job with a Wall Street law firm and would be moving in a few days, starting work on January 1, 1945 (I prayed that his move wasn't prompted by the shame of being a cuckold and that he'd make nice friends to protect him from his own crackpot enthusiasms). Although en famille we'd been sworn not to breathe a word of what I'd done, everyone at school knew all about it anyway, so I saw no reason to keep it from Rex. Appealing overwhelmingly to his impish rottenness, the story proved entirely too much for Rex. When Rex had been a kid, my father, a great athlete, had been Rex's idol— some distillation of machismo, strength, and courage— and Rex, in an urgent attempt to visualize every delicious detail, kept saying, among drunken peals of laughter, "So what'd Earl say then? Ho, ho, ho! And your sister is holler-ing what? 'Don't hurt him, Dad'? Ho, ho, ho! I mean, marvelous Jesus, my darling pal, I love it, I love it, *I luuuhhhfffff it!* I ain't ever gonna forget this one! Ho, ho, ho!"

Rex of course had a plate in his head to remind him what siblings were capable of doing to each other. Then we made our good-byes, and when he said he'd miss me, my luscious pal, I told him I'd miss him too and was sorry he wouldn't get to see me play as I'd doubtless make the jayvees the next year.

"The jayvees, my ass. With what I taught you, you'll make the fucking varsity. Besides, I'll be getting home to see you play."

Rex was both right and wrong. I did make the varsity but Rex never got home again until they brought him back in a box to be interred. And, alas for me, Rex did remember the shooting of my sister until the end of his brief life.

Now abruptly it is three years later, a brilliant February Sunday afternoon in Manhattan, and, together with team-mates from the John Jay High School, Katonah, upper Westchester, New York, I am swaggering—in only the way guys destined to win the sectionals in White Plains could swagger—west on Forty-second Street, heading for the Paramount to see one of what nowadays are called the Big Bands, when who should be coming straight at me but Rex on his way to pick up a date for "brunch," a word I'd only learned since moving to la-di-da Westchester. When Rex at last convinced himself it was I (for I had gone through puberty and had changed a good deal more than he), he startled everyone by kissing me full on the mouth and all the time we talked he kept patting me, pinching me, em-bracing me. At first unable to understand that my friends weren't also from Watertown, Rex finally grasped that though I'd graduated from there, my grades were too low for college, and to get them up I'd attempted to take a post-graduate, had been vigorously denied admittance, and hence had been forced to go live with my aunt in Katonah. Certainly I was playing ball, I assured Rex. He was looking at the best team in north Westchester (four of our five starters got scholarships: University of Texas, Bowling Green, Springfield, and Bradley). Our next game was Friday night at home.

"I'll be there. You better fucking believe I'll be there! I know where that Katonah is. That's way the hell up and gone on that twisting fucking Route 22! Right?"

It was coming back from the game on that twisting fucking Route 22 that Rex bought it all. The autopsy would reveal that the metal plate had outworn it usefulness, something had exploded in Rex's head, and he'd been dead even before his Ford Sportsman Convertible hit the tree.

How I played so well that night is beyond understanding, at least beyond my understanding, though of course I wanted desperately to play well for Rex and, under the circumstances, am glad that I did. I do know that in the first minute of the game I withdrew into myself utterly, perhaps became some pure essence of basketball, and everything I threw up went in. We scored first, went into our full-court press, as we did against "running" teams, and I intercepted their first in-bounds pass, broke for the basket and though I was coming in from the left side decided to take the lay-up with my more sure right hand. Suddenly, though, a previously unseen defender was up in the air with me to block, I simply shifted the ball to my left hand and made the play. When I was pressing this same defender, who was taking the ball out, frantically waving my arms in his face, he sneered, "You lucky piece of shit," and Rex, who was standing right next to him—all that night Rex would run up and down the side of the court to wherever the action was—heard it.

"Lucky?" Rex cried in anguish. "Lucky? Why, you dumb Guinea! Lucky? I taught him how to do that! Right, Ex? You better believe it, Guinzo! I taught him that! In the days before he shot his sister! Right, Ex? That's a fact! In the days before Ex shot his sister! Ho, ho, ho!"

And it goes without saying that every time I scored

‡ 233

that night Rex continued to chant his high awful hysterical liturgy. That proper John Jay crowd—some of those kids used to arrive at the games in chauffeur-driven Cadillacs (a long way from Watertown indeed)—sat in stunned pop-eyed disbelief. And Ex?—well, a redfaced Ex just withdrew further and further and further into basketball.

"Yeah! I taught him that! Right, Ex? In the days before he shot his sister! Ho, ho, ho!"

8

As incredible as it may seem to you, Alissa, and as an indication of how badly my incarceration is affecting me, do you know what I almost asked you—*you*, the most cloyingly shameless Anglophile it's ever been my great misfortune to be in love with? I almost asked you if you'd read Evelyn Waugh's *A Handful of Dust*. It was you, for Christ's sake, who would give me no peace until I'd read all of Waugh, you, Al, who tried so eloquently, with all your legal sophistry and psychological legerdemain, to convince me, while I said nary a word, that Anthony Last's being held prisoner in the Amazon jungle by the mad blind Mr. Todd, surrounded by Pie-wie Indians, dining on farine and dried beef and forced to read aloud to the menacing Mr. Todd from Todd's library of Dickens, *Bleak House, Dombey and Son, Martin Chuzzlewit, Little Dorrit, Nicholas Nickleby*—that, you cried, was a vision of the ultimate damnation, the Promethean Hell.

But it never was, Alissa, despite my refusing to dampen your girllike enthusiasm for what you considered your startling acuteness. From page one Tony Last was never alive, with his tenacious love of the conventional and his infantile passion for that nothing pile of stone called Hetton Abbey, falling battlements, Morgan le Fay ceiling, and so forth. One can hardly empathize with the anguished un-allayable sorrow of a man born dead. Had that been Waugh's Basil Seal, the one true character Waugh ever created, I could have agreed and said, "Yes, Alissa, that indeed is hell." But of course, among his other endearing attributes—being a liar, a roué, a cheat, a cad, and so forth—Basil Seal was altogether too resourceful, would never have sat still for his imprisonment by Todd, and eventually, like Hemingway or a gorilla, would have walked from the rain forests chomping jovially on bananas, as I hope one day to do, though in my case I'll walk out munching pineapple.

At his more sober moments O'Twoomey has in fact admitted to keeping me prisoner, as when he tells me that when his "business is done" I shall be free to go as I please "with a nice lurverly bonus from me, my dear, for the inconvenience, don't you know," for the most part he insists that Random House has waited quite long enough for my book, thank you, ma'am, and that I shall damn well honor the financial obligation of my advance even if it kills him, O'Twoomey. Of course he calls Random House "Whimsical House."

"I mean, really, my dear Frederick, it sounds so aim-less, 'random' does. Rather as if needing ten manuscripts to publish, they throw a hundred from the roof and put the first ten they pick up between covers. Random indeed!"

When I pointed out—and why do I bother to do this, Alissa?—that the house he was so sneeringly mocking was the first this side of the Atlantic to publish his compatriot's *Ulysses*, not only that but that the late Bennett Cerf had taken it to the U.S. Supreme Court to get a ruling on its alleged obscenity, O'Twoomey cried, "Precisely, my dear

Frederick. Who but a bunch of godless anarchist nits would devote that much time, energy, and money to heaping that pile of feelthy vile trash on an ingenuous unsuspecting America!"

Forget about Waugh's Todd, Alissa. There is really no end to O'Twoomey's dementia, though I expect schizophrenia to be the besetting malaise of the Irish. Not only can O'Twoomey quote at endless length from Joyce's *Ulysses*, and often does, including the Nighttown section ("I'll wring the bastard fucker's bleeding blasted fucking windpipe!") and the Molly Bloom soliloquy (". . . *feel my breasts all perfume yes and his heart was going like mad and yes I said yes I will Yes*.") but he does so with a gustatory relish that borders on the rapturous sexuality of the drooling impotent.

Although O'Twoomey has an extremely dear apparatus called a dish installed atop Lanai Lodge, where our party permanently occupies six of the eleven rooms, or the entire north side of the motel, and can pick up thirty channels, on the theory that it's not "substantive enough for a writer" and will do my "genius ghastly irreparable damage," he refuses to allow me a TV in my room (O'Twoomey himself watches the box all the morning and all the evening). He has, however, allowed me a great expensive clock radio, the function of 90 percent of whose feverishly glittering dials I don't understand, and I am awakened mornings, at five, to the croakings and rantings of the Honolulu disc jockey J. Akuhead Pupule, said to be the highest paid in the world. The J. stands for nothing, an aku is a bonito, a fish much relished here as sushi, *pupule* is Hawaiian for "crazy." Hence his name translates as J. Crazy Fishhead, under the circumstances a most appropriate guy to whom to awaken.

Aku's real name is Hal Lewis. Years ago he played the violin in drawing-room and honky-tonk bands in the Bay area. He found his way to Hawaii and married a Hawaiian woman with operatic pretensions named Emma. Recently I saw in *The Advertiser* that in his autobiography

Robert Merrill assessed Emma's voice as falling between lacking and painful, and for days I have to no avail been waiting for Aku to start rending the airwaves about Merrill's indiscretion. Once Teddy Kennedy said he might challenge President Carter's incumbency and seek the Democratic nomination in the primaries. President Carter's mother, Miss Lillian, said she hoped no one would shoot Kennedy. On reading this, Aku said, "What a tacky broad." Other than waiting breathlessly to hear what J. Akuhead Pupule might say next, and to get the news and the weather on the half hour, there aren't any melodic reasons for listening. For the past year Aku's favorite record has been Englebert Humperdinck's "After the Loving." When one of Aku's idolaters telephoned and asked why he played it so often, Aku snapped, "Emma likes it." The diva likes it? On occasion Aku plays an Emma record, but I don't have the musical savvy to gauge Merill's assessment.

Hannibal knocks at my door at 5:15, unlocks it, we repair to the Lodge's screened-in veranda for the Kona coffee he has already prepared, and we read the morning *Honolulu Advertiser*, Hannibal the funnies and I anything that strikes my interest. Hannibal laughs a lot and exclaims, "Eeese goot, *eeese goot!*" then asks me to read what he's just laughed at and explain it to him. Tell me about that, will you, Al? At six, after four or five mugs of coffee and a half dozen True blues, Hannibal returns me to my room, locks me in, I have my morning evacuation, sit at my desk, half listen to Crazy Fishhead, and survey my writing paraphernalia, books, paper, ballpoint pens, pencils, erasers, typewriters, even a used Xerox machine.

When O'Twoomey asked me how I wrote—I knew of course that he wanted to know what material I used—I told him I wrote in longhand on legal-size tablets, typed the material on cheap paper, rewrote, then put it all onto a high-quality rag-content bond. Two days later this room was stacked with enough boxes of paper to produce Trollope's shelf, with enough left over to copy *War and Peace* and four or five of Dostoyevski's in triple space. As one example, to the right of my desk in easy reach is a stack of virginal legal-size tablets three feet high. The four- and five-foot stacks of books, scattered aimlessly about the room like an intellectual recluse's formidable maze, are—or were until O'Twoomey got my number—a ploy of mine.

While reading the morning *Advertiser* and the Sunday *Advertiser and Star-Bulletin*, I made mental notes of every reviewed book. On my return to my room I'd write the titles down, then every two weeks or so I'd present a long list to O'Twoomey, telling him there were things in these volumes I felt might be of use to me. O'Twoomey would hand me three or four hundred-dollar bills and have Toby fly Hannibal and me over to Honolulu in the Cessna. As O'Twoomey won't allow any of us to have a drink until 6:30, when he switches from his imported Guinness stout (by then he's drunk at least a case) to his deep-dish Boodles martinis (four ounces of gin on ice, no vermouth), I use these semimonthly outings to get drunk and to look at the shoppers.

In the rented Jeep O'Twoomey keeps in Honolulu airport's long-term parking lot Toby would drop Hannibal and me at the Walden bookstore in the Ala Moana Shopping Plaza and we'd make arrangements to meet in the Hano Hano room in the Sheraton Waikiki. Because Toby had six or eight girls in Honolulu, Hannibal and I were never pressed for time. Toby was always late (he was into his "Chink period doing strange things" he never got around to detailing for me, taking Oriental herbs that allowed him to sustain two-hour erections or some such thing) and I, with Hannibal never more than a step away, would select eight to ten books that had nothing to do with any titles on my list, after which we'd stroll about the plaza staring achingly at the Eurasian girls in their muumuus or—grant me peace—high-slit cheongsams. We'd pick up some underwear, leather thongs and sandals, aloha shirts, golf balls and tees, occasionally a small gift for O'Twoomey. O'Twoomey never asks for change, Alissa, and I have over four thousand dollars lying loosely in one of my cabinet drawers.

Then we'd take a taxi to the Sheraton, the outdoor glass elevator to the top of the building, and, while waiting for Toby, we'd sit at the bar of the Hano Hano Room overlooking Waikiki. I'd have a double vodka and grapefruit juice, Hannibal a Coke, and he'd go one for one with me even if Toby was two hours late and I had time for fifteen. Hannibal always said, "You no tell Mr. O." and I'd say, "No, I won't tell him, Hannibal," meaning I wouldn't tell O'Twoomey Hannibal had sullied the sacred rules of our alluring palm-shrouded Yaddo by allowing me to drink before six.

Some time ago—I've lost all track of time, Alissa—when I presented my book list to O'Twoomey, he asked obliquely why I didn't finish the books I already had. When I protested I had finished them, having read some of them twice, he reached fiercely under his chair, pulled out a fat R. F. Delderfield paperback, snatched up his letter opener, and with a grand flourish, as though he were a swashbuckler brandishing a cutlass, began lustily separating the pages which, alas, the binder's machines had obviously neglected cutting. It was the first indication I had that O'Twoomey was spying on me when I was out of the room. The next day, having exposed himself for the Jerry Sneak he is, he had a peephole installed in my door, one he can see in but I can't see out.

It does little good, Alissa. O'Twoomey's leg has never healed properly; every time the surgeons took the pins out the leg collapsed from his monstrous weight. Now he refuses to have the pins removed altogether, despite admonitions of possible severe infection (I pray for gangrene compounded by irreversible blood poisoning). In any event, were I forced to, I could hear his clamorous gimpy walk from here across the Maui Channel to Lahaina. Hence, I'm always at my desk, either reading or composing this letter, by the time the fat old sybarite hobbles down the hallway and puts his booze-rheumy eye to the peephole.

I've insisted that because the Lodge is such a tinderbox I rent a safety deposit box for my manuscript. Late every

Friday afternoon Hannibal and I stroll over to the Lanai branch of the Royal Hawaiian Bank, where I deposit six or seven pages of this letter, plus thirty or so pages of blank manuscript, all dated and sealed snugly with masking tape in a ten-by-twelve manila envelope. On my return I'm invariably met with O'Twoomey's "all safe and cumfy, lurve?" I nod. "Good." For emphasis Hannibal adds, "Eeese goot, *eeese goot.*"

At a quarter to nine Hannibal fetches me back to the veranda for breakfast. While O'Twoomey swills his second or third bottle of room-temperature stout (vile enough stuff cold), the thick dark malted liquid spilling over his chin and chins, scalloping down from what actually might once have been a jawline and onto his custom-made (he's outgrown double XL) white linen golf shirts with clusters of vivid green shamrocks stitched over the pockets, I have poached eggs on dry wheat toast, with a glass of skim milk, and try not to ruin my appetite by looking at O'Twoomey. Like Anthony Burgess's Sikh, Katar Singh, O'Twoomey's fatness has gone beyond obesity and become O'Twoomey himself, some majestic pinnacle or essence of corpulent drooping flesh. "Watching my weight," he says and lovingly pats his immense belly. O'Twoomey does not eat breakfast but sits there stupidly smug, his morning flushed face as red as the rising sun, watching me fuel my "genius."

Ironically, when I go next door to the medical center for my semimonthly blood pressure checks, O'Twoomey accompanies me, his blood pressure is invariably normal, and, despite my three different pills a day, I get tut-tutted by Dr. Jim because my diastolic hovers around ninety. Hannibal, who does not believe in medicines other than the ubiquitous liliaceous aloe plant he boils down in milk, refrigerates in gallon jars, and drinks a glass of daily (my unabridged claims it a purgative, Hannibal esteems it an immunizer against all disease), says, "Mr. O's eese goot, very goot. Fred's eese bad, very bad. I know. You ast me. I know. *Oooooh.*" In dismay Hannibal shakes his great weak noodle from side to side.

At two minutes to nine, the dining room having cleared of its half dozen farers, we stroll there and turn on O'Twoomey's Advent TV, which throws its picture onto a movielike screen mounted above the mantel of the great brick fireplace. If Toby is in residence (and more often than not he is off in the Cessna "on business"), Hannibal drives him the eleven miles down to White Manele Beach, from which Toby jogs back. Even walking the steep twisting badly potted two-lane road from White Manele to the village, fourteen hundred feet above the sea, would send the average man in good shape to bed for ten hours' sleep. Toby's condition is truly miraculous, Alissa, I can see that even Hannibal fears him, and it is yet another daydream of mine that my jailers one day have it out and neutralize each other. Although Hannibal goes out of his way to please Toby, Toby refuses to acknowledge Hannibal's humanity, simple and savage though it is, by saying a single word to him, considering him little more than a robot to watch me while Toby is off doing O'Twoomey's bidding.

Having something to do with my chiding him for his abominable Irish taste in food, and in the hope that he can cultivate a more sophisticated palate, O'Twoomey and I daily watch *The French Chef*, which is hosted by an alien, or what would appear to be an alien, named Julia Child. I am using the one in ten dishes O'Twoomey favors to assure that if the insane bastard doesn't go with blood poisoning he'll do so with a heart attack, massive, I expect. Ordinarily poor Julia no sooner forms the cooing Bostonian "O" of her flexible lips and announces, "*Soupe aux Moules*, today on *The French Chef*!" than O'Twoomey shrivels up his nose in horrified mock distaste and with sublime disgust cries, "*Wrong*-GOE! We'll have no bleeding Frog dishes from the likes of you, you insufferable old faggot!" What other than Frog dishes O'Twoomey hopes to get from *The French Chef* is beyond me, and my unabridged allows no clue as to what an Irishman means when he calls a peculiar though likeable enough aging woman a faggot. More unbearable than anything, when Hannibal watches with us he repeats, throughout the half hour, everything O'Twoomey says, in a kind of Polynesian pidgin. "*Wong*-GOE! No Fog shee-it, 'sufferable old 'aggot!" It is when the *wrong*-GOEs stop and O'Twoomey's salivary glands start pumping passionately, wet thwap, thwap, thwaps, Pavlovian noises his swigs of stout are quite unable to stay, that I know Miss Julia has hit on a dish that strikes O'Twoomey's fancy. You can be sure, too, Alissa, that it is a dish fit for swine. Or at least it is when Exley gets through with it. Three days ago, for example, Julia prepared a "Cassoulet for a Crowd," dry white beans baked with goose, lamb, and sausage.

"Can you do that, lurve?"

"Nothing to it," I said. "Of course I'll need a couple days for the *confit d'oie* and to soak the beans against intestinal motility."

"Speak English."

"You mean Irish?"

"Please, lurve, *do not push your bleeding fucking luck.*"

"*Confit d'oie* is preserved goose, a simple matter of pan frying the goose, then storing it in its own fat. As your dear departed mother"—here I actually blessed myself, Alissa—"should have taught you, one has to soak the beans a couple days to prevent flatulence or farting, a condition you already suffer from to such a degree, Seamus, that should I neglect this step you'd doubtless blow yourself to pieces and expire in your own vile stench."

Preserved goose and soaked beans, my ass, Al! For the goose I bought a dozen turkey legs and fried them in globs of lard, garlic, and heaps of pharmaceutical saltpeter. Then I cut a lamb shoulder into thick cubes, sliced some Italian sausage O'Twoomey has specially prepared by a Honolulu butcher, and braised this mixture in more lard, garlic, and saltpeter. Stripping the bone from the turkey, I broke this meat into edible pieces, then took the sausage and lamb, added it to the turkey, with its fatty skin, and stored it all overnight in the lard, garlic, and saltpeter drippings. The following day, having washed the beans and given them a twenty-minute boil so they'd at least be chewable, I prepared the casserole, a layer of beans here, then a layer of turkey, lamb, and El Wopo sausage in this marvelously glutinous, spreadable, and nauseous-looking fat, then another layer of beans and so forth. Before we went to the golf course yesterday, I put the casserole in the oven at 275 degrees Fahrenheit and let it go all the afternoon, telling Sissy, who ran the lodge, to check it every hour or so. If the top layer of beans appeared dry, I told her, throw two or three tablespoons of butter, together with a dash of saltpeter, on top of it. Last night O'Twoomey and Hannibal ate the whole thing, doused in ketchup.

Today on the golf course, on the 158-yard par three ninth hole, having bet me a thousand dollars he could put the ball from the tee onto the green with an eight iron, and do this straight into a hard wind, O'Twoomey came slowly to the top of his backswing, paused ever so slightly, came ferociously forward, and at the impact of iron with ball evacuated.

It was beautiful, Alissa. All the way round the course I'd seen—I should say heard and smelled—it coming. It is O'Twoomey's left or power leg which contains the pins. Unable to plant it, he is forced on every stroke to go to the very top of his backswing and come into the ball with all the force of his upper body and arms. It requires the kind of terrible strain, really, that one employs when sitting on the throne after three days without voiding. Hence on every swing that afternoon his flatulence had been such that even Rabelais would have been shy of detailing it, so bad that even in that fierce hard wind one could hear its thunderous rumbles, occasionally even pick up its odor at thirty paces. But I do not own the poetry to do it justice. These noises were no warm-up arabesques. There was something symphonic about them, the darkly vibrating romanticism of Wagner, something so debilitating one knew the composition had exhausted the composer. One had no doubt O'Twoomey's evacuation was complete.

As I dug a hole with my pitching wedge to bury

O'Twoomey's pants and underwear, Hannibal ran O'Twoomey's electric golf cart (he makes us walk, "for the exercise, lurve") back to the Lodge for fresh underwear, clean slacks, and a bucket of hot water, soap, and towels. While I dug, O'Twoomey stood hiding in the woods a few feet from me, his fat fishy face compressed tightly between a V limb, sneering hatefully.

"Are you sure you washed those beans with detergent?"

I laughed. "You don't wash them in soap, Jimmy. You have to soak them. I did so for two days. So help me." I raised my right hand and invoked the Almighty. I don't know why I did that, Alissa. It was almost a dead giveaway that I was lying. And, save on those occasions I'm trying to wheedle a concession from the sinister bastard, I never, never call him Jimmy.

After Hannibal completed the unhappy chore of scrubbing down and drying O'Twoomey's monumental backside and got him into fresh linen and slacks, we made our way up the steep hill to the eighteenth green, which is so steep Hannibal often has to get behind O'Twoomey's cart and assist the electric engine by pushing. The eighteenth green is, in fact, so elevated it is hidden from the tee, showing the driver only the top half of the pin and the flag. When we got to the top, alas, there was O'Twoomey's ball three inches from the pin, a "gimme."

O'Twoomey smirked. "Let me see. That's thirty-five hundred dollars you owe me on the day. Uhmmm." He wet his scorecard pencil with his tongue. "For a total of a hundred and four thousand dollars altogether. And if you don't think this is coming out of your bonus, Frederick, you have another think coming, sir. Indeed you have, sir."

I can't imagine what my bonus is going to be, Alissa, but apparently it's going to be a hefty one, "for the inconvenience, lurve."

9

Tonight we returned to our usual mode of dining. After Hannibal woke us from our siestas at 6:15, we repaired to the backyard and the picnic table next to the outdoor fireplace. On the top grill, farthest from the coals, Hannibal already had O'Twoomey's favorite dish simmering, one O'Twoomey claims not to eat but more often than not does. O'Twoomey claims he merely wants the odors pervading his senses, his very being. "Ambrosial, *utterly ambrosial.*" His mouth waters, thwap, thwap, thwap. After lining a great iron skillet with olive oil and garlic powder, Hannibal throws in a half dozen Italian sausages, a dozen chopped bell peppers, and two or three sliced Maui onions. Often this mixture simmers away to blackness and nothing. O'Twoomey eats it anyway.

At one end of the picnic table was the ice chest full of cubes, O'Twoomey's Boodles gin and postprandial J&B Scotch, the bottle of Noilly Prat vermouth that has gone unopened for two years, and my Smirnoff red label vodka, along with a pitcher of freshly squeezed grapefruit juice. Besides her other staggering daily tip, Sissy gets an additional thirty dollars just for that pitcher of fresh juice. In front of that were seven inch-thick Delmonicos thawing on the morning *Advertiser,* three for Toby, who had returned from one of his nefarious errands, three for Hannibal, who is so in awe of Toby he does everything Toby does, even tries to dress like him, and one for me. Before the steaks lay a kettle of Toby's special salad, one taught to him by one of his Chinese girls. As nearly as I can determine, there are two kinds of lettuce, iceberg and romaine, cucumber, tomato, bamboo shoots, avocado, apple, and walnuts, topped by a delicious dressing whose ingredients Toby typically refuses to reveal. If it contains those prurience-inducing herbs, Alissa, I don't appear to be getting any more than my customary infrequent hard-ons or having visions of sullying *Playboy* centerfolds (my blood pressure medication, don't you know?). Next to the salad lay six Kona Gold joints, rolled so immaculately by Toby they honestly look like Camels. Hannibal is a mess after one, but because Toby smokes three during the course of an evening Hannibal smokes three also.

Walking to the outdoor wooden pantry, I unlocked it, opened a twelve-ounce can of Planters mixed nuts and one of cashews, then opened two cans of macadamia nuts, put the various nuts into three imitation cut glass ruby canapé dishes I picked up on sale at Liberty House at the Ala Moana Plaza, a set of four I bought as a present for O'Twoomey from his own money. "Aren't you the thoughtful one, lurve?" He used to eat the fattening nuts directly from the cans, but in that way he could gauge how many he was eating and I wasn't able to add more salt, as I do now, hidden behind the pantry. Nobody but O'Twoomey eats the nuts or the extra-sharp Monterey Jack cheddar cheese I cut up and put in the final canapé dish, along with four or five tablespoons of Plochman's horseradish mustard. O'Twoomey hasn't figured out why we forego the snacks. Like so many grossly obese people, O'Twoomey has affected a politesse of eating so grotesque as to be laughable. Until he gets a couple of those Boodles into him and goes for a fistful at a time, O'Twoomey airily picks up one or two nuts, with loving delicacy places them on his salivating tongue, chews elegantly, swallows, washes them down with a sip of Boodles, then in some shanty-Irish parody of fastidiousness extravagantly licks his fingers, thwap, thwap, thwap, all the while his eyes closed, moaning in orgasmic pleasure. Within three or four minutes every dish of nuts and a good deal of the cheese is covered, like heavy dew, with a nauseating film of his saliva.

O'Twoomey has no idea why he keeps balooning up "on snacks," he lives in blissful ignorance of the calories in a single Queensland nut, and one night I saw him eat two cans of these, one each of the mixed and cashew nuts and better than two pounds of the cheese, topped off by three or four shrunken sausages and the blackened peppers and onions swimming in olive oil and sausage fat. If his weight, the booze, the fat, and the salt don't get him soon, Alissa, I don't know what will. O'Twoomey manifests all the symptoms of a walking time bomb, but I worry so much about ridding the world of him that I expect I'll be in a wheelchair before him and my hope is that high blood pressure is in fact, as the cautionary advertisements proclaim, the hidden disease.

I'd be able to kill him a lot sooner if he didn't take his "business calls" during Julia Child and was thereby able to listen to her prepare her Gratin of Potatoes *à la Lyonnaise* or her desserts, caramel-topped pear poached in white wine and set in gooey chocolate tarts, perhaps her *Bombe aux Trois Chocolates,* dishes I'm sure he'd have wanted prepared. At one time O'Twoomey took his calls—it is 9 P.M. in Ireland—on the wall phone of the veranda, but he talked so loudly, and the calls are often of such a sinisterly personal nature, that I suggested he have his own phone installed. He must have thought I meant installed near the TV so we wouldn't miss Miss Julia, for that is where we found it when we came one afternoon from the golf course, a brilliant kelly green wall phone, with a long cord so Hannibal or I could hand it to him, mounted on the side of the fireplace. On the day—it was two days after Lord Mountbatten was blown up on his fishing boat, *Shadow V*, on Donegal Bay— that Julia did various pizzas, including an onion one that would have been great with Maui onions and on which I could have tripled the amount of provolone, O'Twoomey took one of his calls from Eire and talked so long I couldn't get the go-ahead for six or eight of these. "Pizza? But that's wog food, Frederick. You know I refuse to eat wog food." O'Twoomey wouldn't eat wog sausage, Alissa, until Toby and I ordered some in Honolulu and he decided to sample ours. The next thing we knew he was asking the proprietor where he got it, which led him to the butcher who now makes up twenty pounds a week for him and has it flown over, iced. It is these calls from Eire that make me certain O'Twoomey is with the provisional wing of the IRA and that, at the very least, whatever illicit monies—way too much to be realized from sweepstakes tickets—he and Toby are raking in hand over fist—are being channeled to those madmen, perhaps in the form of guns and explosives. But how, and why, from Hawaii, Alissa?

"Yes, poor, poor Mountbatten. A lurverly chap, they tell me. Educated at Osbourne and all that tommyrot, don't you know? Liz and the family called him 'Uncle Dickie'? That intimate, huh? Oh, but it'll be a lurverly wake. Yes, yes, I know all about it. So they have McGirl and McMahon. They don't know anything—stupid, stupid boyos. And the bleeding bastard fucking press. I told you it had to be spelled out for them. Who was supposed to paint a map of a partitioned India on the jetty? Every report I've seen thinks it's just a senseless terrorist attack on a harmless senile old man because he's royalty. I thought this was to be an act of war against the monster who partitioned India, then pulled out and left in his bleeding wake one of the great bleeding bloodbaths of fucking history. I thought it was supposed to be an illustration of what the bleeding Limeys might expect in Ireland—another India, that is—if they don't soon get their troops out of there. Of course, they have twenty-two less troops now. Dear me, the shame of it all. I thought this was supposed to illustrate what the historical result of partition has always been. And always will be."

On and on it went. Because I didn't want to hear I twice tried to walk away, but O'Twoomey signaled Hannibal to sit me back down, then pointed impatiently at the TV screen to inform me I should mind my business and watch Julia make her onion pizzas. Afterward—and I must have been temporarily deranged by O'Twoomey's insouciant smugness, Alissa, for ordinarily I pretend I hear nary a word—I said, "Anybody who'd do that to Lord Mountbatten, a seventy-nine-year-old man out for a little fishing, is nothing but a cowardly savage."

O'Twoomey laughed raucously, cracked his fat hand against his fat thigh, and cried, "You may be right, lurve, you may just be right! But then, the Brit imperialists wrote the book on pusillanimity and savagery and assuredly it's something they understand. In fact, lurve, it may be the only thing they understand!"

Although as a citizen of the Republic O'Twoomey isn't allowed to take his seat in the House of Lords, he claims to be a peer of the realm, the Duke of Lisdoonvarna. His heraldic crest is a Boheena, a freshwater mermaid passionately clasping to her ample bosom—so her nipples will be hidden to the Irish clerics, I assume—a great cumbersome knightly sword, a veritable Excalibur. Of course O'Twoomey refuses to mock his lineage by personally displaying his crest (he leaves that to us!)—says he won't do so until Ireland is reunited—but his tailor does have it stitched in red, green, gold, and black into the fly of his custom-made skivvies. Since 1921, when the Irish Free State declared its independence of England, Irish peers have not only been denied their seats in Parliament, they have, ironically, been refused the apostate gesture of disavowing their titles and, according to O'Twoomey, he is Lord Lisdoonvarna whether he chooses to be or not. Hence I expect his pee-stained heraldic crest is in a sense a tacit protest against what he appears to be attacking in a more devious and alarming way.

As with everything else, O'Twoomey's schizophrenia regarding his lineage is striking. Because the Dole field workers—O'Twoomey calls them rice-eyes—have Saturdays and Sundays off and take over the E. B. Cavendish Golf Course and White Manele Beach, O'Twoomey refuses to stay on Lanai and mingle with the wogs, and on Saturday mornings Toby flies us to Honolulu, where we check into the legendary Pink Palace, the Royal Hawaiian, invariably into the same rooms, a two-bedroom suite on the second floor of the main building for O'Twoomey and an armed Toby and adjoining rooms, 1600 and 1602, for Hannibal and me on the top floor of the relatively new Towers, overlooking the pool and Waikiki Beach. Except in our rooms or at the pool and beach, we are required at all times to wear the tailor-made kelly green linen jackets with O'Twoomey's heraldic crest stitched on the pockets—we are, I gather, O'Twoomey's royal entourage—over the heart, we all have kelly green bathing trunks with the crest on the right thigh, we even have it on our laundry bags. Doubtless we are the only group in history who ever checked into the Royal Hawaiian weekly, were taken to their rooms and immediately dialed room service to have a week or two weeks' soiled linen picked up for twenty-four-hour service. If you can believe this, Alissa, whenever on these weekends we are in O'Twoomey's presence we are required to address him as "your grace." One late Saturday afternoon O'Twoomey, Toby, Hannibal, Robin, and I were seated at the outdoor Mai Tai bar debating where to go for dinner, O'Twoomey asked if I were ready for another vodka (*whatkah* in Hawaii, as in the Bahamas), without thinking I said, "No thanks, Seamus," and the next thing I knew Toby was, as punishment for my indiscretion, flying Hannibal and me back to Lanai, only to drop us off at the airport and fly back to Oahu to complete his weekend guarding Lord Lisdoonvarna. For that reason, Al, in Honolulu I no longer address O'Twoomey by name at all, simply respond to his queries with a yes or no.

10

O'Twoomey had this idea that because of his illicit activities (whatever they are) he ought to maintain harmonious relations with the wogs, that he ought to become a *bruh* to the vanquished and downtrodden against the day he and Toby get busted, hoping, I expect, that the natives will raise such a hue and cry in protest that he and Toby will get off lightly. Hence he set Robin up in her own public relations firm, Lisdoonvarna Ltd., gave her unlimited funds, office space on the ground floor of the hotel, and has her greasing every extended palm in the islands, as well, no doubt, as lathering no few on-the-take wog *lingams* with K-Y jelly. Furnished by Antiques Pacifica, which also has commercial space in the hotel, the Lisdoonvarna Ltd. office is, save for the banal Gauguin prints on the walls, genuinely splendid, especially when Ms. Robin Glenn, seated at her great bare teakwood desk and seen easily from the lobby corridor through the floor-to-ceiling glass, is triumphantly barking orders into her gold leaf antique French desk phone. The goggle-eyed tourists are not in the least aware she is probably talking to one of her lovers.

Robin's main outside account is a group called Ohana, which an authority on Hawaiian writing in *The Advertiser* said best translates as "an extension of the family," that is, Alissa, if you'd spent some time here and were told by a Hawaiian that you had become *ohana* he would be paying you the ultimate compliment of saying you were now blood of his blood, all very nonsensically romantic and highfalutin'. With this group Robin has the unhappy—unhappy to a sane person—task of convincing them that to support their activities she is raising thousands of dollars from sympathizers around the islands at the same time they understand completely that the anonymous donors are Lord Lisdoonvarna period.

As a group they are much given to self-dramatization and remind me of our mainland Indians, wear faded Levi's, Levi vests displaying their mahogany biceps, puka necklaces, gold pirate earrings, and Aunt Jemima bandanas on their heads. Their beards also come out in black splotchy patches, but to no avail I've asked Robin to try to persuade them to remain a businesslike clean shaven. Not to be outdone, Robin's outfits of denim pants and jackets, made by O'Twoomey's tailor, are something to behold, done as they are in guava, lemon, Natal plum red, honeydew, pineapple, avocado, plantain, pistachio, papaya, cantaloupe, and so forth, with bandanas dyed to match. Beneath the jackets Robin wears white silk shirts, invariably unbuttoned and revealing heartbreakingly ripe décolletage. She also has her shirttails hauled up and knotted at her diaphragm. Because her pants are tailored to her hips, there is always on display a great triangle of golden brown flesh, comely with a whisper of down, and dotted in the lower middle with an erotically buried belly button. Beneath her breeches she wears white bikini panties, the appetizing outlines of which can more often than not be seen in the striking Hawaiian light. Up home, as you know, Al, the guys call this the VPL, for visible panty line, a Woody Allen *mot*. When she struts, statuesquely, about the hotel, her hair pulled tautly beneath her honeydew bandana, her long opihi shell earrings aglitter, all heads turn, and turn, and turn yet again. Believe it, Alissa, when I say I've heard audible gasps. So inviting as to be absurd, Robin is a torture to the blood. If only she'd been struck dumb at birth.

The other day Mr. Einhorn, the hotel manager, called during the Julia Child hour and asked Lord Lisdoonvarna if he might persuade Robin to wear her shirt tucked into her trousers, perhaps give the mainlanders a little less décolletage. There had, it seems, been an unfortunate incident. One Percival Applegate, a fifty-eight-year-old sugarcane broker from San Francisco who has been checking into the Royal Hawaiian twice a year for better than three decades, had in his lust for Robin gone beserk and been guilty of an indiscretion. Although Percival was an admitted alcoholic—he'd been dry for fifteen years—he'd got drunk and strangled the switchboard operator until she'd revealed Robin's address at the marina in Hawaii Kai. He'd gone to the *Cirrhosis of the River* at 4 A.M., kicked in the door of the houseboat, and had been badly beaten up by one of Robin's Ohana chums before the cops arrived and arrested him for aggravated assault, breaking and entering, drunkenness, and public lewdness. Apparently the poor drip—a grandfather to four spewing brats in Marin County—had burst through the door with his fly unzipped and his manhood all afluster.

I picked up most of what happened when O'Twoomey called Robin back to tell her he wanted the charges dropped immediately and detailed how she might comport herself in a more pristine manner. Before he hung up he listened a moment, smiling impatiently, then said, "Oh, Frederick? Frederick is in his room working on the masterpiece." He winked outrageously at me. "No, don't worry, Robin. Frederick shall be none the wiser, my dear. Frederick shall be none the wiser."

What a field day I was going to have with this, Alissa, having access to information Robin didn't know I had and seeing what she could do with the facts as I understood them. I had no doubt Robin would have been raped repeatedly, and that had not the Ohana dude shown up at 4 A.M.—doubtless he'd be accounted for by saying he'd come to squire her to the windward side of the island to observe some mumbo-jumbo Ohana sunrise ritual over a pile of washed rocks—she'd unquestionably be dead, a lot of tears here, hard proclamations of her innocence and a good deal of wacky disjointed eloquence on the frightening burdens of walking about the dreary world as such a flabbergastingly handsome creature, an accident of birth for which the pitiable Robin could hardly be held responsible.

What always stuns me, Alissa, as a writer, I mean, and owning a natural vanity about my own imagination, is what a paltry thing it is beside Robin's authentically demented one. When she strutted through the door of 1602 that Saturday morning, and Hannibal had locked it behind her, she dropped her alligator leather balloon bag containing her sexual accoutrements (more of that momentarily), flung herself onto the king-size bed, heaved a great sigh, and said, "I suppose you want to fuck me, Frederick. Everyone else does." Robin's white silk shirt was tucked into her hip huggers, buttoned to her regal throat, and a second Natal plum red bandana was being used as a Western necktie.

"Well, no, not if you don't want me to, Robin." She did not respond. She sighed theatrically again, eyes ceilingward, indicating that whatever was bugging her would have to be elicited, it was utterly too awful to be freely volunteered. "You somehow look different, Robin. Oh, I know what it is. You have on a necktie! And your blouse is tucked in!"

Robin began to sob, savagely. Were not people cruel beyond belief, Frederick? Cruel, cruel, *cruel*? A man—"a drunken fucking *haole* tourist" (naturally)—had come up to her in the lobby and told her how much more attractive she'd be if she wore her shirt in such a way that didn't expose her stretch marks. Stretch marks? Now listen closely, Alissa, as I cry out to you as a trained analyst. It wasn't so much that I knew Robin had never had a child, but that only the weekend before and before and before ad infinitum throughout my now endless incarceration my tongue had spent all kinds of time lapping about that astonishingly golden area so free of any marks whatever as to drive poor grandpappy Percival Applegate mad with lust. My first reaction was, of course, one of hopeless futility, which instantly turned into that frustrating fury you must have long ago learned to control, my impulse to leap up, charge to the bed, now grab her fiercely by the nape of the neck, bend her over double so that her eyes were two inches from that lovely tum-tum and cry, "Look, look, look! There are no fucking marks whatever, for Jesus Almighty's sake!"

If you'd taught me nothing else, Alissa, you'd taught me the patience to know that in order to learn the extent of her fantasies and therefore her malaise I'd have to hear her out—hear Robin out if, in my case, for no other reason than not to offend her and thereby risk one of her haughty, regal-necked exits, sit there and listen dumbfounded, my yellow poplin golf shorts bulging with desire, offend her, and risk her leaving me with a week's harbored and coddled lust. Robin was working on the assumption that I of course knew all about the child—but was she really, Alissa? You'll have to answer that for me—and hence, taking a deep breath, I took a chance on gender (it was after all 50–50, better than roulette's red or black at Vegas, which is 26–24) and said, "How is the boy anyway, Robin?"

"Oh, he's fine, getting to be quite the little man. Still living with Denno's sister in Waimea. The sister claims to have adopted him and young Denno bears her married name. It'll be no time at all before Denno has him in Punahoe, thence it'll be off to the mainland and Harvard, then either Harvard or Columbia Law, Denno thinks. He'll be governor of the islands by the time he's thirty, president I should say before he's forty-five. And you know what's the worst part of the shit Denno pulled on me, Frederick? Even after I agreed to have his child?—I mean, Denno knew fucking well no pure Buddha-head, American war hero's son or not, could ever reach the White House unless he possessed a fine-looking strain of *haole* blood—the prick never came through on that Kahoolawe deal. And the only time I ever get to see young Denno—my own flesh and blood, Frederick!—is when Denno's sister brings him to the hotel for a fucking haircut."

Jesus H. Bygoddamn Kheeeriiiiist, Alissa, bear with me on this! Knowing your aversion to TV, I expect you've never seen *Hawaii 5-0*, the usual cops-and-robbers foolishness enhanced only by being set in the islands. In the show the boss, Steve McGarrett (played by Jack Lord), keeps addressing his sidekick, Dan Williams (played—poorly, I might add—by James MacArthur, the adopted son of playwright Charles MacArthur and Helen Hayes and nephew to John D. MacArthur, the Florida billionaire now estimated, since the death of Hughes and Getty, to be the richest man in the world) as Dano. Pronounced here more nearly as Denno ("Book him, Denno, murder one" has become part of our TV mythology), it is the Hawaiian nickname or endearment for Daniel, and the only person Robin ever, *ever* refers to as Denno is none other than—guess?—Senator Daniel Inouye, the legislator you so much admired during the Nixon impeachment proceedings. Or did admire until he started fawning all over ex-CIA chief Richard Helms, congratulating him for his frank and forthright testimony, only for us later to hear that your ughs were right on target and that Helms had been bullshitting those senators all over the place. Not only that but, as you pointed out, Helms at one point reminded them that he'd "been around this town a long time," which, you said, seemed to be Helms's way of saying, "Listen, you little pissants, I've got a file on every one of your indiscretions thicker than Webster's unabridged."

Robin has met Inouye once, at most twice, and I would guess the total time he gave her was only a few minutes. Some months back a splinter group of Ohana called Protect Kahoolawe Ohana attempted to stop the U.S. naval bombing of Kahoolawe, a small (compared with the rest of the islands) pile of rock and shrubs, without water and hence with no commercial value, which on clear days can often be seen from White Manele Beach on Lanai. More than seen. From Lanai one can often hear the navy jets bombing Kahoolawe (it sounds like dynamiting at a distant construction site). Decreed by Presidential Executive Order 10436, the federal courts are not empowered to rescind it. Just as our mainland Indians claim an interstate highway is to be built through consecrated burial grounds, so the Ohana group claims this pile of volcanic rock is sacred acreage. In protest they took an ill-prepared group to Washington, were generally rebuffed by both Hawaii's representatives and a capital press corps that didn't know what they were talking about, and especially were they ignored by Senator Inouye's office. They returned to the islands furious —perhaps Robin had even persuaded them to shave and wash their Levi's before leaving—vowing another Wounded Knee and that blood would flow in rivers. At that time, to console her comrades-in-arms, Robin told them that Inouye owed her a favor—I heard her say this on 1602's phone!— and that she would damn well set things aright.

Now this was only a year ago, and despite her bullshit about Inouye's owing her a favor, Robin had never before met the man. I know because I rewrote her rambling, hysterical, unconsciously amusing, and lofty-minded letter to him, and in a few declarative sentences came directly to the point and asked for a few minutes of his time to discuss the bombing of Kahoolawe. Moreover, when Robin at last heard from him, he gave her that few minutes on a Saturday afternoon when he was back in the islands for a long weekend. Moreover still, because it was a Saturday Hannibal and I, for lack of something to do, accompanied her to Inouye's Honolulu office and waited in the parking lot no more than ten or twelve minutes for her triumphant return. Assuming Inouye saw her right away, Robin could not have had more than seven or eight minutes with him. Dressed in her avocado Levi suit and bandana, displaying plenty of tanned tum-tum and ripe chest, she slammed the door of the

Porsche, sighed contentedly and said, "Well, that's taken care of, Mister Cynical Know-it-all Frederick Exley."

"Eese goot, *eese goot,* 'obin."

"Fat fucking chance."

"But why are you always so negative, Frederick? Why, why, *why*?"

I simply wasn't about to explain it to her again, Alissa. After December 7, 1941, in one of the more notoriously shameful episodes in our history, the Japanese-Americans on the West Coast had their properties confiscated, their asses thrown into peremptorily erected concentration camps, and haven't to this day been formally apologized to by way of adequate federal compensation. In Hawaii an entirely different thing occurred. There the Hawaiian Japanese-Americans were allowed to enlist in the 442nd Regimental Combat Team. Sent to Europe, they were given, literally, some of the most abominable assignments of the European campaign, took staggering casualties (it was where Inouye lost his arm), and for Robin even to imagine she was going to flash a little skin at Inouye or anyone else in the power structure (men well into their fifties and sixties able to remember Pearl Harbor) and have him lift a finger to prevent our navy's being prepared against any such future eventuality was the kind of lunatic fantasizing that permits hack lawyers to allow Indians to believe the government is going to give them a grand an acre for the entire Adirondack State Park or return the Black Hills of the Dakotas to them. Not only are the survivors of the 442nd (many of whom live on Lanai, where I've cautioned Robin against mouthing any Ohana nonsense on the veranda of the Lodge) among the most elitely proud, and rightfully so, private clubs in the world (beside these dudes, your chums at the Harvard Club don't even know what snobbery means, Al) but there was no way that Protect Kahoolawe Ohana was going to elicit anything from them but a sardonic smile, rather as if you'd asked General Patton to stop his armored divisions in the face of .22 target pistols.

This historical digression aside, Robin had taken her

lie to Ohana that Inouye owed her something, when in fact she'd never met the man, and fantasized his debt into her having agreed to give the senator a half-Caucasian son (no doubt Inouye was magnetically drawn to her Smith-Vassar-Sarah Lawrence background and all that tommyrot, don't you know?) who'd soon be old enough to enter Punahoe, the islands' leading *haole* prep school, which forgets all about race when recruiting football players, and thence it was off to your alma mammy, Al, and on to the governor's mansion and the White House long before he even reached my enfeebled age. *Hi yoooohhhhh, Silver!* By now, I was seated on the edge of the bed, my golf shorts cramping my embarrassing lust, I had my legs crossed, one bare thigh resting atop the other cramping my ardor, and I was gently massaging Robin's stomach through her silk shirt. One of my ex-wives, Alissa, had had an inordinate aversion to stretch marks, I had spent the latter months of her pregnancy nightly rubbing cocoa butter into her bulge (to no avail), and, because the moment still wasn't right for Robin, I was using this finger rubbing motion I'd used in that long-ago, nearly obliterated time.

"How old would young Denno be now, Robin?"

"Oh, Frederick, *Frederick*, he's almost nine! Almost nine! On March 28 he'll be nine!"

March 28 is, of course, my birthday, Alissa. But that is no matter, it was nearly time. This was no banal soap opera, this was opera on the epic perches. Robin's arms were about my neck, she'd reverted to her savage sobbing (her tears against my cheek were as scalding as those of any other creature in pain), and as her tear flow began to subside, I removed my massaging fingers from her torso, took them to her breasts and continued gently rubbing there, through the silk shirt. When at length the tears stopped, and her arms dropped laxly to her sides, I rose, unbuttoned and unzipped her Natal plum hip huggers, ever so slowly and gently because they were so taut to her skin, removed them, then her white satin bikini panties, in one perfunctory motion dropped my yellow poplin golf and Jockey shorts to the carpeting, and without removing her shirt or mine mounted and penetrated her astonishing wetness; for, before Freud as god, Alissa, I swear Robin's thunderingly deranged stories not only excite me beyond the bounds of anything resembling refinement, but so enrapture her that during her mad monologues she apparently discharges and her backside appears to be covered with a wet coat of shellac. I was, as I say, so agitated that it was strictly a slam-bam-thank-you-ma'am. But then, Alissa, it had only just begun.

"Are you into imagination, Frederick?" Robin once asked me. Now how about that for a rhetorical question, Alissa, I mean directed to the dude I call Exley who prides himself on an imagination he likes to think runs the gamut from the utterly morbid and diseased to the rarefied and heady heights of the generous and eloquent? And that is how it all began. We had taken a long swim on Waikiki, had washed the sand and sea salt from us at the pool shower, had repaired to 1602, and had no sooner entered the room when Robin threw that one at me.

"Well, I would most certainly hope so."

"No, I mean, you know, Frederick, sexual imagination?"

On that day Robin had on a 1972 Olympic tank suit, blue with red, white, and blue stripes running vertically from her crotch to the V of her breasts, one of those featherweight garments that seem to weigh no more than stealthy fog moving among trees, and I had on His Grace's kelly green trunks with the Boheena crest stitched to the right thigh. Apparently I was supposed to be the coach of the Olympic swim team, hilarious in itself because, though I had in youth been a gifted swimmer—having grown up on the river and Lake Ontario—Robin could now spot me fifty meters and beat me in the hundred-meter freestyle. And I was further, according to Robin, supposed to be screwing all the other girls on the team but poor, poor Robin and as we had now found ourselves alone in the locker room for the first time Robin insisted she needed to unwind from the excruciating rigors of training as badly as the other girls and, great tears of self-pity in her eyes, demanded to know what was so repugnant about her? Robin of course provided me with my own "rational" answer. It was because I found her so breathtaking, intelligent, and high-minded that I was utterly terrified of getting into it with her and finding myself without the ironfisted will to unshackle myself and hence find myself "hooked for life."

Now Robin approached, rubbed her breasts against me, and coyly demanded to know what would be the matter with that, what, what, *what*, could I not, Frederick, envision a life together? *Mrs. Robin Exley* she again and again lolled about her salivating palate. To make a long story infinitely longer, dear old Al, Robin even made me lug the goddamn king-size mattress from the bed onto the carpeting, suggestive, I expect, of those locker room mats swimmers often rest upon. Because distaff swimmers seem to be getting younger every year (one famous coach was quoted as implying you had to get them before they got into guys, that once they started screwing their brains became scrambled and they wouldn't win you doodly-squat, which must have gone down marvelously with Ms. Steinem and Billie Jean and the girls), Robin was only fourteen or fifteen, a virgin, natch, I had of course to go through some painstaking foreplay, be ever so delicate and gentle about penetration, but by the time it was over Robin was crying stuff like, "Oh, this is ever so much better than a blue ribbon! No, it's better than a bronze! Better than a silver! God, God, God, Frederick, it's better than a fucking gold!"

After we'd lain in each other's arms for some time, we rose, removed our shirts, Robin picked up her alligator balloon bag, we went into the bathroom, took a shower together, lathering each other, toweled ourselves dry, and I returned to the bedroom, poured myself a stiff vodka and grapefruit juice and sat down to wait. I never knew, Alissa, what garments Robin had in her bag. What I did know was that we'd long ago exhausted her erotic repertoire, the games had become repetitious to the point—fun though at one time they'd been—of driving me round the bend; and I am now forced to point out to you, Alissa, that despite the incredible hurt we have over the years heaped on one another, in the good times, in the very good times, in the lovely, enchanted times, we never, *never* found the need to fuck anyone but each other, warts and all.

When Robin at last emerged from the bathroom she had her hair in pigtails, she wore a lemon-yellow short-sleeved cashmere sweater, a steel-gray pleated skirt with a slit running from hip to hem and a great outsized decorative gold safety pin joining the slit at the thigh, one of my generation's garments, dark green cabled knee socks, and loafers with fucking pennies in them. Now listen closely, Al, and let me explain the way Robin had taken a perfectly truthful story I told her about an adolescent sexual experience and how she had transformed it; for, as you can well imagine, Robin would keep me up half the night beseeching, imploring, nay, fumingly entreating me to relate, in unsparing detail, every sexual experience I'd ever had, did so until I went quite mad with zany preposterousness and gave her some genuinely wondrous stuff straight from the top of my septic dome. Can you guess, for example, what I told her about you? Do you know those quarter-inch cubes bartenders are now packing into rock glasses? As any drunk knows, Al, and drunks know everything, with these cubes the sleazebags can have their pourers set at half an ounce, give you very little mix, so that whenever I'm in a place that uses these I insist on both a free pour into a shot glass, as well as a bottle of mix on the side, insisting I like to mix my own. Well, ma'am, I told Robin you liked to have your vagina plugged with these cubes before intercourse.

"*What in the world does that do, Frederick?*"

"Christ, Robin, what a sexual novice you are! A guy can keep a hard-on for about six hours that way!"

And I'll be goddamned, Alissa, if Robin didn't insist on trying it. You know of course what happened. The frightful hog shriveled to the size of a sun-baked grape, and

I had to explain it away by saying there was apparently some mysterious and unaccountable anatomical difference between you and Robin. Yeah, I know, Alissa, thanks a lot, Ex.

Be that as it may, when I was a hotshot high school basketball player, one night after a game I came up from the locker room with the guys, was handed a sealed envelope by a girl I didn't know, I put it into my overcoat pocket, and the guys and I piled into a couple cars and drove to the top of Washington Street hill to the Circle Inn, where they weren't finicky about checking draft cards—the legal age was then eighteen and most of us were seventeen and eighteen in any event—and where you could get a bottle of Genesee for twenty cents, so that if a guy had three bucks he was, as we then said, "holding the heavy."

Halfway through my first beer, I took the note over to the light of the jukebox, discovered it was from a very attractive classmate I'd never known had any feeling for me one way or another, she said she was babysitting for a wealthy couple who'd gone to Syracuse for the evening and if after the game I came over I could do with her what I must. After I'd finished a couple Ginnys, I had one of the guys drive me into the city, naturally making him drop me six blocks from my destination so he wouldn't know where I was going, then walked to the address I'd been given in the note.

What I could "do with her what I must" turned out to entail—oh, ecstasy!—being allowed to kiss her breasts, play a little "stink finger"—I wasn't even allowed to remove her panties, had to slide my hand under them—and I received a hand job. Halfway through this, she asked if I had a handkerchief and when I said no, she fled to the kitchen, came back with a still damp dishrag, and all the time I was coming into it, she had the dishrag strangled fiercely over the head of my penis, her head was turned away, she was making nauseous *ugh* sounds and over and over, repeating "*disgusting, disgusting, disgusting, ugh—*"

Now listen, Alissa, the only reasonably accurate thing Robin drew from this story was what the girl was wearing, the fact that my generation was without the pill and hence deathly afraid of becoming pregnant or inducing pregnancy, and by mental gymnastic leaps across the years Robin transposed my rather grotesquely amusing tale a generation or two to her more "enlightened" adolescence. First Robin would give me a blowjob, so she could keep her teeny-bopper outfit on, I'd then lift her steel-gray wool skirt, remove her panties, perform cunnilingus, after which she'd orally bring me up again, just happen, at age seventeen mind you, to have a ribbed Trojan and some K-Y jelly handy—I never heard of K-Y until I was forty and a fag friend, an entertainer I much admired, told me about it—and then we'd have anal intercourse to prevent pregnancy, all this supposed to have taken place in Watertown fucking New York in the forties! Listen, Al, coming from my generation I never had the guts to get down between the lovely old thighs and take a look at one until I was twenty-five, never performed cunnilingus until I did so with you, I was twenty-eight then, you were seventeen and would never be so lovely again, no offense intended because you are now so much lovelier in other ways. So as we now began on the bed, I was naked next to a clothed Robin, for her imagination was such that, thank God, she never required that I get myself up in what-ever in the hell it was I wore in high school, and she began blowing me, having forever and forever and forever been denied the truth that I'd been blown frequently in high school. But that is another story, one that one does not tell to loonies like Robin, for in that story there is sorrow beyond measure, grief so deep it resides in those darkest pits where damning life abides, not a little unavoidable black humor and a guilt so terrible that there are times, after all these years, I can hardly bear to think upon it.

Part Four

BLOWJOB

Her name was Cassandra "Cass" McIntyre,
Cassandra of course being a healer of men, and she was an
orphan and lived in the Jefferson County Home for Children
on outer State Street in Watertown. I know now, in my
fifties when with any luck and any smarts one might just
begin to acquire that elusive thing called wisdom, that I
loved her more than any woman I ever knew, more than
Alissa, more even than dear, loony Robin. Of course I
then did not know that I'd end by both denying and be-
traying Cass, or that backing a high school football line
and loving to whack and put hurt on an opponent have
nothing whatever to do with courage.

Long before I heard the Brigadier was involved with
Cass, I had had a thing for her that had begun in junior
high school when I was in the ninth grade and Cass in the
eighth. It was, I expect, not unlike a case of angina where,
when the patient walks too rapidly or goes abruptly up a

‡   269

staircase, a steady burning ache below the sternum begins, an illness that might easily be rectified by the afflicted's losing twenty pounds and throwing away his cigarettes. When one learns, as I did when I first asked about Cass, that he is unable, be he the most iron-willed dude in Christendom, to shred either the weight or the weeds and must continue to live with the moroseness of a valetudinarian, it is no happy discovery.

Cass was, I was told, an orphan and lived at the orphan's home on State Street. In what way was I told? In a way of course that emphatically signaled any further discussion of Cass as a human being, least of all a lass to be wooed, was precluded if not boringly time-consuming. In the first place, and this is what was so finally and formidably tacit among the guys, the girls at the Home were so rigorously supervised and confined that the idea of getting them alone long enough to hold hands was an insurmountable one. Even as seniors in high school, if one could persuade one's mother to write a note to the head of the Home seeking permission to escort one of the girls to a dance, one had to have her back to the Home by 10 P.M., have her back, in effect, when the dance was only beginning.

And the idea of making such a request of one's mother was an even more insurmountable one. Lord, how easily and smugly mothers transferred the stigma of abandoning parents to those faultless children, in their ignorance not in the least realizing, my mother included, that what they were really saying was that if they had to put up with their spouses and four spewing brats the rest of the world could damn well abide by the same schismless rules. Looking back, and I say this in utter sincerity, I doubt I had a single friend during the forties and fifties whose parents wouldn't have split a dozen times—I know mine would have—had they not been bound together by an evangelical trepidation of a vengeful God visiting his wrath for violating their marriage vows and, foremostly, being blistered together by a Depression poverty so exacerbating they simply hadn't the wampum to split. If the postwar affluence has done nothing else, then, it has allowed a man or a woman the exhilarating freedom to say, "Toodle-oooo, asshole, I can't hack this shit one second longer," a gesture, I hasten to add, that two ex-wifes and uncountable girls have visited upon me.

So from the ninth grade to my senior year in high school, I learned to live with the burning ache, never in my wildest imagination dreaming that the angina would be cured by the cause of it, Cass herself. Although it is doubtless physiologically impossible, I cannot remember Cass changing in the four years from the day, in the halls of South Junior High, I first became smitten with her to the day I denied and betrayed her. In everyone's past there is the pipsqueak adolescent who, like the Jolly Green Giant, sprouts eight inches over the summer holiday and is miraculously transmogrified from a perky runt to the star who leads his school to the state basketball championship. But what happened to Cass between the seventh grade, when I was totally oblivious to her, and the eighth grade was even more miraculous. Cass became a woman.

And, as I have said, and though I'm certain that by the eleventh grade the lines of her figure must have grown more alarmingly feminine, her flesh more pulpously appetizing, I stared at Cass so much during those four years— and I could hardly have been alone in this furtive, gnawing watching—it was as impossible to detect changes as it is for a spouse to detect the day-to-day weight loss of his scrupulously dieting mate. In an orange-and-white checkerboard cotton dress with a white dickey collar and a little orange bow, she came at me in the halls, her mountain of books cradled in her arms and quashed firmly to her lovely new-formed breasts, disguising them from guys buoyant with an inarticulated screaming lust. Thinking her a new addition to the school, and wanting to lay groundwork for a blissful future, I stared at her in the hope that she would look my way that I might play Joe Good Guy and give her a welcoming nod. As I gazed, I detected a habit Cass never lost in all the time I knew her. Deep in long thoughts, and I can understand now that Cass was beleaguered, distraught, stunned by how foolish—nay, downright simpleminded— her recent anatomical changes had rendered the young men about her, Cass's response to perplexity was to lay the tip of her tongue on her lower lip and grip it with her upper, so that it looked the tip of a juicy peach suspended between puckered moist lips. When Cass came abruptly up from her heavy thoughts, a child drowning in a new sexuality that was frightening her beyond the bounds, her lovely blue eyes gone alarmingly wide at finding herself back in the pedestrian world of rowdy classmates and clanging lockers, and I gave her my nice-guy, strictly aboveboard, nothing-up-my-sleeves smile of greeting, not only Cass's light copper-colored face but her entire body, ears and throat, dimpled knees and sturdy calves, seemed to diffuse instantly with the blood of self-conscious shyness, she nodded in response, the delectable peach was withdrawn and her enticing lips formed a word that sounded very like—surprise!—"Fred."

It is now two, perhaps three, weeks later and, having ascended Thompson Boulevard on my bicycle, I am riding over Park Drive toward my home on Moffett Street. A walking Cass, whom I've met at the top of Thompson Boulevard near Gotham Street, is now an invited though reluctant passenger on the crossbar of my silver-gray balloon-tired beauty. In the two or three weeks since I learned, with that "Fred" spoken out of her moist lips, that Cass knew who I was, I have also learned that she is an orphan and has been since at least kindergarten when she enrolled in the Thompson Park Grammar School where the orphans went. Moreover, and talk about putting her out of reach, my informant told me Cass was so nice, and shy, she found it impossible to say hello to a guy without her face diffusing with blood.

Unless they were very special and trusted kids, which Cass obviously was, the Home kids had to return to the orphanage directly on school's closing. Hence, coming from junior jayvee football practice, I was therefore mildly surprised to find Cass making her way home so long after the final bell. She was, I would learn, vice-president of her eighth-grade class and had attended a meeting of officers. If anyone from the Home saw her ensconced on my crossbar, Cass told me, she wouldn't in the future be able to attend those meetings. Still, the meeting had run over, Cass was already late, abruptly she was on the crossbar, and I was the knight errant pumping like mad and flying over Park Drive, intent on getting the princess home before the foreboding stroke of midnight.

To say that during the past days I had in my mind fabricated such a chance and isolated encounter with Cass is putting it mildly; literally, I had thought of nothing else, even to forming in my mind those things I might say to most impress Cass. What those things were, I do not now recall. At fourteen, one is a long way from perfecting the high and ruthless art of guile, and I expect that something as preposterous as describing the rowdy, impoverished, argumentative, disorderly Exley clan as an adoring, high-minded, brilliant, dedicated, serene ménage—to Cass, who of course had no family—was as far as I'd carried my mental courtship. Whatever, and however practiced and stylish this encounter was to have been, I ended saying nothing whatever.

Because Cass was in such a desperate rush, forcing me to lean into her as I strainingly pumped the pedals, my chin at her shoulder, her flaxen hair piebald with patches of honey at my face, her biscuity odor at my nostrils, the wind catching our hair and bringing her blouse so taut to her breasts she may as well have been nude, the blood now permeating her lovely copper-colored throat, the awful burning angina ache in my lower chest and upper abdomen, then suddenly the most insidiously monstrous erection imaginable, followed almost instantly, and I could not and still cannot credit it, by an effusive—on and on it went—seminal emission into my undershorts and light khaki trousers, the warm damp viscous fluid permeating the light khaki and leaving a dark stain half as big as a washcloth, yes, however practiced my wooing was to have been, I said nary a word, my face and my ears and my throat and my hands as charged with the blood of embarrassment as were those of Cass.

How to describe those four years, years in which my antisocial behavior became so pronounced that even after all this time, when I haven't had a lapse or spell in four decades, it is all but impossible for me to enter a golf foursome with strangers, such is the terrible trepidation of having my long-dormant illness stand abruptly revealed in all its odious horror. Out of morbid curiosity, I have in the intervening years read what little literature (hardly the stuff of *The Reader's Digest*) I could find in the subject. However, I so infrequently displayed the classic symptoms of the malaise that I can't honestly say, *see*, I can cite case histories A, B, C, D, ad infinitum to prove I am at one with other men and as blameless as those dopey teenagers who contract mononucleosis. Hence, let me describe the last spell I had before taking up with Cass and describe this not because it was typical of my interludes but because it manifests those symptoms that would allow me to be at one with humanity.

In the fall of my senior year I was, at 145 pounds, the starting center and noseguard for Watertown. Scheduled to play the Massena Red Raiders, who hadn't been beaten in three years, our coach did not let up on me the entire week preceding the game, telling me Massena had a number of surprises in store for us and particularly for me, at 145 especially vulnerable in the offensive line. What the coach was really saying, it must be understood, was that the year before the center who had preceded me, a 190-pounder named John Barnard, had on defense continually moved from his linebacker position into the scrimmage where he so badly mauled their 150-pound center the guy was eventually removed with a broken arm. Hardly notorious for Christian amnesty, Massena, I was constantly reminded throughout the week, would deem me at my weight too defenseless to resist and would reciprocate in kind by continuing to bring the worst animal they had into the line to play off my nose and put some real hurt on me. Had the coach been the kind of psychologist who spent the week assuring me I'd be up to the challenge, I might have been okay; instead, his style was one of defiance, assuring me I hadn't the stuff to make it and wouldn't make a pimple on a man's ass.

We didn't know how anxious the coach was until the Friday night before the game when, prior to the pep rally, he scheduled a 7 P.M. High Mass at the Holy Family Church on Winthrop Street, a ploy he used only every three or four years. Whether we were Catholic or not, we were expected to attend, those non-Romans among us taking our cues from the anointed, standing when they stood, sitting when they sat, going to our knees in the supplicatory position of prayer when they did. It was while I was in the latter position, nearing the end of the Mass when the Catholics among us had filed to the altar to receive the wafer and the wine, the flesh and blood of the Lamb, that it happened, the abrupt, unforgivable, agonizing, terrible erection, followed immediately by an ejaculation so pronounced that my whole body shuddered to an extent I all but swooned, rather as if I'd actually made contact with the Christ. As, indeed, who knows that I hadn't?

Literature of the malaise confirms that this emission was classic, heralded as it was by a week of threats of pain, fear of failure at public performances, fear of not being able to finish tasks, of not being ready, threats of being punished. Moreover, I filled the bill in that my erection was not induced (in my case it never was!) by what the quack psychologists call "direct sexual precipitants," that is, I was not so hopelessly and lustfully corrupt that during that sacredly serene moment, with my teammates coming together with God to the greater glory of the Watertown Golden Cyclones (did we really call ourselves that?), there abruptly came into my thoughts the vision of a naked Ava Gardner, ivory thighs parted and a gracious hand beckoning me to umber places and a carnal knowledge of her. Oh, no, never that! What always did happen, however, was that at the first seminal discharge, a drip, a drop, there came, obliterating everything in the real world, the overpowering image of Cass on the crossbar of my bicycle, the smell of her flaxen-honey hair, the blood of shyness diffusing her lovely cheeks and throat, the outline of her new breasts directed to the wind, the exhilarating freshness she cast.

If this, then, is a classic example of spontaneous or anxiety-related orgasm, preceded as it was by threats of pain and so forth, most of my attacks, coming at four- to six-month intervals, were so far removed from anxiety or anything I can unearth in psychological tomes as to remove me from the land of men and place me in Satanic worlds. As the reader may have guessed, these spells or lapses began within months of the time I assumed heroic stature, sped a worried Cass to the Home on my bicycle and did not end until four years later when, shortly after my desecration of the High Mass, Cass first performed fellatio on me. So unexpected were these attacks that it required a genuinely ironfisted act of willpower for me to strip myself from my football and basketball gear and step naked into the shower with my teammates.

But, as only one example, and I could relate twenty, look at this can of worms. On Sunday nights in Watertown the high school kids used to congregate on the sidewalk in front of the Avon Theater on Arsenal Street. When the early showing let out at 8:30 or whenever, we'd all crowd through the doors discharging the six o'clock viewers, scoot like mad up the stairs and take seats in the upper balcony. Once seated, and apparently safe, we'd take stock of how many of us had been caught by the ushers, take up a collection of small change, and send someone—usually a volunteer—back to make certain everyone had enough money to get in.

Oh, they were laughing nights, joyous even when the movie was what nowadays is called a turkey, perhaps even sillier then, for when those cynical bastards in Hollywood treated us like a bunch of limp morons, we reacted in kind, took up the challenge, we defied them, we spat in their faces, we gave them Watertown catcalls, we entered into a dialogue with the screen, we said, in effect, *don't patronize us, you phony sons of bitches*. If, for example, the heroine, batting great modest eyes, said, "Do you really love me?" and the hero, played, say, by a bedimpled Richard Greene, proclaimed, "I love you *more than my life*," surely one of the guys would holler, "More than your puny life, Dicky baby, is hardly enough!"

Occasionally such a line came during a good movie, helping to break the tense obeisance we were paying the screen's fantasy. I got off such a line just prior to one of my attacks. The movie was called *The Seventh Cross*. It starred Spencer Tracy and Hume Cronyn. How it would hold up today is irrelevant; if for no other reason than even as adolescents watching Tracy and Cronyn at work, we knew we were in the presence of the goods, we were rapt, we were riveted, we paid these marvelous actors the ultimate homage of our head-tilted silence. Now there came a scene where Tracy, Cronyn, and his wife are seated in the kitchen, Cronyn's young son at distracting play. It is past the son's bedtime. Tracy and Cronyn obviously have weighty matters to discuss, intrigues beyond comprehension, nefarious maneuvers involving courageously single-minded risks, the realignment of states, matters not for the ears of children.

In exasperation the mother finally snaps, "*Come,* kiss your father good night and *go to bed.*" And, possessed by the perverse imps of Sunday-night Avon movie-watching, Exley cried, "Christ, if the poor kid's gotta kiss Hume, no wonder he doesn't want to go to bed!" In retrospect, the line does not seem that funny; but for whatever reason the high school section of the upper balcony broke up in riotous laughter. It was at the moment the hilarity crested that the erection came, the awful emission (thankfully in that darkened theater), and, from the inception of the erection and thereafter, the recurring image of Cass on the crossbar, an image, I repeat, that came only subsequent to the first stirrings in my loins. There was no anxiety whatever. And if there was, it was so deep-seated it would take a dozen Freudians twenty years to unearth it.

2

Until the Brigadier was fourteen or fifteen and I eleven or twelve, we slept together. Then one morning shortly before or after dawn Bill had a nocturnal emission. I know that it happened at this time because when I awoke for school, I rolled over, the warm wetness shocked my back, I leaped from bed only to stare furiously back at a contentedly sleeping Brigadier. At breakfast I did not know how to bring the subject up to my mother. It was not a question of being a tattletale, for I thought the Brigadier had wet the bed, we hadn't to my knowledge ever had a bed wetter in the family, I understood it to be the sign of some inner distress or insecurity. I loved the Brigadier, thought he must be sick, and just before leaving for school told my mother out of solicitation that she might bring her maternal wisdom to healing him. The healing turned out to be very simple. At supper that night we were informed that a new single bed had been added to the room, at the far end fronting the upstairs sleeping porch, and from that day forward I was to occupy that bed. It is only as I write that I smile, imagining, what with my father at work, the desperate logistical maneuvers my mother must have gone through to get a single bed into the room, sheeted, blanketed, and bedspreaded, between nine in the morning and supper time. I smile thinking of the appeals to neighbors for help, the bartering, wondering who carried the bed upstairs, and so forth.

If sex, then, separated the Brigadier and me forever—and it did, *it did*—it also reunited us and healed me in the person of Cass. Or was I in the least surprised that the Brigadier would come to know—even in the biblical sense—an outsider, a shadow person, an orphan like Cass. Almost from the day we were, literally, taken from one another the Brigadier began to inhabit the mysterious nether world of the spy, a world of audacity, silence, stealth, resourcefulness, and intelligence. At fifteen he went to work as a stock and bag boy at the A&P, he began sneaking into our room, shoes in hand, at all hours of the night, occasionally with the ghostly light of dawn diffusing the room. Often wakened by him, I remember hoping it was some older co-worker at the A&P, a ravishing widow perchance, who was showing him the ropes, teaching him how to screw, no, no, not that way, *this way.*

In any event, I knew I'd never learn who it was from the mute and gentlemanly Brigadier. It was not until much later when I heard his older friends say of Bill, "Ex'd screw a snake in the bush—or just the bush if there was no snake there" that it occurred to me that there may have been more than one girl. Nor do I now have any doubt that my parents knew as well as I what time he was getting home. But what does a parent say to someone who is taller, better-looking, and brighter than they, who is getting high Bs and As without cracking a book, and who is self-supporting into the bargain? Yes, the Brigadier left home forever shortly after we were separated from each other by his semen.

The only football game the Brigadier would ever see

me play was the Massena game, when he was on leave. And I am sorry about that, for everything the coach predicted for me came true. His name was Ike Borgosian, a fullback and linebacker (his son, Ike Jr., would later be named All-American at West Point). On the very first play from scrimmage he moved in off my nose, and on the snap of the ball hit me the hardest I'd ever been hit, thereby establishing from the opening whistle who was to control the center of the line. Although I survived until the game's final gun, and though we upset Massena 14–0, I cannot impress enough upon the reader what an excruciatingly long afternoon it was. On one occasion, for example, Borgosian hit me so hard and drove me so quickly backward that I stepped on the foot of our quarterback, who was setting up for a pass, forcing him to trip to the ground. Of course, using Borgosian, the best tackler Massena had, in this way defeated their purposes. The two quarterbacks we alternated, both very bright kids, saw immediately that all we had to do was run away from the center of the line, allowing Borgosian to expend his considerable energies pounding me to a pulp.

"It was a long afternoon for yuh, huh?" the Brigadier said.

"Oh, the very longest," I replied.

It was the following afternoon, Sunday, and the Brigadier and I were walking to the four o'clock showing at the Olympic Theater, after which he'd catch a 7 P.M. bus to Syracuse and connect with a train to whatever base he was returning. The Brigadier did not say any more, and I was grateful for that. As I'd had a lapse only two days before in the Holy Family Church, I was actually debating whether to broach the subject of my abominable illness. As brilliant as I considered the Brigadier, he was only twenty on that Sunday afternoon and because I did not begin my own research into spontaneous ejaculation until I was well into my thirties, I knew his only horrified advice would have been that it was a grave matter indeed and that, now that Dad was dead, I hadn't any choice but consulting the family physician, who of course would have been just as

horrified and bewildered as the Brigadier. On the verge—
the words dancing on the tip of my tongue—of telling Bill
what had happened to me during the High Mass, and but-
tressing this spell with a dozen other equally shameful,
obscene, and insane interludes, I was suddenly stunned by
what the Brigadier was wondering aloud. Had he said that?

"Pardon?"

"Do you know Cass McIntyre?"

I stopped dead in my tracks, the blood zoomed upward, I became giddy, somewhat nauseous, thinking I was
literally going to faint. Among his other accomplishments,
was the Brigadier telepathic?

In the end, what it amounted to was this. Cass was one
of the girls the Brigadier was "seeing" during his seven-day
pass; and the only reason he was bringing her up to me—as
I say, the Brigadier was too much of a gentleman to discuss
his love life—was that on the two occasions he'd been with
Cass all she'd done was talk about me.

"She talked about me?"

The Brigadier laughed, at my naïveté no doubt. "She
said you stare at her all the time, and that she knows you
like her."

"Oh, she knows that, does she?"

The Brigadier laughed again. "C'mon, stupid, don't
get sore. Cass feels the same way about you."

What the Brigadier told me next was to account for a
number of things, including how the Brigadier was to elude
the Home's rigid security long enough to spend any time
with Cass. Cass hadn't lived at the Home since the previous
spring, when she'd become a foster child and live-in baby
sitter for Fairley Parish's ten-year-old son, Howie.

"Fairley Parish, for Christ's sake?"

That the Brigadier was a friend of Fairley Parish says
more about Bill than any words could, for I doubt another
twenty-year-old in Watertown had a first-name back-
slapping familiarity with Fairley. Fairley was a bookmaker
and gambler. For a percentage of the pots he ran the card
and crap games at the American Legion, the VFW, and the

Elks Club, supplied the cards and dice, and settled disputes. He ran an Italian domino game in a loft on the north side of Public Square. At one time, for a two-year period before the city forced Fairley to take them out, he had a couple dozen dime, quarter, and half-dollar one-armed bandits in the American Legion. With monotonous regularity, at about yearly intervals, Fairley was arrested, paid a hundred-dollar fine, went back to work that night, and our more seemly citizens balmed themselves with the notion that we didn't allow anything as diabolical as gaming in Watertown.

Fairley was a very handsome guy, with a cinema star's slender dark good looks, though his skin always seemed to me to have the pasty jailhouse pallor of people who inhabit the night, so much so that even freshly shaven his black beard was strikingly evident against his milky complexion. His wife, Cookie Parish, who had committed suicide the previous June by hanging herself in the garage, was, I thought, the most beautiful woman I'd ever known, a natural blonde with a trim athletic figure and strikingly even white teeth. From the time I was twelve until I was fourteen, I had caddied at the Thompson Park Golf Course. Cookie played two or three mornings a week and would refuse to go out on a round unless I caddied for her, so that the caddy master, Karl, often had to send another caddy out onto the links to find and replace me and I'd return to the first tee and an impatiently cursing Cookie.

How a psychiatrist would have diagnosed Cookie is beyond me, but there were elements of both the schizophrenic and the manic-depressive in her. Because of Fairley's occupation, Cookie was a social pariah, she always played alone, and because, as she never wearied of reminding me, my father had taken her virginity when she was fifteen and "a dumb piece of catshit from the North Side," my father the lifeguard at the St. Mary's Pool who had taught her how to swim, Cookie felt we were bound by crummy impoverished beginnings and assumed I was the only caddy with whom she'd feel comfortable. Cookie was a superb golfer (I did not know how good until years later when I myself took up the game). There were days when, after a muffed shot, her language was the foulest I'd ever heard, she'd furiously throw her seven iron twenty yards, bellow, "Fuck, suck, cuntlicking cocksucker," and still come in three over par for eighteen. As I say, she must have thought it tacit between us that both she and my father were "catshit North Siders," when in fact I not only now lived on the South Side, as did Cookie, but came from a household in which a guy could have his mouth soaped for saying "shit."

On the other hand, and I never knew in what mood to expect Cookie, there were days when she had a dreadful round, say, twelve or fifteen over par, and she'd laugh joyously at her every mistake, saying things like, "Holy Crimminy, Ex, I mean, am I terrible, or what? I mean, did you ever?" Even on those days, however, she never completed a round without at some point reminding me that my father had been her "first love," though in her high moods her language was considerably more digestible than when she was on a bummer. Whereas in the latter mood Cookie would be sanguine with self-loathing as well as hateful recriminations against my father, saying things like, "Yeah, every noon when the pool closed for lunch, that prick Earl would drag my ass into the bathhouse, stick that disgusting cock into me, and fuck me half to death"; on Cookie's highs these animal scenes took on a kind of lace-curtain purity and she'd tell me that Earl had been her first and only love and how happy she'd been "making love" and sharing the sandwiches "Ex's mom had made for him." Of course I never knew if any of it were true, for I certainly wasn't about to confront Earl with it. The only reason I have for suspecting it was true was that once, studying his high school annual, I saw that no few of the females had an inked X over their heads and when I asked my mother what this signified, her face reddened and she said that my father had marked, like Hawthorne's Hester, I expect, the classmates he'd "kissed." What was beyond dispute, though, was that Cookie contained within her sad and troubled being the impossible polarity of an arrant romantic solopsism, which she tried to anchor in a bedrock of the most distressingly corrupt vileness. Cookie hadn't needed a psychiatrist. So unalloyable were her component parts, she needed one of those brilliant physicists capable of bringing polonium together with lithium to activate a nuke. Whatever, God had assuredly dealt Cookie an impossible hand. It was as though He'd conceived her, full-blown, with a pin in her left hand and a fully inflated balloon in her right and unfairly—as the expression goes: "nobody said it would be fair"—demanded from her the incredibly ironfisted feat of not bringing the two together. One does not need a psychiatric bent to know Cookie eventually went bang.

When the Brigadier was sixteen the A&P began to use him to deliver, in the red-and-white-paneled pickup, groceries customers had ordered by phone. Almost immediately enamored of Fairley and Cookie Parish, the Brigadier never ceased telling me what great people they were, and characters into the bargain. Delivering the groceries about five in the afternoon, the Brigadier was always invited to sit at the kitchen table with Fairley, was given a Coke or a 7-Up and a two- or three-dollar tip, depending on how many cardboard boxes of groceries he'd delivered. Invariably, having just risen, Fairley was seated at the kitchen table in a midnight-blue satin dressing robe, drinking black coffee and chain-smoking Lucky Strikes, the green of which had gone to war, and his first words to the Brigadier were always, " 'Cha get laid last night, Ex?" He'd then throw his head back and roar with laughter. Oh, Fairley was a card all right! Cookie, however, was nuttier than a fruitcake, according to the Brigadier, a fact I certainly wouldn't have challenged, having already told him how she'd acted and the things she'd said during my caddying days. Subject to her highs and lows, and as she busied herself putting the groceries away, she'd either say, "Oh, Fairley, Ex's just a baby; would you for crying out loud leave the poor boy alone?" or, feet first, jump right into Fairley's perverseness and say, "I can tell by the evil smile on Ex's face he screwed himself silly last night." She'd then join Fairley in his ribald laughter.

Two or three nights a week Cookie went out to Morgia's or Canale's to dinner with Fairley (he would, I heard, order scrambled eggs, bacon, and English muffins), after which Cookie would take in a movie while Fairley went from club to club checking the nightly action. On those occasions they'd use Cass, who was a niece to Cookie, as a babysitter for Howie and because Cookie often joined Fairley for two or three drinks after the movie, and she'd find Cass asleep on the couch on her 1 A.M. return, Cookie'd decide to let Cass sleep, waking her in the early morning and driving her to the Home in time for her to bathe and change for school. After exasperatingly explaining a dozen times that they couldn't keep Cass overnight unless they signed papers to become her foster parents, the head of the Home sighed with relief (another less mouth to feed, another stunningly nubile girl about whom he hadn't to fret) when Fairley and Cookie did sign the papers, fixed up a bedroom for Cass, furnished it beautifully, as I recall, and moved her into the house, ordering that brat Howie to call her Sis. Cass would have been nearly seventeen then, a woman since she was thirteen.

It was only after I was well into my thirties that a number of things about the Brigadier, Fairley, and Cass became clear to me. At seventeen almost none of us is demi-world enough to understand that screwing is merely another bodily function, to be sure a rather more exalted one than one's morning movement. A legend in our family has it that the Brigadier hardly spoke until he was six or seven (it was actually considered that he was "slow"), at which time, an ear of fresh corn in hand, he said, "Pass the butter, please," that being, as it were, the first time he felt the urgency to communicate with the dummies around him. It was when I began to understand that Cookie, for all her foul mouth, was, like me, an intractably inconsolable romantic —Earl had been "my first love"—that I also came to see that on one of her bummers she'd hanged herself. She'd done this, the Brigadier informed me, with the midnight-blue sash of Fairley's morning robe, a romantic gesture if there ever was one.

No, as I later thought all this through, the Brigadier had too much respect and affection for Fairley—an authentic meeting of two minds born effete—for him to enter Fairley's house without Fairley's encouraging and condoning it. What Fairley told him about Cass is lost to history, but when the Brigadier was home on leave Fairley must have convinced him—one hopes not too crudely—that a trip to his lovely home on Park Circle would bear erotic fruit. In defense of the Brigadier, he loved, worshiped, and adored women, in the way a man loves his first automobile; unlike his asshole sentimentalist kid brother he did not, even at his tender age, consider any girl he slept with a whore. To the Brigadier all conquests were "one sweet petunia," "some kind of lovely chick," and, "I mean, a really great person," which I now have no doubt was the reason he did so well with women, their sensing instinctively that the mute mysterious Brigadier, who would later become such an adept spy, had too much class and too many other things on his mind to mention anything as casually offhand as inserting a penis into them. Although I'm sure the Brigadier could have spelled "epicurean" at twenty, and probably could have hewn a rough definition of it, I'm also sure he was by nature an acolyte of that philosopher, a hedonist of the very first order, and believed that whatever sensuous pleasure could be derived in the face of the void was good.

Hence, even as I walked to the movie and grappled with the terrifying notion of telling the Brigadier of my malaise, he must have been solemnly pondering how to tell me Cass liked me and wondering further whether I were weather-beaten enough to handle what he had to tell me about her, wondering if I understood that a piece of ass was a piece of ass, if, as it were, I was the kind of guy who could walk through a fuck without getting angel dust on my shoulders. Moreover, and I cannot emphasize this enough, before he got around, in his gentlemanly polite tones (he was constitutionally incapable of epithets like *cocksucker*), to telling me Cass would please me "with her mouth" (as I write I can of course see Fairley telling the Brigadier the same thing) and that all that would be required of me was that I tell a fib and say I loved her, even before he got this far I became wild and flushed, dizzy and nauseous with anger and raging jealousy, I wanted to smash the Brigadier in the mouth, knock him down and beat him half to death. Could he not, for Jesus's sake, see that I did love Cass? It goes without saying that I saw nothing of the movie, that twice I had to flee to the lavatory and throw up the roast pork dinner my mother had prepared specially for the Brigadier's farewell, and remember hardly anything of putting him on that bus taking him back into a world in which people killed each other in a lot less subtle and considerably kinder ways. Ah, disenchantment, so this is all life was, a roast pork dinner, doing it to the Gook before he did it to you, and a blowjob? If that were so, I knew all about the pleasures of the dinner, I would reverently dedicate myself to unearthing the forbidden raptures of the blowjob, and that would leave only a Fort Benning Georgia Top to get me into fighting trim, show me how to use an M-1, and point me in the direction of the Gook.

When I said that on learning Cass had become a foster child to Fairley and Cookie accounted for a number of things, I meant that in March of the previous spring I had sensed a new, shockingly confident, near-brazen Cass. At first unable to fathom it, it suddenly occurred to me what it was. Whereas I'd previously been moved to immeasurable sadness at how cleanly immaculate she'd kept her four or five outfits, two of which were faded cotton dresses so sprightly and starchy-looking that I had visions of things Dickensian, of this shy angel staying up half the night washing and mending her outfits to keep herself as presentable as she always was, abruptly something very strange was happening. Hardly detectable at first, and about three months before Cookie hanged herself, Cass began wearing expensive cashmere sweaters, pleated Black Watch plaid skirts, and those expensive buckskin saddle shoes (how Cookie must have relished dressing Cass up!) worn by the daughters of doctors and lawyers who lived west of Washington Street; after school I began seeing her in Musselman's ice cream emporium drinking Fru-Tang with her classmates, once even overhearing her say "my treat" and ostentatiously laying a five-dollar bill on the Formica table; and finally, and wonder of wonders, about ten days after Cookie died, Cass came to our junior prom (she was a sophomore then) dressed in a lovely clinging black gown, without all those awful gaudy bosom frills and ruffles indigenous to the period, escorted by a poncy classmate of mine—a nice guy, for all that—who was active in little theater, band, and glee club. Further, and I could not keep my eyes from her the entire evening, she stayed until 1 A.M. and the final dance. What the hell was going on?

In the four years from the time I first fell in love with Cass until, my courage bolstered by Genesee at the Circle Inn, I at last mustered the nerve to call her at Fairley's, knowing he'd be checking the nightly action, I'd spoken to her only twice, the first time when I'd sped her home on my bicycle. The previous fall, when I was a junior and Cass a sophomore, we'd drawn a first-period study hall together, in which Cass was seated next to me. One morning the teacher who manned the large hall, seated omnisciently on an elevated platform overlooking us, had had an auto accident on his way to school, had been taken to the emergency room with a concussion, and the period was nearly over before the noise level and the rowdiness announced to the rest of the building that there was no teacher present.

Having taken a deep breath, praying my face didn't redden as badly as Cass's, the spitballs and erasers flying furiously around me, I asked Cass—I was so very earnest—how she planned to spend her life. As she pondered this, her face reddening to that strange arousing copperish ocher, in perplexity her appetizing salmon-pink tongue suspended between her moist lips, I thought I would faint, so buoyant was I with love; and I may as well have fainted, for I later learned that everything Cass told me was fantasy. When she was two, she said, her mother had died of poliomyelitis (her mother was living in Palatka, Florida, with a gambler friend of Fairley who ran the cockfights in Putnam County) and that her father was a navy regular and warrant officer now stationed on a carrier in the Pacific. In two years, Cass said, her father intended to take his pension and Cass would go live with him in San Diego and study nursing. Cass would do this, devote her life to healing, because of what had happened to her mom, who, as I would also learn, hadn't the foggiest idea who Cass's father was, learn this from the Brigadier, who in turn had heard Cass's story from Fairley. Be that as it may, on hearing Cass's story in that clamorous, potentially explosive study hall, I was more in love with her than ever.

How, then, to live with this deviant, this loathsome, this aberrant Cass? Oh, I still stared at Cass in the oiled halls of the old high school, make no mistake about that, but I now stared at her in an entirely new way, grim-visaged, my jaw and my mouth set in lofty disdain, as though I were saying, "I know all about you, you no-good bitch." Cookie, I would think, may have taught Cass the high, wily, and feminine arts of shaving her marvelously audacious legs, taught her how to do her brows and lashes, explained to Cass that with her wondrously stunning complexion she needed only a minimum of lipstick, Cookie may have armored Cass in pleated wool skirts, cashmere sweaters, and buckskin shoes, but for all that Cass was still a grubby orphan whore; whereas the astonishingly imperturbable Brigadier had merely meant to tell me that sex was the best of life and that I should enjoy. Lord, how the Brigadier had overestimated his sexually infantile brother.

Now Cass, alarmingly, began broaching my gaze by riveting those great blue eyes on me; and though she hadn't yet cultivated enough serene self-assurance to stay her face from reddening, she yet seemed to be suggesting, with that blatantly disarming return of my stare, that she was glad, glad, glad that the Brigadier had told me—it was what Cass had intended!—and that she was confident she could please me ever so much more than those sanctimonious, endearing girl-children with whom she'd so often seen me.

In any event, there now came the time of the great wash in which for thirteen heart-quickening days, between the Sunday I put the Brigadier on the bus and I made my first trembling call to Cass, that in shuddering anticipation I had the cleanest penis, scrotum, and backside in upstate New York. Whereas, as I've already indicated, I had previously, because of my oddity, been charged with anxiety at the mere thought of entering the shower with my teammates, often lingering until most of the guys were dressed and departing, after practice I was now the first guy into the shower, devoting—oh, *devotion* does not adequately describe it—so much time to lathering my genitalia and backside, only to rinse and relather, that the guys grew amused at my bathhouse fastidiousness and laughingly chided me.

"Hey, guys, you think Ex's going down to Severance Studios and have it photographed?" "Naw, Ex's going to have it bronzed; you know, the way his mummy bronzed his baby shoe!" Or, "Naw, Ex had his first wet dream last night, he just discovered his cock and is trying to scrub the hair away so it won't grow on his palms!"

Mornings I started rising half an hour early, drawing a scalding bath to which, from a cut glass container, I'd pour my sister's pink crystal salts—the genitals were going to smell ambrosial too—and linger in the bathtub until the other members of my family were so anguished they were ready to bash in the door. Shaking my penis after urinating was hardly enough. I'd wait for the boy's room to empty, would bring my hands to a ripe foaming lather, would apply it to my crotch, scrub the area thoroughly, rinse, and dry myself with paper towels. Caught once in a lavatory whose towel supply was exhausted, I began to carry in my back pocket one of those farmer's great red bandanas, so poised I was to experience the thrillingly forbidden. How exactly

I knew that the moment Cass brought me to climax, I'd be forever rid of the daimon within me, I don't know; but know I did, I swear I'd become clairvoyant, perhaps even numinous, an inspired augur capable of seeing a long, happy, and damnless life in my future.

The Saturday following the Massena game we played on the road, defeating Oswego 47–0; on the next Saturday we were back in Watertown for a home game. I knew it had to be that night. From the Brigadier I'd learned that Saturday was Fairley's busiest night and that he was often still making his rounds when the Romans were making their way to early Mass. To bolster my courage I waited too long, drinking five or six Ginnys with the guys at the Circle Inn, hoping they'd give the jukebox a rest so Cass wouldn't know I was in a bar, as the minutes ticked away practicing in my mind what I'd say. "Golly, Cass, I only just looked at the clock when you were picking up the phone. I'm *really sorry* about the hour. Did I wake you?" Neither the Genesee nor the contrived script was necessary. At Cass's abrupt and lively hello on the phone's first ring, I said, "This is Fred," Cass said something I didn't catch, I drunkenly appended "Exley," and embarked on my mock good-guy profusions of apology for the lateness of the hour and my unforgivable boorishness for calling at 11 P.M. Until it occurred to me what Cass had said—"Do you want to come over?"—I was sanguine with all kinds of preposterous rhetoric, would Cass maybe go to a movie some night and so forth. Then, like an unexpected blow to the diaphragm, it occurred to me what Cass had said on my announcing my name and I now said, "Well, sure, I'll be there in twenty minutes."

As in most dives, there was no lock on the men's room door of the Circle Inn—fear of a drunk's passing out on the seat and having to break in—and whenever one of the guys had to ascend the throne, he'd have a buddy guard the door for him, a silent solemn sentinel, arms crossed forbiddingly over the chest, standing watch over, of all things, a broken-mirrored, graffiti-walled, urine- and excrement-odored water closet. Corralling a guy for whom I'd just stood watch, I entered the men's room, removed my pants and underwear, laid them neatly over the toilet well, from my jacket took a bar of Camay wrapped in toilet paper, did my reverently fastidious business, returned to the barroom, told a friend with a car that the beer was making me dizzy, and asked for a ride to town. Outside Fairley's house I paced, heart-thumpingly, for some moments, then taking the bull by the horns walked up the steps and gingerly rang the bell.

Most of what happened that night is lost to memory. What is not lost is that I neither got pleased "with her mouth" nor in fact sexually sated by Cass in any way at all. Explaining that she had some homework to finish, as she was going to the movies "with the girls" (she was becoming a regular social butterfly) the next afternoon, Cass took a chair at a lovely, ponderous, textbook-strewn mahogany desk at my right, I sat on a beautiful deep peach-colored brocaded couch (three decades later I would find myself sitting on this very same couch), stared about the room marveling at what seemed to me, at seventeen, to have been the mad Cookie's exquisite taste in interior decorating (probably done by a professional, it occurs to me now), everything seemed so neat, tasteful, and well placed. So many years before I had detected Cass's response to per-plexity, so that even now as she pored over a textbook, scribbling answers on a piece of scrap paper, that pink tongue—oh, my heart!—was gently gripped and suspended between Cass's moist lips.

When at length Cass joined me on the couch, sitting very close to me, I had again to hear Cass's fantasy about her parents, with a good deal of new and colorful detail. Although her mother and Cookie had indeed been sisters, there had of course been no poliomyelitis, there was no warrant officer serving in the Pacific, and so forth—this having been told me by the Brigadier as we had waited for the bus that would take him back to whatever war he was going. And indeed, why the need for Cass to continue this tale? Had Cass the grades, Fairley had the dough—mostly tax-free, I might add—to send her off to Vassar wheeling a Cadillac convertible. At one point, too, having heard our voices and claiming he thought Fairley had come home early, the ten-year-old Howie descended the staircase dressed in playing-field-green flannel pajamas patterned with small beige footballs and I was dumbstruck at how much he resembled his late mother, the natural blond hair, the fine nose, the perfect teeth. Even at ten Howie owned Cookie's athletic swagger, something of her arrogance in the way he carried his body, and I had no doubt Howie was going to be a killer with the girls. "You know darn well your father never gets home before morning on Saturday nights. You weren't even asleep. You had that radio on tuned low. Get to bed, Howie, I'm warning you. If I tell your father, he won't take you to the New Parrot for hot dogs tomorrow night." Cass then introduced us, reluctantly and curtly.

"Goddamn," Howie said, "are you the football player?"

"Stop that swearing," Cass said.

Smiling, I was sure that Howie, having grown up clutching the skirts of the breathtakingly bedeviled Cookie, owned a considerably larger stock of obscenities, any of which would make *goddamn* seem an epithet issuing from the mouth of a ten-year-old maiden. As Howie started up the staircase, in sneering defiance of Cass, he hollered, *"Goddamn, goddamn, goddamn,* Exley, that's what I want to be—a center!"

Cass sighed. "What a brat."

Outside, one of those terrible late autumn rains, heralding the winter months, had begun blistering the storm windows. I moaned. We had only two more games, Onondaga Valley of Syracuse the following Saturday before closing out against Lackawanna of Buffalo on Thanksgiving Day. Both of these games, I was sure, would be played on wet cold muddy fields. It wasn't so much that our running backs were so fleet, with great maneuverability, which would be severely hampered, but that we used the T, and I would be expected to lay the slimy ball into the quarterback's opened hands on every offensive play, as well as make those long wet snaps back to our placekicker and punter. I hated cold wet fields.

When Cass at last asked what was bothering me, wondering aloud if it had something to do with the brat Howie's interruption, I said hell no and told her the truth of what was so distressing me. As there didn't seem to be any appropriate response Cass could make, and as she probably understood football as little as most girls (half the time our own cheerleaders, like a bunch of stick-legged mongoloids, were clapping and jumping idiotically up and down when they should have been hooting with derision), Cass abruptly rose, turned out the light on my mahogany end table, then the one on her side, we were suddenly laid out on the couch, with Cass facing me from the inside and were into some heavy petting, tongues exploring each other's mouth, my right hand going up under her sweater to her bra-covered breasts, up her skirt to her smooth copper-toned thighs, we went through the goofy mock-ritualistic bumping and grinding of teenagers. How long it took, I don't know, but not long. When my erection was most unbearable, I furtively reached down, unbuttoned my trousers, struggled to get it out of my underwear, then ardently took Cass's left hand and placed it there.

"Jesus!" Cass cried, struggling out from behind me, bolting stiffly upright and snapping on the light, while I, as red-faced as I'd ever seen Cass, furiously forced my penis back into my underwear and with shaking hands buttoned my fly. "What do you think you're doing?"

"But I thought—"

"I know what you thought. Your brother told you about me, didn't he? The difference between you and him is that he's a gentleman. Besides, he was going back to his base." Here was that entire nursing healer-of-men syndrome again, one that I wouldn't understand until many years later. "And I thought you were going to take me to the movies." Was it as simple as that with Cass? In retrospect I expect that it was, this unctuous pathetic need for Cass, who had for so long, all her short life, been deprived not only of normal family intimacy but of any normal access to her school friends—I had had to speed her "home" from something as ludicrously mundane as a class meeting—so that Cass wanted nothing less than the bogus dignity that would accrue to her should she date a jock. Perhaps I would even give her one of my cleats on a gold chain? Lord, what a pompous, arrogant, aloof, pampered, snot-nosed bunch we jocks were and how I now loathe (even thinking of it causes the sinuses to contract and the neck muscles to stiffen) every moment of that epoch of my life, so much so that, whereas I should be boundlessly sympathetic, I now smile with sadistic relish at the nemesis of an athlete, to drugs, to armed robbery, to exposing himself to little girls in the park.

Apparently I had been that drunk in the phone booth. Certainly I remembered thinking of suggesting a movie to Cass. "I will, I will," I said. "Who takes care of Howie?" Cass mentioned a friend from the Home. We sat in sulky silence, watching the rain pelt the windows, and unless I was much mistaken some of it had turned to snow.

"God," Cass said, "you'll never be able to walk home in this." She rose, walked to the desk, took a slip of paper from the upper right-hand drawer and looked back at the mantlepiece clock, which read five till two. It was apparently a list of phone numbers at which Fairley could be reached at certain hours. Cass got him at the second number she tried (in those day we didn't dial and instead asked the operator for a four-digit number) and I heard her say things like, "Yes, Bill's got a brother. Fred. He's in the class ahead of mine. He's only got this old silk basketball warm-up jacket and he'll get soaked." A long pause. "Okay, Uncle Fairley, I understand. If he's not asleep, though, I'll kill him." Cass laughed. "Okay, Uncle Fairley, if he's not asleep, I'll tell him you'll kill him."

Cradling the black receiver, Cass made a shush gesture with a finger to her lips, slipped from her loafers to her baby-pink anklets or bobby socks, and started stealthily up the staircase. Suddenly I heard Cass shout, "Damn you,

Howie! There won't be any hot dogs for you tomorrow!" As Cass bounded down the carpeted staircase two at a time, I heard her hiss *"shit,"* an epithet doubtless acquired during her own long proximity to her aunt Cookie. "What's the problem, anyway?" Her uncle Fairley, Cass said, had told her she could drive me home if Howie was asleep. Don't worry about it, I said, I'll be all right and picked up the basketball jacket from a chair across the room. "Hold it!" In her bobby socks Cass fled through the kitchen into an enclosed back porch or shed. When she returned, she had a long rubberized wool-lined yellow raincoat and one of those yellow hats Maine lobstermen wear in nor'easters. As I was putting on the coat, I detected that on its inside WATERTOWN FIRE DEPT. was stenciled. Smiling, I was recalling the Brigadier's tales about how much money Fairley spread around among every department in our municipality (once they had caught city workers paving his driveway). Fairley was doubtless an "honorary fireman" but even imagining him got up in that outfit tickled the funny bone. When I was going down the front steps, Cass said, "Don't be too hard on Howie, Ex. It was he who found Cookie that day in the garage. He really hasn't slept well since then."

3

It was the longest walk I'd ever endured—and not because of the rain, the snow, and the wind. I was giddy—giddy with love, I thought—and suffered two or three bad spells of vertigo, against the northwesterly winds moved at a snail's pace, feeling oddly weakened and diminished. It hadn't been love, I would discover within the next few days. For the past two weeks I had been playing with a moldering case of athlete's foot on my right foot, one that had become so putrescent that the callused skin on the balls had begun coming out in mushy chunks. On that day, I had played with the spaces between my toes and my sole sloshed with sickly purple calamine over the infected areas, after which thick globs of cotton had been stuffed between my toes to absorb the blood and the pus, the balls of my foot bandaged and taped (I no longer hear of cases as exacerbated as this and assume the disinfectant in the wells leading to a shower is more potent, or that the doctors have unearthed some better ways of treating the infection than calamine).

After the game, I'd had to remove the blood and pus globs of cotton from between my toes, the bloodied bandage from my foot. I'd then scrubbed the foot clean in a pail of near-scalding water, loaded with disinfectant, was given a tight shoe rubber, and was allowed to complete my shower. When this was done and I'd thoroughly dried myself and my foot (the towel would be thrown away), the trainer repainted the infected areas and gave me a new white silk sock to wear under my regular one. He also gave me two extra socks and two towels, to be used Sunday and Monday mornings. When at last, through the rain, snow, and gale winds, I reached home and struggled up the stairs, I slipped from my loafers, dropped the WATERTOWN FIRE DEPT. raincoat and wide-brimmed nor'easter cap to the foot of the bed, threw back the covers, and, fully clothed, crawled into bed and slept soundly until five the following afternoon.

Waking somewhat refreshed, I put on a new white silk sock, a slipper on my right foot, and made my way downstairs, for the first time detecting an odd throbbing soreness in my right foot. As with most lower-middle-class families, the Exleys ate their main meal between noon and one on Sundays; on Sunday nights it was popcorn, fudge, and radio night. My mother had, however, kept my dinner —chicken, chicken gravy, mashed potatoes, and peas— warm; at the kitchen table I ate what I could of it (not much), repaired to the living room, tried to concentrate on the radio, but could think only of Cass, and forsaking the popcorn ate two or three large pieces of chocolate fudge. By eight I was back upstairs, where I slept until I was forcibly awakened for school.

Had the coach ordered me to run the first two days, he would have seen immediately that I wasn't up to it. Instead, for fear of further aggravating my foot, he had it dressed in the same way as he did for a game, allowed me to wear a loosely tied sneaker on my right foot, and excused me from calisthenics and the mandatory two-mile run that closed our practices. All I had to do was run offensive plays against cutoff telephone poles, creosoted and buried in the ground, these to make sure everyone understood his blocking assignment. Only Bruno Grant (the best football player I ever played with), our fullback, middle linebacker, and punter—against Rome Free Academy that year, and to the ooohs and moans of their alien crowd, he'd boomed his first punt sixty yards in the air—saw that something was terribly wrong with me.

Ordinarily we spent twenty to thirty minutes a day practicing the snap from center, after which Bruno would punt away to guys in our defensive secondary, who alternated fielding the ball. "Jesus, Ex," Bruno kept crying, "what the hell yuh doin'?" My snaps were literally dribbling along the ground, so that he had to scoop them from the turf. When Bruno became particularly irate and I put all my strength into my snaps, the ball came in such a slow-motion underwater banana loop it had a hang time longer than a pro's sixty-yard pass, which would have allowed the entire Onondaga Valley line to be atop Bruno before he took his first step into the ball. "I'll be okay," I kept assuring Bruno. But in my heart I knew that I wouldn't. Even when I bent over to frame Bruno between the inverted V of my legs, the vertigo would seize me instantly and, like a drunk, between my legs I'd see two and three Brunos, a phenomenon I'm sure our opponents were glad they never saw.

To see a Red Skelton movie at the Olympic, Cass had suggested she pick me up at the corner of Franklin and Moffett Streets at 6:45 P.M. Tuesday, this in order to see the early screening. To that I'd laughed disparagingly. Misinterpreting, an irritated Cass said, "I know I've only got a junior operator's, but if I get caught Uncle Fairley can fix it. Uncle Fairley can fix anything." Explaining to Cass that I wasn't laughing at her driving at night, I said the coach often kept us until eight or later and that we'd be safer to plan on the late showing.

"He makes you practice in the dark?"

In weather like this, I said, we didn't even practice

on the main field, we'd do too much damage to the turf. Instead we practiced in the area bordering South Hamilton Street between the track and the street. He had a telephone pole over there, mounted with klieg lights, and though the visibility was hardly that of high noon or that of the fully lighted playing field one could see enough to go through the motions.

"He's crazy, isn't he? Uncle Fairley says he's crazy." Cass also thought he was crazy. She said he spoke to all the best-looking girls in the halls, including Cass, not so much spoke as growled like a rabid police dog (for the first time it struck me how easily saliva came to the coach's lips). The only thing that rendered his growl friendly, Cass added, was that he actually conjured something like a smiling leer. When the coach was angry and brought his face next to an offending player, afterward the guy needed a towel to dry his face. From the opening whistle, the coach was as oblivious to the crowd as the players. During the Massena game, when I was being so punished by Borgosian that I tripped up our own quarterback, he substituted for me; while leaving the field I made the grievous mistake of removing my helmet and in view of a crowd estimated at ten thousand he hit me over the head with the clipboard on which he diagrammed plays, let me brood on that for two series of downs, then returned me to the game. Whether the coach was crazy depended upon the point from which he was viewed.

When Cass picked me up Tuesday night at nine, I saw immediately that she was driving Cookie's yellow Lincoln coupe, either a '40 or '41, the last they made prior to the war (though the postwar cars were now coming out and Cass would doubtless have a new one soon), and it was a beautiful piece of machinery, with that yellow-and-chrome-encased spare tire mounted on the rigidly right-angled outside of what our Limey cousins call "the boot." Alarmingly, and though Cass was an average five-five, I thought the automobile way too much for her, something about the strain it took for her lovely legs to reach the brake and clutch pedals, the petiteness of her leather-gloved hands on the wheel. It soon became apparent that Cass, like her aunt Cookie, was wonderfully dextrous and wheeled that baby around as if it was one of those miniature electric vehicles that bump each other on the wooden board tracks in the carnival section of a state fair. When we reached lower State Street, we found all the parking places taken, we circled Public Square a number of times trying to find a place at the east end of the square, in exasperated impudence, Cass, finally giving it up, turned the Lincoln into a no-parking zone in front of a fire hydrant. When I pointed out we'd probably get a ticket, perhaps even hauled away, Cass snapped, once again after the arrogant manner of her Aunt Cookie's shooting a scratch round, "They wouldn't dare touch a car owned by Uncle Fairley." Increasingly disarmed by Cassandra "Cass" McIntyre's newly acquired and blatant confidence, I nonetheless wasn't surprised when we left the theater and discovered that though lower State Street and the square were all but empty of cars there was no ticket on Cass's windshield.

Wherever the occupants of the cars were (probably at a supper and social in the First Baptist Church across the street, the church whose high limestone tower's four facades held the town clocks), they weren't in the theater. Allowing Cass to lead the way, I found myself following her up into an empty balcony and coming out on a landing that separated the balcony into two parts. At this juncture we could have gone down left, which would have taken us into the loge seats closer to the screen and overlooking the spottily occupied orchestra. Instead, Cass turned boldly right and started up into the Alpine regions of the upper balcony. Cass may as well have proclaimed, "I haven't come here for chit-chat, Exley." Following her, I was again seized by a spell of vertigo, again thought it had to do with being dizzy with love, and to steady myself I gripped the outermost aisle seats as we ascended toward forbidden altitudes. We ended in the back row of the balcony, in the two seats against the easternmost wall, so far away one needed opera glasses to see the screen. As I had been with our punter Bruno, I was in any event seeing two and three images. Red Skelton was then at his prime. I'd never found him in the least funny or endearing and over the years, as he made the transition to television, I was appalled to find he was, if possible, becoming increasingly slapstick and even less amusing. Whenever I accidentally tuned him in, though, that night in the Olympic Theater in all its horrific ecstasy would rush nightmarishly back to me and I'd immediately switch channels.

After neatly folding a beautiful double-breasted midnight-blue cashmere polo coat, with great mother-of-pearl buttons and asking me to put it in the seat next to mine, Cass sat by the wall, I removed Uncle Fairley's fire department slicker I'd worn with a view to returning it and placed it atop Cass's. In those days I had a butch cut (imagine a guy today saying his hair was "butch"? Ah, semantics and the peculiar history of words), which due to frequent showers and lack of tending caused the hair to lie down in all directions, including down my forehead in piquant little bangs. I wore basketball sneakers, my best slacks, an old much-washed and faded football jersey, over which—the ultimate concession to the ritual of dating —I sported a beige corduroy jacket with dark brown leather patches at the elbows.

Abruptly Cass reached over and took my hand to hold, then as abruptly reached over with her left hand and placed her palm on my cheek. She said, "God, Ex, you're burning up. And sweating too." She laughed impishly and said, "Is this what you guys call 'having the hots' for someone?" I laughed too and said, "Probably." And just as abruptly we were again into some heavy petting, my hand discovering when it went under Cass's sweater that she hadn't worn a bra, then finding she was directing me by gently clasping the back of my head and leading my lips from one nipple to the other, back and forth, back and forth. At last she pushed me gently away and, incredibly, began unbuttoning my trousers. When she had me out, she tried coming to me over the high rigid armrest. But this proved impossible. Hence Cass rose, took Uncle Fairley's raincoat from the seat, spread it on the carpet at my tennis sneakers, and moved to her knees before me.

Other than Cass's twice performing fellatio on me in that lightless balcony, I remember very little else and certainly nothing of the movie. On the first occasion I recall that with my thumb and forefinger I fiercely strangled my penis at my scrotum and that Cass kept prying my fingers away and mock-slapping my hand, as if demanding I allow her mouth to control the act. Then, too, when the ejaculation was imminent, I touched her lightly on the head, leaned over, and whisperingly stammered. "I'm . . . I'm going . . . I'm going to do it." Although I couldn't see well, when Cass looked momentarily up at me I sensed a movement indicating a so-what shrug and she was back at her business. Never, never shall I be able to draw a true analogy or accurately describe my unbridled terror, my immeasurable anguish, my boundless pleasure. I think of a memsahib of Empire experimenting with a wog servant while her husband, Captain Smathers-Welles, is out on the plains of India shooting dacoits, the stricken bewilderment and heart-pounding terror diffusing the wog's entire being, realizing that if caught he'll be chopped into bits and fed to pariah dogs at the same time he is utterly unable to stay himself from sitting there paralyzed, stunned by enormities beyond his comprehension, ravished by the damnably excruciating pleasure.

When Cass had finished, obviously having taken my semen into her, she rose and as if it were the most natural thing in the world picked up her pocketbook, took out a stick of gum, offered me one (I declined), sat, and almost instantly was laughing at Red Skelton. She sat as far from me as possible, as if she were trying to make a shoulder impression in the plaster of the wall, and I found myself sitting as far from her as I could, two strangers warily circling one another and trying to decide if it would be worth pursuing a friendship. But this is not, I think, entirely accurate. No doubt Cass knew exactly who I was, another goofy

‡ 303

awkward male. What was needed, Cass seemed to be saying, was time for a rube like me to get used to who Cass not only was but who she had now become in my eyes. Apparently Cass decided I had had time enough. Fifteen minutes before the movie ended, she was back on the WATERTOWN FIRE DEPT. slicker at my feet.

But I never learned to live with that night. No one who didn't live through the forties and fifties has any comprehension of the tyrannical precepts, decorums, rules, and restrictions with which we were instilled and to have fellatio performed on one as well as to perform it was a good deal more damning to the participants than a simple loss of innocence, it was absolutely, believe me, nothing less than a fall from grace and a consignment to eternal hellfires. Moreover, and this is what would so shamefully beriddle me over the years, Cass saw me as some kind of jock-guru, like all converts she was embracing the faith with an outrageous passion that would have disarmed those born to the belief, metaphorically and literally she humbled and humiliated herself at my feet and with a kind of terrifyingly pathetic and gaspingly oral gratitude—that is what I loathed, the suggestion of gratitude—took my body's sap into her as though it were the nectar of some reverent being rather than the sperm of a conniving wretch.

4

Unable to rise from bed the following morning, I thought I'd finally done myself for sure. In those days, one must understand, The Big Three of things proscribed for athletes were cigarettes, alcohol, and masturbation. "It saps the energies, boys. You may as well swim the English Channel, then try and play a football game." (As an ironical aside, and in the cyclical nature of things, coaches now prefer their athletes to have healthy sex lives, and pros take their wives and girls to Super Bowls for the week preceding the game.) Be that as it may, whatever I'd done had assuredly sapped my energies. When my mother took my temperature, she found it pushing an alarming 103, she disappeared and returned momentarily with some clean flannel pajamas and told me the family doctor, Stubby, was on his way. Stubby verified the temperature, then spotted the white silk sock, splotched now with purplish blood-and-pus stains. Taking it gently off, Stubby took one look and said,

"Jesus Christ!" then, "Look, would you get me a pan of boiling water, Charlotte?" When Charlotte had gone, Stubby ordered me to take off my pajama bottoms. Reluctantly, I did so, timorously terrified that Stubby, no man for mincing words, could in some miraculously gnomic way detect what had taken place the previous evening.

"Jesus Christ, look at that!" And Exley, in his appalling ignorance, dwelled lingeringly on his limp dick, looking to no avail for lipstick stains. I cried, "What?"

"Can't you see the red line running up the inside of your leg and the swelling in your right nut? The goddamn infection has gone to your right nut!"

When Charlotte returned, Stubby scrubbed the foot clean with soap and water, followed again by swabbing the area with cotton balls dipped in alcohol. This done, Stubby gave me a shot, explained to Charlotte that some patients reacted badly to the medication (it occurs to me it was my first shot of penicillin, the miracle drug of World War II), and told to her to call immediately if any one of a number of symptons showed up. He also told her to keep my foot elevated and exposed on a pillow, gave her a bottle of capsules I was to take at three-hour intervals with orange juice, and said he'd return at noon to give me another shot. When he did return and he and Charlotte were ascending the stairs, I heard him say, "You know what that crazy bastard said to me, Charlotte?"

"Who?"

"The coach, *the coach*. He tracked me down at the hospital making morning rounds, demanded I be interrupted, then ordered—not asked, mind you—me to have Fred ready to play by Saturday. I just laughed and hung up. Ex'll be lucky if he's running by Christmas. I mean, is he crazy, or what, Charlotte?" I smiled, thinking it was the second time in a week I'd heard the coach referred to as crazy, the first being Cass's parroting Uncle Fairley's opinion.

Penicillin was indeed a miracle drug. The infection had pretty much cleared up by the following Monday, the telling red line running up the inside of my leg vaporized, the swelling in my nut abated. The fever, however, had laid heavily on me through Wednesday, Thursday, and Friday. For those days I was only able to take juice, milk, cocoa, and beef and chicken broth with crackers and my weight loss was eight pounds. Jack Case, the sports editor of *The Watertown Times*, announced the games on the radio and though I tuned in the game, and because it was that wavering fluctuating tricky time before a fever breaks, I fell asleep before the end of the first quarter and that night had to ask my sister, a cheerleader, to discover we'd beaten Onondaga Valley. Early that night a number of players, including Hotdog Wiley, my substitute, who was considerably bigger and stronger than I, paid me a courtesy visit prior to their pilgrimage to the Circle Inn. Hotdog was kind enough to say he'd taken an awful beating that day and sure hoped I'd be back by Thanksgiving. A girl named Cass, my mother informed me, called religiously twice daily, inquiring after me. My sister, as curious as most sisters, continued to wonder aloud in my mute ironically smiling presence what Cass that could be? She said, "It can't be Cass McIntyre. She's way too beautiful and way too nice for the likes of you." I took counsel of my silence, which of course infuriated my sister. Siblings never understand what suitors see in their pain-in-the-ass brothers and sisters, in the way it took me years to understand what women saw in the Brigadier.

When I returned to school and practice (Stubby told my mother he'd assume no responsibility for the latter goddamn madness), the coach weighed me, had my game uniform taken in, and, unwilling to leave it to chance, in practice made me take calisthenics and run full out. It didn't matter much. Thanksgiving Day against Lackawanna, the field was wet, cold, and muddy, precisely the field I abhorred, I was yet so weak and inept I was replaced by Hotdog at the end of the first quarter; and for the last three quarters I stood on the sidelines shivering in a Golden Cyclone parka, the occasional burst of rain matted my hair to my head, and knew, despite my continuing with basketball, that I was saying good-bye to all this, the rain and the cold and the infections and the pain and the brutality. After we'd had the family Thanksgiving meal, I called Cass, she invited me over and said she'd pick me up as she had a terrific surprise for me.

I wasn't surprised. It was a postwar Lincoln coupe, precisely like Cookie's save that it was a blindingly snow-trooper white and was, Cass squealed, "registered in my own name!" What did suprise me was that Fairley was at the house and that they were just preparing to eat, having been joined by a beautiful dark-haired woman in her mid-twenties, one of Cookie's possible replacements I had no doubt. Knowing I'd already eaten, Fairley told me to join them anyway and asked Cass to get me a bottle of Genesee 12-Horse Ale. Howie said, "You stunk today, Exley." "Howie!" Cass cried. "I told you before we went to the game Fred had a bad foot. God, you're rude. Isn't he rude, Uncle Fairley?" "What's the matter with it?" "Fred doesn't want to talk about it when we're eating." Howie was an in-sistent little bastard. "For cryin' out loud, Ex," Fairley said. "Take 'im into the kitchen and show it to 'im. Then maybe we can eat in peace. Maybe Howie'll learn what football is all about." When we returned to the table, Howie, not only a brat but a born ballbuster, said, "You ought to see it, Fairley. It's got all this purple and red blood oozing out of it and all these pussy-looking scabs." "Jesus Christ, Howie, would you *please* shut up!" Fairley slammed his fork onto the beautiful white linen tablecloth. And though by then I'd be long gone and moving lethargically about in a free-spinning disenchanting world, I should here append that whatever Howie saw that day, he accepted, learned to live with it, and years later I heard he'd captained both Watertown High School and the Colgate Red Raiders and had actually been given a free-agent tryout as a defensive back with Vince Lombardi's Green Bay Packers. Howie was, I understood, the last player Lombardi, with the great-est reluctance, cut from his roster before the regular season began.

When Cass and Fairley's friend came from doing the

dishes, Cass told Fairley we were going to a movie. Having forgotten what a busy moviegoing night Thanksgiving was, we actually went, too, but stayed only ten minutes and ended at the Thompson Park Pavilion (it would be snowed under within days) overlooking the east end of the city, the Lincoln's engine and heater running. And so began my endless season of the "blowjob," though I'm not at all sure that in those days we used such a word. Many believe our century was dramatically and traumatically divided into two parts, the first half ending with our use of the atomic bomb against the Japanese in 1945. Certainly guys but a few years my senior were coming back from Europe, Asia, and the Pacific and bringing with them not only terrible memories of war but the language with which they had confronted the madness and it was only a matter of time before "fuck" and "suck" and "motherfucker" and "cocksucker" became such a part of our nature that over the years I've often found myself with lovely, intelligent women who would feel quite at ease at a Jackie Presser teamsters' convention.

But to have someone as lovely and intelligent as Cass perform fellatio on me night after night, week after week, month after month, and to have her do so in what seemed such an enthusiastically unself-conscious way was a quantum leap into the second half of the century for which I wasn't prepared. And the worst part was that among the antediluvians of my epoch there was absolutely no one I could tell, primarily because I was all but illiterate, hadn't the language, had I even known who he was, to either comprehend or articulate the unabashedly crude joy of a Rabelais, and had further come to see that none of the guys would believe me in any event. Long since I'd come to see locker room talk for what it was, fantasy. And in retrospect I wish I could, having heard that So-and-so was a great fuck, enumerate the wasted hours I spent in pusuit of these fantasies, only in my case to get these wantons alone and get nothing whatever. In those days we had no roll-ons and I spent so much time rubbing my sister's Mum salve—"Mum's the word," we said of someone with body odor—

into my armpits that I developed something like exudating canker sores under my arms and had to carry them away from my body, as if continually poised for a wingless flight from the top of the six-story YMCA building.

But what tore me asunder, what ripped my intestines out and fed them back to me, was that on the one hand what Cass was doing seemed so unspeakably crass and damning, on the other hand there seemed to be something so spiritual and seraphic in the way this healer of men went about her ministrations that, despite my continuing to pester Cass demanding—often I bellowed and swatted her—to know where she'd learned these things and how many guys there had been other than the Brigadier with whom she'd indulged these "aberrations," Cass would give me only a chilling, "*Haaaay,*" as though demanding her own airspace at the same time she was insisting that whatever the case there was presently no one but me. My paranoia was zooming toward ethereal heights, and if the thought of the Brigadier and Cass together made me damn near rabid, the image of Cass with anyone else made me smash and despoil things and I became one of those hooligans who break men's room mirrors and purposely miss urinals so the piss goes all over the floor for the next poor bastard to step in.

In the way of intuitive women Cass sensed that I was expanding, ballooning up with rage, and poised to burst; and though I didn't know what she was up to, in late spring she began earnestly inquiring, over and over, what I intended to do on my graduation in June. What possessed me to lie, other than the desire to see where Cass was taking me, I don't know; but in fact I'd already been told by the guidance instructor that my grades were an abomination, that I hadn't enough credit hours to graduate and would have to return in the fall and take my diploma in January. To Cass I said, "Get a job, I guess, like everyone else." Once Cass said, "When you're eighteen, maybe Fairley'll put you to work. He's always bitching about no longer having the energy or any time to spend with Howie." My heart leaped at the prospect. Other than my mother's raising holy hell,

I didn't see why not. In any event, Fairley was always handing Cass and me twenty-dollar bills the way other parents dispensed half-dollars and singles and I felt I may as well be doing something for the money.

Then one day, in the first week in June in the halls of the high school, Cass handed me a note written on lined notebook paper. It was scrupulously folded, had enough staples in it to secure a summer cottage for the winter, and I took it into a stall in the boys' room to read. Its tone was pugnacious and defiant and said that if for one second I believed there was anyone else but me I could that night do Cass "in the normal way" and that I needn't bring "one of those things"—obviously a prophylactic—as she knew from cleaning the house where Fairley kept his. Lord, Cass's self-possession had so come to verge on contrariness that I was surprised she hadn't used "rubber" or for that matter "cocksafe."

For months now, Howie again having started to sleep soundly, Cass had abandoned nearly all pretense at demureness. As "I like to see what I'm doing," she'd even begun to leave the lights on. After a minimum of petting, she'd assist me from my trousers, do what she had to do, after which she'd masturbate by rubbing herself back and forth on the length of my bare thigh, while I kissed a copper-colored throat that was the epitome of strength and grace. At the first sign of shuddering orgasm, however, Cass invariably wept chokingly and exclaimed, "Oh, Ex, I'm . . . I'm so embarrassed." Although Cass never removed her panties, afterward my thigh was often so aqueously slick that on one occasion on donning my pants the corduroy stuck momentarily to my leg. It was a good thing, too, that Cass had access to Fairley's condoms. It is not folklore that guys of my generation carried a condom so long in their wallets—boy, were we ready!—that smack in the middle of the imitation alligator leather there eventually rose a moldy lump the size of a silver dollar. In trepidation of my mother's coming across mine (she doubtless already had), I'd flushed it down the toilet only to discover the hideous great circular lump never did vanish, a recurring reminder, if there ever was one, of the Christian admonition that thinking fornication is as grave as committing it.

What happened that night, as well as the repercussions therefrom, I would shut from my mind for years. I could not have functioned in the world otherwise. That I was later institutionalized proves I'd repressed what happened on only the most triflingly conscious level. Although Cass did not remove her blouse or skirt, beneath them she was braless and pantless, she lay on the carpet before the peach couch, placed an old orange-and-white candy-striped beach towel beneath her haunches, then unbuttoned her blouse and pulled up her skirts, exposing herself. If I have learned nothing else in attempting to write, it is that a description of the act is beyond the pale of any artist, however gifted, so that even a Nobel laureate as talented as Hemingway makes us laugh aloud when his fecund earth starts trembling and rumbling, rather as if it were a tum-tum deprived of sufficient gruel, beneath his noble interwined lovers. In retrospect there is no question that in my youthful feverish lust I brutalized Cass or that at some point, or points, she cried out—if I never heard her, how then could I presume to describe the act?—in pained hurtful anguish. I know this happened inasmuch as sometime later when, having donned another of Uncle Fairley's condoms, I reentered Cass, I abruptly became aware of a shoe ardently poking my bare backside, heard someone say, "C'mon, Exley, get the hell up," and turned to find two Watertown policemen, both of whom I knew, hovering over Cass and me.

As nearly as I could later determine, Howie had heard Cass's heartfelt cries, had come unseen down the staircase to find Cass and me lying side by side, Cass in her virginal blood staining the beach towel and sobbingly clutching my neck. Howie had then gone upstairs, called the police and said "Fred Exley is hurting Sis bad." Hesitant to heed a ten-year-old's word and enter Fairley's house unbidden, the police had in turn called Fairley, were told where the key was and ordered to enter the house immediately. Fairley would, he said, be there momentarily. After I'd put on my skivvies, pants, and loafers (when I at last undressed that night, the rubber was still in my underwear), Cass having fled upstairs, I was taken, a cop fiercely clutching each arm, out onto the sidewalk where the officers, Sid and Pat, threatened to charge me with everything from breaking and entering to first-degree assault to statutory and/or first-degree rape. If this weren't sufficient, and if Fairley so wished, Sid and Pat promised they'd beat the shit out of me. What I have to say about those times, or that particular moment in those times, does not in any way exculpate the lies I told about Cass. Still, and whether it excuses me or not, I shall never cease shouting what a stifling, stultifying world the forties and fifties were, how there hovered over our every word, deed, and thought the trepidation of a fearful despotism wreaking its awful vengeance for any distressing act or thought, how we all in one way or another bartered our soul to the rigidly puritanical image the public held of itself, so that if, in terrible fear of those apes carrying out their threats I cowardly and cringingly laid it all at Cass's feet, spitting out unforgivable things like, "She's screwing everybody in town," and so forth. If the times do not exonerate me, and they do not, *they do not,* nevertheless my spinelessness must be seen against a backdrop whereon all one's thoughts and actions were suppressed so that this great abstract high-minded self-righteous lump that called itself America could sleep in blissful ignorance of not only the sleazy but what was, in the case of Cass and Exley, nothing less than love.

Fairley seemed as unflappable as ever, rather as if he were going over the nightly figures at one of his gambling emporiums. He told one of the cops, Sid, to take me up onto the porch, then went into a lengthy mumbled huddle with Pat, interrupted once by Fairley and Pat's going to the back seat of the police car to examine what appeared to be—oh, my Lord!—the orange-and-white beach towel. The only sign of Fairley's ire was his frequently poking Pat severely on the chest with his index finger, as if admonishing him that Fairley did not ever, *ever* expect to hear a word of this again. When the police finally went, smiling and making weak jokes with Fairley as they pulled away from the curb, I bolted from the porch and started across the lawn. I never made it. Moving swiftly, Fairley intercepted me, grabbed me by the arm, swirled me around, and with doubled fist smashed me furiously in the face, knocking me to the ground. When I tried to get up, Fairley knocked me down again and this time the blood was gushing from my nose.

From the Brigadier I'd learned many things about Fairley, precisely the kind of detail that would have held the Brigadier in thrall. Fairley was, for example, a Mangione on his mother's side but I'd never until that moment seen the Sicilian in him. The Brigadier had told me that all Fairley's business was conducted with "the guys in Utica." It was from Utica that the weekly football pools came, and it was to someone in Utica that Fairley laid off his bets; that is, if Fairley had too much Notre Dame money on the USC–Notre Dame game, the guys in Utica were honor-bound to help him cover his bets. It turned out, too, that Fairley, for all his notions of Sicilian honor, cared little about Cass's virginity. What had infuriated Fairley was my insisting to the cops, for Pat had apparently told him, that I was only one of regiments of guys who were screwing Cass.

Still sitting on the wet grass, afraid to rise again, I began weeping. Fairley said, "For Christ's sake, Ex, if Cass was fucking everyone, what the hell was that on the towel? Iodine? What do you want? To have Cass sent back to that fucking Home?" Furious saliva was coming from Fairley's twisted mouth. "I ought to have your legs broken, Ex. I just wish your dad was alive. He'd break them for me. You'd better damn well know your brother Bill is going to hear about this anyway." When he was going up the lawn toward the house, he turned abruptly back, pointed the finger with which he'd poked Pat on his chest, and very evenly said, "If you ever come around here again, Ex, your legs will get broken."

If my work has frequently evidenced a hatred for women, it is not women I hate but a woman, Cass—for Cass copped out, as assuredly as if she'd made that exhilarating leap from the Golden Gate Bridge, copped out with all the loops untied, with all the fences unmended, without giving me the chance to grovel in apology at her feet, without allowing Cass and me the time to grow into that happy maturity which would have permitted us to laugh heartily in the knowledge that we hadn't—or at least Cass hadn't—done anything at all, copped out and left me with a grief and guilt so burdensome it is something of a marvel that I survived. Oh, they have a fancy name for it today, anorexia nervosa, and every alternate month the women's magazines have a piece on it, written in that ghoulish chitchat style, rather as if halitosis or feminine hygiene was under discussion. Of course I doubt any Watertown physician in the late forties had diagnosed Cass as anorectic-bulimic and it wasn't until many years later, when I did my own researches into anxiety-related ejaculation, that I also unearthed what had happened to Cass.

When she hadn't shown up for the first two weeks of the fall semester, in alarm I sought out Shirl Carpenter, the babysitter from the Home whom Cass and I had used when we went out, and asked her where Cass was. Shirl told me Cass was "awful sick, Fred. She won't eat, and even if she does, she sticks her finger down her throat and throws it all up again. All she does is sleep. She thinks she's too fat. Imagine, Fred! Cass? Fat? God, Fred, there isn't a girl in this school who wouldn't give her eyeteeth to have Cass's figure!"

Cass died near the end of October, goddamn her rotten selfish soul. Even when years later I read the psychological claptrap suggesting the patient-victim refuses to eat "in response to an unconscious urge to make herself unattractive to boys" or, and more telling in Cass's case, "there is an association between eating and oral sex and a refusal to eat is a refusal to admit the idea of fellation," above and beyond all this pontificating dribble, yet the thing was to survive

‡ 315

in order to discover just how innocuous and paltry our sins had been. As ridiculously ironical as it may seem, considering my own cringing cowardice in the matter, I never did forgive Cass.

It took me a quarter of a century and a lot of living even to say good-bye to Cass. One autumn day I bought a dozen long-stemmed white roses, went to the lovely shaded Brookside Cemetery on the south side of the city, and asked the caretaker to direct me to Cass's grave, which, as it happened, wasn't far from my father's stone. Believe me when I say I'd fully intended to tell Cass I'd forgiven her as well as myself. But when I got to the grave I found I was sobbing so uncontrollably that snot was leaking from my nose, between terrifying, gasping sobs I spat out, *"Fuck you, Cass,"* then walked to my father's grave and laid the long-stemmed white roses there, which in a way was really the first time I'd been mature enough to say good-bye to Dad.

5

After my January graduation, I worked on the railroad for months, loading great canvas bags of mail onto dolly carts that were taken by freight elevators up to platforms and thrown onto the boxcars of mail trains. It was dim-witted, backbreaking, brutalizing work; and in the fall, having at last heeded those teachers who for years had told me I should be getting Bs by just showing up for class, I went to stay with my aunt in Goldens Bridge, New York, and enrolled in the John Jay High School in Katonah for a postgraduate course. In one year I took physics, chemistry, biology, plane geometry, intermediate algebra, and trigonometry and stabbed Spanish II for my college entrance language requirement. Although I'm told it is no longer allowed, in those days stabbing meant that the student did not attend classes and either studied the material on his own or was tutored, or both (as in my case), and then took the New York State Regents Examination, the only obstacle being that, whereas a 65 was ordinarily a passing grade, on a stab a student had to get 75.

Two days before the test, while cleaning my aunt's garage, I took a Coke break (Coca-Cola in those ingenuous days) and skimmed an ancient dog-eared dust-ridden *Reader's Digest*. In it there was an article on Bolivia or Argentina or Chile, one of those countries, and because I was at the time studying Spanish I naturally read it. On the test two days later, the student was asked to translate an article from Spanish to English and I hadn't read three sentences before it occurred to me, my stomach in my mouth (as though I'd done something spooky, I actually looked over both shoulders), that it was the article I'd just read in my aunt's garage, obviously taken from the *Digest*'s Spanish edition. Effortlessly I slipped through the translation, had it come out in glibly idiomatic English, was given twenty-nine of thirty points, a pat on the head from my proud tutor, and an overall 86 Regents grade. As I was that year named to the North Westchester Interscholastic League all-star basketball team, it was in many ways the most productive year of my life. As I've said elsewhere, four of our five starters got basketball scholarships, to Springfield College, Bowling Green, Bradley, and the University of Texas. The reason I didn't was that my five-ten height, though not as grotesquely impossible as it would be today, mitigated against me.

Perhaps my reason for not recognizing Fairley nearly thirty years later was that, like Dorian Gray, he had changed so incredibly little. I was staying with friends on Singer Island, Florida, where I had spent a good deal of my adulthood. Whenever, at four, I made my afternoon pilgrimage to the Beer Barrel for draft beer, I'd find I'd no sooner be seated than Fairley and Howie, the latter now well into his thirties, would wheel their ten-speed bicycles into the bar, lean them against the brick wall fronting the street, take stools on the opposite side of the bar from me, and order two cans of Budweiser. They'd be sweating from their afternoon exertions. Although we invariably nodded politely at each other, there was on their part no sign of recognition either, and they invariably asked for blank paper and a ballpoint and went into a whispering huddle that seemed to involve a good deal of adding and subtracting. Fairley and Howie, I later learned, were buying and selling a good deal of Florida real estate, lots, homes, condominiums.

Not recognizing Fairley may have been understandable, not seeing Cookie Parish written all over Howie's handsome mug was unforgivable. Of course Fairley was the last guy in the world anyone would have expected to see taking daily exercise, his hair was still a vigorish black, and where his pallor had once evidenced the sickly gray of night people the sun had now turned him an olive dark and for the second time he manifested the Siciliano in him. Fairley had to be sixty-five, he looked forty-five; Howie had to be late thirties, he looked mid-twenties, athlete written all over him, including the badge of all contact sport jocks, a partial plate in the uppers of what were otherwise perfect teeth. One afternoon, having nodded politely at each other and going immediately to our own things, Exley to dreams, Fairley and Howie to the reality of figures, from the far end of the room the bartender Jaylene hollered, "Hey, Exley, you're wanted on the phone."

It was my hostess informing me that her husband had called from his office and was actually taking her to the Top of the Spray for dinner that night. "Can you believe that shit, Ex?" In fact, Moose invariably took Veronica out once a week but it utterly behooved Veronica's homemaker martyrdom to see the mysterious miracle of an ongoing *affaire de coeur* in something as unredeemably American as a New York strip steak and a baked potato with sour cream and chives.

As Moose and Veronica had long since given up suggesting I put on a necktie and join them, I was, one must understand, getting directions for the preparation of my supper. There was a tuna casserole and a tossed salad in the refrigerator. Veronica told me at what temperature to set the oven and how long to bake the casserole. As for the tossed salad, all I had to do was put the dressing of my choice on it. Exley is saying yeah, yeah. Veronica also told me that a Hemingway short story was being dramatized on the public TV channel that night. Exley gave his bored yeah, bored because I knew when I got home all this would be neatly spelled out (itemized A, B, C, etc.) on a note under the salt and pepper mills on the kitchen table. If I dwell at length, laughingly imagining my liberated woman reader cringing at what a loutish subservient boob this Veronica must be, I dwell at this length so that I might disarm that reader by saying that Veronica is one of the brightest, most competent, and tough-minded women I've ever known, and I defy any honest reader, however exaltedly liberated, to challenge the truth that a woman never, never gets over the intransigent myth that there is something basically and despicably infantile—as indeed there may be—in a man. My all-time favorite came from a girl—a Berkeley Phi Beta Kappa—with whom I once lived briefly. "Dearest Ex, When you do our laundry today, please, *please* don't roll your socks into balls. Naturally, for convenience's sake, you'll want to pair them. But just lay them flat, one atop the other. Rolling them wrecks the elastic that holds them up, shortens their life span, and if one day you dress hurriedly—and you, asshole, never dress any other way!—and go to some nice place, you'll find that in embarrassment you are continually reaching down to your ankles to pull them up to your calves. Where they belong! Love and XXXXXXXXs, G."

When I returned to my barstool, I sensed immediately that there was something terribly wrong in the room, some palpable absence of motion and muted sound, an eerie feeling that time had suspended itself, no, that time had fleetingly regressed and, my face already reddening in abruptly queasy recognition, my breathing stayed, my jaw slack, I looked up and across the bar to find both Fairley and Howie equally agape in astonishment.

"Fred?" Fairley said.

"Fairley? Howie? *Howie?*"

Fairley and Howie had adjoining spacious apartments

on one of the top floors of the Côte d'Azur, one of the new, extremely costly condominiums that had sprung up on and all but ruined the Singer Island I'd first known twenty years earlier. The island had then been a place of first-name familiarity, of one-story sidewalk cafes where, in one's bathing trunks, a guy could buy a can or shell of beer and with it in hand wander from one cafe to the next in search of friends, a place where (and I kid you not) the billionaire, John D. MacArthur, had electric eye doors installed in his Colonnades Beach Hotel so that a buddy of his, a tramp Basset hound with one ball (that one dragged on the pavement, too!), could enter the lobby, walk through the dining room, exit the back door, and take a dip in the pool. And screw the sensibilities of the guests.

On the lower floors of the Côte d'Azur Fairley owned four other condominiums, three of which he leased, the fourth a one-bedroom he kept for guests from "up home." I expect it was at this point in our conversation, for Fairley and Howie, after vigorous handshakes and embraces, had immediately asked me over for a drink, that Fairley suggested that any time I wanted the one-bedroom—"You know what I mean, Ex, to write or somethin' "—for the winter, I shouldn't hesitate to ask, I expect it was at this point that I was finally and relievedly certain that Fairley hadn't brought me to his apartment for ancient and futile recriminations. There was, in fact, something so touchingly urgent and self-effacing in his invitation that I had no doubt Fairley genuinely wanted me in that apartment, that for whatever reason he desperately yearned for some proximity to me. Unless we are psychopathic, we spend our lives as psychologically self-flagellating penitents and Fairley was in some odd way making amends, struggling mightily to articulate apologies that weren't necessary, being crumbled into old age by all the days and acts that waste the soul. And for what was Fairley trying to apologize? For smashing and bloodying my nose? No, if anyone ever had it coming, I had. In his contrivedly dramatic way, Fairley was groping for something quite else.

Although I could see Howie fidgeting anxiously, irritably repressing the urge to help his father put into words what he must have known Fairley was building up to, for a time at least Howie neither intruded on whatever Fairley felt was between himself and me nor once interrupted the don. When I say don, I of course do so in the most blatantly tongue-in-cheek way. If Fairley was part of an organization, as he most certainly was, he would have been something a good deal more than what romance novelists call "a soldier." It was, however, obviously a question that out of simple courtesy—not fear—one did not put to Fairley. For all that, I had no doubt whatever that had I, in an academic way, put such a question to Fairley, he knew enough about me, I about him, to know that without blinking an eye he would have given me the larger upstate New York picture, chapter, verse, and numbers.

Fairley and Howie, for example, had recently seen *The Godfather* and Howie told me how "Pop" had, to the consternation and extreme ire of those viewers seated around them, laughed all the way through it, including laughing at those places the audience was accepting with a reverent solemnity. When they were leaving the theater, Howie said, Pop, still chuckling helplessly, had turned to him and said, "Howie, that was the most hilarious Guinea fairy tale I ever saw." Caught up in the spirit of it, and laughing in reminiscence, Fairley leaped from his chair, disappeared and returned wearing a shoulder holster over his cyclist's sweatshirt, bearing a great iron skillet in his right hand. For my present edification, Fairley now put on his best mock-Siciliano accent, with his left hand made an urgent stirring motion in the skillet and said, "You know, Ex, first-ah we make-ah up some-ah nice-ah spicy meatballs, then we go make-ah duh hits." Howie and I laughed. Fairley couldn't have more eloquently exonerated himself from any notion that however he'd spent his days, it had been just as dreary and time-consuming—though doubtless extremely more lucrative—than an insurance man's showing up at the same underwriter's desk for thirty years.

Howie blew his stack only once. An hour and three vodka and tonics into the conversation we were on to the subject of Cookie. "It was what the shrinks call—what is it they call it, Howie?"

"*Schizophrenia. She was a goddamn hopeless schizophrenic, Pop.*" Howie was fuming.

"There's no need to get nasty about it. And it's your mother we're talking about!"

"Yes, there is a need to get nasty. I hate it when you do that to me, Pop. Use me for your straight man, your educated son from Colgate. I got a B.A. in business—with a C minus average, I might add—and learned more in a month working for you than I did in four years at Hamilton. I was a fucking jock, Pop. I don't give a goddamn if you do it in front of people we don't care about. But this is Ex, for Christ's sake. He's family, he was there at the beginning and don't think he can't see through that dumb wop facade of yours. It's humiliating, Pop. It's goddamn humiliating."

Fairley was stony with shame, for that fleeting moment sagging under the weight of his sixty-five years.

Howie turned to me and spoke, his voice considerably moderated. "You know what he did, Ex? He paid some quack shrink across the inlet in Palm Beach a hundred and fifty clams an hour for a solid year so he could talk about Cookie and her sister, Cass's mom that is, and Cass. Before he even went to this clown, he must have read twenty volumes on schizophrenia. I'll take you into his bedroom and show them to you. He tortures himself with it. After a year of being reassured that he couldn't have done anything to help either of them—the fucking quack even told Fairley he knew more about schizophrenia than the quack did—Fairley still tortures himself with the notion that he didn't do enough. He refuses to dwell on the nice things he's done for people. If I ever told you, Ex, you'd shit—the people's houses and cars he saved from the banks, the fuel and grocery bills he paid so kids wouldn't freeze or starve, I'm talking here about thousands and thousands of dollars. When he mentioned buying your brother Bill that Pontiac, it was the first time I ever heard him admit to having done anything for anyone. And what happens? He gets so flustered for having let that kindness slip out, he can't talk for five minutes. He thought Bill had told you." He turned back to Fairley. "Admit it, Fairley. You thought Bill had told Fred, didn't you? *Admit it, Fairley.*"

Fairley didn't speak.

After Howie had mixed the drinks and we'd seated ourselves, the subject of the Brigadier was nearly the first order of business. Fairley had told me how proud he was of Bill and how sorry he was to have heard of his death. "Forty-six, Ex, that's too young. *Too young.* I cried. Yeah, Ex, I bawled like a baby. Ask Howie." As Fairley and Howie had been in Florida eight years, having I gathered made a lot of money (whether for Fairley or for Fairley and "the guys in Utica," one didn't ask) in the Orlando–Disney World boom and having come south to Palm Beach County two years before, I expressed surprise they'd heard of the Brigadier's death. *"Heard about it?"* Howie said. "Come here and look at this shit, Ex." Off the lavish master bedroom there was a tastefully furnished den with three oak filing cabinets, atop which lay a dozen or so copies of the most recent *Watertown Times*, apparently copies Fairley had yet to read and clip.

Laughing and pulling out the appropriate drawer, Howie took out three manila folders astonishingly bearing the legends EXLEY I, II, and III. In my father's Fairley had all kinds of clippings, concluding with his obituary, in Bill's he had chronologically arranged clippings detailing his military career, his Silver Star, and his two Purple Hearts and I detected that those Fairley must have deemed most important, as Bill's being awarded the Legion of Merit, were laminated so the newsprint wouldn't fade. Fairley, Howie said, had a file on everyone he'd ever known "up home." Howie repeated, "Look at this shit, Ex."

Going to another drawer and ripping out a thick file labeled ME, Howie, quite beside himself with laughter by now, pulled from a stack of tamer clippings two or three relating to Fairley's having pleaded *nolo contendere* to violation of the gambling laws. "I mean, listen, Ex, he's done this all his life. Nothing's real to him until he reads it in *The Watertown Times*. I mean, anybody else in America says 'I read it in the *Times,*' they're talking about the big guy in New York City, right? Not Fairley!" In mock exasperation Howie sighed and wagged his head. That wagging was charged with overwhelming affection for "Pop."

Back in the living room, Fairley was saying, "The last time I saw Bill was when he was home on leave after Korea. Remember, Ex, he was limping and had a cane? The jeep he was in was strafed by a MIG, rolled over on him, squashing his pelvis and hip? Remember the new Pontiac with all the trimmings?"

"Sure do. Borrowed it to go on a date and ran it into a snowbank. Didn't have the money to have it towed out, so I called the Brigadier. Boy, was he pissed. Fortunately for my ass, there was no damage."

"I bought him that Pontiac. But I'm sure you knew that. Yeah, I was so proud of Bill, winning the Congressional Medal and all."

"It was the Silver Star, Pop. For Christ's sake, we're talking to Ex now. He knows what medals Bill won." By way of apology, Howie turned back to me. "Pop always does that. As though the Silver Star wasn't good enough. Pop has to make it the Congressional. He does that with everybody he knows. Vince Lombardi never really cut me. I just decided because Pop was alone I'd come home and help him with business. Like you, Ex. You were only nominated for a National Book Award, right? Not when Pop tells it! *You won. You better goddamn well believe you won.* And Cookie, Mom, I should say. She was more beautiful than Elizabeth Taylor. And Cass was going to be even more beautiful than that!"

"I don't mean to sound phony, Howie, but I'd have rather had your mom on my arm any day than Liz."

As no one spoke for a moment, I said, "I didn't know you bought that Pontiac for Bill." And I was almost as immediately sorry; for everything Howie later pointed out to Fairley about himself was true. Instantly Fairley became flustered and jumpy, no, he withdrew into himself utterly and became near stricken, downright overwrought that he'd allowed anything as endearing as his own generosity to stand revealed. There was something awesomely decent and civilized about Fairley; and whether or not he'd spent his life in the company of thugs from what the fiction writers call "the brotherhood" or "la cosa nostra," it occurred to me, at that moment came to me as an absolute fact, that for Fairley there were bonds a good deal more tenacious than those theatrical ones and that these ties were nothing other than what I shall here call "the bonds of home."

In *Daniel Martin* John Fowles has his narrator speak eloquently to the idea of Robin Hood and his merry men in Sherwood Forest being the quintessential British myth, that is, the myth of "hiding" and how he—the narrator—had once made the egregious error of penning a grimly realistic movie script based on this myth, not at the time realizing that, whether we were English or American "colonists," Errol Flynn and Maid Marion and Friar Tuck and Little John sitting about the fireside deep, deep in the green, green forest, all gnawing ravenously on shanks of venison, was absolutely indispensable to the health of our psyches—this notion that there was actually a place—hence Heaven, perhaps the ultimate myth—to which we could all repair and be at peace. Fowles calls it both "the sacred combe" and "la bonna vaux" or "the valley of abundance." And what else was Fairley's den with its oak filing cabinets stuffed with *Watertown Times* clippings but a place for Fairley to go and hide and lovingly finger, caress, fondle, and ponder these articles while fantasizing that there was actually a time when the world was a younger, greener, and more lovely place?

Not long ago I had a prominent editor and publisher call me from Utah, where he'd gone to ski. The day before he'd called from New York City to reject a piece of mine (a very flattering form of rejection), saying that though he'd loved it and how much he'd laughed at it, he found it too inward and explained it belonged "in the Exley corner." When I countered with the truth that—despite nitwits (rushing to exclude the editor from this company) who persist in believing I write about nothing but myself—I have never written a single sentence about Frederick Exley except as he exists as a created character—Robert Penn Warren was perceptive enough to see this years ago—and that Watertown was nothing other than a state of mind, he sighed and said okay and asked for a couple more weeks to think about the piece. When he'd gone out to the tow that morning—"Listen to this, Ex!"—the first guy he'd encountered had a baseball cap bearing the legend WATERTOWN. The editor was roaring with laughter. "I mean, what is it with you fucking guys?" Seeing my opening, I said, "But if he'd come from Bellow country, it could as easily have said CHICAGO. From Styron country, TIDEWATER. From Cheever country, WESTCHESTER. From James Jones country, SCHOFIELD BARRACKS. From O'Hara country, SCRANTON. Give me a break and try to understand." "I'm trying, Ex, I'm trying."

When Fairley got on to Cass, I sensed instantly it was something I couldn't bear to hear. Howie had come up on the edge of his chair, his wonderfully athletic body rigid, no, paralyzed with tension, the cords in his neck popping as though he were pumping iron, his entire being screaming, "Leave it alone, Pop." But Fairley would have none of it. He had his hand up in the manner of a pompously imperious traffic cop signaling *Stop*. Directed squarely at Howie, Fairley's entire demeanor was telling Howie that in this matter he wouldn't under any circumstances be interrupted. When in reply to Fairley's query whether I knew why Cass had come to live with him and Cookie, I related Cass's version of the head of the Home's not permitting her to stay overnight unless Fairley became her foster father, Fairley smiled sadly and said that hadn't been the case at all.

In the early years, Cookie hadn't wanted to take Cass for fear of becoming too attached to her—"An easy kid to love, right, Ex?"—and then have Cookie's sister come back from Florida and take Cass from her. When it became apparent Cass's mother and "that shithead" she was living with in Florida were never coming back, Cookie and Fairley had begged Cass to come and live with them but by then Cass was into her fantasy about her admiral father—"Warrant officer," Howie interjected, only to be cut dead by Fairley's icy stare—and absolutely refused to come and live with them as "the admiral" would be sending for her any day.

One day Fairley's attorney had come unannounced to Fairley's kitchen when he was having coffee—in his midnight-blue robe?—and asked Cookie if he might speak with Fairley alone. One of the attorney's present clients, who had gone down twice before, was now being held on a breaking and entering, a potential three-time loser unable to make bail and in return for Fairley's posting bond, the client had information he wanted to trade.

Fairley said, "The creep's going to run, isn't he?"

"Probably. Look, Fairley, I'm only here as an intermediary and I'm so goddamn nervous—look at my hands—about even passing on this information that all my courtroom decorum and diplomacy will of necessity be cast to the winds. You've got to bear with me on this, Fairley."

"Shoot."

It seems that for a couple years past Cass had been going out the window of the Home nights, by prearranged appointments had met with three, four, and five guys in a car, by Cass's requirements men over twenty-five and unlikely to have contact with her classmates, and for five dollars apiece had gone down on them. Removing a scrap of paper from his pocket, the attorney had shown Fairley the inked figure $2,225, which, the attorney said, was Cass's current balance—"Obviously a good deal of it babysitting money," the attorney had said, nervously attempting to balm Fairley —in the Watertown National Bank. Although he needn't have told me, Fairley said he went crazy, headed immediately to the Home and on the pretext of using Cass as a babysitter that night had brought her back to Park Circle and to Cookie and Howie's horror, screams, and sobs, for

Cookie and Howie were totally ignorant of what was taking place, had beaten Cass half to death with his belt.

When I looked over at Howie, he had in memory of it collapsed utterly, his mother's great blue eyes pools of shimmering grief. It was all coming back to me now, but I of course daren't say what I now knew. When I was a kid, the client in question had been a great high school halfback, everything after that was downhill and though we were all saddened by his steady deterioration we were all nevertheless shocked when we picked up *The Watertown Times* and saw that the aging halfback—he was twenty-five—had "hanged" himself in his cell. Apparently the halfback's information hadn't been forthcoming soon enough or whipping Cass hadn't by any means sated Fiorello Mangione Parish's fury.

"You gotta understand, Ex, Cass was going to come to me and Cookie with a check for three grand or so and tell us it was from the admiral and she was off to study nursing in San Diego. And remember, Ex, I was only thirty-five and dumber than dogshit. When I told Bill about her, though I certainly didn't tell him what she'd done at the Home—and he in turn told you, right?—I thought poor Cass had enjoyed what she'd done. I was so fucking stupid it didn't occur to me 'til years later that she'd loathed every minute of it. You know, I thought that with Bill I'd at least know who she was with. And by then she was so terrified of me—"

"That's not true, Pop! *Cass worshipped you!*"

"—she was so terrified of me, she probably thought she had to do it. You know, Ex, a horny USO hostess or somethin' giving her all for the good of the services."

When I had first entered the apartment I had been struck immediately by the couch to which Fairley had directed me. Detecting that I was bouncing nervously about on it, that I kept looking down on it and was actually lovingly and bewilderingly fingering the brocade, Fairley started laughing and said, "Yeah, Ex, it's the same couch, Cookie's favorite. Of course it's been redone a few times since those days." Howie laughed, too. "Redone? *Redone?* Listen, Ex, the last time we couldn't find the material and had to have the material made. Hey, we're not talking here about an accomplished carpenter remaking a leg. We're talking about a small fortune creating material from scratch. Fairley better live to be Methuselah's age—the old bastard probably will. Looks great, doesn't he, Ex? We've got enough material up home in storage to last until four thousand A.D."

Now I was sitting there stricken with distress at what I'd just heard about Cass, staring down at the floor, my head throbbing with a grief burdensome enough to detonate the cosmos. Then suddenly, lo, there was Cass as I'd seen her last, on the carpet at my feet, her blouse unbuttoned, her skirts pulled up, the orange-and-white candy-striped beach towel beneath her shanks, her arms outstretched to me in urgent, desperate, utterly unfettered invitation, yes, despite what I'd just heard about Cass, at that long-ago moment it had been on Cass's part nothing less than a tendering of love. Then I fainted dead away.

When I came round, I was on the carpet between the couch and the great Danish coffee table, Howie had my head bent over between my legs, and I heard him say, "God, Pop, he's wet himself. You go too far, Pop. *Too far.*" When I got to my feet, it was terrible, with Fairley as jittery and ashamed as a maiden aunt, in the Italian way jumping excitedly about and begging me to take a shower, put on some of his underwear and trousers, and not leave him at that moment. "Not now, Ex, not now, *please.* I've got some baked ziti we can warm up, we'll have an oil-and-vinegar salad, a glass or two of vino, and a few laughs. Like the old days, Ex. Like the old days."

I did not of course stay. When Howie was driving me home, I said, "I don't mean to be alarmist, Howie, but how do you feel? Your Mom's illness, I've read, can be endemic in families." Howie said that when he'd been teasing Pop about his visits to the suave Palm Beach psychiatrist, he'd neglected to mention he'd gone every day Pop had and the quack had assured him he was one of the sanest people he knew. "He said the Mangione in me saved me." As I was getting out of his Aston Martin, Howie told me how lonely Fairley was and said that I had, absolutely had, to come back and see Fairley. "I will, I will." When Howie asked for my phone number, I substituted an eight for the nine in the final digit.

After showering and pouring myself a stiff vodka, I lay down on the couch and stared unseeing at the dramatization of the Hemingway story, thinking instead of a TV interview I'd seen some years before with an intellectual who'd been in Paris in the twenties with Hemingway, Joyce, et al. The intellectual was utterly perplexed by the Joyce-Hemingway friendship and saw them as a kind of Mutt and Jeff strolling the boulevards and hitting the bistros of Paris together. An odd couple, to the intellectual's way of thinking, this big brusque laconic midwestern Hemingway with his contemptible high school diploma out of Oak Park, Illinois, mucking about with this petite half-blind vitriolic Irish genius educated to Latin and Greek by the Jesuits. As with most intellectuals and academics, the interviewee had missed the point of the relationship entirely. Hemingway had only to read a single paragraph of Joyce, Joyce reciprocate, to understand that Joyce and Hemingway were bound together by being on the same arduous, near-reverent pilgrimage, that is, of what the French call "breaking the language," of doing nothing less than taking English and making it their very own. And this in turn got me laughing as I thought of yet another academic myth, that of Joyce's bold brave lonely impoverished exile on the Continent. Joyce never approached paper with pen, however indignantly and sardonically, without finding himself smack dab in the middle of his loathed and beloved Dublin. Joyce never left home. And though I shouldn't, in my zaniest and most ill fantasies, presume to mention my name in the same sentence with Joyce or Hemingway, this is precisely what I'd been trying to tell the editor who'd called me from that ski resort off yonder there in Utah.

Part Five

MARRIAGE
AND
RESURRECTION

1

Frederick Exley, the author, is going to have a good long slumbering sleep, Alissa. With any luck, perhaps he won't wake up. This afternoon, in the company of Ms. Robin Glenn and his warder Hannibal, he walked for two and a half hours on the breathtaking White Manele Beach, back and forth, back and forth, the three of them taking a dip in the natural coral pool at the east end of the beach on the completion of every fifth lap. By the third lap, the tide was up, the ocean broke crashingly on the coral barrier, creating a spray luminous with rainbow colors stunning enough to break the heart. What, you might well ask, prompts this sudden health kick? On getting from bed two mornings ago, Frederick detected not only that his head was continually snapping to the right side, like so, but that these snaps were compounded by an alarming vertigo. Worse still, after slipping into his T-shirt and Bermuda shorts intent on joining Hannibal on the Lodge's porch for coffee and his snarling arguments—Hannibal likes the latter very much—with the morning *Advertiser*'s ghastly headlines (a world gone mad?), he took four steps, his legs gave out completely, and, falling sideways, he crashed into his writing table, toppling his Olympia portable, fortunately for once secured in its plastic case, onto the linoleum floor, creating a thunderous thud. You shall be pleased to hear, Alissa, in fact, I suspect you shall gloat, that at that moment Exley, the guy you have so often dubbed the Terminal Skeptic, appealed to God. Yes he did. As he was going down, Frederick Exley said, "Dear God, if this be a stroke, don't let me come round leaking spittle from the side of my mouth, my typing fingers gone—let me, Christ, you fatherless bastard, take the deep six now."

2

In her grief and panic Ms. Robin Glenn was nothing less than majestic. Leaping naked from bed, her hair in disarray, she ran out onto the porch shrieking, *"Hannibal, Hannibal, Frederick's dying!"* Surprisingly, that oaf Hannibal wasn't much more composed than Ms. Robin Glenn, though he was of course considerably more utilitarian. For whatever reason, probably nothing other than his constant proximity to me, Hannibal has in his groping inarticulate way become fond of me and while Robin grew more hysterical Hannibal began weeping, running his incredible hands through his hair, and saying, *"Eese bad, eese bad, Frederick bad boy."* Both Robin and Hannibal knew, however, that I hadn't had a drink in two days. Hannibal then reached down and as though I were a hundred-pound sack of cement—my weight, Alissa, is 180!—picked me up, the three of us exited to the porch, went down the steps, and started across the lawn toward the hospital, with Hannibal's abominable snowman feet crunching the cones beneath the towering Norfolk pines. As we hurried, Hannibal continued his "Frederick bad boy, Frederick bad boy," while Robin, having donned a blue terry cloth robe and not to be outdone, kept patting her lovely tum-tum and crying, "Oh, Frederick, don't die and leave your son fatherless. Not fatherless! I only got pregnant to give you a son!" It was all rather like Ophelia's marvelous burial scene in *Hamlet*, the players absolutely determined to upstage one another in their grief. Here I might add, Alissa, that Robin is the only pregnant woman I've known who still has her monthly periods.

Dr. Jim, in his pajamas, his mustaches twitching as they do in dismay, pissed off at being roused from sleep at 5 A.M., twice took my blood pressure in both arms, angrily shaking his head. He then asked the two night nurses to do the same. They did so, forbiddingly. Afterward the three of them walked to the far end of the emergency room and went into one of those grave handwringing whispering consultation. When Dr. Jim came back to us, I could see he was furious. "What a pain in the ass you are, Exley." "Frederick's dying," Robin shrieked. "The father of my son is dying!" "His blood pressure is 140 over 90, goddamn good for him." When he asked how much I'd been drinking, I indignantly replied that I hadn't had a drink for two whole days. *"Two whole days,"* Robin reiterated. With equal indignation Dr. Jim snapped, "Well, you're suffering delirium tremens, *that's what you're suffering.*"

"I've never had the shakes in my goddamn life!"
"Never!" Robin cried.
"Now look, Exley, let me practice the medicine around here, will yuh? I spent half my internship in an alcoholic ward and can tell without even a blood test, which I will of course take anyway, that all the potassium is gone from your body, causing your legs to give out. I've warned you repeatedly about taking those diuretics with alcohol. Alcohol is a diuretic, too." Dr. Jim then told Hannibal to pick me up, to throw me on the bed in Room 12, asked one of the nurses to draw some blood, and said he was going to feed me some

potassium intravenously. It would, he said, take most of the day and half the night. He would give me something to help me sleep the next few nights. When he released me in the morning, after having given me a couple massive doses of Vitamin B_{12}, he wanted Hannibal and me to walk leisurely around Lanai City's village square, or do so until my legs tired. The following day, which was of course today, Dr. Jim recommended we go down to White Manele Beach and do the same. He also gave me a photocopied sheet listing foods high in potassium content. Personally he recommended I bake up a half dozen potatoes at a crack, scoop out the pulp, and eat the skins with a salt substitute.

But I am yet being so very evasive, Alissa. As you above all must know, I have always had this dream of the two of us ending together, married, and in the hope you'd have the son you've always professed to have wanted, despite having turned down at least three guys I feel would have been perfectly suitable. Like most writers, I had this sappy vision of finishing the third volume of my trilogy, having it come out to great acclaim, realizing that this in turn would send the readers, in droves, back to the first two volumes. Oh, Alissa, it was a fantasy of nothing less than millions. I'd persuade you to give up your practice (I mean, you'd have quite enough on your hands with me!) and we'd spend half the year in London and the other half on Belgravia Island. Let's face it, Alissa, by your own admission most of your patients are wealthy matronly broads who are into six whole martinis a day (big fucking deal!), have let themselves get too wide in the arse, and have husbands who are mucking about with younger chicks. Still, and I must remind you that you yourself told me this, these women actually believe they have problems of monumental *gravitas,* when in fact the solution is nothing other than accepting the normal aging process and working reverently to keep themselves in shape. I mean, what would there have been for you to give up, Alissa?

Still, I have put aside this fantasy once and for all. And, as I've said, I very much doubt that this letter shall reach you in any event and I now know beyond a shadow of a doubt that I shall never finish my trilogy, least of all shall I finish it to acclaim and the inevitable millions that necessarily accrue to that acclaim. But I still zig and zag, Alissa, play the elusive phantom, so let me at last come to the point and confess to you that I have married Ms. Robin Glenn and that I wanted to be sober when explaining my reasons. It is a long, complex, guilt-ridden, doubtless unintentionally funny tale and I ask you, dear, dearest Alissa, to bear with me through this.

3

In the early morning hours of March 16, 1968, to the everlasting shame and discomfort of the American people, units of the Americal Division's Eleventh Light Infantry Brigade had been set down by helicopter outside the villages of My Lai 1 and My Lai 4 where, they had been told, they would encounter the Vietcong's elite and lethally capable Forty-eighth Battalion. After a five-minute artillery barrage or "prepping" of both villages, a Charlie Company platoon, commanded in the field by twenty-six-year-old 1st Lt. William L. Calley, Jr., was put down near My Lai 4, platoons of Bravo Company, commanded eventually (after the quick death of Lt. Roy B. Cochran) by Lt. Thomas K. Willingham, set down outside My Lai 1. Encountering heavily hedgerowed, booby-trapped, and mined fields in the approaches to My Lai 1, and immediately beginning to sustain casualties, including the aforementioned Lieutenant Cochran, the Bravo Company platoons were ordered to abandon their part of the operation and proceed south to a shantytown of mud and straw hutches or "hootches." They there killed between fifty and a hundred women, children, and old men.

Walking unimpeded into My Lai 4, Lieutenant Calley's Charlie Company platoon, using their M-16 rifles and M-60 machine guns, with a kind of workaday blood lunacy, slaughtered approximately 130 women, children, and old men. On that day the artillery barrages, the gunships (helicopters armed to the gunwales with heavy-caliber machine guns and rockets), and the ground troops or "grunts" accounted for the deaths of 500 (the real count will never be known) civilians, for which they would claim the capture of at most three enemy rifles. At a debriefing the next day at the American Division headquarters at Chu Lai, called to pass on the stunning news of Task Force Barker's grandiose success, a number of officers were heard to sneer and laugh derisively at the ratio of the number of the enemy claimed killed in action (KIAs) as against the absurdity of a mere three weapons captured.

Although the scandal would ultimately reach all the way to Maj. Gen. Samuel W. Koster, the superintendent of the United States Military Academy at West Point, who on March 16, 1968, had been the American Division's top honcho, and would involve scores of lesser officers and enlisted men, only five soldiers eventually stood trial, four being acquitted and Lieutenant Calley being convicted. If there was anything more senseless than the slaughter of these innocents, it had been the incompetence and lack of communication in army intelligence. The dreaded Vietcong Forty-eighth Battalion comprised 400 men. Employing hit-and-run tactics, they had inflicted heavy casualties upon and severely demoralized units of the American Division. It was therefore no tactical accident that platoons of the American were selected to go into My Lais 1 and 4 to wreak vengeance on the Cong's Forty-eighth, Americans chosen precisely because they had lost so many friends to that deadly battalion. On the very day the men of Task Force Barker began their sanguinary work, however, it was known at our intelligence headquarters at Quang Ngai that the Cong's feared and loathed Forty-eighth Battalion was an astonishing nine miles from either My Lai 1 or My Lai 4.

On March 16, 1968, Lt. Col. William R. Exley, of the 500th Military Intelligence Group, was stationed at the airport or what in Saigon was called Pentagon East. It was the Brigadier's job to "isolate targets." Like most lay people I at one time assumed that the Brigadier studied maps and enemy troop movements and passed this information on to field commanders, though of course I was assured that he did that, too. In intelligence jargon, however, and as all people interested in such things now know, isolating targets is a euphemism for isolating human beings as possible sources of information, the spies (Vietnamese in this case) who come in from the cold, buying information from them, then separating the wheat from the chaff by continuing to do business with only those agents who appear to be feeding accurate information. And though I have been assured by a number of Bill's friends that the intelligence that placed the Cong's Forty-eighth Battalion at My Lai 4 would have emanated from the American Division's brigade or divisional level, I have never been entirely certain that Lt. Col. Oran K. Henderson would have ordered Lieutenant Calley to waste anything that moved at My Lai 4 (Henderson claims to have ordered no such thing) without those orders coming directly from Saigon.

At the Brigadier's wake, for example, his widow Judy told me Bill hadn't really died of cancer. She said he'd hardly slept in the last years of the Vietnamese farce and it was the information that continued to pass over his desk that killed him. At least once a week, a man who'd served with him told me, Bill came down from upstairs, dressed in his combat boots and fatigues, and went through the same awesomely furious ritual, kicking the side of his desk, so that he not only had his desk scuffed up but the guy was surprised he hadn't caved in the side of it. On the pretext that he didn't always have "a need to know" (I'll bet), the man also told me he wasn't sure what many of these tantrums were about. He also emphasized that he himself had not known about My Lai 4 until, some years later, he read about it in the newspapers at the time everyone else read about it. Still, I have over the years suffered myself this fantasy that Bill was trying through channels to make it understood that the Cong was never going to come out of the jungle, meet us on a West Point textbook front, and permit Westmoreland's field commanders to pretend they were General Patton.

4

Several years ago, Alissa, after a story on the Brigadier's death appeared in a national magazine, I abruptly received a letter from a friend of his, a high GS in the Department of Defense Intelligence. He told me how much he'd enjoyed the piece and went on to flatter Bill highly by saying he'd always found him one of the better, sharper types in the intelligence community. Then he astonished me by saying that anytime I wanted to come to Washington and meet Bill's "friends," he'd be more than pleased to make the introductions. I couldn't pack a Gladstone quickly enough, and one can't imagine how naïve I was. I went armed with a tape recorder, as though I actually expected these spooks to talk into it and tell me everything they could about the Brigadier.

They put me up in a motel across from the main officers' club in Arlington. As Bill was one of their own, they treated me royally—couldn't have been more gracious

—and it wasn't until the second day, my lunatic tape recorder running, that it came to me that they weren't going to tell me a goddamn thing and doubtless were a good deal more interested in what the Brigadier had possibly told me over the years.

As they were talking to a novelist, they pretended to believe I'd be more interested in Bill's boozing and alleged wenching—the "Ex'd fuck a snake in the bush" notion—than in exactly what it was my only brother had done with his life. It must have been because of hearing this nonsense, Alissa, that I began to suspect these guys were feeding me pap, for not only did I know the Brigadier had dearly loved his wife Judy and his son Scott and though I was playing my drunken upstate New York rube role to the hilt, I was actually beginning to wonder if all this crap hadn't been orchestrated.

As you may or may not know, Alissa, these guys were a terribly embittered group, having taken no small part of the blame for our failure in Vietnam. The quack scientists had convinced the spook community that there was no longer any need for human intelligence (HUMINT), that it was too unreliable, that there was too much room for double-dealing, and that they had now perfected satellites capable of looking down the front of Dolly Parton's dress and defining the aurora borealis around her right nipple. One guy had gone all the way back with the Brigadier and I began to understand, by the very nature of the things he revealed, that, like Judy, he too was sure it was those documents crossing my brother's desk that had killed Bill.

The guy and Bill had met when Castro and his bearded boys came out of the hills of Cuba and sent that tinhorn brutish tyrant Batista flying into exile. The Brigadier, then a captain, had recently been teaching at the intelligence center at Ft. Holabird and had been placed in charge of what in Pentagon jargon was called the Cuban Desk. The guy said the army then borrowed him from Langley and got him up in a master sergeant's uniform and assigned him to our embassy in Havana as a military attaché. It was his job in Cuba to keep eyes and ears alert, as the agency so diligently trains its operatives to do, and do his best to determine how many men Castro had under arms, what weaponry was available to them, in other words where and where not the Cubans were vulnerable, what in military talk is called the Order of Battle.

He then fed that information to Bill, who in turn wrote it up "in language that even generals can understand, as Bill used to say" (and I can just hear him saying it, Alissa!), and then sent the reports "upstairs." After we severed diplomatic relations with Cuba, he said he went back to Langley and though he and the Brigadier's paths crossed from time to time socially, they didn't really work together until eight years later, at which time the Brigadier spotted his name on a list of men available to him and he was brought to Saigon, now dressed as a lieutenant colonel, and acted as an aide to Bill.

Even after Bill had made full colonel, that is, so many years after Korea, there were days he was limping so badly from the jeep rolling over on him—not to mention the shrapnel scars on his back and leg from an earlier wound— that he seemed almost in need of a cane. Therefore I waited until the appropriate moment, then said to these guys that with Bill's combat experience in Korea he would have appeared to be a natural to have been assigned a regimental field command. Had he been ordered to do so, I asked, in his physical condition would he have been expected to carry out those orders?

"Certainly," these guys assured me, hastening to add that he had been away from combat units so long and due to his particularly sensitive MOS in intelligence, it would have been a ridiculous bureaucratic screwup had the Brigadier drawn a field command.

If my brother was going to continue the heavy drinking that had begun during his intelligence career, he had struck a bargain with his wife to start attending church again and together they'd gone to an Episcopal Church in Arlington. One Sunday, in his sermon, the Episcopal priest began a long adoring paen to Martin Luther King, Jr., whereupon the Brigadier abruptly stood from his aisle seat, in the military way pivoted, and to Judy's redfaced embarrassment stormed from the church, his heels clacking in parade fashion. Some months later, en route to Florida, I stopped at Bill's house in Springfield and asked the Brigadier what his problem with King was? Thereupon Bill was off on a furious tirade about King's philandering and whore-mongering (this, mind you, Alissa, coming from my brother!), his depravity, his utter lack of morals, and so forth and so on. Without then having any confirmation, I was nonetheless certain that at that time someone was tapping King's phone, bugging his office, and conducting a surveillance of him and that for whatever reason Bill had access to these files. Bill sighed and spoke.

"It doesn't matter a hot damn anyway, Ex. *Martin Luther King is a dead man*."

And it wasn't three months later that I picked up *The Palm Beach Post* and discovered that King was indeed a dead man, felled by an assassin's bullet as he stood on the balcony of a Memphis motel. When I told his Washington friends what he had revealed to me, one of them, flustered, said I shouldn't forget just how bright a dude Bill was, how extremely controversial King was at the time, that the Brigadier was merely perceptive enough to prognosticate such an end for King, nor should I further forget that for the last two years of his life King was predicting just such an end for himself. For all that, Alissa, King's assassin, James Earl Ray, has maintained to this day that he was prompted into the act, as Brutus was by Cassius, by an army officer with a Spanish name and accent, and I couldn't help believing if these dudes had a guy bright enough to quote, in old Finnish, from P. Cajander's (1846–1913) translation of Shakespeare's *Hamlet,* which one of them had done for me, they'd hardly have trouble coming up with a guy who could cultivate a Spanish accent. Hence, Alissa, I've never felt comfortable with the notion that James Earl Ray was entirely into fantasy.

5

James Seamus Finbarr O'Twoomey was utterly in thrall to what little I'd been able to learn in search of a brother I'd never find—mute and agape would best describe Jimmy or rather His Grace's intense listening posture. And because of our nearness, our constant and damn near unbreathable proximity to one another, he was always desperately appealing to my memory to summon up every little last detail I could about the Brigadier. And no matter how irrelevant or insignificant the detail seemed to me, Jimmy would invariably sigh theatrically and say, "Boyo, boyo, boyo, could I have used a grand Irish lad like that! And it wouldn't have been for selling sea shacks on the sunny shores of Wogland either. Not by a long shot, sir! I'd have paid him ten, twenty, thirty times what he'd have made selling bleeding real estate!"

"Doing precisely what, Your Lordship?"

"Now, Frederick, me lurverly, there you go again,

being a naughty, naughty boyo. You know it's against the game to ask questions like that."

"Listen, Your Grace, I wish I could get it through that thick Irish skull of yours that I haven't the foggiest notion what you and Toby are up to. The other night I heard—as did half the guests in this Lodge!—you barking into that asshole kelly green phone of yours about a shipment arriving at Vladivostok at such and such oh-hundred hours, Greenwich Mean Time, and if that shipment was, let's say, arms intended to be transported across Siberia to the Russkis, thence rerouted to your thug pals in the IRA, and had you even approached the Brigadier with any such lunatic scheme as this, you'd have found that lardass of yours—excuse the personal aspersion, Your Grace—in a federal prison quicker than the time it takes to kiss the bleeding fucking Blarney Stone."

"Oh, but my dear Frederick, there you go speculating again, which I've repeatedly warned you, my dear, is also against the game, oh, *very, very much against the game*. And I doubt very much that your brother would have reacted in any such way. Remember, laddie, it took me three years to get you to admit that on your mother's side you are a Maguire—the veritable warring clan of Ulster, years ago broken up and dispersed all over Eire by the bleeding Limeys, so in terror of the Maguires were the skulking cravenly Brits!—ergo, your brother was a Maguire, too, and had he been born in Derry I have no doubt whatever that he'd have been in the very thick of the Troubles. Further, let me remind you, me lurverly, that I've made it through both your books—true, it was a struggle, a monumental effort on my part, they never would have seen typeface in Dublin!—and beneath that gross syntactical clumsiness there nonetheless resides the mentality of a born radical, no, an out-and-out bleeding anarchist! Certainly two brothers born as close together as you could not vary that much in their ways of viewing the world. No way, me lurverly!"

I held my peace because I knew in my heart that had Bill and I been born in Londonderry we would indeed have been in the thick of it. Whether with the Provos or the Prods is open to question but not too much of a question. Somewhere along the dim line of our heritage, we had let go of our Catholicism, rather like releasing a kite to the indifferent winds; but we had nonetheless both been confirmed in the Anglican or High Church and I had no doubt whatever that the Brigadier bought it all, which cushioned him between Heaven and those acts duty demanded he perform on earth. Too, I have a provision in my will requesting that our local priest in Alexandria Bay, Father Meehan, who is everything a priest ought to be, perform a brief lay ceremony over my ashes. Hence I've never had any doubt that had I returned to the church, it would have been to the Roman. It was as though my brother and I had released the kite and instead of blowing out of view, the kite had got caught in shifting winds and hovered immovable there in azure skies. Many years ago, when *The New Yorker* did those marvelous parodies of famous writers, a guy did a beauty on Graham Greene, making the hero the pilot of a monoplane who wrote messages in the sky; and I suspect that as a writer my fear of returning to something as entrenched as our Maguire Catholicism is nothing other than the fear of cluttering up a yarn with the temptation to send messages from on high. O'Twoomey was right. Bill and I would most assuredly have been counted with the Provos.

The question most often posed by O'Twoomey, and the one that drove me completely round the bend, that would lead eventually to all our problems, including my "marriage," was why, with the Brigadier's distinguished career, he hadn't at his interment been accorded full military honors.

"Now listen, Jimmy, for Christ's sake, for goddamn once listen to what I'm telling you! *Puowaina* is an extinct volcanic crater—they don't call it Punchbowl for nothing! —the breezes are minimal there and when my sister-in-law

saw the weather report, she felt full military honors, what
with the caisson, the band, and so forth, would simply be
too long a time to ask his comrades, the enlisted men's
firing squad, my elderly mother, et cetera, to stand in the
heat for such a portentous ceremony. Why do you have to
keep asking that question?"

Soon enough it became apparent why.

6

Each Saturday morning, as I've said, Toby would fly His Grace, Hannibal, and me to Honolulu where O'Twoomey and Toby, the latter armed with a .32-caliber Walther, invariably took the same two-bedroom suite in the main building and Hannibal and I the same adjoining rooms on the twelfth floor on the newer addition to the Royal Hawaiian, the Towers, overlooking Waikiki Beach. It was a weekend to rest my "clumsy syntactical labors," a weekend to sate myself on the luscious favors of Ms. Robin Glenn (for which, I had no doubt, James Seamus Finbarr O'Twoomey paid her dearly), and also a weekend to pay homage to the Brigadier.

As we did not return to Lanai until first light on Monday, I made a practice of going to Punchbowl with Robin and Hannibal before dusk on Sundays. First I'd buy a couple leis from a fat jolly Hawaiian woman who had a kiosk on Kalakaua, then Robin, Hannibal, and I would pile into her Porsche, drive to Punchbowl, and place the leis on the Brigadier's grave. I'd then briefly bow my head, Hannibal would do the same and pray aloud in either Hawaiian or that odd abrupt pidgin, often weeping for a man he hadn't known. And all the while Robin would be recording—for posterity no doubt—on her expensive Nikon, which she clicked with the rapidity of a silenced automatic weapon. As often as not, and as was her helpless wont, Robin turned this brief commemoration into a farce. While she was clicking away, she'd holler, "Jesus Christ, Exley, can't you pray or weep or do something? Look at Hannibal! Look at Hannibal! I mean, you really are an aloof haughty cocksucker!" Yes, Robin turned these brief moments into high comedy and I would, I swear, often hear the Brigadier laughing beneath the sacred earth of *Puowaina*. Hannibal was another matter entirely and his grief rose from some strange spirituality in his soul.

7

O ne Sunday O'Twoomey informed me that he and Toby would be joining us at Punchbowl and that we shouldn't bother with "those bleeding cheap leis" we were getting from "that fat wog swindler on Kalakaua" as Jimmy had taken care of the floral arrangements. When Robin, Hannibal, and I arrived at Bill's grave, we found a smiling Toby and an impatient Jimmy already there, Jimmy gimpily pacing round and round the Brigadier's headstone bearing the legend SS LM BSM JSCM PH, for Silver Star, Legion of Merit, Bronze Star Medal, Joint Services Commendation Medal, and Purple Heart. Atop the grave there now stood a metal wicker stand overflowing with the most flagrantly beautiful leis I'd ever seen, and though the mad O'Twoomey would be as mute on the subject of where he got the leis as he was on his and Toby's "business," Robin said they could only have been made by the woman the islanders had dubbed the Divine Kapiolani, after the ancient Queen

Kapiolani. Robin said the Divine Kapiolani was legendary for her leis and "charged a small fortune for just one," and one can be sure Robin would have known about the latter, not to mention—"Whoooeeeee"—what that mountain of leis must have cost O'Twoomey.

What came next was even more astonishing. On the headstone I had already noticed an expensive tape recorder, and it suddenly occurred to me that where the Brigadier's family, I included, had failed him, Jimmy would now damn well rectify. In the manner of a sergeant in the Irish Guards, Jimmy called us to attention, bent over, pressed the play button, and we were startled to hear what Jimmy later told us was the official U.S. Army Band beginning the A part of Frédéric Chopin's "Funeral March" done in *lento* tempo. At the conclusion of the A part, the drum cadences used to keep everyone in step began, one could hear the sound of a single caisson rolling over what sounded a cobbled pavement, the sound now muted, and someone who sounded very like Richard Burton began reading selected passages from Pericles' funeral oration:

"So died these men as became Athenians. You, their survivors, must determine to have as unaltering a resolution in the field, though you may pray that it may have a happier issue . . . you must realize yourselves the power of Athens, and feed your hearts upon her from day to day, till love of her fills your hearts; and then when all her greatness shall break upon you, you must reflect that it was by courage, sense of duty, and a keen feeling of honor in action that men were enabled to win all this, and that no personal failure in an enterprise could make them consent to deprive their country of their valor, but that they laid it at her feet as the most glorious contribution that they could offer."

The tape then went into the more cheerful, almost lullaby tempo of the B part, after which the drum cadences began again, again muted, and again someone who sounded very like Burton:

"Turning to the sons and brothers of the dead, I see

an arduous struggle before you. When a man is gone, all are wont to praise him, and should your merit be ever so transcendent, you will still find it difficult not merely to overtake, but even to approach, their renown. The living have envy to contend with, while those who are no longer in our path are honored with a goodwill into which rivalry does not enter."

The tape then returned to the grave A theme of Chopin's work, and this was followed by what was obviously a twelve-gun salute, going immediately after into the most moving—it broke one's heart—rendition of Taps I've ever heard. The entire ceremony took no more than fifteen minutes, and when we returned to the Royal Hawaiian we repaired to a table at the outdoor Mai Tai bar and Jimmy ordered a round of drinks. When I thanked and toasted him for his kindness, I said to Jimmy that the voice reading sounded very like Richard Burton's. "And just who in the bleeding hell's voice do you think it was, you bleeding culchie! Of course it was Dickie's voice! Dickie's been one of us for years, contributed more cash than I could ever tell you. You of course must know that Welshmen hate the bleeding Limeys more even than the Irish do, and that, me lurverly, would have to make it the very essence of loathing. Even Dickie's drinking buddy, Dylan, as broke as he was and no matter the unhappy circumstance of his drunken demise, contributed a fiver from time to time." How did one enter a conversation with this fat mad Irishman? "And who do you think was playing Taps?"

As I knew it wouldn't be in the least necessary to say *who* I held my peace.

"Chuck Mangione."

"*Chuck Mangione, for Christ's sake?* You mean Chuck hates the bleeding Limeys, too?"

"But of course, you silly oaf. He's one of us, always has been. Mangione is not just one of those bleeding wog El Wopos, he's Siciliano"—didn't I know it!—"from that gorgeous island of rebellious, Machiavellian dukes and princes. The bugle has no range, me lurverly, and though Chuck's flügelhorn has a lower range than the trumpet, my guess is, me lad, that you never heard Taps played like that before." I just sat there, agape, staring at this madman, then poured down my vodka and grapefruit juice and, while O'Twoomey smirked and lovingly caressed his great belly, ordered another, adding, "Make that a double."

On a Sunday at the Punchbowl two months later, O'Twoomey had no sooner pressed the PLAY button than dark thunderheads rushed over the head of Columbia's statue, an immediate tropical downpour began, we fled to the vehicles—I to Jimmy's enclosed Jeep—and we were no sooner into the semicircular drive of the Royal Hawaiian when the sun broke brilliantly through azure skies. In the manner of General Rommel ordering his corporal back to the front, O'Twoomey told Toby to return to Punchbowl, then stuck his arm out the window and violently signaled for a rain-drenched Robin and Hannibal to follow us. At the cemetery we were shocked and enraged—*"Bleeding fucking grave looters!"*—to discover all the Divine Kapiolani's leis had been stolen. Prior to this time we had always assumed that Punchbowl's caretakers had removed them as they rotted during the week, or that the Divine Kapiolani had had them removed when she had fresh ones delivered before our weekly dusk ceremony. Obviously this hadn't been the case and Robin, herself the possessor of a larcenous heart, came up with the most trenchant solution. Early on someone had spotted the leis as the work of Kapiolani, and that someone had waited for our weekly departure from Punchbowl and had doubtless stolen them to sell at a kiosk on Kalakaua. "Probably that bleeding fucking fat wog swindler with whom Exley does business. The Maguires were a warring clan. They knew bleeding nothing about barter. The Maguires just took what they bleeding well wanted!"

Among relaxing rounds of golf, we spent the following week on Lanai mapping strategy for ensnaring the miscreants, O'Twoomey, on his kelly green phone, filling in Robin as the plan matured and resolved itself. With a credit card Toby would steal from a hotel room on Saturday night (a trifling matter for Toby), he and I would go to the Honolulu International Airport on Sunday morning and rent two nondescript Fords or Chevrolets, preferably basic black or gray. On Sunday afternoon Toby, Hannibal, and I would drive one of the cars to the back of the memorial, then make our way down past the frangipani trees (*Plumeria acuminata*) and the Courts of the Missing and hide behind the enclosure of Court Two, from which we could get the best view of section T, in which the Brigadier was buried in grave 358. At the usual time, Robin and O'Twoomey would come to the grave and proceed with the service, then depart in the other rented car.

Everything went exactly as planned. Toby was wearing a black wig. Naturally a master at this sort of thing, Toby said that should anyone come up with an accurate description of Hannibal the cops would feel it so exaggerated as to be farcical. Robin and O'Twoomey's rented black Ford was hardly off the grounds of Punchbowl when two Samoans, damn near as tall as Hannibal but a good deal fatter, began taking the leis off the wicker stand and began stringing them along their massive forearms as though they were beads. Reaching under the flowing aloha shirt he wore when armed, Toby went to the small of his back, unclipped the holster holding the Walther, handed it to me and whispered, "You won't be worth a shit on this caper, Exley. I just want you in the car with the motor running when Hannibal and I get back there."

To Hannibal he then said, "Look, Hannibal, and listen closely. I don't need your help with these fat slobs. Even if their arms weren't encumbered with those leis, those gobs of puke couldn't move fast enough to get their hands up against me. Agreed?" Hannibal nodded solemnly. "Okay, then, all I want you to do is make sure we get every one of those leis, every blessed one of them, back to the car. I don't want a petal left behind, any indication whatever of what this fight was about. Got it?" As the two Samoans had already started walking nonchalantly away from the grave, Toby said, "Let's go," and he and Hannibal broke into a feverish run toward them, while I, Toby's holster and .32 stuffed in my belt at my belly, started back up the marble stairs past the Courts of the Missing. When I reached the Court of Honor and was passing Bruce Moore's statue of Columbia, who has breasts almost as beautiful as Robin's, standing on the prow of a carrier, I for the first time noticed the words inscribed below the carrier's prow, Lincoln's message to a bereaved mother: THE SOLEMN PRIDE THAT MUST BE YOURS TO HAVE LAID SO COSTLY A SACRIFICE UPON THE ALTAR OF FREEDOM.

Presently Toby and Hannibal jumped into the car. Both were garlanded about the neck and arms with the Divine Kapiolani's leis, both were sweating profusely, and both were laughing like hyenas, Toby, among gasping breaths, saying, "Jesus, Hannibal, Jesus, Hannibal, that slob's moronic head split like a fucking pumpkin!" Hannibal said, "Like a fuckin' papaya. That prick no rob no more grave." Later, Toby was even to remember the name of the master sergeant whose gravestone the Samoan's head had hit: Peter Rasbeck, also the winner of a Silver Star, state: New York. And Hannibal could not have described the Samoan's condition more succinctly.

The article was buried in the morning *Advertiser*. Fortunately for us the Samoans had a rap sheet longer than Hannibal's lingam, everything from breaking and entering to aggravated assault to sodomy to incest, both had twice done time in the state penitentiary and their description of Toby as "a black-haired skinny guy" and Hannibal as "the biggest meanest bruh" they'd ever seen was said to be taken lightly by the state police as they felt it was some nitpicking "lower-echelon thug feud." After O'Twoomey read the article, he sighed relievedly and said, "Serves the bleeding fucking grave robbers right."

When we were checking out at first light, I heard O'Twoomey tell the deferential desk clerk he wouldn't need his suite and Towers rooms for two months. Lord Lisdoonvarna had always had a hankering, he said, to see Australia and he and his court would be flying down to Melbourne and taking a leisurely train trip across the Outback, disembarking at Alice Springs or wherever en route to Perth the fancy moved them. Unable to resist it, O'Twoomey had of course to add, "Yes, siree, I'm going to take me an elephant gun and bag me a couple wog aboriginees." The clerk, knowing Jimmy was going to lay a C-note on him, pretended to find this hilarious and assured O'Twoomey that space would always be available to him at the Pink Palace. On the Cessna going back to Lanai, I said, "Are we really going to Australia?"

"Don't be stupid, Frederick! We're simply going to lay low on Lanai for a couple months. Don't you think that the wisest thing to do, me lurverly? I mean, your extremely competent pal Toby—and I shall always, Frederick, be immeasurably in your debt for having introduced me to Toby —has, after all, damn near killed a bleeding wog. Don't you think it might be the wiser course for us to respect your chum's privacy and whereabouts for a couple months?"

"What about Robin?"

"What about bleeding Robin?"

"You mean, I won't be able to see her weekends?"

"But of course not. How can I make it any plainer that none of this group is going anywhere near Honolulu for weeks?"

"Then I'll have to have Robin fly over here weekends."

"Miss Robin will most assuredly not be coming to Lanai. Your chum Hannibal informs me that the two of you make noises like whales mating in the Maui Channel, and I'm certainly not going to expose these wog children on Lanai—*total innocents all!*—to any such feelthy bestial shenanigans as the two of you shaking the flimsy walls of the Lodge with your reprehensible piglike grunting, groaning, and oinking. It shall not happen under my roof, sir!"

A self-righteous O'Twoomey was genuinely something to behold. "But I can't live without Robin for two months!"

"You mean, me lurverly, that you can't live without that disgusting, nauseating feelth for two months. Isn't that what you mean, Frederick?"

"Put it any goddamn way you want, Jimmy."

"It's Your Grace, Mr. Exley, until this plane settles onto the tarmac of Lanai."

"Your fucking Grace."

"Keep it up, Frederick, and I shall have Hannibal punish you. Oh, punish you severely, me boyo!" Sensing my acutely pained frustration, O'Twoomey sighed and said, "There is a way, Frederick. You might marry Robin, you know? And at least that feelthy oinking would be sanctified in the eyes of Our Lord Jesus!"

"Marry Robin? Are you fucking crazy, O'Twoomey? But of course you're fucking bonkers. I've known that since the day we met! Absolutely and unequivocally bonkers!"

Even Toby and Hannibal, who hadn't been missing a word, found the vision of Robin and me living in connubial bliss somewhat more than they could handle. Toby, who had been making his approach to Lanai, called the airport and, among the silliest laughter I'd ever heard from him, told the guy he was circling back and asked him if he was cleared for yet another approach.

8

So it was, Alissa, that Frederick Exley of Alexandria Bay, New York, and Lanai City, Hawaii, virtually unknown and unheralded author, drunk, child abandoner, and ex-mental patient, and Ms. Robin Glenn of Queens, New York, and Hawaii Kai, Hawaii, onetime stewardess, would-be Emilio Pucci model, extortionately priced hooker, and of an unquestionably batshit mental condition, came to be joined in holy matrimony.

Robin would be three weeks closing the public relations office. I suspected Robin had to give her various Ohana clients a few final fucks. Many articles were then appearing about herpes and I told the new demure virginal soon-to-be-betrothed Robin that if she ever infected me, I'd kill her. Robin of course became hysterically indignant, screaming, "You even have to wreck my marriage, my one and only marriage, *you prick*!"

I spent those days exhausting myself attempting to

explain to O'Twoomey that I could not in any dilatory fashion take "lessons" to marry Robin in the Catholic Church, that for my own mental peace, or what was left of it, I had to go all the way to conversion. Finally, more from his own exhaustion than any eloquence on my part, Jimmy said it was okay to marry outside his and Robin's church. He added the rider, however, that though he would out of courtesy attend the ceremony he would not give the bride away, as he had been scheduled to do.

"I'll have no bleeding part in any such bleeding pagan rite."

Jimmy then gave Toby a check for a thousand dollars, made payable to the Jehovah's Witness minister on Lanai, told Robin about it, and Robin got the sizes of everyone in the wedding party, as Jimmy's tailor would be making up the appropriate attire. She also told Toby to tell the minister she would be writing the ceremony—the creative Robin, Alissa!—and gave Toby a Saturday four weeks hence, the Saturday just prior to Easter, as the date we would be married at Hulapoe or White Manele Beach. The reverend's only stipulation was that he would of course "baptize" both Robin and me in the blue Pacific (but I can hear you chuckling and already ghoulishly anticipating, Alissa!).

At some point Robin must have asked O'Twoomey about my state of mind, for I heard him say, "Frederick? He's fine. I've never seen him more industrious." I hadn't as yet sobered up, Alissa, and was of course trying, to no avail, to write you these words while hung over.

9

Robin arrived on Lanai the Monday before our marriage. She had only two overnight bags and as one of these contained our marriage outfits, I asked her if she didn't intend staying on Lanai. Possibly, she said, but O'Twoomey had arranged a week's honeymoon for us at the Royal Hawaiian and at that time she could pick up her clothes, which were all packed in boxes and stacked inside the door of the *Cirrhosis of the River*.

As Robin knew I was "too frigging insensitive" to have picked up a wedding band, she handed me a small felt green ring case, making me swear not to lose it and suggesting that I give it to Wiley, my best man, as he would in any event be holding it during the ceremony. When I opened the case, I saw it was the same jade band bordered in gold—"the friendship ring"—with which she'd allowed O'Twoomey to simulate his making of thump on the plane on that long-ago day the three of us had met; and as Robin

‡ 365

had already told me O'Twoomey had wanted to give us the honeymoon suite but she had insisted we take our usual room on the twelfth floor of the Towers—later I learned Robin took the price difference in cash!—I was being made to understand that now that we were to be a responsible married couple a new penuriousness was being introduced into our relationship. Would Hannibal, I asked, sleep with us or take his usual adjoining room? "Hannibal is most certainly not going on our honeymoon." Fat chance of that, I said. But as it happened Robin was right. Hannibal didn't go on our honeymoon.

Fortunately for me I did at last agree to a marriage rehearsal at White Manele Beach on the Friday afternoon, Good Friday, before our marriage. Had I not agreed, I wouldn't have made it through the ceremony. Whether Robin intended to send the details of the wedding to Tony, the retired plumber, and Evelyn Glenn, the retired Con Ed secretary, for publication in *The New York Times* I don't know, but if that is what she had in mind, this is what the *Times'* society editor would have had to digest.

For Wiley, my best man, and me—because Robin knew that the Rev. Mr. Dimmesdale, or whoever the Jehovah's Witness guy was, intended dipping us in the ocean in the concluding baptismal exercise—Robin had had O'Twoomey's tailor stitch the Lord Lisdoonvarna Boheena crest into two old-fashioned black tank suits with shoulder straps. Wiley—and I despised him for it—looked great in his but both my belly and my flabby pectoral muscles sagged droopily in mine and I was simply too tired and too bored to object. For Malia, the maid of honor, O'Twoomey's tailor had made a beautiful tank suit of cranberry taffeta lined with a white lightweight waterproof material and for Robin he had outdone himself. Her tank suit was ivory, the panty section lined with a virginal white lace that protruded suggestively from the thigh's suitline, rather like the lace underwear the tennis player Gussie Moran used to wear under her shorts to titillate dirty old men. Both Malia and Robin would wear ivory bathing caps topped with a halo of baby's breath flowers—I called it "hog's breath"—and minuet roses, Robin would carry a bouquet of white roses and Malia a bouquet of minuet roses.

As if all this weren't grotesque enough, the Rev. Mr. Dimmesdale would begin, in Robin's words, by saying, "We all come together today in peace and love to witness this union of man, woman, and nature," after which Robin would say, "Being born of woman, I have consented to give freely of myself to Frederick," then, substituting Robin's name for mine, I would repeat the line. Listen, Alissa, I kept a straight face at the rehearsal until we came to one of the lines Robin had written for the reverend.

"Do you agree to live together with Frederick as his woman, to meet his mind"—there's no way I'm ever that drunk, Alissa!—"be not puffed out, not put him down, crowd his space, or be an oppressive person as long as you both shall love?" At one point I was expected to say to Robin—and I ask you, Alissa, how could I be expected to get through this sober?—"Come to me, Robin, be a part of my aura, live in peace and love, follow the seasons with me," to which Robin says, "When the ground is cold," and Frederick enjoins, "Lie with me and be warm." And Robin says, "When strawberries ripen in spring," and Frederick, "So, too, shall you, Robin, and bear me many sons." On and on this lunatic rehearsal went, while Frederick, the seed bearer for these many sons, bit a hole in his lower lip in an attempt to stay both the mirth and the terror.

After the rehearsal I kept telling everyone that we had been practicing the ceremony in the beginnings of a Kona wind and that I'd be damned if I'd allow myself to be baptized in the kind of majestic surf that always accompanies these winds. But everyone, including Wiley who should have known better, pooh-poohed this, told me I had premarriage jitters, told me I was just a pouty spoilsport, and even suggested that as I fancied myself the writer I was just jealous that Robin had written such a beautiful and sensitive ceremony. We were at the picnic tables behind the Lodge, having a prenuptial Eucharist of Delmonico steaks and Toby's herb salad, and O'Twoomey, toasting Robin, said, "That was the most lovely and moving ceremony ever I did hear. Indeed it was, ma'am. I only wish my faith didn't preclude my giving such a beautiful and brilliant woman to Frederick in holy matrimony. Indeed, that is my wish, Ms. Robin." We were barely halfway through our steaks and salad when the Kona rains penetrated those dense towering pines that rose above the picnic tables, we scooped up the food and booze and fled to the screened-in veranda to complete the meal. When we had done so, I looked very evenly at Wiley and said, "Are you shitting me, Wiley?" Wiley laughed.

10

As you know, Alissa, I have never finished—finished? never got past page ten of—a Michener book since his *Tales of the South Pacific*. Still, I have never been as phony about it as you. Whenever you wade through one of his endless tomes, in shrieking embarrassment you protest your horny appetite for sheer escapist pulp, whinnyingly asking, *"How can a Harvard summa cum laude read this shit?"* whereas I have never, never begrudged Michener or Irving Wallace or Harold Robbins or any of their ilk a single nickel he's made. As with any other business, publishing comes down to a question of red or black ink and I've always felt that any one of the aforementioned made it possible for a publisher to see into print a hundred clowns like me.

For your sake I did, however, sit through the movie version of *Hawaii* (and I ask you Alissa, is this love or isn't it?). Of course, and even though you brought along an iced twelve-pack of Budweiser, you made sure we went to a drive-in ten miles out in the country so I couldn't flee to the nearest saloon to wait for you. To this day I don't know what the flick was about. But having read the book, and been further ennobled by the flick, you'll recall Hollywood's version of these winds. There comes the scene where the fat Wahini, who is married to her own brother, is dying. And her son says to the Yankee minister, Max von Sydow, who looked as bewildered by his lines as the rest of the cast, "She will die," ominously adding, "And then the whistling winds will come."

Those foreboding whistling winds, Alissa, are what are known in the islands as Kona winds. And ominous they are, believe me. Some months ago we had one that lasted a mere four days. When the weather broke clear and Hannibal and I went to White Manele Beach for a swim there was no beach, literally. Having come here from American Samoa when he was three and grown up in the islands, Hannibal wasn't in the least surprised but I was agape with astonishment, so much so that Hannibal still does a passable imitation of my expression. At the picnic tables behind the Lodge O'Twoomey will say, "Do Frederick, Han, when he looked at the beach; do Frederick when he looked at the beach after the Kona storm." Hannibal will thereupon let his long muscular arms and his long jaw go slack, his eyes will bulge out like those of Lugosi or Frankenstein in acute pain and everyone, me too, will laugh.

To say that I looked at the beach is inaccurate, for there was, I repeat, literally no beach. It was as though some contractor had run amok, had moved in overnight with ten thousand heavy equipment operators and as many bull-dozers and just carted off a billion tons of sand. The surf had taken the entire beach right up to the line of the Kiave trees, under which sit the cinder block cooking grilles and the picnic tables, and at the precise point of the tree line the wet sand dropped away as sheer as a cliff for thirty feet until it met sharply the place where the beach had been, a mud-colored sand as hard and as flat as Daytona or concrete, with here and there broken shards of brown, orange, and bottle-green glass, coins of all denominations, and patches of white coral standing exposed. That, Alissa, is what a Kona wind and the surf that accompanies it will do. And it would be eight to ten weeks before a normal surf had restored the beach to its white shimmering beauty.

Ms. Robin Glenn was due to become Mrs. Frederick Exley at White Manele Beach at 5 P.M., a sunset observance. By 3 P.M., however, the Kona winds and rains were coming with such screaming whistling monotony that I'd long since put to rest the thought of anyone's considering holding the ceremony on the beach, was smug in the knowledge that we hadn't any alternative but to get hitched in the tan clapboard Church of Jesus Christ or in the Lodge, so smug indeed that though O'Twoomey wouldn't allow me any vodka until after the rites he said I could drink a few cans of Budweiser and for the better part of the day I'd spartanly denied myself even these in the straitlaced hope that a sober Frederick would have at least a chance of getting through the marriage without collapsing in mirth.

At 3 P.M. Hannibal and I were sitting at our table at the screened-in veranda discussing my attire for an indoor ceremony, having decided that my black Florsheims, my beige chinos, a tan silk shirt, and a red-and-gold dotted four-in-hand (Giuseppe of Milano: Made in Canada) I'd found in the hall of the Lodge would not be inappropriate for that climate. I'd even tried everything on and though the breeches were somewhat snug, my outfit, Hannibal indicated (*"Eese good, eese good"*), looked fine. At 2 P.M., over the day having had six or eight cups of black coffee and numerous glasses of ice water, I'd gone into the men's room and along with the remains of the previous evening's supper had thrown up the coffee and water.

Shortly thereafter the dry heaves that invariably accompany my going cold turkey began, coming at about twenty-minute intervals, and if anything at all came up it was only this sickly yellow bile. Experts on alcoholism state unequivocally that weaning yourself off a quart and a half of booze a day with a few cans of beer is only compounding the problem; but as an admitted alcoholic, Alissa, and therefore having wasted my life in the company of drunks discussing the ways and means, the pain and the intricacies of drying out, I can only say the experts are, as usual, wrong. Moreover, I knew that without three beers, the first of which I'd also throw up, I would in awful embarrassment have to claim a brief illness during the ceremony. At 3 P.M., then, having already thrown up the first of the Budweisers, I was nursing the second, knowing I was going to be just fine. Then abruptly Toby's Jeep braked to a screeching rocking halt in front of the Lodge, out leaped Toby and Robin, now running frantically up the sidewalk toward us so as not to get soaked, and Ms. Robin Glenn was joyously shouting, "The sun is shining at White Manele! The sun is out at White Manele!"

I could hardly credit it, Alissa. There is an old Filipino dude in the village, retired from the pineapple fields, and at sunrise every morning he drives to White Manele and if it is raining high up in the village everyone calls him on his breakfast return to see if it is doing the same at the beach. Such is the nature of Hawaiian weather, about half the time it is raining in the village it is not doing so at the beach, eleven miles down to the sea. But during a Kona storm? I vehemently challenged this, but Toby verified that they'd just driven from White Manele and that indeed the sun was shining. And so we all dressed in our bathing attire.

Our Jeep caravan arrived at the beach about ten to five. It was a hazy red sun dropping off into the Pacific to our west and the surf had already taken out about thirty feet of beach, so that to get down to the mud-colored concrete-hard sand we had, firmly spiking our heels into the wet sand, to descend a steep eight-foot precipice to the surf. Even the Reverend Mr. Dimmesdale, recognizing there was no way he was going to stay dry, removed his shoes and socks, rolled his white linen trousers to above his knees, and took out his wallet and handkerchief and gave them over to Mrs.

Dimmesdale's safekeeping. The thunderous surf was enough to stay even the thought of laughter, and the minister finally pronounced Robin and me as one and the same and at peace with the cosmos. Robin had decided at the last moment that she and I were to face each other and from mimeographed sheets read aloud and in its entirety John Donne's versifying about no man being an island. Obviously too chagrined and alarmed to be at peace with the cosmos, and to Mr. Dimmesdale's pained expression, I snapped, "Jesus Christ, Robin, would you get your ass the hell on with our baptism and let's get the screw out of here!"

Robin opened her mouth to protest but instantly I doubled my fist and shook it violently under her veiled nose, thereby letting both Robin and the matrimonial assemblage know that though Robin was for the nonce in a state of connubial bliss, her fall from grace was going to come extremely early on—even before the marriage's consummation!—in the form of a grand manly healthy husbandly Maguire thrashing if she didn't toe the mark and stop waxing poetical. O'Twoomey, being the wonderful Irish lad that he is, broke up in raucous laughter and thereby enlisted the others in his hilarity. "Now, that's a grand boyo, Frederick. Give her a solid crack on the noggin and let her know from the outset who the cock of the walk is!"

Although Robin and the Reverend Mr. Dimmesdale only went into the water up to their shins, when he was lowering her face-up into the surf—Robin's Catholicism erupting in the form of her repeatedly making the sign of the cross at forehead, chest, and shoulder—an incredible wave broke over them, knocking them violently straight up and into Wiley and me, with Robin's head cracking my left eyebrow with such ferocious impact that I'd spend my honeymoon with a lump over my eye as big as an extra large egg.

The Reverend Mr. Dimmesdale needn't lower me, thank you. I simply laid down in the surf, face up, with my head toward Tahiti and my feet toward the marriage party. What I remember after that is scant. I remember Mr.

Dimmesdale bending over me and mumbling his rites, and the laying on of the hands, with his right palm coming to my forehead, his left palm to my chest, then suddenly all was turbulent, breathless, terrifying, and painful blackness and I had what appeared to be a Great White's jaws clasped to my ankle and rushing me out to sea to partake of his own wedding feast. How long it was before it occurred to me that I was caught in an undertow and that the Great White was a heartstricken Reverend Mr. Dimmesdale brutishly strangling my ankle, I don't know; but the moment it did, with my right foot I laid a violent kick on the good reverend's dome, the memory of which he'll take to his heaven with him. For all that, he was luckier than I because in my own boundless fear I'd kicked him so fiercely I'd knocked him free of the undercurrent and, I later learned, he bobbed up no more than a hundred yards from the beach, an easy save for a swimmer as strong as Wiley.

Although I couldn't have been in the undertow for more than thirty seconds, it did of course seem an eternity. In Watertown High School, Alissa, we had a game not unlike the present day "Gotcha," where the kids shoot each other with water or cap pistols, though the Watertown jocks played the game with considerably more vigor and lunacy. The idea was to catch a teammate completely unawares, say, coming round a blind corner in the school halls, then with a doubled fist giving him the best shot one had right at the solar plexus or heart. One night at the Avon Theater, Bubba Fox, having seconds before me gone through the swinging doors discharging moviegoers into the lobby, caught me in the diaphragm as I came through those doors, the pain was excruciating, everything went black, and sensing myself going to my knees I gave myself utterly up to the darkness.

How odd it was that as the undercurrent continued to rush, bump, and surge me outward that that memory should flood back upon me and, remembering, I surrendered myself to the burning, chest-constricting darkness. Doubtless I wasn't, as I say, under for more than a half minute,

and when at last my head did bob up, I found myself tread-
ing in twenty-foot seas puking saltwater and booze bile, so
bad I thought my stomach was turning inside out. Once as a
wave broke I caught sight of White Manele, which seemed
a mile away, only later to discover I'd been a mere quarter
mile away. It says a good deal of Mrs. Exley's lung power
that into the face of a Kona wind I could yet hear her
crying, "Oh, Frederick, my darling, my husband, I'm
coming, *I'm coming*," and though I had of course often
heard this, Alissa, in quite another context, it was not
without its comfort to know that Robin had me in view.
When at length she came over the crest of a huge wave
and dropped rapidly down to me, as if in free fall, she instantly started giving me a lifeguard's rote litany of primer
rules, which may be the first complete sentences a kid from
our neck of America—the St. Lawrence River–Lake
Ontario region—learns to speak, pedantically ordering me
to relax my body and heave to so she could cup me under
the chin and sidestroke me back to paradise.

Actually, Alissa, and despite my continuing to gag up
bile seawater, I could have easily made my own way back
to the beach; but I've always been of the opinion that bad
theater or vile poetry needs more than an urbanely verbal
panning, often the playwright and actors need nothing less
than rotten eggs, soggy tomatoes, and mildewed cabbages
cast upon the stage, the pedestrian poet a good caning.
Moreover, I had high hopes that were I to exhaust my rather
too exuberant bride she might not that night demand my
manly connubial services and, even more than that, she
might for once in her life be too weary to talk. Why I
didn't just leave it at that, I don't know; save the very
real possibility that I am at heart a beast, so that when I at
last turned my head and saw the kiave trees but a few yards
aft and knew that momentarily the surf would be crashing
Robin and me onto the concrete-hard beach, I spoke to a
panting, ever-tiring Robin.

"You know what you've done with this zany marriage
service of yours, don't you, Robin? *You know what you've*

done, don't you? You've just acted your way into a celibate honeymoon! I mean, listen here, Robin, you don't even get to touch my bod the entire week we're at the Pink Palace! I mean, you don't even get to give me a hand job!"

Of course Robin got immediately hysterical, screaming she'd always known I'd find some diabolically vicious excuse, however paltry, to deprive her of her honeymoon, her one and only honeymoon. She then began sobbing mightily, never, I might add, breaking her powerful left-armed sidestroke, my chin still cupped and saddled firmly in her strong right palm. Despite what you might think, Alissa, even Frederick is a sucker for a broad's sobs, as shamelessly crocodilian as they always are in Robin's case, and hence he found himself saying, "Okay, Robin, quiet down. Quiet down. We'll play the honeymoon by ear and if there are no more, none whatever, crass theatrics during it Frederick might—might, I repeat—let you give him a hand job."

ere I a closet Michener reader like you,
Alissa, albeit a troubled self-castigating one much given to
playacting the flagellant penitent slut as the price of your
atonement for 'fessing up to your tastes in literature, I would
stop reading at this bittersweet point and retain the jolly
image of a graying paunchy middle-aged Exley kissing
Robin by way of making it up and thereupon, though with
an airy reluctance, allowing himself to be given a hand job,
rather as if he and Robin were children of the fifties (as
indeed Frederick was!) ingenuously indulging themselves
at a drive-in movie. Of course even this ending might not be
demure enough for Michener readers but having left him
unread for so long I'm forced to leave it to you to stop
reading whenever a pulp element commensurate with your
depravity explodes to the surface.

Robin and I did not check into the Royal Hawaiian
until 11 P.M. On our return from the beach to Lanai City

for champagne and canapés, Dr. Jim checked my blood pressure and recommended an hour's nap, which turned into a four-hour one, after which Toby flew us to Honolulu. When we entered the hotel, a number of employees kissed Robin and presented us with a neatly wrapped gift they had chipped in to buy. Before I'd taken my nap at the Lodge, Sissy had handed me a glass of her own home-brewed emetic—later I learned it was hot bacon grease stirred vigorously into cold grapefruit juice!—to bring up whatever seawater and bile I had left in me; and as Robin and I were ascending the Towers' elevator I suddenly found myself wide awake and famished and suggested I go to the all-night delicatessen on Kalakaua and bring sandwiches back to the room.

Robin, however, pooh-poohed this by saying the half-size refrigerator in our room had been filled with Delmonico steaks—Toby's present to us—and plastic containers of his herb salad, as well as Toby's having placed a bottled gas hibachi on our balcony overlooking Waikiki. There would, of course, be all the champagne and vodka we could imbibe. When we walked into the room I tripped over Robin's alligator balloon bag, which someone—one of her Ohana pals?—had placed just inside the door, and I hadn't even to ask to know it contained the wedding gown of either Grandmother Glenn or Grandmother Flaherty. It was Robin's night both to play the coy ingenuous scandalized virgin and further to elaborate on her privileged family tree, neither for which I was that night prepared.

Stripping to my jockey shorts, I mixed myself a hefty vodka and grapefruit juice, lighted the hibachi, and retrieved two Delmonicos from the refrigerator. After putting them on the ironwork, I seated myself, grilling fork in hand, on one of the two balcony deck chairs intent on lovingly tending Robin's and my first supper together as husband and wife. Even after we'd become airborne in the Cessna over Lanai, I had been unable to accept that Hannibal was not with us—it made me exceedingly uncomfortable—and had half expected him to be waiting at the hotel, however much Robin insisted that not only was Hannibal's job of watching me done but that O'Twoomey neither expected nor wanted us back on Lanai.

"With what I know!" I cried, lunging against my seat belt.

"Christ, Frederick, I wish you'd get that out of your head. They were never worried about you in that respect. And what do you really know? That O'Twoomey's a filthy rich loony with all kinds of imagined contacts in the IRA and the intelligence services of half the countries of the world. It's all in his head. He reads too many Le Carré novels. Half his phone calls are to his stockbroker in Dublin. You know, Frederick, I figured out months ago what he was really up to. He wants to be a character in your book, for Christ's sake. That's why he feels the need for all that mysterious glamour. The main thing he was worried about was your committing suicide before you committed him to paper. If he wanted to read your mail, it was only to assure himself that you hadn't written some long, maudlin, self-pitying farewell to your elderly mother or someone else who cared for you."

"I've never contemplated suicide. Never, never contemplated suicide!"

"And what the hell were you doing the night you were standing on the Pink Palace's balcony railing? A liter or two of vodka in you? Twelve stories up, naked and blaspheming the heavens? Spitting poison at a harmless full moon. Baying, *fucking baying!*"

"I don't remember any such night."

"Well, I do. It was I who got Hannibal to pull you from the railing. And well you might not remember. The doctor kept you sedated for five days afterward and even brought in a psychiatrist to give you an electroshock treatment. O'Twoomey had to say he was your father and sign a release to get it done. It was during those five days that Jimmy decided you couldn't be left alone and rented one whole side of the Lodge so he could watch you. I mean, listen, Frederick, you'll never, never have a friend who cares for you more than O'Twoomey."

"But why doesn't he want us back on Lanai?"

"He says you've always wanted to live in London, much to his stupefied consternation, and he thinks you ought to go there for a couple years because the company of those wogs on Lanai is turning your brains to mush."

"How the hell would he know I've ever dreamed of living in London?"

"He says the whole latter part of your new book is in the form of a letter from your narrator to an imagined psychiatrist—Alissa?—whom he takes to be modeled on me, and that in that letter your narrator expresses the desire to live in London with this Alissa, ergo, a wish to live in London with me."

I hadn't, of course, Alissa, any need to learn how O'Twoomey had got into my safety deposit box. Even as Robin spoke I was recalling that the box was in Hannibal's name. What would later astonish me was in learning that no sooner would I deposit some pages to you than Hannibal would remove them and have them photocopied, after which O'Twoomey would send the copies to a Honolulu psychiatrist (apparently the same one who had administered the electroshock) for analysis. A Chinese-American named Dr. Ulysses Lee, his reports to O'Twoomey indicated that I suffered from a common and simple form of delusional paranoid schizophrenia and the last of his analyses had offered professionally reasoned doubt—thank God—that I was a danger to myself or to anyone else.

From revving the engines to takeoff to sitdown to discharging passengers, the flight from Lanai to Honolulu takes no more than forty minutes, and I think, Alissa, you'll find the fantasy that followed this exchange on the Cessna, and for the final twenty minutes of the flight, more than a little instructional. Whereas at one moment I'd no future before me but eighteen holes a day, nightly steaks and salad, and buckets of vodka, my slim margin of sanity maintained by scribbling on a letter to you I never, I can see now, had any intention of mailing, now suddenly I was living with my striking but loonily garrulous wife in a tastefully furnished flat (it was all deep mahogany and prints of guys riding to the hounds) on Leinster Terrace—Robin had already been in touch with an estate agent friend of O'Twoomey—London W2, but a few short steps from Kensington Gardens.

And who precisely was I supposed to be in this new incarnation? At forty-eight, I expect I was a writer with a dozen major novels behind me, for in my fantasy my Chesterfield and cashmere topcoats, my demurely pinstriped dark-blue-and-gray and obviously Savile Row-cut suits, my maroon Aston Martin sedan, all conspired to speak to the notion that "major talent" is occasionally rewarded. I am retiring, inward, not immodest, debt-paying, a good though occasionally philandering husband, I jog daily in Kensington Gardens with those many sons Robin has bore me, to assure Robin will be well taken care of I have a prodigious policy against my life, and so forth and so forth. What a farce, Alissa! I've never known a writer worth a tinker's damn—and as you know I have a first-name familiarity with many of the best writers of our time—who wouldn't sacrifice everything to pull off one major novel. Hence this slimy yearning of writers to be at one with the bourgeoisie is so patently fake as to be reprehensible.

There is a hateful, baleful, alienating darkness in all good writers that can never be disguised by a Brooks Brothers suit, and whenever I see a good writer so got up he always seems to me to exude the notion of soiled undergarments and foul socks. Moreover, and particularly in my case, as the son of a power company lineman I have all but missed my life in pursuit of what I assumed were my educated betters, when in fact it began occurring to me years ago that I was always turning those betters—including you, Alissa—on to books of which I was stunned and pained to discover they'd never even heard. At any one of those moments I could easily have said, *"All right, already, enough of reading—get a pencil and a piece of paper."*

It wasn't that this fantasy of a world-renowned writer wasn't exceedingly satisfying. It was that all my material comforts were being realized without my having done anything to merit them, without sensing, as it were, the sweat of painful labors on my brow. For example, Robin had in her bag my long letter to you, which Hannibal had delivered over to her, as well as nearly four thousand dollars I'd had in my desk. As I had no clothes on Lanai but tattered shorts and T-shirts, there'd be no need, she said, to return for anything in the way of possessions. Moreover, Robin showed me what she said was our wedding present from O'Twoomey, a check for twenty thousand pounds drawn against Barclay's Bank of London. As the check was made out to Frederick Exley period, I hardly saw it as "our present." Further, and in huffy response to my suggestion that that amount wouldn't last us eighteen months in London the way we lived, Robin said she'd managed to save sixty thousand dollars from her public relations job —public relations!—and though she was by inclination opposed to an able-bodied and talented man living off a woman, she had that very day and in a ceremony she herself had written been bound to me in a union of man, woman, and nature. As on her own oath she'd sworn to give freely of herself to Frederick, she assumed, however reluctantly, that this giving included her hard-won wages. Of course, Alissa, I was too kind to suggest that in the earning of those wages she must have occasionally experienced a little forbidden and delicious titillation, or that those monies were tax free and that the remainder of her "earnings" might as well have been lifted from O'Twoomey's fat wallet when he slept.

And though our honeymoon (about which more presently) was an abominable joke lasting a mere two days, and though to appease Robin I visited O'Twoomey's tailor and had myself measured for a London wardrobe before we returned to Lanai, for I had decided to forestall my London trip until I was damn good and ready, Robin was for once, for once, right in her claim that O'Twoomey hadn't wanted me back on Lanai. He was furious, spittingly so. He would, he said, have nothing to do with me, stating that he had offered me a new life, that I had spurned that life, and that though Hannibal would continue to watch over me, he would not do so out of any affection O'Twoomey had for me—"It has ceased to exist, Frederick!"—but because O'Twoomey would not bear the guilt of my untimely death.

If I wished, however, to drink myself to a slow sloppy death, he'd already told Hannibal that there would be no restrictions on the amounts I consumed or the hours I was free to consume them. Moreover, were I not interested in pursuing that new life—and I obviously wasn't—O'Twoomey felt I might do the gentlemanly thing and return his twenty thousand pounds. Robin was naturally dumbstruck at this suggestion, and it was an anguished two minutes before, above those stricken gurgling noises rising up from her strong regal throat, as if she were choking on her own blood (she was in fact choking on twenty thousand pounds, something dearer than her blood), O'Twoomey and I were able to determine that Robin had deposited the check to the joint London account of Mr. and Mrs. Frederick Exley (I didn't remember endorsing it!), that O'Twoomey's estate agent friend had been paid six months in advance on our Leinster Terrace deep mahogany and doggy flat, and that the only thing that was holding us up was O'Twoomey's tailor preparing a suitable London wardrobe for me, mackintosh and all should I feel the need to play the spy who chose to stay out in the cold.

O'Twoomey, a churlish, stubborn, hard old fart when he chooses to be, Alissa, hasn't let me play golf with him, or Robin and me join the picnic tables at the rear of the Lodge for supper. Since that initial conversation he hasn't spoken a word to me in the two months since our return from our honeymoon, relaying whatever he wants me to know—his golf score, for example, with some *Ha's!* after it—through Hannibal. For the first month I did very well without his company. After having coffee and perusing the morning *Advertiser*—to please Hannibal I got back to arguing with the headlines—Hannibal and I would stroll to the golf course and play eighteen, walking, after which we'd take a shower and, together with Robin, drive to White Manele Beach, where Robin and Hannibal would swim for miles while I drank chilled Budweiser and watched the beach restore itself. After that month, though, I detected that I was persuading Hannibal to return to the Lodge after only playing nine so I could have three or four beers to get me through the back nine, and as another month passed I found that in lieu of beer I was into vodka at the midway of the match until, of course, I was on the vodka all day, every day, trying to write this letter to you, assuring the mad Robin—who was constantly reminding me that my wardrobe had been ready for weeks and that we were scheduled to fly to London the Wednesday after Memorial Day—that I'd dry out any moment now. Then abruptly it was two weeks before our scheduled departure, I detected that no one on the island was speaking to me but Hannibal and Robin, the others turning from me as though stunned by my dissolute appearance, and I sobered up and had what I imagined was a stroke. On the fourth day of my new, oh, my so sober and so earnest, regimen I waited on the veranda for three hours for Hannibal, then in alarm awakened Robin. Robin said that like characters in a bad novel O'Twoomey, Hannibal, and Toby had left under cover of night. "They said they were going to Australia. But who knows with those crazies?"

Robin and I leave for Honolulu tomorrow, where I will pick up my wardrobe, thence to London three days hence, where I will do God only knows what. Jog? Visit the museums and try to recover that archaic form that people used to call a gentleman? Spend my days in the library and become an authority on some minor Edwardian poet? Robin wants no reminders of what she calls "our shitty honeymoon," so she has booked us into the Holiday

Hotel at Kalakaua and Lewers Street, the hotel containing Shipwreck Kelly's Lounge, which she recommended to me on that long-ago day I met her high above the azure Pacific. The Holiday is a block and a half from Waikiki Beach, it is a good deal cheaper than the Royal Hawaiian, and as we shall be paying for it, I suspect that the price also entered into Robin's thinking. In fairness to Robin, our honeymoon did have rather a nightmarish quality.

12

F or me to have imagined I could sit on the balcony with Robin and have a nice long earnest chat, and this on our first night together as husband and wife, in which I would subtly point out that this playing out her fantasies on her sleeve was tricky business in that the awesome stress of keeping one's past straight in one's mind must be very exhausting, to have imagined I could have convinced Robin I had the breadth of character to live with whoever she was and whoever she'd been up to this moment, this very night, and that I saw no way of our making a life together in London or anywhere else should she not make an attempt to come to terms with herself, as well as the slob I was, do this so that I might not be constantly draining myself trying to keep up with Robin's ever-changing history of herself, to imagine that all this could be changed after a quietly reasoned talk with Robin was on my part an utterly demented notion.

Robin, stripping down to her underpants, had joined me on the balcony and demanded my chair next to the hibachi, as well as the grilling fork (a mistake, that!), explaining that now that she was my woman—and, I assume, meeting my mind!—it was her duty to prepare Frederick's nuptial repast. Where Robin purchased her underwear, I don't know; but she may as well have worn none at all, her present panties being little more than a pink silk waistband, a string bikini effect slashed between the mounds of her marvelous behind, and a skimpy silk flap that was drawn from behind between her legs, brought up and snapped with two metal fasteners in her lower loin area. When I asked her if by dropping this to wee-wee, the flap didn't go into the water of the bowl, she said of course not, rose, unsnapped the eyes, then from behind reached between her thighs, clutched the flimsy pink material of the flap and brought it back to the coccyx at the base of her spine. By way of demonstration, Robin then squatted down on the deck chair in the pee-pee position and cast me a contemptuously derisive look, as though to say that men really were blissfully ignorant when it came to the esoteric ways of women. Of course I knew why Robin wore undergarments and expensive ones at that. Robin genuinely believed in coddling, nurturing, and pampering the erotic zones of her body, which, happily, in Robin's case included every square centimeter. I say happily because had I not had her body to love I would have found myself in a quest for a mind so phantasmal as to be beyond the reach of any man, including, as he himself has told us, Dr. Sigmund Freud.

For a long time I had suffered myself the illusion that Robin might have lesbian tendencies, so derisive she was of her sisters and especially hateful when she detected anything about a sister that suggested a lack of demureness or femininity. In all the years I'd known her I'd never heard Robin mention having had a single girlfriend save for her prep school roommate, Ms. Priscilla Saunders, who was of course nonexistent, but even in her nonexistence poor Priscilla had been the recipient of Robin's lofty scorn for having gone to the drugstore and committed the indelicacy of purchasing condoms so that quarterback Dick Brophy, also nonexistent, could nightly service Priscilla and Robin in their dormitory room. Regarding any immediate indelicacy, Robin would grow so rancorous she'd be all but transmogrified into a disruptive lunatic.

Once when Robin, Hannibal, and I were sunning ourselves at the Royal Hawaiian pool, Robin, abruptly charged with bile, suddenly poked me from my slumber and sneered, "Look at that stupid *haole*." The Royal Hawaiian doesn't cater to anyone but *haoles* and as almost everyone at the pool had the pallor of mainlanders, I hadn't the foggiest notion where to look. What Robin, with a genuinely heart-felt disgust, was pointing out to me was a statuesque, even beautiful, woman whose bikini was so skimpy pubic hairs were cascading out the hem and onto the inside of her thighs. "Gross," Robin said. *"Gross."* Even later in the room, she was still spittingly furious. When I suggested that allowing herself to be so upset by a woman's exposing pubic hairs was an overreaction that left her own sex suspect, she countered with something I'd told her about my last stay on Singer Island, Florida.

All the young bucks had taken to wearing satin bikini swimsuits so taut their genitals were prominently exposed. From a bartender I'd heard that many of the guys actually stuffed cotton into their suits, and I spent so much time staring queasily at these erotic mounds, and because of my ongoing self-analysis, I'd begun to wonder if I didn't after all have fag tendencies. "Do you think I'm a fag, Robin?" And now Robin was shouting, "And what did I say, Frederick? What did I say?" In fairness, Robin had said that anyone might stare at an idiot with cotton stuffed into his swimsuit, in the same way a person, unable to help himself, would stare at a grotesque who had been ravaged by some horrible disease. This hardly made me a fag, any more than being repulsed by poolside pubic hairs made her a dyke. The woman looked, Robin said, like the kind of *haole* tourist who would pee in the pool.

When I pointed out that on a dozen occasions I'd heard Robin say, "I'm going to have a swim and make pee-pee," Robin laughed and said, "It's okay in my case. Mine tastes like champagne, as you ought to know. Besides, I've got equity in the islands." For all that, like so many beautiful women Robin absolutely loathed her sisters, with the single exception of Malia who was teaching her how to cook in a wok—her strip steak and mixed vegetables was going to be the hit of London society—and to iron her man's shirts. What fascinated me even more than the fact that all delicacy, propriety, and nicety was abandoned at Robin's bedroom door, and where she wouldn't, had she the Houdini contortions to manage it, have hesitated to massage a guy's prostate gland with her mouth, she'd be transmogrified to an incensed maniac on hearing a woman say "Shit" in the Royal Hawaiian's dining room.

When Robin leaned over to turn up the gas heat on the hibachi, I asked her not to, explaining that I wasn't as hungry as I'd imagined and as I was wide awake I very much wanted the steaks to simmer slowly so that I might savor their odor. Moreover, I said, had I a small skillet, some bell peppers, some olive oil, and some garlic powder I'd soon be into O'Twoomey's ambrosial heaven. "You know," I said, "I'm really going to miss that crazy bastard."

As Robin didn't want a steak, and as I seemed determined to sit on the balcony all night "swilling vodka" and inhaling the odor of simmering Delmonicos, Robin thought she'd take a shower and get ready for bed. To that I said that though I didn't know what was in her balloon bag I wasn't up to sex that night so she shouldn't deck herself out in any honeymoon fantasy. Robin became angry, explaining that in the alligator bag was her Great-grandmother Glenn's wedding gown, a marvel of gossamer, satin, and lace that had found its way down the family's hearty stock lines. Her great-grandmother, Edna O'Brien, had married John Glenn in a whaler's chapel on Nantucket. It had always been the family wish that Robin also be married in that discreet rustic place, and Robin hoped that on our return from London we might further sanctify our marriage by being rejoined in that Nantucket chapel.

I sighed and said, "Speaking of your noble lineage, Robin, did you ever let your mom and dad know you were being married?"

"No. But after we're settled comfy into Leinster Terrace, our first order of business will be to hop over to Paris to my parents' Île St.-Louis apartment so you can meet them. I was just afraid, you see, that knowing what you know about dad you might beat the shit out of him."

I sighed yet again, not daring to look at Robin. "Look, Robin, Tony Glenn is a retired plumber from Queens, your mother Evelyn a retired Con Ed secretary originally from the Prospect Park section of Brooklyn. You graduated, as valedictorian to be sure, from Bayside High School, spent two years at SUNY at New Paltz, then took a job as stewardess with American Airlines. And what, what, *what, for Christ's sake,* is the matter with that? Isn't just such a background what makes us so uniquely American, what lends the American his astonishing vitality? For the life of me, I've never understood those people, like you, who trace their ancestry to the Mayflower. Who'd want to be descended from those self-righteous, puritanical, malcontented quacks? Had they stayed in England they'd have been hung for the seditious rabble they were. And good riddance!"

"That's a lie," Robin cried. "That's a fucking lie!" It was then she hurled the grilling fork at me, lodging it firmly in the flabby pectoral muscles just above my left nipple. "Ouch." To say that Robin hurled it is perhaps inaccurate. As she was seated but three feet from me, the fork no sooner left her hand and began its trajectory than it was into my chest, the blood exploded, immediately slowed to a rushing stream, then, as I started wiping it away with my chef's apron, a trickle. Of course Robin became hysterical, tried to pull the fork from my chest, but I swatted her hand and told her to take a shower and go to bed before I got really pissed and slapped the shit out of her. Robin rose and started to the bathroom. Then I heard her pause, and she was back on the balcony telling me she hoped I drank myself to death and slamming an unopened liter of Smirnoff red label on the folding TV dinner table before me. For a half hour or more, above the weighty rush of the shower, I heard Robin's stricken sobs and when at length both sounds were stayed, I waited as long as I dared, so afraid I was of something Robin might do in her present condition —Lord, she was unpredictable enough in her rational moments—then cranked my head round and, sighing with relief, saw that Robin was naked on the king-size bed and preparing to dry her hair with her ivory-and-gold-leaf hand dryer.

By then it was nearly 3 A.M. and I'd already decided that after I slept, if ever I got tired, I'd travel alone to Punchbowl and make my final farewells to the Brigadier, knowing that he would give me up to the living, knowing really that he'd long since wanted me to go back among the quick. Then I'd go to O'Twoomey's tailor and have myself measured, after which, and whether Robin approved or not, I'd return to Lanai, drink for a day or two, maybe a week, perhaps a month, perhaps two, then I'd sober up, put these words down to you, Alissa, do a lot of golfing and swimming, and get ready for our new life in London, where I'd walk in Kensington Gardens during the week, weekends taking the Underground to walk in the bracken and gorse of Hampstead Heath. The grilling fork was still in my chest —some martyr, I!—and though the chef's apron was by now a bloody cerise mess, the blood had all but coagulated and the steaks were simmering so slowly I didn't need the fork and occasionally reached over and turned them with my fingers.

Abruptly I became aware that Robin had turned off the hair dryer. I was conscious of movement behind me, a whispering, some indistinct ruffling noises, and when at length Robin reappeared on the balcony she was dressed in her grandmother's wedding gown—doubtless purchased at Liberty House—and, dropping to her knees, she grasped my bare thighs and begged me to please, please, *please* remove the grilling fork from my chest. Lifting Robin's veil, I saw that her eyes were red and swollen from her tears; but even as close as I was, my eyes all but lying atop her bruised vacuous blue eyes, even then I couldn't help remarking her astonishing handsomeness. Robin was truly a stunning, heart-stopping, head-turning young woman even in her present distraught condition. Even were she dressed in a nun's habit, I thought, she would have been helpless to prevent the crude lust of vain swinish men. She ultimately had become nothing other than that brute American male fantasy of the cornbred princess and, in her awful fragility, she had devoted her life to living up to that fantasy, however unsought it had been on her part, only to have had it all turn to ashes in her mouth. God, she was America.

"It's Easter Sunday, Robin. Like Christ, I shall be resurrected by sunrise. Until then, I want to contemplate the—what is it you call it? Cosmos?—*cosmos* as fantasy. If, for example, Christ was into the fantasy—and I'm not saying he was—of being the son of God, does that negate the possibility that he was indeed the son of God? Moreover, who is the Jesus of Nazareth we fashion in our minds?—a secular, bearded, sweet-faced man—in Hollywood, ah, Hollywood, listen to this one, Robin, his armpits are hairless!—with a genius for metaphor, and doubtless the greatest gift for creating a personal mythology of anyone who ever walked the earth. And who are you and I, Robin, but a couple of unconscious worshipers who emulate Him with our every breath and gesture, you with your half-baked quackery about autumnal New England ancestors and Seven Sisters colleges and me with my own quackery of being a novelist—should I capitalize Novelist?—when I know that my grasp of the metaphor is at best a paltry, pedestrian thing—yes, Robin, just a couple pathetic bohunks striving in our separate ways to create personal mythologies we deem worthy of us."

Robin had begun to weep again, quietly, and lifting her eyes to me she said, "Please don't talk like this,

Frederick. I hate it when you talk like this. It's sick, it's insane."

"I like your eyes when they're tear-covered. They change from that startling paleness to a lovely violet. That blank paleness scares the shit out of me, Robin. In that state they have a disarming innocence, the scary spine-chilling frankness of the satanically fallen. Forsooth, you are the devil's daughter and I'd know you anywhere. Ah, but the tears bring on a depth of tenderness and compassion."

"Please, *please*."

"Give me this night to myself, Robin, and I make you this promise. I shall never, never again condemn nor reprimand you for babbling out your fantasies for all the world to hear. Ultimately my condemnation of you resides in my feeling that your waking, articulated dreams were never grand enough. Why an Emilio Pucci model? Why not the next Marilyn Monroe? But even now I am being unkind and unfair to you. Believe me when I say that you are nicer than Marilyn Monroe. In high school we used to play Eastwood of Syracuse, and Marilyn always reminded me, what with her wide low-slung ass and simpering kisser, of one of those Polack cheerleaders from Eastwood. And yet in death this broad who couldn't walk, who couldn't talk, who couldn't act has become an icon who preoccupies more of the intellectual dodos' time than ever Christ did. But you, Robin?— you have more regality in your little finger than Marilyn had in her entire presence, hyped presence at that, and had I not met your lovely parents on one of my flights over here I might have believed most of your stories, well, I might have believed some of them, well, one or two of them. And I am no better than you, Robin, save that my fantasies dwell within. In one of my books I have my narrator say something to the effect that he wanted nothing less than to stick his dirty fingers into posterity, my dreary fantasy, and if you allow me my august, presumptuous, and risible dream, I shall, I repeat, leave your fantasies—however troubling I find them—becalmed and unsullied by anything as garish as facts."

Robin rose, said, "I'm not listening to this shit one second longer," and disappeared into the bedroom.

Shortly before dawn I began to hear voices, whispers from across the dark sea, then suddenly a startling and joyous, "*Whoooeeee,* you asshole!" What the hell was going on? Was that directed at me? My first inclination was of course to check the vodka bottle, where I discovered that since Robin had in rancor slammed an unopened bottle on the TV tray I'd barely consumed an inch of it and hence couldn't lay the voices to auditory hallucinations. As the sky gradually lightened, the voices grew more numerous and murmurous, there was excitement in them, and laughter, a sense of heightened anticipation, an unbridled joy, and though I didn't again hear anything as distinct as that startling imprecation, I caught isolated scraps, "Howzit, bruh?" and so forth. Just before sunup, at that moment the sky was a lazy, stunning ocher gray, I found that I was standing, drink in hand, leaning into the concrete parapet and straining mightily to see the sea's horizon, now here and there catching glimpses of ships with stubby movable outriggers clawing at the distant dawn. The entire horizon seemed taken over by these odd mechanical craft and, for whatever reason, I called back that Nazi in his Normandy bunker on D-Day watching the English Channel filling up, one ship after another, forming the greatest armada the world had ever seen, the Nazi sitting there at first too benumbed by the evidence of his eyes to pick up the phone and sound the alarm that the Allies not only were coming, they were coming in a force hitherto inconceivable to man. And now the sun jumped and exploded over the horizon, I heard the first waves lapping at the previously undisturbed beach and saw—incredibly—what was happening.

The surf was up on Waikiki and the horizon was full of those golden Hawaiian girls and boys lying belly down on their surfboards, paddling with their hands and arms to maintain their positions, laughing, chatting, waiting for the first great wave to take them up and up and up and riding into Waikiki. Throughout the velvet night radio stations carried bulletins on where the surf was, Waikiki was of course on the leeward side of Oahu, and it was damn near miraculous for the winds to be such—one could almost hear the announcer croaking, "The surf is up on Waikiki!"—that the kids would find themselves surfing for the swank hotel guests on an Easter Sunday morning. I can't say how many Saturday nights I'd told Hannibal that the following morning I was going to the windward side of the islands and watch these kids, along with the Aussies the best in the world, but I'd never followed through and now, when I was about ready to leave Oahu, and perhaps forever, I was at last, and finally, going to see them.

In her alligator bag Robin always carried a first aid kit, for what I don't know unless she was, sooner or later, planning on getting me into a little S and M, and after finding a Band-Aid and the iodine I pulled the grilling fork from my chest, doctored my wound, and gave Robin, who in her wedding gown was sleeping facedown on her as yet virginal wedding bed, a hearty smart swat on her sculptor's-dream behind, shouting, "The surf is up on Waikiki!"

Robin, in Grandma's wedding gown still, I in a pair of khaki shorts and a blue golf shirt with a Giants helmet where the alligator should have been, went down to the beach, I agape and without the art or the surfer's lexicon to describe what I was seeing, settling for such meager words as, "God, this is terrific, I mean, this is incredible," until Robin, exasperated with my triteness, said, "These guys aren't that good. Some of the best surfers on the island aren't even here today. I'm better than most of these creeps."

Despite my solemn vow to my bride, made in the witching hours of that very special night, never again to disparage or to hold up to ridicule her fantasies, however excessive, I turned to give Robin what I hoped would be a moderately peeved look only to discover she was greeting a big handsome kanaka dude, wet red bandana tied about his forehead, who'd just ridden his board into the beach. "Hey, John-john, howzit, bruh? Leave me duh board, huh?" "Hey, Robin, howzit, *howzit*? Whoooeeee! What you do? Marry dis tubby *haole*? *Whoooeeee!*" Tubby *haole*? Jesus, the arrogance of these Ohana kanaka dudes—and the worst part of it was that though they always appeared flabbier than swine there was, I'd heard often enough, something inherent in their Polynesian racial characteristics that lent them a deceptive, often savage power and strength. Before I could protest the kanaka's rudeness, Robin had snatched John-john's board, had slipped from her satin silver slippers, laid her veil atop them, and, still begowned, had charged into the sea, slammed belly down on her board into the surf, like a child onto his snow sled on the shimmering winter hills of home, and stroking over a huge wave, dropped quickly off, disappeared momentarily, came back into view, then with long fluid powerful strokes was seen making her way to the horizon, the while John-john crying, "Geevum, Robin, *geevum*," until the other surfers, who obviously also knew who Robin was, got caught up in the chant of "Geevum, Robin, geevum."

When at last Robin reached the horizon she let one wave after another go by, her head continually turning over first her right shoulder, then her left, seeking as they do the perfect wave. Then I sensed her body tense, she was looking straight into Waikiki, now her arms were stroking mightily to bring her board to the wave's crest, then as effortlessly as I'd ever seen it done she was atop her board and coming home. First she rode way across to her right and when abruptly she slalomed sharp left and rode down the backside of her own wave I saw, astonishingly, what she was up to—running a tunnel created by the monstrous wave immediately behind hers and now breaking over her head and spitting itself to pieces, a sound like the long, lazy, indulgent belching of the eternally smug and sated gods. She couldn't have been in the tunnel but a few seconds, which seemed to me a few hours, and when to the grand cheers— "*Geevum, Robin*"—of the other surfers she rode the furious tunnel clear she was so high up on her board and so strainingly crouched over I thought she was going to topple over the board's bow. She didn't though. Recovering herself, she suddenly took another sharp left and was riding this dying but still raging wave right into me. For what seemed like the last hundred yards, I swore I could make out every nuance of her body, the way her beautiful soaked gown so clung to her I could see the outline of her marvelous tanned thighs, the embarrassingly suggestive lines of her white string bikini underpanties, her audacious, assertive breasts; and now in their wetness her blue eyes had assumed those violet depths and that depth registered a monumental hauteur as furious as the surf, as though Robin were saying, "Don't you patronize me and question everything I say, you toady tubby—yes, tubby!—mealy-mouthed little wimp!" It was, literally, so scary I hadn't any alternative but to laugh, thinking what an incredibly joyous and intricate business life indeed was. Yet I held the power over Robin, despite the way she was now riding down the seas as though to overwhelm and bury me in the warm white sands of Waikiki.

Ah, yes, were I able to cultivate the willful awesome power of silence, perhaps I'd never ask Robin another question for as long as I lived. In that way I would in a very real sense deprive Robin of her very essence, her artistry, her need for melodrama, humbuggery, mendacity, elaboration, camp theater, pretense, hyperbole, dissembling, sophistry, improvisation, fantasy—is not one fantasist per family quite enough?—ad infinitum. And now as Robin's board beached itself and she bounded off and leaped toward me in search of accolades I looked directly at her—oh, I was as steady and as steely-eyed as Lugosi—as though to say, tubby wimp or not, I shall in the end defeat you, Miss America, shall defeat you, learn to live with you, and make you mine.

Acknowledgments

Acknowledgments are made to the following, without whose kindness and encouragement this book would not have been finished: Mike Bresnahan, Jr.; Concetta and Frank Cavallario; Feliza and Jo Cole; Francis Costanzo; Ms. Pat Hall Dunton; George Hebert, Sr.; Audrey and Bill Horsefield; The National Institute of Arts and Letters; P.E.N.; Gordon Phillips; Robert Renzi, Esq.; Baba Riedel; Brenda Riedl; Vince and Frank Rose; H. W. Rouse, Jr.; Jack Scordo, Esq.; Richard and Wally Tamashiro.

FREDERICK EXLEY is the author of *A Fan's Notes* and *Pages from a Cold Island*, and *Last Notes from Home*, the final volume of his trilogy.

He has been nominated for a National Book Award, was the recipient of the William Faulkner Award, received the National Institute of Arts and Letters Rosenthal Award, and won a *Playboy* silver medal for the best nonfiction piece of 1974. He has also received a Rockefeller Foundation grant, a Harper-Saxton Fellowship, and a John Simon Guggenheim Fellowship.

V I N T A G E
CONTEMPORARIES

VINTAGE
CONTEMPORARIES

ALSO BY

"The best novel written in the English language since THE GREAT GATSBY." — <u>Newsday</u>

"The second volume in Fred Exley's autobiographical trilogy is in every way a worthy sequel to A FAN'S NOTES.

Lunatic, funny, sad and infuriating. A work of art." — <u>The New York Times</u>

V I N T A G E
CONTEMPORARIES